THE RIGHTNESS OF THINGS

Novels of the Joad Cycle

Book 1: The Golden Rule
Book 2: Profit
Book 3: Circle of Life
Book 4: The Rightness of Things

Join us for a discussion about America's future at
WWW.Joadcycle.com

THE RIGHTNESS OF THINGS

Book IV of the Joad Cycle

GARY LEVEY

iUniverse, Inc.
Bloomington

THE RIGHTNESS OF THINGS
Book IV of the Joad Cycle

iUniverse books may be ordered through booksellers or by contacting:

iUniverse
1663 Liberty Drive
Bloomington, IN 47403
www.iuniverse.com
1-800-Authors (1-800-288-4677)

ISBN: 978-1-4697-7900-3 (sc)
ISBN: 978-1-4697-7902-7 (hc)
ISBN: 978-1-4697-7901-0 (ebk)

Printed in the United States of America

iUniverse rev. date: 03/01/2012

I dedicate *The Joad Cycle* series to my wife, June who made our future and to my children Daniel and Elena who are adults now and building a future of their own.

Most of all, *The Joad Cycle* is dedicated to my granddaughter, Dyllon, who, at eight, deserves a better future than that which responsible adults who run and lead this country's institutions are providing with their avarice and thoughtlessness.

For her sake and for the sake of all the grandchildren, I hope that love and kindness can triumph in our world like it does in novels.

Gary Levey
12/25/2011

Gulf of Delmarva—*Weather changed, climate changed, but humans didn't and an oversexed economy spewed industrial filth bringing forth a fury birthed in scorn; the shallow, churning coffee waters of Delmarva, our wondrous, unholy Gulf.*

America's most highly valued real estate, Jersey, Delaware, Maryland and Virginia are no more. This sad, sad, bitter deluge is proof that despite warnings, Industrial Age entrepreneurs and politicians could not outgrow their lust for wealth.

Our first Eastern Gulf was a child of arrogance and unbridled capitalist free market rape; its mother, the serene, aloof Chesapeake, its cuckold father, the risen wrath of the great Atlantic, whose fury settles all scores.

And so, unchained, nature's waters rose over the wealthy and the pitiable sending entrepreneurs into retreat, to watch in distant luxury as coastal assets drowned, even at low tide, while climate refugees, funneled by highways, fled inland, in mass desperation, to unfriendly, taken places.

Diaspora for the rich is different, for the greedy rich own everywhere.

Diaspora, from the only performance of the Broadway stage musical-comedy: "Entrepreneurs?" 2026; Music and Libretto by Dyllon Tomas.

—Archive

Monroe, District of Columbia—*Resort towns from Maine to Anchorage retreated in the wake of global tides and new shoreline was recapitalized leading to the Supreme Court decision, Allen Casinos and Resorts v. Vineland, NJ Shoreline LLC, that ceded new beach improvements to those who could best develop them.*

With assets sinking under water, American corporations fought back with as much technology, steel, and concrete as they could muster in a down economy in order to mitigate any risks that submerging balance sheets couldn't mask.

To fund the financial disaster, whatever entitlement programs remained for the poor and downtrodden evaporated as corporate interests influenced advantage they could believe in into legislation that created the public funding for a mammoth system of dunes and dikes constructed to bolster the economy long enough to allow diversification of assets while seeking forbearance from a no-nonsense and very troubled Stock Market.

Nature runs its course and it soon became apparent that any capital project would be inadequate and merely add moments and debt, yet still larger dikes were funded to add more moments and more debt. In this universe, unproductive money spent yesterday isn't available tomorrow and the product of Mother Nature's revenge resulted in a more concentrated country in so many ways and the only decision left was to admit defeat and move on.

To mitigate the negative impact on corporate balance sheets and price per share, special laws were passed that gave favored accounting treatment to massive asset write-offs and delivered enticements and relief to those who controlled law making apparatus. But where the money went, that trail has long grown cold.

In 2038, at an historic conference at the new Gulfport city of Hammonton, NJ, professionally licensed forensic environmentalists, actuaries, and cost and general accountants met to confirm that Nature's encroachment would stabilize enough so that funds could be allocated to reconstruct our flooded nation's capital.

President of the United States, Andrew Crelli, spearheaded a vast architectural and landscaping venture to replace America's nearby, deluged former capital, Washington, D.C. The project rivaled the World Islands of

Dubai in scale and cost and the Pyramids of Egypt in use of slave labor and though Chairman Crelli never saw it complete, it was named in honor of his beloved mother, Phoebe Monroe.

The great resort capital of Monroe is a secure community of multi-colored palm and date trees on man-made hills that overlook and protect a lush administrative land that begins near the great salt bog expanse on the western shore of the Gulf of Delmarva. The land around Monroe slopes gradually down and away, flattening as it approaches Gulf waters where once verdant green hills are now blanched into an expanse of sterile dunes tiled in beige cracked earth that colors the coffee waters and delays the Gulf from its relentless mission, payback for centuries of petrochemical frenzy.

An unsafe distance south and east of Monroe stands the partially submerged and mostly deserted former capital, Washington, D.C. Where once a new and naïve republic exerted its might, today, vast empty skyscrapers pierce the horizon but serve no function other than as a reminder that Capitalism fought and won, at best, a pyrrhic victory here.

Washington had always been a prison to the poor who had no means to escape and nowhere to go. The former Capital died functioning as a prison for procrastinating businesses whose leaders ignored the science until there was no means to avoid free-falling property values. Free markets require two things above all, and Washington D.C. real estate had sellers a plenty with great incentive to deal, but as the tides rose, there was no market because they lacked even a single buyer.

Today, Monroe is the jewel of the Second Republic. It is an oasis of brilliance and regal elegance, surrounded by palm-lined paths and lagoons, shelters for the residents' yachts along a fresh water lake large enough to satisfy even the most demanding vacationers while the magnificent homes represent the glory of being rich and powerful in America in a rebounding economy. Monroe is the symbol of America's new greatness

—Archive

Chapter 1

Monroe, D.C.—Spring, 2083

The cabin shook. Vivid, loud explosions turned the trees black and the sky grey with bursts of white, yellow and red. Frightened from a troubling sleep, he grasped his mattress tight, his screams squelched by the throbbing bass of shells detonating while his sparse possessions skittered along a shelf to fall on the cabin floor and continuing to vibrate with each new blast. Outside, evergreens ignited in bursts of reddish white flames and his world was painted orange.

With his ears ringing in unnatural silence, he flung his cabin door open to stare as terrified villagers fled into the night. A man wearing a white dishdasha dragged a chained and near-naked blonde slave girl past his door. He paused and turned, rolling one side of his pencil thin mustache between the thumb and index finger of one hand while pressing the slave girl to her knees with the other. He smiled grandly.

"This one could have been yours if you had cared. Now, I have her. And I will have her whenever I wish and when I no longer want her, she will want me that much more. She will beg for me. She will cry for me and she will do my bidding in hopes of winning my love back. That is the cost of your indifference."

Fearfully, the slave girl looked up at him. He recognized her and looked away. With her green eyes red with tears, Stacey Grant spoke in a sad, broken voice.

"Why can't you be worth it? Why can't ever you be worth it?"

His heart was broken, again.

His own dream-induced moaning woke him. Shivering and sweating, it took a moment to realize that it was a dream—that dream. He took a deep breath and tried to calm himself. He was, shirtless, lounging on his lanai, floating on a translucent nano-fiber hammock while warm, artificial breezes gusted gently over the lake and through his lagoon, gently rocking his yacht. This was his peace—an inadequate peace, but it was all the peace available to him.

In nearby fields, indentured servants, shirtless, even the women, labored in the hot sun under large conical plastic hats, a sheen of sweat on their worthless bodies as they landscaped, earning another day of life doing the back-breaking, thankless, unrewarding job required to appreciate the assets on these executive luxury homes.

The weary gait of the exhausted slaves was disturbing so Gil focused his attention on the more productive movements of the experimental agribots working tirelessly, oblivious to the employment threat they posed to their less fungible human counterparts. He put his hand up to shade his eyes from the scattered sunlight reflecting off the lagoon. Time had taught him that to survive, he must quarantine what hurt, but sometimes that lesson didn't take. He wiped away tears caused by the sun and closed his eyes.

Gil Rose was a free man, Chairwoman Brandt had decreed it, but he felt as imprisoned as any free man can be. Ten years of dread, acrimony, and disappointment, mostly with himself, along with guilt and shame, will do that to a man and it certainly did it to him. And the worst part was that he could never let on, even if he found someone who cared. That his death, by any means imaginable, was but an insane ruler's whim away, only added to his stress. He was an adult. He had the proof. Life had seared his soul and numbed his heart, turning the defensive boundaries that he'd built to survive into insurmountable prison walls.

Rejected by Joad and captured by Chairwoman Tanya Brandt, survival required that he be on constant guard, anticipate correctly, and speak the precise right thing while reading others' reactions and remembering what was safe to say and do. And mostly, he did that but his thoughts were of other things, wrongs that shouldn't exist so he forced himself to keep busy and stay away from Monroe for as long as he could so as not to slip, and yes, he was required to deliver the best consulting work that a Morgan missionary could possibly deliver. So far his performance had been enough to keep him thriving, but barely living.

After his capture, for some unfathomable reason, he had been commanded by the Chairwoman to enter the Morgan Missionary College with its requirement that interns gain experience through long-term overseas consulting assignments. Each time he returned from an assignment, he found that his wealth had grown. And each time he returned he had a larger mortgage and a more expensive home located closer and closer to the seat of power, Chairwoman Brandt's mansion. To add to his misery, he and the Chairwoman were neighbors, now.

He had just returned from his final foreign missionary engagement, this one in Bolivia, and for the first time since he was arrested by Reverend General Tucker, he was facing the high risk of real down time where, in this center of intrigue, even closing his eyes and thinking other thoughts could be a life threatening blunder.

On assignment, it was easier to act like a consultant and be in control. It was the free time that terrified him but even fear couldn't stop his guilty mind from wandering where it didn't belong so he could never relax. It was concentrate or die.

He requested shade from his nano-hammock and once the sun was blocked, he stared out at the lake where perfect, man-made three-foot mint-green breakers formed in the center, swelling outward in a quiet rush, crested and broke, painting a foaming lacey gash along the otherwise pristine white-sand lakeshore before washing into a gentle ripple in his private cove. He stared at the water, unable to escape; as it was sucked back out and forced to reform again.

He had come far from those days and nights on the run. He had come far, too, from those nights long ago in Aeden when his father, Howard, had employed him to genetically alter his prized Dionysius flowers. Gil smiled at that. How naïve Howard had been, expecting flowers alone to gain him promotion to an Executive town inferior to the one Gil now lived in. Howard's goal was impossible, and not being able to inform him of that made him feel duplicitous. Maybe someday, when he had proven himself, when he was more successful, richer, freer, he would be allowed to contact Howard. Once again, his eyes fluttered open and he stared at the waves, searching for the cue that would bring on the needed calm that he had learned to show but never feel.

Somewhere above him, in addition to shade, a nano-fan generated a pleasantly synchronized breeze and once again he closed his eyes and his thoughts drifted. It had been almost twenty years since he had last seen Howard. Twenty years! He had been alive longer without Howard than with him. And because the Chairwoman forbade him from communicating, he knew little more than that Howard was still alive.

The Executive town of Monroe was his home now, but nothing here felt right. Even the guarantee from the nano-hammock manufacturer, which advertised that floating on a cloud with nothing apparent below, was the best relaxation that money could buy, even that wasn't quite right. Like so much in his life, those marketing claims weren't satisfied because he could never relax.

Gil was thirty-two, Howard's age on that fateful, life-altering day when his great-grandfather, Bernie, conned him into aiding a stillborn revolution by saving his grandfather and former President, Mark Rose. That day, that fateful decision, it changed his life because it involved him in the kidnapping of former Chairman Andrew Crelli, and that began a long, perilous, and surreal ordeal that ironically led here to Monroe, to Gil becoming a Morgan Christian missionary with Executive status, and to his palatial estate.

His troubled thoughts drifted to Presque Isle, Michigan, to Annie and her daughter—his daughter—who he would never see. Mary Khadijeh—that's what Annie had said she'd name her. That child, no, his daughter, she would be the same age now that he was when he had first met Bernie and it troubled him that Archive had no record of Annie or their child—as if they didn't matter; an uncomfortable thought given his culpability. He took what comfort he could from knowing that Annie was a *Toller* leader's niece and that information about *Tollers* simply wasn't worth the cost to accumulate it and he was left to hope that they were alive and productive, and not *disappeared* like so many millions. He squelched the guilt before it rose up to defeat him.

Once again, he opened his eyes and tried to concentrate on his most recent consulting assignment in Bolivia. It had been successful and he felt that this time he had truly helped people and not just converted the poor to Morgan while increasing a corporate client's profits. Anyway, it was satisfying to believe that. He needed to keep that focus and relaxing triggered bad or sad memories that were a dangerous way to live.

As a focused consultant, he had achieved successes for his clients, but in unguarded moments, his mind sought troubled purpose, forcing him to face all of his failures. But Joad had failed him, too, and her duplicity was the hardest thing to accept. She had caused his capture outside Presque Isle the morning after Clarke Jackell had instilled in him renewed purpose. There was yet another of life's ironies. Just when Clarke's story had convinced him to join the revolution, an utterly hopeless revolution, almost immediately after he'd made that decision, he'd been captured by Ginger Tucker, the Chairwoman's Reverend General. But even Joad's treachery couldn't assuage Gil's guilt. He had procrastinated so long that what he felt he should have done became irrelevant.

He tried not to dwell on Joad because when he did he felt the uncomfortable tug of the love he had once felt for her as a naïve teenager and she was his avatar lover. He hated her now. She was a two-faced bitch who had trapped him into this life. That moment when he saw Reverend General Tucker, he knew that Joad's rival avatar, Gecko, was the avatar with true power and with that knowledge, his interest in revolution vanished.

After capture, he had endured months in isolation, fearing for his life before fate provided an unexpected turn. He met the Chairwoman. In many ways, she was exactly what Bernie and Mark had described, yet different. Extraordinarily beautiful for an older woman, she had striking, violet eyes that had staggered him at first because he'd seen another, better version of them in Bree, his faux wife from Profit. But when it should have been Brandt's breathtaking beauty, it was her radiant, yet hard and insincere smile that defined her.

His audience with the Chairwoman was not what he expected. Brandt had been affable, and though he was under great stress, he found himself enjoying her wild, rambling conceit. She was all but omnipotent, yet she was bawdy and alluringly brash as she acted as if nothing but her was sacred. When the audience ended, he was escorted out, unsure whether he would live or die. More months of isolation followed and then, to his astonishment, he was provided a scholarship to the Morgan Unified Colleges of Theological Economics, Liturgical Sciences, and Faith Based Technologies.

Three years of virtual studies at Morgan University at Monroe led him to an Advanced Missionary degree in Technological Spirituality with a field of concentration in Moribund Societies. He spent the next three years in an intense internship where he learned everything a consultant needed to know about interpreting body language and understanding brain chemistries. In the College of the Rule-of-Law he added classes in Applied Blessings and Value Added Mysticism and in the daily stock market analyses and prayer services he attended, he learned the essentials of Morgan dogma required of all consultants representing Church enterprises in overseas locales. After a post-intern assignment at a Morgan-run *keiretsu* in Kyoto, Japan, he spent three years concentrating on Economic Visioning and God-based Supply-side economics at

Thomas Gorman University. Upon completing his coursework, he was assigned to Bolivia from which he had just returned.

Before becoming a true Morgan Missionary Master of Commerce with his chosen specialty in Consensus Building, he had one last hurdle. He need only pass his final exam to claim a Missionary Master Degree that would assure his financial future far more certainly than developing unique botanicals ever would for Howard. The curious thing was that not one of the Morgan consultants on his team would divulge anything about the exam that he had to pass or he wouldn't survive.

Would Bernie have been proud? He knew that answer and so tried his best to avoid thinking about Bernie.

A sound distracted him and he chastised himself for letting his mind wander again and so easily. He was so close to his goal that reminiscing about unhappy pasts and miserable futures was distracting, and worse, it was potentially lethal.

He flipped on his headgear to access *Archive* so he could check on his exam schedule. In virtual, he walked down color-coded streets to the repository that housed his final requirements. He meandered through his schedule, careful to avoid the virtual classrooms that were in session and he was busy confirming his final study plan when he failed to notice the blinking yellow caution light that signaled a real person needing attention. When he didn't respond in the allotted time, Archive faded and he saw his gardener, Keven Daig, standing beside his hammock.

"Oh, sorry, Keven."

Keven was a fair haired brute of a man with an easy smile. "No problem, sir, I'm sorry to bother you but you haven't approved this year's landscaping budget. I trust there's no problem. We're getting back-logged and I need to schedule your workers before it's too late."

Gil put his headset aside. "Why would there be any problems? I invested pretty heavily in landscaping before I left for Bolivia and now that I've seen it, I'm happy with it. Everything's where it needs to be. I've been away a long time and I'd like to enjoy what's already been done before doing more."

"Right, sir, but we have some exciting new botanical concepts this season. Current trends are showing more decadent, global warming themes and I'm pushing a tropical look that the climate in Monroe supports.

"Frankly, sir, the botanicals I'm recommending are becoming more abundant as climate changes so there are real price opportunities, if you catch my drift. We've had great success with Royal Dutch palms that were evolved a few years ago in Discipline, the Iowa Corporate Agricultural community. Its creator earned the Management Town Landscaping Entrepreneur of the Year Award for his achievement with these sturdy, sub-temperate climate palms. You've just returned so you need to be aware, Madam Chairwoman loves them so much she's contracted for fifty to encircle her personal ice skating rink. By summer, these trees will be the rage and prices will be through the roof.

"Excuse me for saying so, sir, but an up-and-comer like yourself won't want to appear so 'last year' and we have palms aplenty. I can make them available at our delivered cost—plus labor and material—and we offer a long term maintenance contract that includes replacement at cost plus labor and other materials."

"Maybe next year, Keven. We'll talk in the fall."

Assuming his landscaper was leaving, Gil put his headgear back on but before he could reach his study plan, the yellow caution light was blinking so he pulled off his gear.

"Yes, Keven?" He tried not to sound annoyed.

"I'm sorry, sir, you've just returned and perhaps you don't realize the situation. My landscaping firm has never lost a job in Monroe and I have a team of a hundred yard men and two hundred indentured servants under contract with that assumption. They depend on these jobs, you know, to support their families and all."

Negotiations, Gil understood. "You're not losing a job; I'm delaying it. You said you have plenty of work and maybe by autumn the style will change."

"Sir, am I free to talk?"

"Why wouldn't you be?"

"Delicacy, sir. I have a full spring schedule, yes, but as you know, you live and we work in the highest per capita net worth Executive Community in the world and as a Missionary Consultant, I'm certain that you understand that our overhead expenses are extraordinarily high. As you're quite aware, the only highway into this community is hidden from view of the residents and that constrains the size of what can be shipped in economically. And to show concern for global climate changes, the Chairwoman prohibits internal combustion machines in her paradise, except, of course, for the Zamboni that resurfaces her skating rink. This adds to the complexity of our efforts. It means we haul trees and shrubbery through the hills using high maintenance livestock because slaves haven't proved to be a cost effective solution. Oxen react much more favorably than do slaves to the whip but they require more food and water.

"Sir, logistics can be quite expensive, so if we lose or delay even one project, the servants will . . . well, you know." Keven shrugged.

Gil disliked sales pressure but the implications were too concerning to ignore. "At the rates you charge, you must make a good profit. Trees and bushes can't cost much."

"Sir, you're embarrassing me," the gardener said. "To provide the service that a high level executive like yourself requires, our staff must live nearby so we can respond to any emergency. Being close and ready is very expensive."

"We're talking shrubbery, Keven, what emergency service does that require?"

"I know you're trying not to be offensive but you must have no idea how difficult it is in a free market to obtain the type of shrubbery, as you call it, *Executives* require and do it at a price that satisfies them and my stockholders. More than most, *Executives* hate to be reminded of failure and they're disappointed when their planting investments don't perform."

"But you recommend the shrubs," Gil pointed out.

"As usual, your grasp of the situation is very sure but every business has its uniqueness and we prefer not to burden our customers with ours. We work on very tight margins so to lose a top end customer, well it means reductions."

"You can't be serious."

Keven nodded, glumly. "In all likelihood, the servants who delivered your landscaping with such heartfelt verve assuredly will be the first to go. It's unfortunate but budgets are intolerant masters, and Morgan tells us that we must be slaves to our fiscal responsibilities. I'm not saying this to make you feel responsible but . . ."

"But if I do feel responsible . . ."

"Sir, we're Morgans. This is business. Let's take the workers out of the equation. You must do what you believe creates the most value, but before you decide, consider that my recommendations are entirely about keeping your property values up for appearance and appreciation. While the masses believe real estate value is all about location, location, location, you and I know it's about appreciation, don't we sir?"

"And life is about choices."

"That is an odd way to put it but exactly, sir. That's why I love working in this community. The executives in residence are so extraordinarily successful. You know that I would never ask a customer to decide on landscaping based on the affect it has on something fungible like workers and their families. This is about you and your long-term worth. It is for that life-and-death reason that I implore you to reconsider."

Gil was getting frustrated. "But I'm really not that interested in landscaping."

"Forgive me for being so bold, Mr. Rose, but I've always taken your apparent lack of interest as effective negotiating skill. The reality is a successful professional like you simply must landscape. To not compete with your neighbors well . . . you simply must, or our entire free enterprise system unravels."

"I invested so much already. Certainly that is still rippling through the economy."

"Sir, you better than I know how *Executives* are; how they search for every advantage. Should some observe others skimping, well sir, ugly rumors will circulate and there will be embarrassing questions asked. There will be concerns as to whether you're overextended, or perhaps have even fallen out of favor with the Chairwoman, or others will surmise that you have simply lost your edge, your competitiveness.

"It happens, and when it does, it leaves the scent of blood in the air and you know how dangerous that can be to careers. There is great potential in rumors and it may seem like none of my business but I assure you, it is. The Daig family has performed landscaping consulting since '32 and we have always provided value-added service. That's why I consider it my responsibility to protect you from wrong thinking that can destroy your career momentum as well as the confidence other executives have in you. If people believe you're scrimping, failing, think how it affects every negotiation. I've found that a well-placed rumor is often the first step in career devaluation. Of course, if the rumors are true, I'll be discrete until such time as you turn your finances around or the next owner of this lovely property presents me with his landscape budget."

Gil was anxious to return to his study schedule and Keven was taking far too much of his time. "Thanks. I can't tell you how much I appreciate what you're saying."

"No, thank you," Keven said with a slight bow. "And I assure you, Mr. Rose, only you, Archive, our beloved Chairwoman, and the competitive writers who evaluate landscaping for their subscribing followers—*Conducers*—with an exhaustive faith in the ultimate fairness of capitalism—will know the truth. I know you're aware of how rumors chase facts until they become them and can be unfortunate but those dynamics are what make the markets what we worship and admire. More spending is just the ticket to ward off the nasty innuendoes that ruin careers. I'm not saying this to get business . . ."

"I know. It's a service you provide."

Keven nodded. "A value added service, sir, but if you're having . . . difficulties, say no more. Your secret is safe with me and hopefully; when your worth stabilizes we'll talk again. One thing is certain. Whoever owns this property, I will landscape it."

Gil sighed, audibly. "Keven, you're very good."

"Thank you, Mr. Rose. I would never, and I mean never, say anything to anyone about this conversation or your declining worth. Far be it for me to press you to do something you can't afford, regardless of the signals that sends. Still, since you're relatively new to our community and you may not be aware of the implications, I feel that it is my professional obligation to enlighten you."

"Please believe me, Keven, I truly don't care what people think about my estate."

The landscaper smiled. "You have a reputation for being special that way."

Gil was desperate to end this. "Okay, reduce your bill ten percent and I'll approve it. I'm doing this for the workers, so I want assurances you'll keep them on."

"Ten percent, very good, sir. I may have neglected to point out that the nasty, persistent drought and the cost and availability of water has driven costs up. I can offer a five percent professional courtesy discount instead." Keven pulled out his order pad.

"Seven and a half and that's final," Gil haggled. "And I expect to see all the workers assigned from my previous project. I don't want to find out later that you allowed some to . . . disappear."

Keven looked horrified. "Mr. Rose, never! That is not me. When can I start?"

"I'll be leaving on assignment after my exam. Start then. I want my site lines to the lake maintained and I want as much open land as possible. If you can't adhere to those specifications, I'll live with the rumors. Are we done?"

"Yes, sir, thank you. If you don't love my choices, we'll replace them at cost."

"If I don't like it, you eat the cost."

"You drive a hard bargain. One other thing, if I may?"

Gil eyed his headgear. "What is it?"

"Bluto Dubai, the head of my Interior Decorating division, wishes to meet with you at your earliest convenience. He has some luscious ideas for growing internal home values. Once Bluto performs his magic, you're assured international exposure for your magnificently redecorated home in Bluto's MESH magazine. His displays are marketed with the Chairwoman's *Preferred Status* imprimatur, and they appear in the *Executive* Homes and Gardens MESH site where *Conducers* and low end *Entrepreneurs* in every Management, Production, Agricultural, Financial and Service town in America will see how a hot, up and coming young executive like yourself lives. It'll greatly enhance your media presence and that correlates with enhanced future worth. I won't lie, Bluto's decorating tastes are expensive, but for an *Executive* like yourself, that's the cost of greatness."

Tired of being pitched, Gil ended the conversation. "Keven, we're done here."

"Sir, you must reconsider. Interior decorating, in conjunction with landscaping, shows the world a stunning picture of a true business executive in full bloom."

"Keven, I have to study."

"I understand, but because you're relatively new, you may not be aware of how much value there is in demonstrating to the simple *Conducer* rabble how much a true professional must spend to increase his worth. You are also probably unaware, but the masses thirst for inside information about celebrity tastes and they hunger to mimic those tastes in their filthy little abodes and insignificant lives. There is stunning economics in that for *Entrepreneurs* like yourself. It's such a wonderful dynamic and such a grand display of herd mentality when millions of

Conducers risk bankruptcy every day to spend their limited disposable income in order to emulate a favorite *Executive* celebrity like you. I can offer three opinions from three respected Certified Forensic Accountants attesting that Bluto's recommendations will enhance your worth and reputation by a significant multiple and as a Morgan; you know how fame enhances wealth accretion. You simply must take advantage of this; it's a guaranteed win-win."

"Decorating really isn't how I want to enhance my reputation. Tell Bluto that I'm busy and stop selling me or I'll cancel my order."

Keven nodded reluctantly, and left. Gil watched him go, unsure whether he was sorry for the distraction or thankful. When he was certain that Keven was gone, he put his headgear on and re-entered Archive to complete his schedule. Once he was done, he closed his eyes and faced with nothing but free time, he tried to relax but once again his past wedged into his thoughts.

The Chairwoman had been surprisingly conciliatory, making just two demands of him once it was clear she didn't want him executed just yet. He complied with her requirement for a formal Morgan Missionary education, but he had balked at her second demand.

He had refused the Chairwoman. Gil smiled at that. Even though it would greatly enhance his performance, his career, and extend his life, he refused to accept implantation of a computer chip, a PID that would facilitate direct access to Archive. After considering how much worse his life would have been with Gecko omnipresent in his mind, Gil was as insistent as a prisoner of war could be. He'd had enough of treacherous avatars and didn't want the most powerful one incessantly rattling around in his skull launching virulent thoughts. Surprisingly, the Chairwoman had acquiesced and he was relieved to pursue his new career with a small victory in hand.

He was startled awake by a chilling, wet sensation on his neck. He shivered and opened his eyes. The tongue that gently teased its way around his carotid artery belonged to his dark brown haired, live-in girlfriend, Gale. Instinctively, he embraced her and she folded into him, cooing warmly in his ear.

"Slow down, honey, I'm on vacation," he laughed. "How was your day?"

"Apparently it was more stressful than yours," she said as she kissed his cheek. "The kids were horrid. I swear, every year they get worse. I know it's not their fault; we just don't fund the right resources to keep them interested. Every time we request money from our sponsors at *Global Solar*, their administrative liaison tells us we have to make do because funds aren't available due to cost reductions. Make do, what a joke. *ANGS* has a multi-trillion *Yuan* advertising budget, yet they won't offer a single extra *Yuan* to help my students." She reduced her voice to a whisper. "Honestly, I think it was better before they bought the school system from the city."

"Don't say that, you never know who is listening."

She laughed. "If they're listening to me, they're wasting bandwidth." Gale cared deeply about her kids and he longed for that kind of passion in his own life. "The kids are so bored and why wouldn't they be? With their parents working all the time, the few who live at home live in a carnival of unlimited access with far more interesting virtual experiences than they will ever enjoy with me at school. And our resident kids live every waking moment to test limits. They do things virtually and without restrictions and they do it without adult supervision. The freedom they have is really scary. In school, there are rules and limits and teachers like me hound them. Even with the *Pharma* treatments we're permitted to dose them with to get them to focus or just calm down, it's no wonder they're incorrigible.

"It's frustrating because education doesn't have to be this way. I'd blame the parents to their faces if I ever saw one but parents lose the responsibility for raising children as soon as the pregnancy stipend pays off. I understand that parents are more productive if they live separate lives from their kids and I don't blame them but their lack of involvement is just permission for their children to become poor students and then teachers get our wages dunned because the kids fail to perform. They're good kids but they fight to be the center of attention because it's their only chance to get any attention at all. They rarely see an adult human face looking at them, let alone talking to them and so my classroom becomes a platform for acting out.

"The kids expect to be entertained every minute and as teachers we're expected to satisfy their need for attention while at the same time we're required to keep them focused and passing the ANGS Standardized

Commercial Education Outcome exams so they can qualify for employment someday.

"I love my kids, you know that, Gil, but I wonder who'll hire them. We get them everyday for sixteen hours, and we do what we can for what little they pay us. If my kids test below standard again this year and I don't quality for a raise, I'll . . ."

"You'll teach again next year, Gale," Gil interrupted. "You're a teacher and a damn good one."

She refused to accept that. "I mean it, I'll find other work." Her sad brown eyes stared at him. "I do love to teach. Why must free markets make teaching so horrid?"

He patted her head. "Gale, every generation grows up doing the same things. Take me, for instance. I was home-schooled by my father, but mostly, I had free reign in Archive while most of my Mesh friends went to real schools and hated it. They would have loved to stay home with unlimited access to virtual technology, yet I always felt virtual learning was boring. I'm sure you and the other teachers will find a way to convince *ANGS* to provide more robust technology. I saw a report that some nursery universities have started a business adoption plan, whereby corporations select the most promising kids and sign them up to long term contracts. They pay all the kids' expenses until they reach the point where the corporation needs to see a return, and then the kids turn professional to fulfill their contract. You should bring that up with your school management."

"If we still had a union, maybe I'd recommend it," she said. "But as independent contributors, teachers can't convince ownership to do anything. First they destroyed my union and then they forced us to accept private industry oversight in return for reduced wages and limited funding. What a joke! It took years before our private sponsors realized what we were doing to their bottom line and, as a result, now they ignore us in their budgets. If there was a government to buy us back, I'd jump at the chance to go back and work for them. Frankly, it's only because my specialty is wealthy middle children that I even have a job. Most of my associates have lost their teaching careers to Archive.

"What makes it so sad and hard to accept is that my kids understand technology in ways I never will. They know how to bypass Archive firewalls to access *Virtuoso* and then I'm responsible for what they do in there, even though I don't know how they do it. We forbid them from showing initiative but these are kids, they find ways. The CEO of my school insists that the harder it is for them, the better they learn Capitalist skills, but I don't think so. It can't take much funding to reinforce *Virtuoso* firewalls and still provide the kids with a better learning experience, but the money never comes. It's not like business is content with the employees they're getting. You're a consultant, can you do something?"

"I'm not that much into business, Gale. You know that."

"Well, when you are, please do something. Today, during quiet time, Roboto Marvin, a ten-year-old boy in my class, he was discovered by his Home Room Avatar playing in *Virtuoso*. Somehow, he'd geeked into my Comparative Civilizations lesson plan and morphed it into an early Rome *Virtuoso* scenario. He was caught actively participating in an orgy, a Roman orgy. A ten year old! I was fortunate our bandwidth is so limited. The transmission was too pixilated and choppy or the *ANGS* Oversight Board would've fined me big time. As it was, I'm no longer allowed to instruct my students about anything Roman, which is ludicrous if you're teaching Theology and Capitalism in Western Civilization.

"I'm so frustrated. If these poor kids don't qualify for work, they'll become *Wasters* and die, and I'll feel somewhat responsible. I know they're young, but I take it professionally. All my kids want is to have fun and screw their tiny, immature, virtual brains out instead of focusing on the coursework that will make them productive *Conducers.* I seem to be the only one who cares.

"They're bright kids when it comes to satisfying themselves but they are so undisciplined when learning and utilizing what I'm teaching. If they don't turn it around, they'll never achieve high value careers and I'll never get the raise I deserve."

"It's unfortunate," Gil offered, "but the process of creative destruction is quite good at winnowing out the underachievers and it has to be ingrained when they're young to be effective. If a child can't grasp how important forever is and what he has to do to get there, it's safe to assume he'll be a cost burden and business has the right to eliminate him. That's the way of our world."

She contemplated it unhappily.

"Don't be discouraged. When I was their age, I thought about sex, too."

She frowned at that. "Thanks for trying to cheer me up but I don't believe that for a second." He'd made a mistake. He had brought sex up but he didn't want to continue in that direction because it was unsafe territory. Gale, seeing an opportunity, pressed on.

"When you were a boy," she continued, "*Virtuoso* wasn't sophisticated enough for sex." He decided not to correct her but as she always did, she read something in his silence. "You did, why you rascal." She always considered his silence license to persist. "I never would have thought that you . . . Studies show that when kids are involved in sex prematurely, particularly virtual sex, it affects their adult relationships and . . ."

Too late, she realized she'd crossed a line and her face flushed red. In horror, she put her hand to her mouth and tried desperately to recover. "No, I wasn't . . . I'm not talking about you, us . . . I'm sorry, Gil. I just meant . . . It slipped out. I'm sorry" Tears formed and not knowing what else to do, she snuggled close.

He accepted her embrace and stared out in search of calming waves. It wasn't her fault and of course she was sorry. She did sorry good.

She started to say something but he put his finger to her lips, silencing her. "I just got back," he said. "I've been away a long time and it's too soon to scratch at old wounds. Let's not ruin today. Be happy that I'm here."

"I am happy. When I heard you were coming back for good, I told my students and we counted the days together. I was so tired of your short visits back, not that I wasn't glad to see you, but you were always so stressed and we never . . ." To silence her, he returned his finger to her lips. They returned to resting quietly in the gentle embrace of the almost invisible hammock.

"Maybe after the exam you'll be more at ease," she added. "That would be nice."

"Gale . . ."

"Is it so wrong to . . . to want you? I know you prefer to be cerebral, but I can't help it if I find you sexy. I see the way you look at me. You think I'm attractive, too."

"You are. You're a sexy woman, smart and caring."

"I should thank you, but—"

"Why do there have to be buts?" he asked. "I respect your profession even though few appreciate it enough to provide better funding. In fact, I feel guilty living in luxury, significantly overpaid for doing something not nearly as important as what you do."

"I don't understand you," Gale maintained. "We're all worth what we're worth. This is free enterprise at its best and there's no fairer way to live. It's what made America great. I explain that every day to my kids and it's a critical lesson because, like few things in our world, it's true everywhere and for all time. If it's the only lesson that ever gets through to them it'll be worth it, well almost. Besides, if the Chairwoman didn't think you had great value, you wouldn't be living like this. She doesn't invest in bad assets."

He inventoried his list of safe replies and carefully applied one. "Thanks, Gale."

"Gil Rose, you are so frustrating. For all you've been through, why can't you just be grateful for what you have? You're living better than 99.9999 percent of the world's population. That's something to be proud of."

He reminded himself that this was her way of cheering him up but it had the opposite effect. He liked and respected her. He even found her attractive, but she was a product of a system that he hated, and because of it, she would never understand him. If he was ungrateful or unemotional, or if he chose his words too carefully, sometimes, it was because he knew who was listening and he never knew what part of what innocent sound bite Gecko might find intriguing enough to recommend to Chairwoman Brandt for her listening pleasure. But even more important, he mustn't ever encourage her.

He gently disengaged and stood, leaving Gale alone, suspended, and gently swaying, in the invisible hammock. Walking to the edge of his swimming cove, he stared at the digital projection of fish and plants that made the cove appear alive. His eyes followed the water to the lake where cresting waves crashed against his dock causing his sailboat to bob and roll. In her way, Gail had identified the issue. What was his value to Brandt? And how much longer would Brandt value it?

He continued to stare out at the waves. She walked to him but stopped short as if frightened to close the distance. Their relationship would have been easier if he could have given her what she wanted most, a forever financial commitment, some regular lovemaking, and liabilities—children in the vernacular—but he couldn't, he simply couldn't. Her requirements were reasonable and by anyone's standards she was an appreciable asset and she only wanted to make life better for him in ways she believed it could be better. So she hung on dearly to what she thought they had, believing that eventually her persistence would define their relationship, while he found it sad that she endured his passivity, his lack of commitment, and when his patience waned, his indifference. He wouldn't mislead her and so in the little time they spent together she ineffectively hid her hurt and he his guilt.

She sought intimacy and commitment while he warded it off, preferring mere companionship. What he wanted most, he knew was impossible but that wouldn't spare her the inevitable harm. If he had been cruel or more certain, he would've ended their relationship because her unrelenting efforts to sustain it made it impossible for her to consider that it must end.

When he had departed for his consulting gig in Bolivia, he decided not to communicate with her; hoping that what cowardice couldn't achieve, maybe isolation would. Each brief and occasional visit home ended more awkwardly and unsatisfactorily. In her way, she loved him and forgave him everything, and that only made it worse, for he was weary of disappointing good people. Still, he endured the misery he caused her and correctly blamed himself for perpetuating it.

"I know your life has been sad," she said, striking that tapped-out vein again. "But for a long time, everyone's life was sad. We all lost family and friends, but things have settled down now, and life is easier and way better. Bad stuff doesn't happen so much and we live more profitably now so isn't it time for you to put those feelings aside?

"We're not . . ."

"If you were a failure, I could understand why you feel like you do. But you're a high net worth guy and what bothers you is that everyone respects and honors the value you provide yet you don't feel worthy."

What bothered him right then was the splitting headache of a migraine gaining dominion. She had the knack for doing that to him.

He walked her back to the hammock.

"Don't look at me like that," she said. "I've said it before; you'll implode if you don't commission a psych avatar to talk to about this, or at least work it out in virtual treatments with a good, solid healthcare avatar. If that doesn't work, there are palliatives for everything. I understand you, Gil, but think how confusing your attitude is to your business associates."

"I don't care about them."

"Why is it so easy for you to simply disengage? A productive person cares about what peers and superiors think. Is it any wonder that your associates mistake your attitude for ego? They think you think you're superior because you're the grandson of a former president who once was a favorite of Madam Brandt. They don't see the brilliant and tough consensus builder. How can they know what you're selling if you don't try to sell them on it? Your attitude was unsettling to me at first; think what it's like for them." Her words continued to feed energy into the tightening vortex of a strengthening migraine.

"There, see, see what I mean? I'm just talking and you act like I'm stealing money from you. Why can't you enjoy the life you've earned? You deserve it or you wouldn't have it. It's that simple. There's that face again. You do deserve it.

"When we go out, I hear people talking. They say you have mad skills and a bright future. The Chairwoman likes you and there's nothing wrong with that, it's what everyone strives for. With her on your side, nothing will get in the way of your career so stop waiting for bad luck to ruin everything. You're way past that."

He closed his eyes and took a deep breath. "I appreciate what you're saying, Gale. I've been fortunate. It's just that, that . . ."

"Talk to me honey. I love you." She said it softly and simply and so directly he didn't have time to prepare. Worse, he was staring into her eyes when she said it and he could tell that whatever expectations she had hoped for in that moment, she was horribly disappointed. Her expectant look became defensive and her eyes glistened with tears. Then, seeing the reaction in his eyes of what he was seeing in hers, she turned away. If she had hoped to pick the right moment to offer those words, she knew instantly, she hadn't thought it through.

He felt weary and overpoweringly sad for both of them and wanted nothing more than to be alone but that wouldn't be kind so he tried to calm her.

"Gale, please. I'm sorry. You know . . . I can't," he said it softly but the panic in her eyes sucked dread into his heart. His head was throbbing now and even staring out at the waves only amplified it. He had tried so hard to avoid confrontation, but hurting good people came far too easily.

She looked down, tears poured from her cheeks, dripping through the invisible netting to pool on the stone below as she waited for him to deliver the death blow.

Throughout their relationship, he was never able to draw on the right words that would articulate his feelings and spare her the pain, so he had long ago stopped groping for the wrong ones. In the past, she reacted in various ways but acceptance was never one. She was desperate now and showed courage trying to salvage the moment. She blinked her tears away.

"I said I love you. I wasn't asking you to reciprocate. Its how I feel and I want you to know . . . that's all . . . whatever happens."

"Thank you," he said. It wasn't eloquent but it was accurate.

She lifted her hands to his chest. "I would gladly go bankrupt to know what's rooted in your past that makes a really terrific guy like you act like such a creep." Tears began again and she turned away.

What happened next was instinct. He reached for her before realizing his mistake.

"I'm sorry, he offered. "I don't want it to be like this. I care about you but I'm not who you want or need."

"You make me sound like a poor investment."

"No, I mean . . . wait," he steeled himself. "The truth, you deserve the truth."

She let out a little yip of a scream and put her hand to her mouth to stifle another.

He persevered into uncharted territory. "Gale, what you need, I can't ever give you. I wish I could, but I can't. We've been together since before Bolivia, so why this now? I'm here and that's something. I wish you could accept and appreciate it."

"I know you're scared to commit, but why must you be so hurtful?"

"Things were going well, weren't they? We attend the best parties, we eat at the best restaurants, and we live in the most sought after location in the world. You know what it's like out there. Can't this be enough?"

Her chin slumped to her chest. Her eyes looked up and she sounded exhausted. "How can it be good enough for me when it isn't for you?" It was like her to say something that hurt so much.

"This is how I need to live," he said. "To continue—and I'm not suggesting we should—can't you accept it and not ask for more—there isn't more, I promise you."

She made as if to slap him. "How can you say that to me? I've done nothing but accept you. I changed my life for you. I put mom and dad in a facility even though I couldn't afford it without your financial support, knowing they'd die if you broke up with me. I accepted that risk gratefully." She stopped. He said nothing so she continued.

"You're nice to me, mostly, and unlike everyone I've ever met, you're kind and fair and you're so rich! I look around your home and I love how you spend your money. You'd be perfect except you sleepwalk through life and I don't understand why. What's wrong with commitment—not just financial but to me? Do you know what living like this is doing to me?"

Like some disobedient middle child, he nodded, contritely.

"What happens to me in your future? You're a wealthy Morgan who is definitely fast tracked to live large and forever. You've refused Singularity treatments, but someday, because of your career, or an illness, or you don't like the way you feel when you get up in the morning or go to bed at night, you'll see the advantage of the infinite and begin treatments. Like every executive, you'll decide on forever. There's no choice, really. I don't hold that against you, no one does. You'll be immortal and you deserve it, you've worked for it. But where will I be without you as a partner? I'm a commodity, a doomed mortal; I live with that because I lack economic potential and fantasizing about having potential will only reduce my lifespan. The best it can ever be for me is to know that when I die, you'll live happily long after and love so many other women that you'll forget everything about me, including my name. I live in fear of that."

"I have no interest in living forever."

"You aren't listening," she said angrily. "You say that but no sane person gives up forever when it's offered so why even argue? I'll die and you'll forget ever having known me." She began to cry and stood to run. He knew she expected it so he grabbed her arm and gently turned her toward him.

"Stop it," he demanded. "Stop beating me with words. Maybe you'll convert or maybe Tanya will change the rules. I don't know. Maybe the treatments will get cheaper, I don't know that either. Who does? They may not even work, for God's sake. I mean how do you prove you're getting what you pay for and if you don't, who do you sue? Something will happen, we're capitalists and something always does. It's important to you, so I promise I'll take care of your parents no matter what happens to us. If you want to move them closer or to a better facility, I'll pay for that, too. If you want Singularity, I'll find a way to have you qualified and I'll pay for it. What more can I offer?"

"I want to be your partner!" she screamed. "What good does it do me to have all eternity to miss you and regret having known you? If that's how it will be, I'll gladly stay mortal so that regret dies with me. And I won't allow my parents to become tokens of a former relationship. It isn't their fault. They were born Christian in the First Republic and they never learned to live as capitalists. But they were good to me, they bought me what I needed and they allowed me to follow my career instincts, they just weren't highly motivated enough to build their capital account and when they were no longer economically viable, they had years left. Gil, I'm happy that you're offering to take care of them, but think about it. When I'm history and you find someone else, and you will, she won't understand why you're funding a former girlfriend's parents and she'll be right. Don't be naïve. It'll happen; everything is possible in the infinite. And what I fear most, there will come a time during your eternal life when you will hate me long before you forget me. In the end, all I'll have is my net worth, which is inadequate, and I'll be forced to take care of my parents until they die and then I'll die alone. But before I die, I'll have nothing but regret and I'll hate you. I'll hate you." She began to sob anew.

She was too good at worst-case scenarios.

"Gale, partnerships don't guarantee anything. They are easily deconstructed. And your parents, I'm sorry, but how many years do they have? Surely a few decades in a luxurious assisted living facility is better than what you just described? I'll sign a contract. I'll take care of them, in perpetuity and anonymity if that's what you want."

"That's not the problem I want solved. You don't understand. I love you and I value you. If you truly value me, you'd show it in the only way that matters. In my heart, I know that if you had no value and I had wealth and promise, I would gladly protect your assets in every possible way for all time. You make it obvious that you don't value me that way and that much."

He blinked away the blow. There it was: the truth. It seems so elusive until it kicks you in the gut. Begrudgingly, he gave Gale her do. When all you do is dig, sometimes you unearth a gem. This was his fault. It had come to this and it would only get worse and wouldn't end unless he ended it. Still . . .

"Gale . . ."

She grabbed the first thing she found, his communicator, and threw it. He thought he'd caught it but it bounced off his fingertips and hit him in the throat. Tears formed as he coughed and choked briefly. Thinking she'd hurt him, she stepped toward him and then seeing that he was okay, she ran away crying.

Instead of following her, he searched for his communicator. He found it broken so he tossed it from hand to hand before angrily hurling it as far as he could. It skittered across the beach and landed at the water's edge, where it was immediately inundated by a wave and was soon buried in sand.

Frustrated, he dove into his cove to swim away his frustrations. When he was finished, dripping wet, exhausted, and depressed, he entered his sunlit study where she lay sleeping curled on a couch. He fought his instinct to comfort her and decided against it so he returned to the lanai. Before he could try to relax, another communicator announced a call from the White House.

Chapter 2

Tianrong Zhang—2083

This was Tanya Brandt's favorite meeting room in her White House. She swore by this room but rarely used it so as not to exhaust the good fortune she attributed to the fear that oozed from errant petitioners who capitulated to her will here. And she had been looking forward to this meeting, this joust, and maybe even this tryst. But unusual for her, she wasn't certain, not of today's guest, and that made the meeting even more exciting. She wore her favorite lavender business suit that accentuated her eyes and accented it with an off-white blouse that made her tiny waist seem tinier while accentuating her world class boobs. She also wore one of her lucky purple polka dot floppy bowties but left it suggestively untied. And mindful that it contrasted sharply with her lavender and purple outfit, she wore her American Second Republic flag pin, the alternating green and silver stripes flowing from a gold corner square populated by six rows of eight Almighty Dollars in green and silver.

Sitting across from her was Tianrong Zhang, the current CEO of *Global Solar* and the most powerful businesswoman in China, and thus the world outside of the United States. In a world still dominated by silly men, Tian was the single most important pure capitalist to percolate out of China's free markets since China committed to free market gospel. She was reputed to be more ruthless and dominating than anyone Tanya had ever faced, having employed her immense corporate power to turn the aging and decaying Chinese Communist Central Committee Board of Directors into an ineffectual advisory council. She was here today as a supplicant.

Tanya thought back to the last time a CEO from *Global Solar* had been entertained at the White House. *Global Solar* was *Mobile Global* then, and the meeting took place early in Andy's reign in that horrid, old and decrepit, and not yet soggy Washington D. C. White House. She hadn't been invited, one of the slights she had nurtured into revenge.

Seated across from her, CEO Zhang was lean and seemed lithe, a vibrant young woman of sixty, with tight, unwrinkled, and mostly unflawed skin, long flowing straight and shiny black hair, accented with streaks of gray and dark red, and she possessed not unattractive deep chocolate almond eyes. The Chinese leader was elegantly dressed in a black and pink formal *cheongsam* that fit with an exquisite tightness, accentuating shapely legs that went on precisely as far as they had to. And though her breasts were small, they seemed firm. The one flaw in her otherwise unblemished presentation were her freckled cheeks, but a small, button nose standing guard over a fetching smile made the freckles forgivable. She wasn't Tanya's usual taste, by any means, but unusual was a turn on too, and for good deals to get done; the lights need not be on.

At Tanya's command, a servant poured her CEO guest a glass of exquisite 2061 vintage Chinese claret from the world famous Hu Vineyards of Shandong Province. Tian picked up her glass, nodded at the label, and foregoing tasting tradition, slowly imbibed and then asked for more. With the second glass, she held the wine in her mouth overlong before swallowing and sucking in air. "We make marvelous wines." She spoke in an American dialect that was curiously Midwestern. Tian then nodded toward Tanya's servant. "It's good that your America permits slavery. Free market capitalism doesn't work as well without it. Here's to you, Tanya dear. Here's to all the great things that you've done. You will be revered forever."

Tanya purred at the compliment, smiled, and then took a sip of her wine. "America's First Republic tried to evolve a more egalitarian society, more egal than you ever faced in China, my dearest. Allow *Us* to compliment you, Tian, sweetness. You speak divine, impeccable English but please speak Mandarin; *We* love the sound of your native tongue and I have onboard AI that translates faultlessly."

"Of course," Zhang agreed, readily. "But how will I know how effective your translator is unless I hear her for myself? We've done studies. Nuance is still too hard for AI to translate accurately. My own AI is sorely lacking in that area."

"Still, let *Us* try. I insist. I will have the translation spoken aloud so you can judge the accuracy for yourself. Now where are we? Oh, yes, you have come to offer a deal. Splendid. Before we discuss it, it is important for you to know that I consider you the dearest executive in the entire world, but your tired old offer is no longer valid. Since last it was offered, America has returned to the zenith of global economies. Surely you recognize that?"

"*Global* is pleased to have you join us as a world economic leader once again, my sweet, soon to be partner." Tian spoke in Mandarin and then waited for the translation. After hearing it, she approved. "Your AI is perfect. She sounds just like me. We may proceed." She paused and then said, admiringly, "Her inflection really is quite good."

Tanya smiled. "Thank you, Tian dearest; *he* fills an important role in my world."

The *he* seemed to give Tianrong pause, but she allowed it to pass.

Tanya quickly moved on. "America's great social experiment has succeeded far beyond anything our global competitors believed possible and so *We* have once again forced the world to play by *Our* rules or lose market share. Given all the grief they caused *Us*, it will pleasure me greatly, Tian, to watch how the Christian Democrats in their silly European Union implement their downsizing solution which, of course, they must do to stay competitive. *Our* Missionaries are trained and available."

"I suspect that the cost of nurturing the world to crisis and then having the precise resources to solve that crisis is going to be quite expensive."

Tanya laughed. "The world must pay restitution for their affronts while *We* were vulnerable as we built *Our* Capitalist utopia. They will be financially gracious and they will apologize or our fees will grow."

The CEO said nothing but the voice of her translator added in a sincere, almost repentant voice, "I'm sorry." At those words, Tian squirmed ever so slightly before protesting. "Tanya, I most assuredly did not say thank you. That was your translator's doing. I can't continue if your translator takes liberties."

"I apologize. The AI was merely suggesting the proper response. Let us move on to more profitable discussions, shall we." It felt soothing to display her very best smile.

"Tanya, your efforts are to be congratulated. And certainly, my dove, overseas profits from your missionary efforts should bring astonishing returns given the high number of new poor you've created through advising foreign corporations about new methods of wealth accumulation that have caused severe unemployment. That is why we have determined that this is a wonderful time to invest in America, LLC. We've been monitoring progress of America 2.0, as you so creatively call it, and we are impressed. For decades, our American subsidiary, ANGS, has benefited greatly doing business on the cutting edge of the libertarian Liquidation solution that your great revolution implemented to save the profits of American Capitalists."

Tanya never tired of hearing praise. "Yes, ever since before the 'Mission Accomplished' ceremony that marked the official end to *Our* Circle of Life law and the great downsizing, *Our* corporations have reported the lowest costs in the world as well as record profits."

"There isn't a boardroom in the world that doesn't revere you as the first true Capitalist revolutionary. My dear Tanya, you are so young and vibrant. It's hard to believe you were there when Capitalism won. You are fortunate to have lived through in reality what I could only experience in virtual."

She smiled demurely. "Yes, I'm so revered that some Asian corporations sell my likeness to support their brands but they refuse to pay *Us* royalties." She laughed as Tian struggled to smile. "As a principled leader, I could consider that an act of war but as a businesswoman, I never shit where *We* eat. You understand." She smiled, serenely, and continued. "There is social and economic unrest throughout the world, but in America, everything is productive and calm because *We* know that prolific business profits require a predictable and secure environment. Armed with that knowledge, *We* will turn America into a free market Garden of Eden just like *Our* Morgan Bible says existed in biblical times."

"Yes, of course, your vision is to be . . . commended."

"In spite of great international pressure, *We* stay our course, on course, of course, until all waste is eliminated."

"Of course, dear, your draconian handling of labor is taught in business schools throughout the world. It has often been tried but never duplicated. Please, may I get to the point of my visit?"

Tanya nodded, thrilled that Tianrong had broken first.

"*Global Solar's* subsidiaries are facing civil unrest in Africa and Asia, much of it fomented by your Morgan missionary consultants and that has added a great deal of commercial complexity and a significant impediment to growing our price per share. We see similar issues wherever your missionaries perform your 'God's work'. I confess. I wish we had thought of making Capitalism a religion but our consumers worship too many gods as it is. What you did was genius. The Christian world was certainly ripe for a new God and Capitalism was like a religion anyway so, well done." Tian laughed politely. "That said, Tanya, honey, we love free markets as much as anyone but no one approves of Capitalist on Capitalist crime and this turmoil created by your missionaries, it has had a deleterious affect on my shareholders so I come to you seeking respectful abeyance. It is time to revisit the proposal we offered to your former Chairman years ago that he rejected."

Tian paused to listen to the interpretation which added to her surprise, "Because of the severe problems that we at *Global* face with *Untouchables* in Christian-Democrat Europe and Buddhist-Mormon Asia, people you call *Wasters,* I have no choice but to make this offer again. My Board is in a panic and they're pressing me hard for results." As the interpreter recited in her voice, words she hadn't spoken, her face registered shock.

"I . . . I never said that." Indignant, she began to rise but seemed to sense something and sat down while working a smile onto her face. "Tanya, love, how do you know that?"

Tanya expanded her advantage. "Sweetheart, let's not forget your issues in Voodoo-Mormon Africa, or in Mormon-Catholic South America. Tian, Tian, *We* respect you so much, but to succeed in a truly unregulated free market Capitalist world, the victory always goes to those who own the most timely, the most perfect information. Please, don't be alarmed with your *Untouchables* or *Wasters. We* lived through similar unrest and although nowhere near as violent as yours, America's troubles were much, much briefer, too. *Conducers* are addle-brained and addicted to work and though they are sometimes angry with *Us*, they fear becoming *Wasters* and so are as compliant as lambs. That's how we grow them but we became lenient and so by the end of *Our* First Republic, *Our* economy was much like yours today. Deluded *Conducers* thought they had real power. Go figure. Once we convinced them that it was the *Wasters* who were dragging them down, we were able to work our plan.

"As principled leaders we do what's necessary. So what if *We* were condemned as mass murderers by outsiders. Fame has its detractors and those foolish decriers never bothered to calculate the expected returns from our actions. That's why *We* never buckled. You break eggs to make a soufflé. Certainly, we lost some businesses and some productive people who might have helped us but the soufflé was worth it, dearest, it was well worth it.

"Look at *Our* economy today. *Our Conducers* and *Entrepreneurs* would never put their jobs or their lives at risk for anything as ephemeral as a cause. The quest for money rules them now completely and supporting a cause never has a good return. For that reason, unions, sabotage, books, fraud, sloth, news, vandalism, voting, and so many other treasonable acts that the rest of the world is fighting to overcome, they all failed here. I swear to you that once *Our* Morgan Missionaries instill that quiescence in the world's workers, global free market Capitalism will triumph and unrest will cease everywhere. And when that happens, *Our* Almighty Dollars will be invested at global Morgan Stock Exchanges and Capitalism will be worshipped in international Morgan Churches."

Suspecting that her conversation might be corrupted, Tian responded in Mandarin, anyway. "Yes, I suppose. You are fortunate, Tanya, whatever God created this earth; she was a jokester who dealt America alone great location cards." She seemed relieved when her exact words and inflection were presented in English and so she continued, cautiously. "*Global Solar* subsidiaries are everywhere yet with two vast oceans to separate America from economic variability, your corporations can service everywhere cheaper than we can. As to my offer, we wish the same terms as were discussed with your predecessor."

Tianrong paused to evaluate the AI translation to English. Once again finding it accurate and not extracurricular; she visibly relaxed.

Tanya clapped her hands excitedly, startling the CEO. "*We* are so delighted with your offer; Tian, my sweetness, but times have changed and so must *Our* relationship. *We* insist on a premium that represents *Our* current advantage. *We* needed you then; today, you need *Us* and that changes the net back equation in *Our* favor."

"*Global* has issues, certainly, but America is not without issues of its own. Your *Circle of Life* legislation delivered astonishing results, but it left you with disadvantages insurmountable without my assistance. Certainly the ocean tides have been an equal opportunity destroyer of assets but as a result of your Circle of Life pogrom, too many of your previously deployed assets have gone dormant generating costs and negative returns. Now in decay, these assets burden balance sheets and you lack the human resources to recover or replace them.

"Tanya, love, you know how much I respect you but American business is desperate because they can't grow fast enough. You need *Global Solar* as a partner because only we have the commercial bandwidth and human assets to more fully utilize your fallow resources. To demonstrate my seriousness, I am prepared to offer America's corporations immediate access to the very same foreign markets that have been boycotting your economy ever since you started eradicating your economic burdens. My experts have done the research. What I propose is a very favorable offer that America's Mayors and *Executives* will gladly support."

Tian paused, but when the interpreter continued on in her voice, all she could do was gape. "What I really want is American land—complete ownership of it," the AI said. "I don't want leasehold rights, those will never do. And I want these lands in perpetuity. The first property my senior management team has selected is an underutilized tract of farmland outside of what was once Sacramento."

Doing her best to cover her rage, Tian listened as her most secret knowledge was divulged by the translator. She swallowed and then spoke, working the concern from her voice. "That you know this and I am here means that you accept my offer. Good. Let's do it and we will allow American corporations to once again tap into markets that a century ago valued that proudest of slogans, 'Made in America'.

"My financial experts assure me the tract of land that we . . . that you just identified for colonization, that it is available and, as you probably know; we will pay twice for it. We will pay what the land is worth today, upfront, and every year we will mark the value of the land to what the market says its worth and pay you the appreciation as well. We will do that for a period of twenty years and then the land passes to us in perpetuity. As you know, this is a great deal so don't toy with my affections, Tanya, and agree in principle to it so that our accountants and lawyers can tidy it up for the photo op."

"*We* love you," Brandt cooed, "and can deny you nothing. I'm truly wet with excitement and can't wait to continue what is destined to be a legendary relationship."

At that, Tian returned to perfect English. "If you please, there is one final condition. I want assurances that the political status quo in America remains just so."

The question took her by surprise. "No, that won't do. *We* are done here. We have completed . . . everything is in order. What could change the status quo, my sweet?"

"You have in your employ a young man purported to be a legendary messiah that your *Waster* community yearns for, the man prophesied to overthrow your government and institute some form of virulent socialism for his supporters. Explain to me why this man is in your employ? How can that be smart?"

Unfamiliar with not knowing, Tanya remained silent awaiting a response that she could use. It felt exciting and a little scary.

"You can imagine my shock, Tanya dearest, when I discovered that this messiah was in your employ. Frankly, I was stunned. You are impulsive, surely, but not this. I can accept happenstance and even serendipity but only about as much as I accept the tooth fairy, so I find the irony of you employing this messiah somewhat disturbing."

Again, she remained silent.

"The situation is farcical. This messiah who will tear down your civilization is also your neighbor! Can that be right? I trust real estate values haven't declined since this messiah invested in your neighborhood." Tianrong laughed.

With a response ready, Tanya returned the laugh. "Where *I* live, Tian," she said, accentuating the *I*, "real estate values never decline."

"Darling, I'm certain that's true. But if we're to be the very best business partners; please explain how having this . . . this messiah is a good business decision."

"How could it be anything else? *Our* economy is great but these are frightening times for certain high risk, low yield *Conducers* and for every remaining *Waster*. As it always does, fear creates an opportunity for a great many enterprising false prophets and messiah-want-to-be's who are searching for a lifestyle they can survive in and a way to fund it. New York City alone is up to my shitter in shit with them," she explained. "If you want, take a few of them home with you," she said, dismissively.

"Every day, *Our* HOMESEC patrols pick up the most enterprising messiahs off the streets. Most are summarily eliminated, but those special few with innate entrepreneurial talent and drive, desperate people searching hard for that one great score to make their mark and live forever, those *We* employ and some provide *Us* with great returns. It seems that once *We* shine *Our* economic light on these . . . holy marketers, what a delight it is to monitor their moral and ethical decay. But if their ardor for Morgan burns hot enough and they are able to dismiss their prior beliefs in order to meet *Our* requirements, their economic situation improves and with that, their rebel habits, their passion for any previous deeply held principles, it all totally evaporates. Some have described that moment of Capitalist infusion as a feeling much like religious communion. *We* are expert at it and have watched millions of them break and I say that it is much more an orgasm than a communion and as you know, you can never experience a bad orgasm . . ."

It was Tian's turn to be speechless so Tanya continued. "This is a teaching moment, my lovely lotus blossom. Capitalism's essence is the force of raw domination and it attracts the most extraordinary and most wonderfully entertaining pets. Let's name this messiah. He is Gil Rose and *We* assure you that *We* enjoy total control over him. Currently, he is earning a post-graduate Morgan Missionary Consulting degree. That's not the usual coursework for a zealot, I assure you."

Tian leaned forward. "As I understand, this Rose is the grandson of the last democratically elected president of your First Republic. How can you be so certain that you control him?"

"Yes, he's Mark Rose's grandson, but what of it? Mark is mine, totally. He always was and always will be. This Rose is simply darker and frankly he lacks Mark's limited brilliance, but other than that, there is no difference, he is a younger version of a long series of incompetents. Let's be done with this conversation. *We* will invite Rose to tonight's banquet. Speak with him. Evaluate him yourself and you will see that with him, there is no risk that needs mitigation."

"Splendid. I will speak with him. But before we conclude our deal, I must know everything that affects me. Why this? Why a messiah?"

"The ultimate goal of our *Circle of Life* legislation conforms to the philosophy of Saints Adam Smith and Ayn Rand—to make economies efficient. It is simply uneconomical to maintain people who can't or won't contribute. No entrepreneur should or ever will again take on the extra tax burden of perpetual handouts and perpetual security that is required to keep wasteful people quiescent.

"Tian honey, the world now faces what we have solved. *Our* Consultant's standard Elevator Speech covers it. 'When you go somewhere you have never been; to insure success, you must take with you someone who has been there'. *Our* Missionaries have been there. They are your guides, the *Circle of Life* is their Roadmap, and Gil Rose is *Our* final solution test case. You see, even now, *Waster* revolts pop up. All are inconsequential and are put down quickly. But there is a cost. Revolts can take the form of protests, boycotts, strikes, and the occasional political nominee, who slips past our screeners in local elections, but we end them and kill most of the *Wasters* involved, but still, like cockroaches, some get away and it has become cost prohibitive to wipe out all of their pesky little hives. Gil Rose is our solution and when we have the results from his actions, we will incorporate that into our *Circle of Life* brand of products and services completing the arc of annihilation that frees world economies to reach their true potential and explore new economic horizons in order to create capitalist paradises of their own."

Tianrong was so deeply absorbed that Tanya felt a sexual warmth building between them. If she could only get past her freckles, maybe this meeting will end with total victory.

"Tian, my beautiful friend, *We* keep Rose in order to enhance his legend as the one. By doing this, it gives every *Waster* rebel hope and even some courage. Already, they have begun to congregate in anticipation of Rose's ascension."

"Why is he working for you? I don't understand."

She liked this part of *Their* plan best of all. "*We* are acting consistent with the original Jesus fable, the one where Christ exposes evil capitalist moneychangers in some great Jew temple. Really, moneychangers in a Jew temple, isn't that racist? Of course, where else would they be, Morgan bless them? Anyway, if you haven't read the story, it is in most Christian bibles and we have stacks of them in old Washington warehouses."

"If it's such a good plan, why hasn't it worked?"

"It is a *terrific* plan. It turns out, blood runs true, but while Mark was a spontaneous ejaculator, this Rose is a namby-pamby procrastinator. Neither delivers the goods."

Tian seemed uncomfortable with that explanation. "So force him."

"To be a proper test, *Wasters* can't see our involvement. For the stupid and lazy bastards who seek to follow him, it must feel right. But don't fear, sweetheart, it will happen very, very soon." Tanya paused before cooing, "I am overwhelmed with your sexuality and your business sense and so *We* fear that I have said too much."

"No, no, I find this interesting and clever, Tanya, but I still believe it is wiser to kill Rose and be done with him. When his followers rise up, eliminate them."

"We have nurtured this Rose resource for too long, it is inefficient to waste him," she explained. "The beauty of stupid people is that they will believe that if he dies, instantly, he is not the One they are waiting for and *Our* investment loses any possibility of return. Kill him and his followers slither back into their holes, causing intermittent cost overruns as they become ever more expensive to eradicate while they await rumors of yet another messiah. No, Tianrong, Rose stays alive until he delivers. It's just like in sex, do it right the first time and every time."

"You know him that well?"

Her smile evaporated. "Am I fucking him? No. I've considered it. I have naked pictures of him, he is attractive and suitably endowed, but my male sex partners become rather useless once I'm done with them and he is far too valuable to waste that way. Maybe I'll indulge once I don't need him anymore. With delicate flowers, Tianrong, *We* must be gentle and Gil Rose is *Our* delicate flower."

"My reports say he is . . . not so delicate."

"Rose is not without career threatening issues. He's a true ambivalent, fortunately among the last of that endangered breed in America. The boy, he's thirty-something by the way, he tries to see both sides of any argument with an annoying equivalence like he doesn't want to be wrong or hurt someone's feelings and it paralyzes him. People who do nothing are abhorrent to the ideals of free market capitalism that *Our* legendary greats, Ayn Rand, Alan Greenspan, Selma Hayek, Milton Friedman and, of course, Thomas Morgan brought down from the mountain to the great people of America. People must succeed or die but they must *do* something. *Executives* and *Entrepreneurs* no longer search for greatness in our country.

"You and I both love the beauty and symmetry of free markets, Tian, sweetie. The weak settle to the bottom to become economic fertilizer while the few, the best and brightest bubble to the top and glory. Those remaining stay suspended in a great capitalist soup, the fiber that helps digestion and these we nurture to deliver clinical exactness. Passion and drive are everything and if someone needs a bridle or a whip, what good are they? Rose, poor Rose, in addition to ambivalence, he is cursed with the worst of all possible afflictions, he values people more than appreciable assets."

"So he cares for people but cannot act on it. *Wasters* are waiting for him to free them and yet he does nothing."

Tanya shrugged. "Yes, it's so frustrating, must we go on?" She reached out, tantalizingly, to straighten the brooch above Tian's small, firm breast letting her palm remain long enough for the CEO to sigh.

"Tell me more." She asked softly.

Tanya moved closer and rested her arms gently on Tian's. Their lips were close, so close it forced a decision but Tian remained motionless as Tanya continued. "*Our* very best researchers have never discovered a single religious writings that documents exactly what happens in this world when a messiah succeeds."

"There was Christian Rome, Tanya."

Tanya stared deeply into Tian's brown eyes looking for the jest. "Rome? I don't think so? Nowhere is it written how a messiah turns worthless, lazy rabble into a viable Socialist state with neither suffering nor inconvenience yet a state that is strong enough to resist an army of entrepreneurs trying to save their shit. Don't be silly. That never happened and never will." She separated slightly from Tian. "Rebels are disgusting, stupid, lazy people who loaf, gripe, and fuck bored rather than show some interest in their lives. Who else but these lazy bastards could fail in *Our* America, the land of opportunity? When they rise to oppose *Us,* Jesus, hisself, armed to the teeth, and hell, *We'll* give him thunderbolts. Even an armed and dangerous Jesus wouldn't stand a chance against *Our* might."

"Rose has killed people."

"My god, sweetie, who hasn't? His scalps were those of trivial *Wasters* and it was all knee jerk, not *pre-medicated.* Rose neglected to learn the commercial laws in Hamilton and killed two drunken *Wasters.* He was fined accordingly. The deed was so inconsequential, his fine wasn't enough to warm his PID. Your reports tell of another murder, this one in Profit, Ohio. My daughter Bree was there. Rose had fallen for her and he was trying to be gallant in front of her when a scuffle occurred and a local, valueless *Waster* malcontent caught a bullet with his brain. It's not worth a rat's ass to worry your sweet self about." Tanya smiled her most alluring smile and leaned in again. It was time to ease her tension.

Tian didn't move away but her eyes became glassy. "When . . . when do you expect his revolt to begin?" She whispered.

"My sweet, you've chosen wisely. The land you want is the home of America's last functioning union, a group of Christian *Wasters* with an expiring labor contract. How sad is that? They strike but before our deal is struck, *We* will break them, take their land, and give it to you, my love, at the agreed upon price. Mr. Gilbert Rose, *Our* messiah, has been assigned to that project."

"You believe Rose will choose the rebels over his career. No one is that foolish."

Tanya licked her lips, her tongue almost touching Tian's lips as she did. She could almost taste the coming Chinese. "That's the beauty of it," she cooed. "He will or he won't. He will attract his flock or not. *We're* prepared for either choice. You see, throughout a missionary consultant's career; every facet of his being is evaluated and constantly updated giving *Us* a detailed map of his value system and propensities. *We* know Rose better than he knows himself. Sacramento will be messy but in the end, he will rebel and America will be free of its last *Wasters* or he will resist his true nature and learn to destroy rebel towns. This will take longer, but I can revel in his torment."

"How can you be sure?"

"The only thing that I am sure about is that you excite me. Your sharp yet tender tongue has left me vulnerable to the thrusts of your concerns. You are my wondrous lotus blossom, and it is time to end this intercourse. About Rose, meet with him later and decide for yourself."

Tanya licked the lipstick on her powerful guest's lips. Then she stared into her chocolate eyes and waited. This was as far as she would go. If *Global Solar* wanted a deal, the next move was the CEO's so she waited patiently, even as Tianrong cautiously reached out to place her hand on Tanya's chin. After a frozen moment, the CEO gently kissed her cheek. Subtly, Tanya turned her head just enough so that their lips met and a cautious, seeking tongue gently insinuated itself into Tanya's mouth causing her to smile.

After CEO Zhang left, Tanya returned to her office where she received word that her daughter had arrived. It had been three years since Bree had last been to Monroe but the greeting was anything but warm. Tanya held out her hand and Bree reached for and dutifully kissed her ring.

She stared at the younger, less attractive version of herself and smiled. "Bree, darling, you're looking fit. Indonesia must have agreed with you."

"Thank you Madam Chairwoman. Indonesia was a great experience. Their management team was cooperative and we made great strides. Thank you again for green-lighting my project."

"No thanks are necessary, dear. *We* always green-light good projects in critical areas managed by strong leaders. Were you seeing anyone?"

"No, Madam Chairwoman. As you're aware, it was a missionary assignment."

"You can use that position if you prefer, I find it mundane. And call *Us* Mother."

"That's disgusting." Then Bree hesitated. "Yes, Mother."

"Now tell *Us,* dear. Was there one man in particular?"

Ever so briefly, Bree seemed embarrassed but then she closed up. "Project Managers see more of each other than anyone else."

"So who is he?"

"He's a prince, Mother. He was educated at the University of Chicago and Nan Yang Tech. It was productive and I learned a great deal about Indonesian culture."

"Did productive translate into the bedroom? You know what they say about Asian princes?"

Bree stiffened. "No, Mother, I don't and I would prefer not to. Besides, that's your area of interest, not mine. We delivered a tight project, on time and under budget. What else is there?"

"Nothing, dear. Gil Rose is here," She said it quietly and watched closely for Bree's reaction. There was a brief flicker, quickly hidden. That was good and bad. She was learning control and that meant she needed to pay more attention to her. "We received your Mr. Rose after a successful consulting engagement in Bolivia. He's taking his final exam in a couple of days. But then you know that."

"He's not my Mr. Rose, Mother, and you know damn well we haven't spoken since . . . since then."

"My, so sensitive. *We* merely assumed that once he fully committed to *Us*, you two would communicate."

"I was in Estonia on a mission when you captured him and in Ouagadougou when he began his studies. Then he went to Bolivia and I went to Indonesia. You know that."

Tanya smiled. "So you have been keeping track of him."

"I staff projects. It's my job to be aware of every resource."

"Very good, Bree. That was the appropriate response."

"It was an accurate response . . . Mother."

"Are you excited to see him?"

Bree hesitated before answering. "It will be nice to see him."

"Then prepare to feel nice. He and his long-term, live-in love will be attending tonight's banquet." She smiled as Bree flinched, ever so slightly at that information.

"You thrive on creating awkward situations. We were nineteen. What are you hoping for? Let me in on it so I can hurry the process along."

"Nothing, dear, *We* treasure loyalty but it must be recalibrated from time to time so *We* know how to reward it properly."

"I'm to be tested. Great, I hope you're disappointed. By the way, your use of the royal 'we' is still as pretentious and annoying as it was the last time."

"*We've* been mother to *Our* country far longer than *I've* been your mother."

"It sounds ridiculous. Excuse me, Mother; I need time to get ready."

"Be at my office by six thirty and be nicer to your mother. You're excused."

When Bree left, Tanya's secretary entered. "Madam Chairwoman, Gil Rose has confirmed your invitation. He'll be here promptly at six thirty."

"Of course, Helen, and he's bringing the bait."

"Yes, Madam, Gale Allen, she's a real teacher teaching middle children at a local school. She's committed to Mr. Rose though he doesn't share her feelings."

Tanya clapped her hands. "It's going to be delightful, Helen. Don't disturb me until it's time."

Chapter 3

Tanya's Party—2083

Gil listened patiently to the Chairwoman's secretary's instructions. He and Gale were to attend a banquet and he was invited to a pre-banquet meeting so they needed to be at the Chairwoman's mansion in a few hours. After disconnecting, he took a deep breath and considered how to approach Gale. The study was empty so he searched until he found her behind her locked bedroom door. He knocked, and though he heard movement, she didn't respond so he explained the situation through the closed door.

"This is a special invitation from the Chairwoman. I know you don't want to go, neither do I, but we can't refuse." There was no response.

He put his forehead against the door as he tried to reason with her. "Please, Gale, I know you're angry and disappointed with me but we can't offend the Chairwoman, it's dangerous. You know how angry she can get if things don't go her way. We have to avoid that so regardless how you feel about me, you can't piss her off. When she's angry . . . there's no guessing how she'll react."

There was no reply.

"She could cut your school funding or just cut off our heads, for Morgan's sake, and I'm not sure I'm kidding about that. You can't turn her down. We have to attend."

He heard her muffled response. "Did she ask for me, or just you and whoever?"

"I can barely hear you," he said. "Please open up." He tried the handle but the door remained locked. "The Chairwoman expects both of us to be there and yes, her secretary mentioned you by name. There's not much time and you have to get ready. Please. I'm sorry. You know that I am. And you know I'm right about this. Neither of us feels like going, but we don't have a choice."

"Go away. I had hoped things would be different. I guess . . ." The door opened suddenly. He was leaning against it and almost stumbled into her but pulled back, startled, and then put his arms out for her. She turned and flung herself onto the bed.

"I don't want to hurt you. I like you and really respect your commitment to your children."

"They're not my children, don't say that they are. And I'm tired of being damned by your faint praise. When will you realize you don't get extra credit for honesty?"

"We'll talk, I promise, but tonight we have to put it behind us."

"That's easy for you. You're a highly-trained professional in a field that honors subterfuge and I'm sorry but my training never covered charm. Can't you see that I'm scared about my future, scared that it will end? Is that so terrible? I can't party feeling like this."

"I understand. I really do. You're angry with me and I'm sorry I'm not who you want me to be, but . . ." He shrugged. "I'm doing my best to stay out of trouble."

She stood. "So I'm trouble. How's that working for you?"

"No, I . . . Please don't force this, Gale—not tonight—not with the Chairwoman. The stakes are too high for both of us. Look, I just got back. Give us some time. Maybe something will change. Once I graduate and my assignments are stateside, I'm sure I'll feel different about a lot of things."

She leaned toward him, her reddened eyes focusing intently on his. "You've never been a sweet talker, that's for sure. You tell me everything is on the line tonight, then you try to win my heart, and that's your best offer? 'Maybe I'll change.' Excuse me if, once again, I'm under whelmed by your less than professional charm."

He stared into her defeated eyes. He couldn't show it, but it hurt him to hurt her and he knew she was angry because she never got angry unless she was hurt. All that mattered right now though was that they attend the Chairwoman's banquet together.

"I won't lie," he admitted. "I don't know what will happen with us but I care about you. I care very much. Please believe me and let's not do this now. After my exam I'll have time, we'll have time. We'll take a few days and go somewhere so we can focus on each other."

"You're just saying that because you want me to attend this party."

"That's true, but it doesn't matter what I want. The Chairwoman wants to see you and no matter how angry you are with me, you must go and you know it. She's irrational and vindictive and a lot of other scary things, so you can't piss her off. Like it or not, we're going and we'll look like we're having fun. You know me. I wouldn't do this if—"

Resigned, she started to turn away from him. As he always did at times like this, he opened his arms for her, but this time, she shook her head and looked down.

"Let's try to have a good time tonight," Gil pleaded. "We need one."

"Don't you dare try to encourage me," she said. "I'll go but that's all."

"I didn't mean . . . you'll see, it will be an interesting evening and hopefully it'll pass quickly. We'll be sitting with some very connected people so you'll have a chance to explain your school issues. There is always a lot of private capital in any room the Chairwoman is in so if you can get someone's ear tonight, maybe you can get the funding you and the kids need."

"Stop working me. No one's interested in my kids but me and if anyone was, it certainly wouldn't be at the Chairwoman's party."

"You're wrong. Executives don't have down time and they appreciate hearing from the people who work in their trenches."

"If they were really interested, my school wouldn't have these problems."

"That's a different issue." He was trying hard to be patient and not cause further damage. "Corporations are interested in anything that will help the economy and an educated, committed work force does that like nothing else. Use this party to help the kids. Convince just one of these guys to spend and you're way ahead."

She refused to make eye contact, "I'm not a public speaker and top level executives and entrepreneurs are pitched every day and they don't suffer people who're far better than me."

"No one's better than you, Gale," he said. "You believe in the kids and you know what you want is right, so you can sell it. Honest, impassioned reasoning impresses the hell out of Corporate Lobbyists and think of the good it will do the kids."

She nodded, her resolve firmed up. "Okay, I'll go. How much time do I have?"

"The Chairwoman wants to meet us in her study in two hours."

"What'll I wear?"

"I ordered a new business suit for you. It will be delivered within the hour."

"That's so thoughtful. If only—" She saw his reaction and stopped. "What color?"

"It's dark purple, the Chairwoman's favorite color. She really likes it when people emulate her. I took the liberty of ordering a mauve blouse and I hope black shoes work."

"What accessories did you get?"

"I'm sorry, I didn't—"

"Men." She appeared reenergized. "Two hours. That's fifteen minutes in the virtual mall with delivery within the hour. I'll have the perfect jewelry just in time."

Before the gondola arrived to take them to the Chairwoman's mansion, Gale walked out of their bedroom, dressed and ready, her hair coiffed and the nano-make-up applied, perfectly accentuating her natural good looks. When he saw her, he remembered how he felt when they first met.

"You look great," he offered. "Everyone will be staring at you."

"It's enough if you stare," she countered. "Every woman who attends the Chairwoman's parties is gorgeous. You'd think she was into women, I mean they are that good-looking. And for her age, she's stunning." She paused. "You'd better not stare at her."

"Never, besides, with today's cosmetics, who isn't gorgeous?"

She put her hands on her hips. "Thank you very much."

"I said I won't stare. I've heard men die horribly after she takes a fancy to them."

"Are you're sure she's not interested in you?"

"How can anyone be sure with her? She and my family have too much bad history. And even with her considerable charms, she could never tempt me and she knows it. I think sometimes that's why she tolerates me."

"I've heard other rumors about her."

"You should keep those to yourself although most are probably true."

"They say she has voracious and unusual appetites and that she's mean enough to eat her young. Maybe that's why there are no kids running around the grounds?" Gail laughed, but on considering it, she turned somber.

When Gale and Gil climbed into their gondola, the sun was near setting over the tall grass and palm-lined hills. Their private gondolier was dressed like a pantaloon-clad French *Zouave* warrior except he carried an automatic rifle draped over his shoulder as he poled through the lagoon toward the Chairwoman's distinctive mansion, a massive structure in lilac-and-white that had been designed to look like a movie house from the glory days of the First Republic including her name and title in lights on a marquee above the entrance.

As the gondola bobbed over forming waves, Gil and Gale sat apart, staring out in opposite directions at the calming liquid-gold reflection of the sun shimmering off the deepening blue-green water. It was a short trip and they arrived at the Chairwoman's dock complex early enough to avoid the inevitable waiting line. A tall, thin austere looking gentleman wearing a laurel wreath on his head and dressed in a formal short white silk toga with lilac sneakers escorted them down the palm-lined pathway. As they walked, the wind blowing through the palm fronds generated calming music. They entered what appeared to be a pink cloud which functioned as an elevator that rose to take them to the second floor entrance to the Chairwoman's personal study. When the door opened, Gil stepped out and held his hand out tentatively for Gale. She grasped it and like untroubled lovers, hand-in-hand, they walked down a long corridor. When they turned a corner, he saw her and stopped abruptly, inadvertently jerking Gale back. She gave him a questioning look but Gil was no longer in that moment. He could only stare at the beautiful dark-haired woman standing at the far end of the room as a flood of memories battered at his emotional levees.

She wore a short, form-fitting, ice-blue, one-strapped gown that looked . . . she looked incredible. At first glance, he'd thought it was the Chairwoman but when their eyes met, hers weren't probing and distrustful eyes. These violet eyes sparkled with liquid warmth that somehow managed to enhance an otherwise perfect and genuine smile, not the subtle reptilian smile the Chairwoman owned. It was a smile that he had committed to memory. She had matured, of course, but if anything, she looked even more strikingly beautiful than he remembered and those memories propelled him toward her.

He was suddenly there and they embraced in a long and liberating event that freed him. Then he pulled back to stare. "Bree, wow, it's been what, fifteen years? You look even better . . . you look . . . wow . . . great." She smiled. He had forgotten how necessary that smile felt.

She laughed. "It was Profit, right? Dan Stacey? It's great to see you." They embraced again. "So," she said, more seriously, "you're a Morgan professional now. How bizarre. How was your mission? Bolivia, right? Interesting as hell, I'd guess."

"I returned this week," he said. "The Bolivian economy is booming and we've received a payment for my service that didn't bounce." She laughed again and he felt recovered, but he wasn't sure from what exactly. "Why are you here and when did you arrive?"

"I just arrived. Mother told me a couple of hours ago you were here but I didn't expect to see you until the banquet."

"I was instructed to meet the Chairwoman here at six-thirty."

Bree smiled again, dimples forming on her perfect, peaches-and-cream skin. As she turned to him, her short, straight hair shifted, exposing a tiny tattoo. He would have to ask her about it. "This is so like Mother. She's probably enjoying watching us."

"Mother? The Chairwoman?"

She hesitated, as if trying to remember something. "How could you not know? Mother must talk about me? No, I guess not."

"I'm a lowly missionary who hears nothing. And it's not like I can ask."

"As if you would," she chided. "You're still as closed as ever I see. It's been a long time. When we met, I'd just run away to find my father and they caught me right after you and I split up. That's when Madam—Mother, finally accepted me as her heir. When they caught you, I was arriving at my first assignment. I saw your image on the Mesh news and it all fit together." Suddenly distracted, Bree looked over his shoulder.

He felt a hand on his shoulder. He had forgotten Gale.

"Who is your friend, honey?" Gail asked, her words dripping with repressed jealousy. "Please introduce us."

Embarrassed, he took Gale's hand. He could see that she was ready to cry but he hoped Bree wouldn't notice. "Yes, Bree Andrews . . . no, it's Brandt, right?" Bree nodded. "Bree, this is Gale Allen. Gale, Bree." They shook hands.

"It's nice to meet you, Bree," Gale said. "How do you know my Gil?"

"When we were teenagers, we met while running away from my mother."

Concerned Gail turned to Gil. "What caused you to run from her mother?"

He caught Bree's stare and they smiled.

"We ran away, but not together," Bree clarified.

"Oh," Gale sounded relieved.

"We each fled at different times and for different reasons," he explained. "We didn't know each other at that point."

Gale still seemed concerned. "Why were you running away?"

Bree laughed. "It's not what you think. At the time, Mother thought Gil was a rebel." She paused. "Has Mother changed her mind?"

He shrugged.

"Now that she has you, you seem to be doing rather well. I guess it only takes one dose of Mother to get the rebel out?"

He had no response for that.

"I hear you live nearby, your Mother's neighbor now."

He nodded.

Gale gave him a questioning look, "Your mother, I don't understand?" Then her eyes widened. "Oh, Brandt, I'm so stupid; you're Chairwoman Brandt's daughter?"

Bree nodded.

"I'm so sorry," Gale said. "I didn't realize. If I was rude, please excuse me. I'm truly sorry."

"Everything's fine, Gale. I'm not my mother."

"So who is your father, the one you were searching for?" Gale asked.

When Bree hesitated, Gil squeezed Gale's hand. "It's not important," he offered.

"No, it's alright. My mother and father did more than run the country. The legendary Chairman of the Board of the Untied States, Andrew Crelli, he is my father."

"What?" It was Gil's turn to be shocked.

"How can that surprise you?"

"I'm not surprised, I'm stunned. You said that you were searching for your father but you never said . . . I . . . I had no idea you were searching for . . . him, for Chairman Crelli. You never mentioned his name and I never guessed. When we split up—"

"You split up?" Gale interrupted. "Nothing serious I hope."

Before responding, Bree stared at Gil, seeking guidance. He stared back until he realized it was up to him to define their relationship to Gale.

"It sounds serious, Gale, but it wasn't," Gil explained. "Bree and I shared a place for a while in an Ohio Production town. We were hiding and we didn't trust anyone, including each other. As I remember, it made for some very uncomfortable evenings." He hoped he sounded more convincing than he felt.

Bree carried the story further. "In order to live in Profit, that was the name of the Production town where we were hiding, the law required that we be married partners, so Gil and I pretended to be married—to protect ourselves, that's all. They even made us renew our vows even though we'd never taken them in the first place." She laughed as she reconsidered the event. "We recited our vows in front of the entire community, remember, Gil? You were using the name . . . Stacey then. You were Dan Stacey."

When Bree saw Gale's face, she stopped. Gil, who had been watching Bree and not Gale, tried to not look so happy.

"We weren't really married," Bree continued. "It was a fabrication so we could stay there and earn enough to continue on. I was looking for my father and Gil . . . what were you doing again?"

"As always, I was just trying to survive. Gale, that's all there is to tell. You can see that there's nothing to be concerned about. We were financial partners, nothing more. In fact, until today, I didn't even know Bree's real name."

Still, Gale looked distressed. "You were Dan Stacey back then. Isn't Stacey the name of that Angel Falls girl who died?"

Gil nodded.

It was Bree's turn to be embarrassed. "Oh, I'm sorry; I didn't know that. I shouldn't have brought it up."

Gale displayed her perpetually hurt and disappointed look and even though the situation was becoming awkward, he had no desire to extricate himself.

"Your partnership with Bree must have been totally insignificant because you never mentioned it to me." Gale persisted.

"More than anything, our arrangement was strange. We had no money, so pretending to be partners was the only way we could find work and survive. It turns out, for a while, we did okay; Bree did, anyway. I had this horrible warehouse job with an annoying avatar supervisor who constantly tried to humiliate me. And no matter how hard I worked, I couldn't earn enough to leave."

Bree smiled at the memory. "He'd come home really frustrated and I was horrid towards him because I was successful."

Now it was his turn to laugh. "Is that how you remember it? I remember something about fraud and the threat of execution. You see," he explained to Gale, "early on, Bree figured out a get-rich-quick scheme using a technology she stole. But Profit has laws against such things. The mayor," he smiled at Bree. "Remember Mayor Doris?"

Bree laughed. "Do I remember Mayor Doris? She was my judge, jury, and almost my executioner."

Gil continued. "The Mayor pressured me to helping her catch Bree in the act." He and Bree shared sad smiles at the memory.

Bree picked right up. "It's true. In my defense, I was young and naïve. I'd never worked before and I absolutely had to succeed out in the real world. I would've died if Mother had to rescue me so just in case; I stole an electronic cloaking device from one of our technology labs and used it to defraud the town merchants and residents. I thought I was being a good businesswoman, after all, we're taught to succeed at all cost, but I'm not proud of what I did. If it wasn't for Gil and Laurence Hilliard . . ."

At the mention of Hilly's name, Gil considered the good man who gave his life to save them and felt sad and guilty for his role in Hilly's death.

"We shared this tiny cottage, a hovel, really," Bree continued. "There was only one bed so I forced Gil to sleep on a small rug by the door like a dog so he wouldn't try anything. He was so sweet and vulnerable. He was my little lap dog. It was cruel but back then I was so full of myself. Then Hilly died because of me and Gil stood up and saved me . . ." Bree stared at him with an intensity that felt exhilarating but it also made him uncomfortable. "I need to say this, Gil. In Profit, with you . . . it really changed me."

In this most awkward of situations, her declaration only made his situation with Gale worse, but it felt great to hear. Gale squeezed his hand hard until he finally had to yank it away.

Bree continued on, oblivious to Gale or Gil's discomfort. "That entire adventure, it's so hard to reconcile. We would've been executed but for . . . well, for Hilly, he was this amazing little man who, for some unknown reason chose to die in order to save us even though he had the worth that people need to pursue forever. The entire Profit experience was . . . it was . . . I haven't experienced anything like it since. What about you Gil?"

By now it was obvious to Gil that the conversation was distressing Gale, but even with that, she seemed interested.

"You were going to be executed." Gale repeated. "And someone was willing to die for you . . ." Before continuing, she offered Gil a look of befuddlement that made him even more uncomfortable. "It sounds like you and Bree had an incredible time. I wish I could've seen you then." She turned to Bree. "He's so different now. My life consists of waiting for him to return from long trips so I can watch him mope around the house and stare mesmerized at the breakers until he leaves for his next assignment. With all that you two went through, it must have been hard to break up."

Bree recognized immediately what Gale was picturing and tried to downplay it. "Gale, it was a long time ago and it sounds more exciting than it really was." Then she smiled. "Except for the escape, that was amazing. We stole a truck and while they shot at us, we fled through a blizzard."

Gil was staring at Bree as she spoke but when he turned to Gail, he could see by the expression on her face that he was in trouble. Still, he allowed Bree to continue.

"We were lucky. The snow was falling so hard that the security team couldn't follow us. And then, as soon as we felt safe, we separated. That's all there was."

"Did you ever find your father?" Gil asked, knowing that by continuing he was upsetting Gail more.

Bree hesitated and gave him a questioning look before answering, sadly. "No. I went north to Hamilton. At a rest stop, I heard a rumor that he was being held in Chicago so I headed there instead but I got careless." She looked down. "Mother sent the Bitch armed with a new search pattern algorithm and I never had a chance . . . and now I'm here." It saddened him to hear her so disappointed.

"Who's the bitch?" Gale asked.

"Reverend General Ginger Tucker, the CEO of HOMESEC," Gil whispered.

Gale shuddered. "You're allowed to call her a bitch? How do you know she's . . . you know?"

"Tucker only has to confront you once for you to know that you don't want to meet her twice." Bree explained and then whispered, more to herself. "And more than twice is an offense against humanity." She crossed her arms and her hands grabbed her shoulders as she shuddered. Then she continued. "Anyway, when Mother assigned Tucker to find us, she didn't know Gil and I were together and so she ended up capturing us separately. Gil, remember the day we met?"

Knowing full well that Gale would make him regret this later, he closed his eyes to remember.

Bree relayed the story. "I was hiding behind a storeroom wall in a deserted village in Ohio while HOMESEC helicopters and foot patrols searched everywhere. I thought they were coming for me even though I was cloaking and in this perfect hiding place but I'm still worried because . . . because it's HOMESEC. My first thought is they've decoded my cloaking device and there's no way out. I was scared.

"I look through a crack in the wall and see this guy here," she taps Gil on his shoulder, "come out of nowhere, frantically slithering across broken glass toward me. He was going to give me away and I wanted to stop him but what could I do? He's staring right at me or at least the crack in the wall and then he makes this funny face. He puts his hand to the wall to test it, slides it away and tumbles inside just as the security team enters the store. I'm furious but I can't yell or I'd give away my hiding place."

In spite of her discomfort, Gale was drawn in. Tales like this weren't told in teaching circles. "What happened next?" she asked.

"Fortunately, my cloaking device held and the patrol never discovered the entrance. Tucker's personal troops are, surprisingly, the sorriest lot. She herself is extraordinary but she's a terrible leader. The units not under Tucker are far better and they probably would have found us." She smiled at Gil. "How's that for irony?"

He nodded.

"When the security team left, there we were in this tiny, dark place and I was even more furious but I had no choice but to stay silent. Later that night, I snuck out, but you know Gil. He traipsed after me."

Gale turned to Gil. "What she's describing doesn't sound anything like you."

Bree offered no help.

"We're making this sound way too exciting," Gil said, adding, "Bree and I just returned from consulting gigs and it takes time to wind down. Yes, I followed her but I did it because I was desperate and I didn't know anyone. She was out there alone so I figured she must be experienced and I could learn something about survival from her. I didn't find out about her cloaking device until much later. Back then, Bree was moody as hell, but I admired her amazing discipline."

Gil and Bree continued to reminisce until he noticed the blank, sad, mourner's stare in Gale's eyes. Before he could react to it, the Chairwoman's secretary appeared.

"Ms. Brandt, good to see you again, dear," the secretary said. "Mr. Rose, Ms. Allen, I'm sorry but Madam Chairwoman has been delayed. She's asked me to escort you to the banquet hall. Afterward, if she has time, she would love to meet with you."

Bree apologized. "I'm sorry, Mother is impolite by nature. I'm sure she set this meeting up hoping it would be awkward. Fortunately, it wasn't, was it? It was nice to meet you, Gale. You've got a great guy here. I travel a great deal, but maybe we can get to know each other better, maybe do something sometime."

Gale nodded.

"It was great catching up, Gil." Disdaining his offer of a handshake, Bree embraced him fondly and then left when Gil and Gale were escorted to the banquet hall by the Chairwoman's secretary.

They were seated at a table with high powered corporate executives representing the League of Major Conglomerate Industries, a mega-Chamber of Commerce. Gil was familiar with such high powered executives, but Gail was nervous. He persevered through dinner by discussing the effects of Missionary Capitalism on consumers in Bolivia with an obviously bored president from the Bio-Fuels Industry, while the vice presidents of the Organics, Inorganics, and Synthetic industries listened politely as Gale explained how inadequate funding for tools like Archive were creating educational and future net worth deficiencies in middle children.

Gil had wanted to help her but Gale refused to look at him, even when he put his arm around her. Finally, because of the size of the room and the crowd noise it became impossible to follow her conversation so, with the band playing and Gale still ignoring him, he excused himself and walked over to a bar.

He watched dispassionately as Gale was invited to dance by one of the VPs and when he turned from the dance floor, Bree was standing there, smiling at him. It felt good to see a happy, friendly face and her form-fitting gown made him even more appreciative.

"I never pictured you here," she said.

"You mean here in Monroe."

She nodded.

"While I was sleeping on that little rug in Profit, Monroe was absolutely the furthest thing from my mind."

She blushed and then laughed at the memory.

"I've thought a lot about this moment. I considered trying to find you but thought it best that I didn't."

Her smile disappeared. "Best for whom?"

He shrugged.

"Growing up, things were always testy between my mother and father. To make matters worse, she and everyone who feared her treated me badly. I only had my father, but at the time, it was enough. No, don't say it. I know I was a bitch, but still. I live at the top of a very competitive food chain and everyone wanted to worship me or destroy me, and usually both. Mother is so demanding and she's incapable of warmth, except toward her bitch and maybe father's clones, my half-siblings who hate me because I'm the legitimate heir and their claim to power has to wait forever which is quite a bit longer than they wish to wait. That was the world I grew up in and to get my way, I was allowed to be wrong, as long as I was never in doubt. When father was taken from me, things got . . . they got rough and I had to flee. Then Profit . . .

"It feels strange not to call you Dan, but Gil, you have no idea how different you were from everyone I have ever known. From the beginning, you treated me like I've come to believe a real person should be treated. Around here, everyone's behavior is carefully calibrated to achieve maximum results which makes everyone so self-centered because if they're not, well, they'll fail and die; it's as simple as that.

"Meeting you . . . you weren't like everyone. You didn't know who I was yet you were . . . nice even though I made you sleep on that rug. I'm the Chairwoman's heir and I've been trained in a great many things and

I specialize in quite a few but nice I never learned because I never saw it displayed to advantage, or ever appreciated its purpose—until you.

"When we split and I knew I'd never see you again, I tried to be nicer, even though doing so might threaten my career. Ever since Profit, I've tried hard to be better because of you. More than anything, Gil, you're the reason mother is both pleased and disappointed with me."

"How could she possibly be disappointed?" Gil asked. "You're a star."

"It took a lot of growing up to figure it out. Mother is disappointed with everyone who isn't her." She moved closer to him, reached out to touch his arm. "What you did for me in Profit . . . Gil, it made me feel and behave differently. It made me want to be better and I thank you."

"I didn't do anything, Bree. You don't have to—"

"It snuck up on me but I treasure those days and because of them, I've changed."

"They were crazy times, weren't they? Alone with no one to rely on and we couldn't even trust each other. What a great way to begin a partnership."

She laughed easily causing him to inadvertently stare at her dress which hinted at her tight stomach muscles contracting to her laugh. "Becoming partners the day after we met goes against standard generally accepted pre-relationship due diligence," she rolled her eyes. "It's not something people do but now that I'm back in town, I hope we can build on what we had."

He wasn't sure what they had had but he knew now wasn't the right time to discuss it. "I've thought about you a lot, too." He said.

"You have?" she blushed, causing her eyes to become even more vibrant.

"Are you kidding? How could you not leave an impression? Relationships . . ."

"Relationships?" she interrupted. "You're not thinking . . . ?

"No, of course not, you're the heir. I was just saying . . ."

"After Profit, driving that truck in the snow, I was free for such a short time before the bitch . . . found me. I should have known that kind of freedom couldn't last, at least not for me."

"So you never found your father?"

"No."

"I'm sorry."

"But you're not surprised." Her head cocked slightly to one side. "You've matured but you're still so closed."

He didn't know what she knew and he was unwilling to lie. "I don't know how to respond to that?" he said honestly.

She punched his arm softly and laughed at him for making fun of her old line. "I guess I deserve that. I kept a lot from you, too. Once Mother and I finally stopped fighting—or at least stopped fighting continually—she explained who you were. What a wild coincidence spending six months with the man who kidnapped my Father."

Gil was surprised that was known.

She noticed and smiled sympathetically. "I'm not angry with you and I don't blame you. You had no idea how great a man he was or who he was to me."

"How did your mother know it was me?"

"Mother knows everything or will, sooner than you'd like her to know it. You should know that by now, just to survive here."

"So you don't blame me for what happened."

"I know what happened to your great grandfather."

"And his wife, my great aunt, my father and mother, my grandfather and . . ."

"I'm sorry. I'm truly sorry. Still, he's my Father and I love him. He is a great patriot and he saved America from a horrible fate—a more horrible fate. But it isn't about that. I was young and didn't know him politically. He was strict, but he was kind, too, and he always had time for me."

Gil felt the same way about his father, Howard. Perhaps it was only absence that made him feel that way. "Excuse me if I can't see Chairman Crelli that way."

"I'm sorry about your family. Is it something we can get past or should I leave?"

"No, stay, I'll be disappointed if you leave. Besides, I've put so much behind me already, what is one more thing. You were an important part of my life, Bree."

She blushed. "It's been a long time for us and getting past things is all we can do sometimes. Yes, I'd like to know about my father but you don't have to tell me if you don't want to. I understand. I do. I don't want to make us about him."

He had missed her more than he thought possible and he wanted to tell her what happened to her father, but he knew so little. If he had known more, he might have told her, just to keep talking to her, but like everything; the more ignorant he was, the safer he was. Besides, not knowing allowed him to answer her honestly. "Bree, I don't know where your father is. If I did know, I don't think I'd tell anyone, particularly your mother and you, at least not now. Don't be mad at me. If your mother asked you . . ."

"She didn't."

"I would do almost anything for you, just not this. I can't because I really don't know anything and I've never been in a position to find out."

"Even in Angel Falls?"

"How do I explain . . . ? I try not to think about it so I never asked. You know me."

She comforted him with a smile. "I understand. Don't worry about Mother. She much likes her role as the stew maker. She makes her goop and mixes people and events in it and then she takes advantage of whatever bubbles up."

"In spite of my career, I'm no fan of hers."

"Yes, Angel Falls, I understand that too, and I'm sorry."

"If you were like either your mother or your father, we wouldn't be talking now."

She nodded. "I should be offended but I'll take that as a compliment. Honestly, if you know where he is, I'm not sure what I would do. I desperately want to see him but if Mother ever found out, he wouldn't be safe."

"I appreciate your concern."

"If she's keeping you here to get that information, I won't make you worthless in her eyes."

"I'm doing a pretty good job of being worthless on my own," he joked.

"You're wrong. I've seen your evaluations, they think highly of you. But if you know about Father . . . I wouldn't tell her." She embraced him and instinctively, his arms wrapped tightly around her. Too soon, she pulled away.

"People are watching," she whispered. They stepped back, awkwardly. "So you're the messiah, huh. Living and working here, that's a pretty big liability."

"How did you know?" She shrugged and he continued, nervously. "It's . . . this isn't the place. Maybe another time."

"You're right. Say, it's been great. I hear you're taking the final on Monday. It's crazy. I mean literally crazy.You'll pass though.About getting together, I'm leaving in a few days for a new domestic assignment and they usually ship new grads out immediately after their exam but, if we can find some time before we go, I'd really like that unless your girlfriend doesn't approve."

He had forgotten about Gale. He wanted to explain about her but had no idea where to start. Mistaking his silence for indecision, Bree added. "Anyway, I'd like to."

"I'd like it, too." He noticed a White House aide signaling for him.

"Gilbert Rose?" a woman came up to him wearing a deep blue military sarong with polished gold buttons and a chest full of ribbons and medallions. She flaunted so many Almighty Dollars icons that Gil thought of football helmets filled with accomplishment emblems from his early gaming experiences. He nodded to her. "Mr. Rose, you're meeting will be in the Gorman Lounge."

"Mother is stirring," Bree smiled. "Good luck in there and on your exam."

Unable to find Gale, he turned to Bree and mouthed, "Call me," and then followed the aide. Instead of staying at the bar, Bree accompanied him.

She stopped at the door, "It's a marvel how mother orchestrates so many concurrent dramas, but she thrives on it. Be careful, she may seem distracted or even downright silly sometimes but she's more devious than you can possibly imagine." With that, she leaned in and kissed his cheek and then turned to leave. Gil stared after her. She was amazing in mint blue. As if she heard his thoughts, she turned, blushing, and smiled. "Hang tough with that final, you'll never forget it." With that, she disappeared into the banquet hall.

The aide knocked on the door and another aide opened it. Inside, an older woman wearing a long, silk gown was sitting near the fire, smoking a cigar. Gil entered as the aide left, closing the door behind him. He walked to the woman through the haze of blue smoke and repugnant odor that was more than the room's nano-atomizers could handle.

"Gil Rose?"

"Yes, Madam, and you are?"

"I am Tianrong Zhang, CEO and President of *Global Solar*."

Gil was surprised. "This is an honor, Madam Zhang. Members of my family worked for one of your subsidiaries, U.S. ANGS, a long time ago. How can I help you?"

"We have much to discuss and my time is precious. That I'm spending some with you should tell you a great deal."

"I'm honored, but you have me at a disadvantage."

"I have everyone at a disadvantage."

"Yes, certainly," Gil said. "You've earned that right."

"I have."

"How can I help you, Madam Zhang?"

"You're an amazing young man. With all the reasons in the world to hate the Chairwoman, you've chosen a career where you are helping her. I applaud your pragmatism if not your courage. One should never put personal animosity above career yet too few follow such wisdom. I'm interested why you do it."

"That's simple. I have no choice."

CEO Zhang was a beautiful older woman with groupings of freckles above and below dark brown eyes intersected by narrow worry lines. When Madam Zhang moved her head, her long dark hair uncovered fresh bruises that looked like teeth marks on her throat and behind her ears. He quickly looked away.

"Don't waste my time. I asked a question and I demand a productive answer."

He looked away from what he was certain were hickeys and forced himself to concentrate on his response. "As a boy, I was taught to respect leaders like Chairman Crelli. As a teen, I learned what he did to my family and to millions of innocent people. Respect should be earned."

"Do you respect Chairwoman Brandt?"

"I work for her because I have no choice and I respect her because I'm not ready to die."

"You are bolder than I was lead to believe."

"Madam Zhang, I'm as bold as I can be, no more, no less and I have no idea why you're interested in an insignificant Morgan consultant like me but I can't imagine it will do me any good to lie to you since you wouldn't be talking to me if you didn't understand my situation."

"You know that former Chairman Crelli is still alive."

Twice in one evening. "No, I don't," he admitted. "I've heard nothing about him in twenty years."

"But you did meet him."

"I did. I was a naive teenager when my great-grandfather asked me to help him. I was unaware that he represented a rebel cell or that their goal was to kidnap the Chairman. When they did, that's when I met him and it was brief, though long enough for him to shoot at me. I once believed he was responsible for creating a better world. I've been convinced otherwise."

"Yet you work for his successor."

"Not to be curt, but who doesn't? To survive in the world, I'm required to create value so I'm doing the best I can. When people entrust me with enhancing their future, I feel that I must be empathetic in order to provide productive service."

"I heard you have strange views. You believe empathy is the magic ingredient."

"Madam Zhang, a man I respected very much once explained to me that perspective is everything in this world, so my strange views, as you say, are merely a different perspective. I chose Consensus Building because I feel I am working to my strength and I can do the most good for my country by helping to end all the destructive zero-sum, win-lose games. It's time we eliminate as much loss as possible from shared outcomes. I know domination is the current fashion but when you factor in the true cost when people's hearts and minds are lost, there has to be a more productive way and I believe that's where empathy and perspective are so critical. There is proven value in seeking win-win outcomes. I believe that they yield greater longer-term benefits for everyone involved. What we have now, this vulture capitalism, the get-wins-quick, get-rich, and get-out philosophy, it really should stop. The accounting for it is faulty. It's not profitable and if you use lifecycle accounting, it's cost prohibitive. The Chairwoman's projects will benefit greater over the long haul through consensus building rather than the win-at-all-cost solutions she's employs with her vulture capital trained missionary specialists."

Zhang sat quietly. When she spoke, she seemed more . . . gracious? "You can't know that. You have no basis and you're assuming softer disciplines can keep order while driving mankind to a better tomorrow. Over and over, history has proven that is a silly dream and a dead end. Over a century ago, my native China committed to Socialism and frankly all the caring and sharing in the world couldn't buy them a viable economy. Ask the hundreds of millions who died due to Socialism. Only Free Market Capitalism, the red-meat kind as you so poetically call it, can do glorious works. And to speak otherwise, to call it vulture capitalism, isn't that blasphemy? As a practicing Morgan who earns his future selling American Capitalist theology, that makes you a very conflicted, if not dangerous young man."

"Madam Zhang, I'm far from dangerous, but I won't make achieving profit goals the primary purpose of my career. That's why I've chosen Consensus Building and, so far, I've received positive feedback for my efforts."

"What an honest fool you are." She chuckled.

"Madam, I can speak to economics, not theology? We are taught that the failed socialists from the past, the Russians and the Chinese, they were never true socialist economies. Mostly, they were autocratic and dictatorial, not dissimilar from those who lead America's government so it's unclear what, if any form of Socialism might work. But I believe that in America, there are a many areas where Socialist economics could work better than Capitalism if someone was serious about making it work for the people."

"The Chairwoman is truly playing with fire. You talk treason and you do it so easily."

"I am responding honestly, Madam, to a superior who has commanded me not to waste her time."

"You are responding recklessly."

"Forgive me. In every consulting engagement, I incorporate something of socialism that I believe is appropriate while implementing overall capitalist dogma as per the specifications. I do this because I'm being pragmatic. My objective is to help every client, to meet their requirements, and to do so I must use every tool in my kit."

The CEO shook her head. "So you are a Socialist and a messiah."

"This is about business and there is no place in it for a messiah." Gil was unsure what the purpose of this audience was but he had no choice but to remain and react.

Tianrong relit her cigar. "Tell me about your future," she said.

"I'm a Morgan missionary consultant and I want to continue to help my country."

She blew foul smelling, grey cigar smoke in his direction with such force that he felt her spittle. "Don't fuck with me. I expect your best answer. I won't be disappointed or turned aside."

The power in her voice was different than Tanya's, less shrill but just as malevolent. It reminded him of Chairman Crelli's voice that day at the hospice all those years ago.

"Honestly, Madam, I have no plans beyond passing my Missionary final exam on Monday. I'm late to this game and I have a lot of catching up to do. Do you know something you're not telling me?"

"I'm not here to answer stupid questions," Zhang shouted. "It is my intention to invest a great deal on the American side of the Pacific and I employ vast teams of immensely overeducated, hard-working overachievers to support my efforts and this allows me to anticipate the future with great confidence. Oddly enough, for this particular investment, you, Mr. Rose, are a critical variable. I'm here to determine if my investment needs further mitigation."

"Madam Zhang, I can't see how I'd impact your investment in any way."

"Let me be clear then. Due to the unrest that plagues the world outside of the United States, your Chairwoman has acceded to the wishes of *Global Solar* and is permitting our senior management and various high-level support functions to acquire choice autonomous locations throughout America which we will resettle."

"Is that what our Chairwoman wants for America?"

The CEO shuddered almost imperceptibly. "Your Chairwoman is a most desirable woman and she has a truly extraordinary feel for the dynamics of global economics and politics. Our agreement will be the first step toward achieving the great dream of capitalists everywhere, to permanently remove meddlesome national governments from free markets and erase all uneconomical national interests from global economies so that unrestrained commerce can thrive and productive people can work for their forever future unburdened by overreaching, overtaxing, and overregulating national bureaucracies that are inefficient and redundant.

"The Chairwoman and I will cleanse the world of government inefficiency, from top to bottom, from local to national. What we will create in its stead is a gloriously efficient new world of truly free enterprise without constraints or bureaucratic inefficiencies, a world where those who can't or won't fend for themselves will be burdens no longer. Ours will be an achievement of surpassing brilliance and scale, something the Chairwoman's mentor, the unlamented former Chairman Crelli did not, and would not consider. The Chairman was a great man for his time. He was a once-in-a-generation intellect who understood the future like few ever have. But alas, he was flawed, he was from an age that nurtured patriots and he was a failed one at heart. That heroic flaw doomed him and you and your rebel coconspirators did the world a great service by removing him. Thanks to your action, patriotism has gone extinct and that provides the space from which we will grow our new international economic order.

"Frankly, Mr. Rose, no one, and that includes me, ever considered your Chairwoman to be in Chairman Crelli's league as a leader and an intellect, but since he disappeared, she has performed extraordinarily. She has organized, marketed, and delivered on the final phases of the Chairman's *Circle of Life* program and she has done it so well, although with unnecessary flare, as his her way, that I felt that it was time to reopen negotiations. Today, meeting her face-to-face for the first time . . ." Briefly the CEO blushed and lost focus, and then she refocused and continued. "It was . . . well, she is stunning, a force of nature.

"Together, we will build a new and glorious future and with it, the reign of nations will finally end. We remake the world and the result will be a corporate golden era where god is what she is but majority stockholders reign supreme.

"Our effort will cost an enormous sum and it will take a great while to accomplish, though we will see it in our infinite lifetime. Together, we create a brave new world of unlimited prosperity. *Global Solar* has the assets, the entrepreneurial resources, and the global commercial relationships while dear Tanya's United States has great complimentary resources, two large and commercially viable coast lines that provide easy access to the world while still being segregated from it and you have unused land in commercially superior locations. America, Mr. Rose, has the honor of becoming the global headquarters for our great and glorious planetary enterprise."

"It sure sounds like an investment worth any risk."

"Don't be banal," Zhang snapped. "The upside profits will be enormous, but there is so much more. With *Global Solar's* management expertise, America will be the financial capital for civilization. But there is more. Our America provides a secure and comfortable residence for the world's economic and financial elite, the most powerful and influential leaders, thinkers, implementers, marketers, manufacturers, logicians, salespeople, and even accountants, the very best from every important industry on every land mass on earth will reside here, all living comfortably on their own estates while they guide the world to commercial paradise as described in your Morgan bible. America will be the land of wealth and opportunity once again; sheltered from every malady that might afflict the world outside. My agreement today with your Chairwoman is the historic first step toward universal economic peace and prosperity, a peace so magnificent that it will provide the Petri dish for nurturing the purest form of free market Capitalism ever devised. Together, we will thrive in a perfect state where every resident luxuriates in his or her own paradise, and in the end, there will never be an end, for nobody with wealth ever need die. All of this comes to fruition if four known variables are managed."

Zhang nodded for Gil to respond.

He offered his view. "What you want will require immense funding, and the burden of building it will rely on massive systems with immense bandwidth, of course. Running that world from a community here will require full integration in real time, both horizontally and vertically, of human and business systems. That requires processing almost infinite data and there's the—I guess you could call it the Noah's Ark issue—identifying and then efficiently relocating the most effective populations to manage and deliver the effort. It will take incalculable funding and resources."

"We have calculated it."

"Then there's the issue of payback. It needs to be rapid enough and significant enough for investors to survive and then recover from the massive debt obligation. And there's the additional investment and debt to keep the global economy functioning and growing."

"Low interest rates and the elimination of all waste make both possible. That's three."

Gil considered it. "Madam, there are so many critical issues."

"Oh, hush. The fourth issue will surprise you. My teams have run every possible scenario and performed multivariate regression analysis on every issue and risk. They have executed sensitivity models, ad nausea, and each has been fully evaluated, with every scenario in every conceivable combination and permutation. In each, to achieve acceptable results within acceptable tolerances, there is one variable alone that presents itself as worthy of singular attention."

"I can't wait to hear it."

"Generally we don't concern ourselves with theology, myth, or local legend because of the infinitesimally small potential impact of the abnormal."

"However . . ."

"My analysts are thorough. When they are certain they have a tight reign on the metrics, they branch out to consider macro-possibilities like population change; regional, political, and economic stability models; changing climate, and even tectonic projections. You may not be aware, but *Global Solar* invests more on geological and meteorological science than all the science teams in all the universities in the world—in fact, we own a great many. After my people squeeze out the merely improbable and the truly gratuitous, our stochastic models delve into more specific, unique event probabilities; anything that could reasonably distort our economic projections."

Gil nodded. "I'm schooled in the methodology."

"There is a legend making the rounds among the *Conducers* and *Untouchables* in America of economic redemption of such breadth that it could shift our carefully constructed outcome projections from wildly positive to negative. We've targeted this single event as worthy of extended scrutiny."

The room seemed warmer to Gil and he began to perspire.

"Have you any thoughts on what that single event might be?"

"No Madam, I don't. I haven't a clue why you're addressing this to me. I haven't even passed my final graduate exams yet. I appreciate the exposure you're providing me to your thought process and your overall concerns about this project and as a consultant, I will help any way I can if I am fortunate enough to be assigned to this extraordinary . . ."

She cut him off. "To the point, Mr. Rose, you are the messiah who will lead *Wasters* to destroy Tanya's and my carefully constructed world. And you will do it just as mankind is reaching its ultimate evolution. We will not allow that to happen."

"I'm sorry, Madam Zhang, but I'm not the messiah. I'm just a lowly Morgan missionary. It's true I don't have the faith of a true believer in unbridled capitalism. I believe it jumped the track somewhere and has become crooked and perverse. Wealth concentrated in the hands of the few keeps a great many people from living decent lives or any life at all, and that isn't what god intends."

Zhang stared at him, a concerned look on her face. When she spoke, she sounded both astounded and cautious. "Oh, so you're not the messiah yet you know what god intends? How have you acquired this belief?"

"From my great grandfather."

"Ah, yes, Rosenthal, an early anti-capitalist."

"He wasn't until capitalism killed his family. Those are my views. I do my job, I do it well, and I will continue to meet my requirements. And I'm not your messiah."

"My research is never wrong."

"With all respect, Madam Zhang, what you believe doesn't matter. If it were up to me, I would redistribute much of our wealth to *Conducers* and *Wasters* because they have suffered too much and it's fair. If life were only about wealth, well then giving it away would be a hardship but life is about more so giving to people in order to satisfy their basic needs, well, it harms no one.

"But for all that, I'm no socialist. I believe redistribution is good business, good capitalism. Redistribution would provide funds to those who spend it fast and totally and by so doing, *Entrepreneurs* and *Executives* who provide the products and services would simply earn that money back as capitalists have done throughout history. The result would be an economy that grows for everyone. Besides being immoral, destroying people is inefficient because each one has the potential to be productive in some important way and America needs that. If it takes a messiah to convince businesses to tap that potential, then I hope a messiah comes along soon—but I am not him."

"What you say is troubling. There is no difference between lithium, molybdenum, coal, and humans—they are all commodities except humans make greater cost demands on the economy."

"Madam Zhang, is this meeting to argue economics and social theory?"

Her eyes brightened and she sat straighter. "You are quite right. You are this messiah of legend and though your Chairwoman insists on coddling you, I must protect my investment so I will know what you're planning."

"You've heard my views, Madam, but I've never been disloyal."

"Do I care?"

"Okay, say I am this messiah. Help me out here, I'm at a loss. Explain to me how I organize widely scattered, dispirited, and disenfranchised *Wasters* with no marketable skills who struggle every day just to survive. And once I organize them, how would you recommend that I turn them into a revolutionary fighting force so effective that it can overthrow the best-organized and most technologically-proficient nation on earth? Did I mention also, the most ruthless?"

Zhang smiled. "So you've given this serious thought. My teams are working on precisely such scenarios. If it's any comfort, they concur. You have a monumental task."

"Monumental! It's impossible. Saying that I'm this messiah changes nothing."

"But you have considered overthrowing your Chairwoman."

He replied, cautiously. "When I was a fugitive, I don't deny it. That a government would murder its own people for any reason, it's unconscionable, and monstrous that they did it because their citizens couldn't provide some arbitrary value or they lacked necessary economic survival instincts. Any government that does that is evil and shouldn't exist. But this," he put his index finger close to his thumb, "is as far as I have come with it."

Her eyes narrowed, her brow furrowed. "What happened to your caution?"

"I'm horrified and embarrassed to be associated with people who accept what my government believes and does but I can't change it so I try to improve what I can. If that makes me a messiah then I'm a great disappointment because all that I'm capable of delivering is incremental change on a project by project basis. That is far from rebellion which, I said and you agreed, is hopeless. And if I were to try, I would cause more pain and many more innocent people would lose even more. I won't do that."

"Your words are rebellion enough. The Chairwoman won't be pleased."

"I'd be disappointed if she wasn't listening."

"You are a curious risk taker."

"What risk. You and she already believe that I'm the messiah. The Chairwoman has technology that allows her to know everything and she can alter anyone's perception of reality so whether I lead it or not, no revolution can find traction in that environment."

"Yet you speak openly of revolution."

"I'm here and living well when I should be dead or in prison. I don't know what the Chairwoman wants, so why guess. If I told her I wasn't interested in rebellion, would she believe me? Would she change her plans? Or you, yours? There's nothing I can do so I may as well be honest, it's all I have left. Who would ever believe that this perverse environment is conducive to candor but, ironically, it's easier to speak the truth when your views are already known."

"You're balancing on a dangerous precipice."

"Aren't we all? My advice—and I'm speaking as a Missionary Consultant, not a messiah—make your best deal with the Chairwoman and then build in whatever risk mitigation factors your analysts feel necessary. Then, using the most obscure derivative strategy you have access to, hedge your bet in the marketplace. If some messiah does come along and turn your world upside down, that strategy will minimize your financial risk. Be careful not to hedge too much because those who monitor the financial tea leaves will see it as enhancing the messiah's reputation in the marketplace and bet against you.

"Hedging too aggressively could make this messiah a reality?"

"It's your call. I have . . ." Gil looked up at the Byzantine clock on the wall. "It can't be midnight already. Madam, please excuse me. I must find my date."

Zhang stood and offered her hand. "Mr. Rose, it was a pleasure to speak with one so conflicted. You've given me much to consider. I won't wish you all possible success for if you decide to take the mantle of the messiah, count me among your worst enemies. Good night." He shook her hand and left.

The banquet was long over and everyone was gone. Gale would be furious with him but he tried to call her anyway. When she didn't answer, he returned home.

She wasn't at home, either. He called her again but she wasn't answering so he waited up, but exhausted, he soon fell asleep. When he awoke in the late morning there was a painfully brief message waiting. Having assumed he'd left with Bree, Gale ended their relationship, begging him not to contact her. Sad because he felt relieved, he walked to his favorite spot on the verandah, sat on the hammock, and stared out at the breakers seeking calm. Instead, he fell asleep.

When he awoke, there was a message from Bree. She wished him luck on his exam but said that she was leaving on her assignment and wouldn't be available to meet with him. That saddened him more.

The exam! He had forgotten all about it. He considered studying but instead, he slept some more.

Chapter 4

The Exam—2083

Gil awoke later that day despondent from all that had transpired the previous day. He tried to study but in the quiet emptiness of his mansion, with his failed relationship insinuating itself into his thoughts, he couldn't find the discipline. It hurt to have caused her pain.

To make studying more difficult, foolish and misguidedly optimistic daydreams of a relationship with Bree slipped into his thoughts. And then there was the issue of the messiah. Maybe Gale's leaving was the herald for a life that needed resolution but he was too conflicted to think that through.

Gale returned for her possessions. He apologized and almost asked her to stay but he knew if he did, she would and he couldn't do that to either of them any longer. When she left, crying, he tried to resume his studies but feeling lethargic, he slumped into his hammock and stared out at the waves thinking of the tomorrows after his exam when his life would have, if not purpose, at least momentum.

That night, he tossed and turned and awoke weary to face exam day. He trudged over to the Gorman University Archive lab in the College of Entrepreneurial Sciences where his Morgan Theology Certification exam was to be administered. He was shown to a private room where he received detailed voice and written instructions that thoroughly confounded him. He re-read and re-listened numerous times but neither the instructions nor the video seemed coherent, let alone informative. Concerned, he frantically queried any source he could find in Archive, but each tended to obfuscate as if the exam itself was some inside joke.

Bewildered, he stared nervously at the various Archive units lined up along a long wall, each uniquely detailed with animated scenes commemorating Tanya Brandt's reign. When a unit acknowledged his existence by calling out his name, he took a deep breath, entered it, and stripped down. He put his lenses in and waited fearfully while searching in vain for a winning attitude. He was distracted by a chill that ran down his spine when he was coated with *Virtual Dust,* the latest *Virtual* product from U.S. ANGS.

Here it was. His real future would begin in virtual. Recognizing the irony, he almost laughed. His vision blurred and then cleared and he was staring at a jowly, heavy-set proctor-avatar standing high above him on a dais that extended from a vast pyramid of gold and silver bullion. The avatar was wearing a glowing green Morgan U.—Monroe Campus sweatshirt under his too tight gold lama business jacket.

"Welcome, Gil Rose and praise God." Without additional ceremony, the avatar began describing the test scenario. "You are the Project Manager leading a team of Morgan Missionary Consultants tasked with expanding our economy so that God's gift, Paradise on earth, can be shared with more hard working and productive citizens. This assignment will take you to the small harvesting town of Buena Vista, California where you and your team will end the labor strike there and return union workers to the fields to restore God's profits. This outcome is vital to the financial interests of the Food Industry and America's stockholders and the harvest must begin no later than one week from today.

"You are provided with the following information: the union strike began when a foreign corporation legally purchased from the rightful property owners the piece of underutilized land that union families currently squat on. The purchase was a fair and righteous deal that became necessary when union families reneged on the sacrament of debt repayment, including interest and penalties, and that put every mortgage in Buena Vista in arrears and underwater, valued at less than owed. The new tenants will squeeze more revenue from that land than can the frivolous union families who refuse to maintain asset values. They do not repair, decorate or landscape and thus are denied God's special advantage, asset appreciation. The bible teaches that under appreciating property is Satan's work and so it must be condemned and then revalued in the glory of a free market. It is sacrilege to oppose that and those who do are subject to punishment consistent with such a capital crime.

"When you arrive, what you will hear is that the union demands better wages and working condition; that they desire respect as human beings, and that they wish to renegotiate their mortgages. Do not be deceived. Satan speaks but believers know God's Truth. The union defies the Holy Word and wants only to bleed God's great economy dry. Praise Jesus and Adam Smith, God's will be done.

"If this union refuses to see the light and end their strike, if they refuse the conditions of the land sale, and if they decline to harvest our crops, God-loving Americans everywhere will face grave hardships as food prices rise far beyond what they can afford and this will have a severe impact on a great many holy Balance Sheets and Income Statements, including those of God's chosen people, the *Entrepreneurs,* who depend on Buena Vista yields to fund other business investments. If allowed to continue, the effect of the strike will ripple through our economy causing ever more desperate *Conducers* to open their minds to the devil's plea for Socialism and they will surely lose their souls, their hard earned wealth, and then their lives.

"Gil Rose, you stand for the glory of God and to prove it, your graduation-victory proposition, the first step in your path to forever is as follows: You and your team will enter Satan's den and gain agreement from the irrational union shaman and devil leader and through the light of Morgan cause him to value right and thus agree to end his demonic strike.

"Using a proven formula, we will decrement your final score every day the strike continues and the exam itself ends when union members vacate their housing and sign their deeds over to God's financial representative at the local Sacramento Goldman Financial Services office or when it is deemed that event will not occur. God's will be done.

"Thirty percent of your final score will be determined by how well you manage your consulting team which consists of three exact representations of Gil Rose as has been determined by Morgan University's world class profiling algorithms. The remaining score is awarded based on the efficacy of your delivered victory or by the lack of same. There are bonus points offered as well in this scenario. Each union member that you extract from Satan's grasp and convert to God's financial love through Morgan will count directly toward your final score and ultimate success in the world.

"If you fail, you will feel the sting of God's great disappointment. It will adversely affect your career and of course, your life expectancy. Should you achieve what is deemed a superior score, when you're scenario is completed, God, in all his glory will look kindly upon you and your investments and you will have earned the right to choose a wonderful surprise gift.

"This graduation scenario has a time limit of one business week in virtual, but it will be accomplished over a four hour period, in real God time. Pray to the Lord and use your time wisely."

Before Gil had a chance to consider these instructions, the scene shifted so quickly that he became momentarily lightheaded. He was wearing a business suit now and he was sitting in a business office. Projected on the office walls around him were process maps, budgets, performance reports, and project timetables, all displaying the symbol of the Almighty Dollar and all being updated continuously. Before he could settle in, three men entered wearing identical business suits. Each was exactly alike, like Gil Rose in triplicate. Oblivious to their shared likeness, the men sat across from Gil and stared at him until he realized he was in charge.

"Welcome, team, I'm your Project Manager, Gil Rose."

Each introduced themselves to him as Gil Rose, also. He started to laugh but remembering the importance of the exam, he caught himself. "Okay, so that we can communicate better and I can assign responsibilities, the first order of business is names."

One of the Gil Roses raised his hand and Gil recognized him. "Yes?"

"You could call us one, two, and three," his facsimile offered.

"We're people and that seems impersonal," said another faux Gil.

The third spoke up. "We're being graded so we shouldn't waste time."

Gil agreed. "Good input, thanks. Each of you, write down an alternative name." Each briefly considered then wrote. "What do we have?" Gil pointed to the Gil on his right.

A likeness spoke. "I chose Bernie Rosenthal," he said proudly. The others two Gils groaned.

"You each chose Bernie?" Gil guessed.

They nodded.

"Okay, I'll assign names." He pointed and recited the first names that came to mind. "You're Abe, Bob, and let's see, Carl. Write the name down and pin it to your suit jacket. The one named Carl raised his hand. "We have nothing to attach it with. I can run out and get some pins or something. Do we have the budget?"

Another likeness added,"If you're going to insult us with fake names, one, two, or three were good enough."

The third offered, "I'd prefer to be either Bob or number three if you don't mind."

The exam had begun, time was at a premium, and here he was already behind and frustrated. "No, we'll keep the names." He pointed to each going clockwise. "You're Abe, Bob, and sorry, you're Carl. Write that on a piece of paper, bend it, and hang it from your shirt pocket so we can all see it." He demonstrated by writing his name and they each complied.

"I wish I was Gil." Carl said, petulantly.

Gil ignored him and asked, "Have you all been briefed on the project?"

Two nodded but Carl looked concerned. It was disorienting to converse with his likenesses but be persisted. "Carl, do you have a question, a real question?"

"No, no, it's okay. I'm comfortable working in the dark all the time. It's what I do. Well, there is one thing . . . It's just . . . we don't have the assets we need to end a strike and besides, the victory condition is impossible, particularly in the time allotted. I mean, if we're going to fail, shouldn't we be upfront about it? None of us has any idea what the union might want and the Procter didn't say anything in the prospectus about . . ."

"You always worry too much," interrupted the likeness named Bob. "Maybe, before we begin we should re-read the prospectus and inventory the assets we bring to the project. We can record all of the issues and then build a plan of attack. Projects are difficult if you don't plan ahead. Remember the old missionary consulting caution: ready, fire, aim. We don't want to do that until we run out of better ideas."

But Carl still looked concerned. "Bob's right about reviewing requirements," he said. "But how can we even start until we know where we're going with this and why? Otherwise, it's like being lost in space and running out of fuel."

"What?" Gil asked, confused. Carl merely smiled and then nodded, knowingly.

Abe chimed in. "In consulting class, they always say, 'begin at the beginning,'"

Carl pushed away from the table angrily before speaking. "Yes, exactly, analyze what doesn't need analyzing? The clock is ticking people, so let's go." Carl paused and added sheepishly, "I'm sorry, I'm not the project manager yet. I didn't mean to overstep."

"No, that's okay Carl," Gil said.

"Okay then, let's review everything."

Gil asked Abe for his opinion.

"What Carl says is okay, I don't know, they gave us quite a problem. I'm sure glad I'm not the project manager on this one." He shrugged and then just stared at Gil.

Gil looked to Bob. "Okay, okay," he said, "We do some preparation but first, we should interview the union leader and if he's amenable, we could win in plenty of time." His look-alikes readily agreed. "How do we contact him?"

Abe stood and walked to the wall organization chart. "Let's see . . . the union leader is Senor Gonzalez Gonzalez y Gonzalez and according to our schedule, he is due to arrive here in three minutes. The prospectus says he likes to be called Peppy."

And so the union leader arrived. He was small, wiry, dark complexioned and of Mexican descent He wore his hair slicked back, shiny, and tied with hemp into a pony-tail. His face had deep pock-marks and some of his teeth were yellowed, some were metal, and some were missing. He sported a pencil thin mustache and was dressed in a shiny yellow silk shirt with a large red guitar stitched on the front and a purple sombrero on the back. His denim jeans were new and his boots were elaborately decorated in colorful stitching.

Gil began the interview. "Thank you for stopping by Mr. Gonzalez y Gonzalez. We would like to talk to you about ending the strike."

The union leader smiled. He spoke good English with a Mexican accent. "Please call me Gonzalez. How may I help you?"

"My team has been assigned to resolve the strike. You and your union are unhappy and we'd like to work out an amicable solution."

"Sorry, we can't do that."

"Why not?"

"I said, sorry, no."

"Gonzalez, we're here to help you. Tell us what your victory proposition is and we will do our best to satisfy it so the strike can end and your people can begin earning wages again."

"You come here with the full faith of the eastern gringo in charge?"

Gil nodded.

"Then this is what I want to end my strike. I want a car, a Cadillac, blue and convertible. And I want permission and funds to return to Guadalajara with my family. I want money, gobs and gobs of money. It's out there and I want it. And I don't want to work for it. That's for other people. People like you who talk so much about having it all the time."

"You're not serious?"

"And I want a perro for my daughter Marlena, her frogs died last week. They were delicious. And for my son Gonzi, I want a Corvette or at least an Audi, but only the sleek one, not the sedan; he'll never accept a sedan and only in silver. And for my wife, she could use new cooking utensils; the wooden ones are worn."

"I can't do any of those things."

Gonzalez y Gonzalez looked up at Gil and sighed. "Yes you can. Late last night, I was praying in the great grotto when a vision appeared to me. It was of a man such as you, but wearing great, flowing white robes, and he was descending from the heavens. I was afraid. Visions have come to me before, but usually they involve naked, big-breasted women and peyote or weed. This vision foretold that my life was to change very, very soon, that he was the great Messiah from the East and he had come at last to free my people from bondage. With the greatest possible humility, he whispered these specific items to me and explained that the man who brings them to me, he will be the true messiah. My vision was clear and the things I am requesting all must be new, not used. This was the promise and it must be delivered."

Gil was at a loss. "Did the messiah in your vision really tell you to go to Guadalajara?"

The union leader nodded.

"Gonzalez, the American economy depends on this harvest and we are concerned that too many will starve if your union doesn't return to the fields. Surely your vision mentioned how well received your return to the fields will be received?"

The union leader's eyes seemed to lose focus. "Of course, that's why the cars and the money. Free markets, supply and demand, all that good stuff you believe in, surely the gringos who sent you have given in to my demands by now."

"But they don't know your demands. There is a great deal we can do for you, but not that, so please take these negotiations seriously."

Gonzalez was offended. "Seriously? Just because I'm Mexican and a lowly harvester of nature's wondrous bounty, that's no reason to talk down to me."

"I didn't mean to insult you. But what you're asking I can't deliver. Personal favors are off the table."

"Since when? Graft is fine for *Executives* and *Entrepreneurs*, but poor lowly union people, we can't get feel the love? We're Americans, too, at least some of us are."

Carl raised his hand and offered to help. "Gonzalez, I've never been to Acapulco but I hear it's nice this time of year."

"Yes it is lovely."

Carl continued, "What else is lovely this time of year?"

Gonzalez seemed confused.

"Watermelon and pecans are lovely this time of year. So are lettuce and avocadoes."

"Yes, they are."

"Well, Gonzalez, we need for you to harvest them so people can enjoy them while they're still lovely." Carl smiled as if he had just solved the problem.

Bob whispered to Gil. "Carl is an idiot. Let me help."

Reluctantly, Gil nodded.

Bob spoke in Spanish. "My friend, I am a very good little friend," he began, "I loved you as a tomato and I would greatly like to taste you as an avocado if you drag a fat old lady from the field for me."

Understanding enough, Gil was embarrassed and exasperated. He turned to his likenesses and stated firmly, "Guys, we need to focus. Time is passing and we haven't come close to achieving our victory condition."

Each nodded and then Abe asked, "When I try to grow jalapeños, they never seem to ripen and then they rot. What am I doing wrong?"

"Plant them in full sun and water them," was Gonzalez's reply.

Before Abe could thank him, Gil stopped him. "Team, we need to get back on task. The strike, it has to end. Gonzalez, it's not helping your people and it's creating issues in the economy. Think about your families and what the strike is doing to the price of food. Food prices are rising for all *Conducers*, particularly those living close to the brink. You don't want to be responsible for that, do you? We can end this quickly if you give me a list of your real demands, not your personal ones. We can help you. I sincerely believe we can help you."

As Gonzalez was about to respond, his image slowly faded away as did those of his team. When his team reappeared, they were wearing different clothes, the wall calendar had incremented a day, and he had no results to show for it.

Days two, three and four were similarly unproductive and confounding as the team bumbled through interviews with unhelpful farm owners, a representative from the California Federal Reserve who would only discuss his mathematical model that predicted union failure, a senior member of the foreign corporation that had acquired Buena Vista, and finally, the Buena Vista mayor, a young woman who deferred to Gonzalez on everything.

When, finally, the mayor's image began to fade, Gil panicked. His career was on the line and he was failing the exam miserably. As, one by one, Abe, Bob and then Carl, his team of Gils, faded from view, he visibly cringed.

"Don't end this now," he shouted to no one in particular. "I'll think of something. I'm getting the feel for this. We're getting closer and I still have time. I still have time." But he was alone now in the project control room.

Then that room faded from view and he was seated below an immense white desk encrusted with rubies, diamonds, emeralds, and sapphires. According to the sign on the desk far above, he was in the office of the avatar in charge of Missionary Education. Above Gil and behind the massive desk sat a balding, heavy-set man wearing a too-tight, brown double-breasted business suit inlaid with fine gold and silver pinstripe threads that, because of the man's obesity, were stretched and becoming decidedly unparallel. On the man's lapel was pinned a large icon of the Almighty Dollar but by the man's unkempt look, Gil wondered if the Graduate program had recently lost funding.

The man looked everywhere but at Gil and when he finally spoke, it was in a nasal monotone drone. "Mr. Rose, Mr. Rose, Mr. Rose, I am Harry Drullo, your Executive Avatar and it is my job to evaluate your performance or lack of same and pass on my recommendations to the Graduate Committee."

Too far below to stand and shake his hand, Gil could only look up like a child and speak. "Mr. Drullo, Harry, it's nice to meet you. Before you begin my evaluation, there is something I need to say. I, I mean we, my team, we had more time. You stopped this too soon. We were close to finding a way. I'm certain we could have met the value proposition and passed the exam if we had a few more moments."

"Yes, yes, time and inclination. Very well put, indeed." Harry pointed to various colored folders that floated above and behind him. He waved some folders away until he found one in particular and double-pointed to it. The folder glowed, opened, and a document fluttered out. Harry made a widening motion with his hands and the document expanded so Gil could read it from his seat below. At a certain passage, Harry pointed and clicked his fingers. The selected passage grew and was highlighted in yellow.

"Aha, here it is," he said. "First, obviously, you and your team receive no special commendations—there were no Morgan conversions, not that any were expected. Incidentally no conversions were attempted and, thank Morgan; no one on your team was so desperate as to try to exorcise the commie out of a union member. I've seen it tried and it's not pretty and I've had to explain the futility of it afterwards to insistent missionary graduates who should know better. It takes more than faith.

"Now as to you, Mr. Rose, although not utterly incompetent, what we witnessed here today was predictably disappointing, certainly within two standard deviations. But if it cheers you, I see worse and more relevant to you, you will be assigned to missions with many who were far worse. But as a word of caution, the Chairwoman isn't looking for missionary consultants who qualify in the 'don't suck' category, so you have no reason to be cocky."

Gil groped for a response. "I certainly don't feel cocky."

"Incompetence may not be the best description of your lack of performance here. Inexcusable comes to mind too, but of course I'm not in the business of apologies. You are sent out to deliver God's holy word and thus our graduate exams, by their nature, must be extraordinarily complex and suitably bizarre so candidates have as little foundation as possible beyond faith with which to comfortably prepare to achieve the victory proposition. One thing of note, along with your best effort, this exercise required an honest effort. That is another important reason why we make scenarios as unfathomable as possible."

Gil wanted to defend himself, but when he opened his mouth, far above him, Drullo held his hand up for quiet.

"Management, as you well know, is, by definition, egotistical, preferring its own point of view on most matters to the exclusion of other, probably better, and possibly more rational points of view. It is one of God's unfathomable mysteries but what good is religion without some mystery? So even if it is not in management's best interest or the best interest of their corporation, management tends to stand unwaveringly on the side of what they know best or what has worked for them previously and they expect you to revere their status and their perspective. I'm not saying that isn't expertise of a sort, but I've been around a long time and I've been involved in the testing of everyone in current management and all I will say is there are lightweights afoot. A great many of God's consultants, more than you would guess, are incapable of creating project synergy, even with like-minded people and even if that is precisely what's required to tap into God's glory and achieve the full economic value of an endeavor. And what could be more like-minded than identical personas?

"I find these exams great theater, but you should be aware that exams have no benefit unless you appreciate their purpose." Harry laughed a loud chortle that caused his jowls to ripple. "I have seen excellent project managers flailing and failing for numerous reasons, but our exam, like the good Lord above, never ever fails. I have witnessed virtual fights among project team members—we even had a knifing once and there was a sexual thing that was pretty violent and very disturbing, but everything got sorted out and eventually that team succeeded—in it's way and unlike your team. They certainly got extra credit for what was called 'bonding', if you catch my drift. I will move on now.

"Frustration is a very useful tool for high net worth people. When it's working right, it erodes just enough confidence to allow the more introspective missionaries among us to uncover amazing personal insights. Confident, strong-willed and highly motivated people often need something outside of themselves to kick start these insights and we aim to please. Failure is useful, too, but not in abundance, of course, and trending in that direction is suicidal. Failure has a useful, debilitating affect on both the under and overconfident but a firm and unwavering faith in God's holy free market covenant is invariably restorative to each, often improving performance on subsequent projects.

"I have seen tears, too frequently, but from my experiences, I much prefer mayhem to great soulful awakenings. It is so much more effective and far easier and more entertaining to watch than to endure great bouts of mournful sobbing among Morgan professionals. You have no idea how difficult it is to keep sobbing jag videos off of our social networks. It only takes one to all but ruin a career before it starts. We invest a great deal in our students so poking fun at their expense only makes sense if there is a suitable return." Harry laughed. "It is why I so love my job. Until you've seen four identicals beating the crap out of each other, so enraged that the irony of it is completely lost on them, you will never appreciate the affect of comic pathos until you see it. Still, this is business so it's all good if it ends well. Do you understand Mr. Rose?"

Unsure where this was leading, Gil just nodded.

"One time," Harry said, leaning forward and peering over the top of his desk, "we had to tranquilize an entire team virtually—including the project manager—and then tranquilize the candidate in real time. When the team awakened, in virtual, you wouldn't believe the ruckus they made. They argued that the exam was unnecessarily cruel and patently unfair as if that has any bearing. And in real, the candidate threatened to sue if we didn't add time back to the exam for the time lost when her team was tranquilized even though she was no closer to meeting her objective than your team was today."

"But we—"

Harry waved his hand dismissively. "We'll get to that. Occasionally, a missionary gets it just right and together with their likenesses, in short order; they simply blow us away with the definitive solution worked to perfect realization. It is a thing of beauty. We've done studies and it seems to be more prevalent among the ladies but other than that, the serendipity is a mystery. The Chairwoman's own daughter had just such an epiphany and drove her team to a successful conclusion. In short order, she recognized the lay of the land, figured out the problem, resolved it—even adding value to the overall strategy and added disciplines that no one had considered—and frankly just delivered an astounding solution. She even managed to convert everyone in latrine services from a form of Anabaptist to God's Kingdom through Morgan. The Chairwoman was so proud that the avatar proctor in charge of the scenario received a merit increase and now the self-satisfied son of a bitch only works with those projected to be the most financially secure—the crème de la crème in Investment Banking. Talk about a sweet job with perks. Any way, your likenesses' performance was nothing like that of the Chairwoman's daughter."

"Did we . . . did I fail? Is that what you're saying?"

Harry caused a graph to slide from another folder and floated it in front of Gil. Appearing on a normal distribution curve was a small flashing red dot denoting his team's performance just to the left of the top of the curve. "Before handing your test scenario over to you and your crew, it was simulated so that we could determine likely outcomes. As you can see your result was entirely expected."

"But . . . but the way it was set up . . . how can what happened be expected?"

"Yes, it's a beautiful thing." Harry smiled and winked as he highlighted a paragraph in another document. This document, too, floated down in front of Gil.

"Here it is," Harry said. "You declined Singularity. Why is that?"

"That's not your business."

"To a point it is. Chip heads with enhanced communication capability are far more productive than antiques like you. You knew that yet declined the enhancement."

Once again, Gil's involvement with Joad was impeding him. "Harry, when I was younger, I had . . . I had a bad experience in *Virtuoso* and I don't want to experience that again so I won't chip. I guess I'm too fond of my own thoughts to—"

"La la la," Harry sang out. "That is far too much information. I'm not here to change your mind. You were selected by the Chairwoman. That is good enough for me. You seem a willing complainer, whereas who would I complain to? What I know is that the chipped make the best Missionary Consultants and have the most potential to achieve their long term net worth goals. Antiques like you, what can I say? Figuring out the Chairwoman's selection process has always proven unfathomable.

"Mr. Rose, as you pursue everlasting life, you will find reason enough to change your mind. When forever is in the mix, no decision is irrevocable and no mind is made up. But that's enough proselytizing. To live forever we must come to God in our own way, or if not, we die bereft of God's love and His financial advice. How you address your immortality is a personal choice, however, I definitely recommend the chip because it will increase your chances of achieving your highest potential. Anyway, that's enough. God or no God, you've made your choice for now. When you change your mind, you may apply to the Human Technologies Department of Singularity, LLC. They have the best surgical teams and the highest satisfaction rate according to JD Powers and as a colleague at Gorman University, they offer financing."

"I'll think on what you're asking."

"Until such time as you elect to chip, our policy is that when you are staffed on projects you will be identified as a consultant who lacks true, blind ambition and true certainty about God and forever. This designation will necessitate that you bust your ass, so to speak, to disprove first impressions. That is what you must do if eternity is what you seek—and who doesn't seek that? Not being a true believer will make it far more difficult for you to get along with your fellow workers so I implore you to not trivialize the importance that imbedded chips can have on your career or the limits not having them will put on your worth and your currently fragile and mortal soul."

"Everything I've done, I've done in an exemplary manner," he argued.

"Until today, Mr. Rose, you mustn't forget today. But I'm not here to contest that with you. What occurred was on the mean, median and the mode of expectations and yet we all hope it is not a trend. I so love irony." With that, Harry motioned and all of the other papers disappeared and a new paper dropped into Gil's lap.

"Before permitting a Morgan missionary to practice in the cold cruel but fair business world of America, we evaluate everything from every possible perspective. We even evaluate acquaintances and generations of family members for correlation. Once again, in this, you have proven to be an anomaly. Your circle of relationships is alarmingly limited statistically, so admittedly our evaluation has a greater margin for error. Other than true belief and being chipped—and not to diminish them—we have found that the one element that most negatively affects your performance is that you consistently give other people too much power in your actions. As detestable as that is, it is also so far beyond the pale that we will monitor you for the eventual onset of mental illness.

"The Church teaches us that concerns for people add unnecessary risk and variability to any project and you have had ample experience to know that pursuing that direction can reduce your business relationships and your worth, yet you do it anyway, and you do it as if it were natural." Drullo shuddered, his jowls rippling. "Frankly, this makes you appear soft-headed, which is never good for a businessman or a missionary, and it puts project deliverables at risk. This behavior has been catalogued along with your other flaws and as I said, it will be monitored. For your sake, you must remediate this, post haste. I know you were trained for better. Never, ever forget, Mr. Rose, you represent the very best America, the great Morgan Church, and our Chairwoman has to offer and not in that order. And God's kingdom on earth, I don't want to forget that. We don't expect you to meet expectations; we expect you to far exceed them. What would this world look like if on the seventh day, instead of creating corporations; God had decided he needed a paid vacation or he wanted to do something that would make him popular with people? Think on that, Mr. Rose, until it sickens you and then buckle down. Today's inferior performance will be with you always to motivate you, focus you, and drive you with the focused frenzy of professionalism to be with God, on earth, forever."

Gil tried to defend himself. "But with more time, we would . . . we could have . . ."

Harry put his fingers in his ears. "La-la-la-la-la. Am I detecting attitude?"

"Mr. Drullo, Harry, if today's performance washes me out, I'll find another way."

"Alas, there is no other way."

"I'm good at what I do."

"You are right to believe that you have unique talent—though talent not in great demand, by the way, but unique in its way. Students who pass through these hallowed booths go on to become the greatest disciples of Morgan. Our graduates become God's bureaucracy on earth and the very best of them levitate to the hallowed halls of Banking where they can plug into God's true power while practicing His great love of the deal. But you are not them, Mr. Rose, you are not them. None of the greats has ever been a consensus builder."

"I've been successful and I would never compromise a project."

Harry stiffened his back, looked down at Gil, and smiled. "Trust me, Mr. Rose, you will. But put your mind at ease. As poorly as you've performed here today, you haven't failed, not yet, anyway. It is time to explore the real purpose of this exam."

Gil was taken aback. "It's not the final evaluation of my capability before graduation and assignment?"

"It is that but so much more," Harry explained. "We script our exams to your first domestic professional assignment—a time when new consultants working with Americans for the first time tend to deliver squishy effort. What did you learn today?"

Gil tried to make sense of it. "Maybe . . . I should have treated the requirements as sacrosanct and we should have worked harder to satisfy our customer's requirements."

"That may be a correct response. Who was your customer?" Gil pointed at Drullo who seemed surprised. "Me your customer? Please explain."

"Well maybe you're not but you're the one grading me and I needed to succeed in your eyes." When Drullo shook his head, Gil recalibrated his response. "I mean, the town, the town is my customer because they are paying for my services." Drullo seemed to smile so Gil continued. "We failed them. We tried to—"

Drullo shook his head, his jowls sashaying from side to side. "Please focus, Mr. Rose. You are talking around the situation. Four Gilbert Roses should have amplified things. Think about strengths and weaknesses. Think. That is what you will be paid to do, within very clearly defined limits."

He considered it. "Yes, well, we . . . I mean, of course I wanted to find the right solution but my team struggled to focus and as Project Manager, I should have forced everyone to work harder on the deliverables. Instead, I allowed my team to get lost in the details to the detriment of the final solution."

"It does no good to speak for my benefit. Before you offer your final response, allow me to help. Who today aided your performance the most and least?"

"Each of them, of me, us, is responsible. Bob was off topic, Abe and Carl . . ."

"No, no, no. You're not getting it. Who are Abe, Carl, and Bob?"

"They're me, at least what the University believes I am. Are you telling me that my profile has me in conflict with . . . with myself?"

"I didn't say that. Do you really care about your profile?"

"No, yes, of course I care. If I'm to graduate and serve, it's important. And if I'm going to get staffed where I can help—"

"If it is so important to you, Mr. Rose, you should come to grips with why you failed to rally your team to deliver a solution that a paying customer demanded."

What answer did Harry want?

"As a Morgan Missionary, expect tougher assignments than this test so figure it out, Mr. Rose, and when you do, you'll understand something essential about your life. Perhaps another time I'll be privy to your well-considered insight but for now—"

Fearing the worst, Gil sat and worried while Drullo rummaged above him at his disorganized desk. Drullo pulled out a small, leather-bound book and a gift-wrapped box. He surveyed the box and then handed it to Gil.

"I present you with a facsimile of your very own *Personometer* 20/20."

Gil reached up for it.

"Please," Drullo said, pulling it back, "allow me to do my job. This is state-of-the-art technology and it is fully integrated for both external and internal use, unfortunately you deferred on the internal. The internal advantages of the *Personometer* brand of solution generators are reason enough to sign up for Singularity treatments, for without that hook-up, you are required to learn the extremely complex method for reading the results of the *Personometer* 20/20 offline through an add-on, the *Integrator* 10/10 which is an extra that you will be billed for and is, out of necessity, quite expensive and comes with a steep learning curve. In fact, the Singularity surgery and the *Integrator* 10/10 cost roughly the same amount. A real *Personometer* 20/20 has been shipped to your home address and will arrive before your first domestic assignment."

It took a moment for Gil to realize what Drullo was saying. He had graduated! Excited, he opened the box and took out the small round black electronic ball about four inches in diameter with the green, silver, and gold Almighty Dollar symbol of the Morgan Church embossed on one side and a small window on the other side that displayed nuanced readings to assist the owner in business negotiations.

"Thank you, Mr. Drullo. This is great. I took a class in Outcomes where we learned how to use an earlier model of the *Personometer*."

"Every successful consultant has used a *Personometer* in the course of negotiations. As I'm sure you know, it provides instantaneous feedback and is guaranteed to optimize and expedite all interpersonal negotiations the first time and every time."

Gil held the *Personometer* in the palm of his hand as if weighing it. He turned it over and slowly a message appeared in the display window.

Outlook not so good

He needed to check the user manual to see what that meant.

"Use this tool prudently, Mr. Rose, for it is a truly remarkable instrument for good in the world. As a new graduate, you have been signed up for the forever maintenance annuity package. There is a not insignificant monthly fee and an annual membership cost, but you will find it all well worth your while. Additionally, during your first negotiations, it is highly recommended that you show restraint at least until you have very carefully recalibrated the unit and learned the nuances between its output metrics and the expectations of your negotiating opponent. Your current personal success profile is already stored in the secure memory of the *Personometer* and this will automatically recalibrate based on your ongoing negotiating success rate. The box includes recalibration instructions, should outcomes turn unsatisfactory. Most consultants find the instructions confusing but as with everything, the manufacturer is not liable for the results which, of course, are not guaranteed because they are dependent upon the individual skills of each negotiator and their ability to read *Personometer* recommendations correctly and, of course, to act appropriately. Value this gift, Mr. Rose; it is our way of thanking you for years of matriculation fees. You will find it a critical instrument in your Consensus Building toolbox and for your journey to God's Kingdom on earth."

"Thank you very much, Mr. Drullo," Gil said, beaming with pride.

Drullo handed him a scroll, tied with a green and silver ribbon. "I am pleased to present you with a degree in Advanced Entrepreneurial Studies in your field of concentration, Consensus Building. You should receive the real document in about two weeks. Once your first domestic assignment begins, your account will be charged monthly until your *Personometer* is paid off. In addition, you are automatically signed up for your Missionary Consultant Association Membership. The dues entitle you to receive the insightful Mesh newsletter; *God's Commitment,* which will help you identify the latest professional opportunities including social marketing activities, church elimination dances, and such that are located near your assignments. By law, I am required to inform you that monthly payments for these benefits, including interest and late fees, will be automatically deducted from your estate. Late fees are often quite punitive and there can be other penalties depending upon your success or rather lack of it in the field. In addition, with graduation, you qualify to receive a perpetual subscription to the Chairwoman's own monthly personal business journal, *My World,* that includes useful job-related recommendations and tasteful landscaping and decorating as well as styling tips for the up and coming consultant-entrepreneur.

"Mr. Rose, I implore you once again. You will achieve quicker and more conspicuous returns if you avail yourself of Singularity." With that, Drullo handed Gil a one-page document. "As a consultant certified to practice, this represents the parameters for your first domestic assignment. Study it because you will need to know everything in order to increase your revenue stream as quickly as possible."

Drullo gave Gil a moment to look over the document. Similar to the exam prospectus, it was far easier to understand.

"You are most fortunate. Your first assignment is critical to the American economy and thus it is highly visible. Succeed here and you will go far. You will operate out of Sacramento, California and under the jurisdiction and control of the Chairman of the Western Federal Reserve Bank, Court and Stock Exchange, Alph Crelli."

He was surprised by the name and Drullo noticed. "Yes, that Mr. Crelli, the first son of our former Chairman. He is quite talented and extremely wealthy."

With that, Drullo stood and appeared beside Gil. He was much smaller than he seemed at his desk above. He shook Gil's hand. "Good luck in your quest for life everlasting on your terms. As soon as you figure it out, I am certain we will meet again."

With that, the simulation ended. He dressed quickly, his elation with passing the exam tempered by his bafflement at what had just transpired. He returned to his empty home and with no one to share his success, he sat on the hammock and once again stared out at the waves. That's when it hit him. Was that what Tanya Brandt thought of him?

Chapter 5

Sacramento—2083

Confidential Memo **Confidential Memo**

To: *President-Elect of the United States, Andrew Crelli January 21, 2032*
cc: Lucille T. Brandt, Mark Rose, Thomas A. Morgan

From: *Gecko*

Subject: *Recession, Liquidation Theory and the Elimination of 100,000,000 Non-viable*

When you take the oath of office tomorrow, the U.S. economy will have been in recession for almost ten years and until you take action, it will get worse. The plan is in place and now is the time to act resolutely because your action, difficult as it may seem, it will lead to long term wealth for Executives and Entrepreneurs and enable the Entrepreneur Party to become dominant, politically while strengthening the economy and enabling significant, long term asset appreciation. Achieving each of these goals will fulfill my primary directive and place you in the pantheon of America's great Presidents.

Background: *For most of its existence, the U.S. economy has been undermined by a two-party political tug of war for power. Rather than support staunch Capitalist principles, politicians have vacillated in order to woo voters and capture votes, the way to power in our current Republic. This incongruous policy began during the World War era, America's Golden Age, a time when global conflict destroyed America's economic competition and unlimited resources were contained in countries without economic capabilities. The unfortunate result of this confluence of fortunate events is that the American people are economically unsophisticated, lack faith, and are not true believers in the benefits of Capitalist business cycles. They believe the fantasy that a robust economy is their god-given right.*

The business cycle can be defined as: Savings generating Investment creating Capital Accumulation spawning Greater Productivity providing "More Stuff" for consumers to acquire. "More Stuff" means a higher standard of living which results in an ever more conservative population voting its regard for the political party that best exemplifies the policies that made "More Stuff" available along with the means to acquire it. The business cycle works best on faith and it works for everyone, every time but one, bad times. Still, the boom times must be worth the bust times or what's a heaven for?

From our current bust economy, we must develop a perpetual boom in order to maintain power and reward the greatest and noblest of our Entrepreneurs who have survived this long term bust cycle. For America to become a Capitalist paradise, for it to generate the wondrous benefits of a forever boom cycle, business must be unfettered from government regulation and taxes. Business must be sacrosanct.

The Issues: *Through the 2028 election, while challenging for supremacy, both the Democrat and Republican Parties have shown flagrant disregard for the lucrative dynamics of the Capitalist business cycle. After taking office and without regard to the promises made during the campaign, each Party, in their turn, has grown government to Socialist proportions until it is now so large that regardless what business people say in public, they can't reach their profit goals without it and the business savvy among them are scared to death that in their America, there is a power greater than business.*

With so many commercial piglets to suckle, to punish, and to reward, the Federal Government has been forced to ever muck around with tax and regulation policies. Unwilling or unable to come to some agreement as to the right size of Government, every administration, regardless of Party, has artificially lowered interest rates in order to stimulate growth. For Booms to occur, Busts are necessary but Government monetary intervention has become so destabilizing that it chokes commercial confidence thus creating the perpetual stagnation and decline that our economy has endured for so long that is has become resistant to all previously attempted remedies and elixirs.

If Government hasn't been destructive enough, every previous Congress and President has provided monumental incentives to their recalcitrant supporters to entice them to vote, adding further discordance to the business cycle by draining savings and investment. Over the last half century, this behavior by seemingly mature, responsible adults and self-claimed patriots, elected by the people to preserve, protect, and defend, has caused America's great economic engine to stall, and then lose dynamics. We are, today, in the crash and burn stage.

The Solution: *In the fully realized Liquidation Theory of Business Cycles lies the antidote. Cycles are natural things that must run their course. That is what cycles do. You must break eggs to make an omelet. For decades, a great many conservatives have been offering this advice but they are cowards for they refuse to live and die by what they preach and know to be right. Boom and bust cycles are the only honest and true way for a free market economy to soar and adherence to the dictates of business cycles offers the distinct bonus of making the right decisions more obvious and easier to implement, and isn't that the essential, true beauty of Capitalism, after all? But the practitioners of American Capitalism have grown soft, not Socialist soft, not yet, but soon if we don't act with resolve beginning tomorrow.*

The true benefit of a bust cycle is that it burns away the inefficient that was created by overconfidence in the economy at the height of the boom. This "liquidation" generates the greatest opportunity for new and vibrant businesses to lead the next boom. Here there is a problem with our political system. The regular, two year political cycle, by its very nature, has a disruptive, dampening affect on much longer economic cycles. How can entrepreneurs run businesses when rules and attitudes change with the wind?

As of tomorrow, government intervention must cease in order to free the business cycle so that the resulting brutal correction will be dependable enough and momentous enough to shock our economy out of this death spiral and back into boom mode. Your administration has this responsibility and obligation because you know that America represents Capitalism at its finest. To save America and Capitalism, the essential issue, one long put off by weak and vacillating politicians must be acted upon as previously agreed. What is required is daunting and it will not be rewarded in the near term. In fact, we, but Mr. President-elect, you most of all, will be considered iniquitous in the short term. Be strong. Forever begs for this opportunity and you must not fail.

The Payout: *The Virtuous Cycle, forever. In bust cycles, demand declines along with investment. It drives boom-generated, mal-invested capital asset values down so that the most inefficient companies, plants and equipment will be forced to shut down and sell-off devalued assets. Over time, the absence of* *demand will drive prices down further which allows for bargain acquisitions by the most efficient remaining businesses. As each industry recapitalizes at lower cost or greater efficiency, a boom bubbles to the surface and the business cycle in America is jump-started, creating a more robust economy. That is how capital rebalances in nature. Labor, unfortunately, is not so fluid or fortunate.*

Critical Factors: *Since the Civil War, the Democrat Party has been desperately prowling for voters. By making deals with the devil and delivering financial security to workers and non-workers alike who haven't earned that right and who have not protected themselves from the worst ravages of the inevitable bust cycles, the Democrat Party found its voters. Without the political courage to fight for right, Republicans perpetuated Democrat welfare economics, leading to the disaster we resolve beginning tomorrow*

Over generations, the Democrat Party's paternalistic policies toward the least contributors in our economy has created a Consumer-Producer class (Production Workers, hereafter called "Conducers"), who are soft, dependent, and economically immature and viable only in the best economic situations. It is these inefficient who now stand in the way of America's great forever. That is why it is essential that we stay true to Liquidation Theory which will create ever expanding cycles to greatness but in order for that to be achieved, faith is essential for unlike mal-invested capital, mal-employed labor must cease entirely and all unproductive human costs eliminated for all time.

Solution: *Beginning tomorrow, government no longer intervenes in the economy and, as planned, all American labor burdening the economy must be eliminated expeditiously, systematically, and permanently. America has ample inventory of human workers to support boom cycles, but in bust cycles, they must disappear—Liquidation Theory in practice so true Capitalism can rule as God intends.*

A memo will follow as to how this disappearance of the nonviable can be best achieved.

Respectfully submitted,

Gecko

Confidential Memo **Confidential Memo**

The morning after Gil's exam, he received his travel instructions in a packet that contained the real *Personometer* 20/20. Before packing the device away, he read the directions over and over until he was able to calibrate it. Then, with his luggage at the door, he waited, unsure whether he wanted Gale to call or not. Finally, when the call didn't come, he boarded a gondola and left for Union Station feeling less confident than a newly accredited, domestic Morgan Missionary consultant should feel. He arrived at the station an hour before the *Entrepreneur Express* was scheduled to depart for Sacramento so he checked his luggage, cleared security, and with time to kill, wandered the ancient Union Station terminal.

He was excited to be traveling to the West Coast for the first time and he walked off his nervous energy admiring the architectural grandeur of the First Republic's Golden Age. He found some areas blocked off due to flooding so he wandered down those that were open, his footsteps echoing past the many statues that guarded the empty marble corridors. As he neared one hallway, a heavy, pungent, sour odor caused him to gag. Instead of turning away, he was curious and persevered down it until he was confronted by an armed, black and yellow-garbed HOMESEC guard stationed in front of large, shiny, copper doors. On an overhead monitor his name appeared in red along with his train number and departure time.

"Mr. Rose, sir, you have no business here," the guard informed him.

Shallow breathing made the odor less intolerable. He smiled at the guard. "Sorry, officer, I was early so I'm sightseeing." He stared at the monitor again. "What is that awful smell? Did something die in there?"

The guard's face remained frozen as he keyed a sequence into his communicator. After carefully reading the response, the guard spoke again, forcefully but polite. "I'm sorry, sir, you are below grade level. I'm not required to respond." Gil waited for the guard to smile but he didn't.

"Doesn't that smell offend travelers?" he asked as he looked around. "I guess that's why the corridor is deserted but how can you stand it?"

"Sir, please go back to the main lobby and follow the green lights on the wall to track thirty-two. The *Entrepreneur Express* is boarding now for Sacramento."

With eyes burning, he turned to leave. "Does it smell like this all the time?"

The guard refocused his attention on the far wall. "Track thirty-two, sir."

Gil retraced his steps. When he reached the main lobby, he followed a set of green lights and soon was on the correct platform where, at the far end sat a sleek, iridescent white train. As he approached, he caught a whiff of fresh air and stopped to reconsider that offensive smell. A distant memory returned. He pictured Clarke Jackell sitting across from the fire in his tiny shack in Presque Isle telling his sad and troublesome story of an ominous scorpion-like death train after he had escaped from the Last Chance Saloon. A chill chased down his spine as he walked past the passenger cars with his hand trailing along their surface.

The *Entrepreneur Express* consisted of four low, sleek, aerodynamic cars coated in a brilliant, white ceramic skin, grooved and yet smooth with an almost leathery finish that felt cool to the touch. He tried to look inside but the windows were opaque so he continued on until he reached a door that opened as soon as he approached.

Inside, in contrast to the whiteness of the exterior, all was dark and rich and it took a moment for his eyes to adjust. Dark stained wood paneling framed midnight-blue carpeting that was so luxurious he could clearly see recent footprints. On one side, a large aquarium filled with colorful tropical fish sat above a glass bar, while on the other side, four large booths each adorned with a set of Archive headgear sat vacant. There was even a *Virtuoso* unit in the rear.

He walked through the car and opened a sliding door. The area between the cars was protected from the outside by the same flexible ceramic skin and was designated as a smoking area with two large, powerful fans set in the ceiling to suck out the offending smoke. By their size, he suspected they could suck smoke from a smoker's lungs.

He entered the next car. On one side was a galley and on the other a series of small tables painted in pastels, their bases made up of shiny metal sculptures. As he walked through, he stared out at the platform. The outside was so different that he paused to consider it. The bare platform that he had just walked down was now a lush jungle of dense, colorful flora and there was a large waterfall near enough for a mist to lightly coat the windows. In disbelief, he pressed his nose against the window. It was definitely a jungle out there. He looked around. Each window projected a consistent scene. This was going to be a fun trip.

As he approached the next car, a sign warned him that it was off limits and a smiling young female avatar's face appeared on the door window. With a soothing voice, she explained. "Please go back to your cabin, Mr. Rose. Ms. Brandt is waiting."

At first, he was surprised and then concerned. "Ms. Brandt? The Chairwoman came to see me off?"

The avatar put her index finger up to her cheek, tilted her head and laughed a high-pitched silly laugh. "There is not one single chance of that, Mr. Rose. I am speaking of the younger Ms. Brandt."

Gil was immediately cheered and retraced his steps.

She was wearing a bulky green and gold Gorman University sweatshirt and tight black linen slacks and was reclining on a chaise. She smiled as soon as she saw him.

"Impressed?" she asked with a smile that never failed to please.

He returned her smile. She was so beautiful that he just stared at her until her smile began to waver. To avoid further embarrassment, his eyes darted around to take in his surroundings. Above was an observation deck with windows and a skylight that ran the length of the car. Although they were inside Union Station, above, the sun was shining in the bluest of blue skies with white wispy clouds hovering off the tops of tall trees in what looked like an immense tropical forest. He was so absorbed by the surroundings that he was startled when she spoke again.

"Impressive isn't it?" she asked again.

"Is this how everyone travels to Sacramento?"

"I'm not everyone, but if you're going west, this is the best way."

She stood and he kissed her on her cheek. "Thanks for seeing me off," he said.

She laughed. "You think far too highly of yourself if you think we'd send a mere rookie anywhere this way. You're assigned to my project and we're traveling together."

He smiled at that. "Great. But I was informed that a Crelli clone was in charge."

"Alph heads our Steering Committee. Project delivery is mine."

"I've never been to Sacramento. Maybe you can show me around."

"There's not much left to see and I doubt we'll have time, anyway." She was silent for a moment. "I spent three years in Indonesia preparing; countless hours stuck in hotel rooms alone while their project team was out celebrating various Muslim holy days. And in order to get access to the right business and engineering personnel, I had to date their Minister of Trade. Boy what a boorish, foul-smelling brute, Amir was, but he was the only one who could move the project along. I endured far too many protracted meals listening to his princely boasts about the thousands of beautiful virgins he devoured at his leisure while searching for Miss Right."

"Let me guess . . ."

"Yes, I was his Miss Right. All that he asked of me was that I convert to Islam, respect his culture, honor him, mother his brood, and look the other way when his eyes wandered in search of another Miss Right. He was, as he liked to boast, a man of great appetites. Fortunately, though his manners left a lot to be desired and his hygiene was sorely lacking, he was serious about the project."

In spite of her description of the man's grossness, Gil felt a little jealous. "Spare me the details of what you had to do for this Amir fellow."

As if he had said something wrong, her face turned red. "Damn it, Gil, do you really think I've changed that much?"

He started to answer but she stopped him. "No jokes. Have you become so stupid you think I'd sleep with someone to get ahead? I'm the daughter of real power and people try to sleep with me, not the other way around." She paused and sighed. "Please don't think that of me or you'll ruin happy memories of our time together in that wonderful little hovel we called home."

He was happy to change the subject. "Hovel?" he asked. "Now I'm offended. I have fond memories of that place. Sometimes, late at night, if I can't sleep, I think back longingly to that tiny rug by the door that was too thin to insulate me from the hard, cold floor. I have great memories of waking to windblown snow melting around my edges."

"You sound bitter."

"Not at all, maybe only that it was always so bitterly cold." He smiled.

"You told me that you were the outdoors type."

He laughed. "I was lying. This train has far better accommodations than our partner cabin. Maybe you can make it up to me on this trip."

She blushed. "Don't be vulgar or presumptuous. That can't happen."

"You sound so sure."

"Now you're being rude," she said. "Nothing will happen. I'm as sure of that as I am of my project."

"So we're traveling together because you like to be tempted or can't be tempted?"

"Gil, stop it. We're together because Mother is being her twisted self."

"I don't know how to respond to that."

"So things haven't changed much since Profit."

"That depends. Are you still fleeing from that fraud rap?"

She looked stern, but a smile burst out ruining the affect. "I'm the Chairwoman's daughter, a certified Morgan Missionary Consulting Reverend Lieutenant, and Project Manager for America's first next generation enhanced profitability project. That fraud charge is merely a youthful indiscretion long forgotten."

"Good to know. So how long before we arrive in Sacramento?"

"We arrive early in the morning for a meeting with Mayor Juana Wua and the Steering Committee."

"Juana Wua?"

"Everyone calls the Mayor, Bunny. She's mayor of what remains of Sacramento."

"The Chairwoman makes travel arrangements now?"

"She's a jokester who enjoys the set up as much as the punch line."

"Is there any chance she trusts us?"

Bree laughed. "Mother?" She pointed to the rear of the train. There are two bedrooms. We'll use both."

"In one night, that could be stimulating."

"Are you demented?" she shouted. "If you want any kind of life going forward, take Mother, me, and yourself very seriously and in that order. And begin now."

"How sweet mommy is."

"Sweet, never, but our relationship has improved. It's purely business now. And regardless how annoying she is; don't doubt she knows I'll be sleeping alone."

He was disappointed, but not really surprised. Her violet eyes had deepened, suppressing the bits of yellow and red that his memory kept trying to put back into the mix but they were no less dazzling than he remembered. He was amazed how the same eyes could appear sinister and cynical in her mother and yet soft and warm on Bree. Her face had matured, too, it was leaner now; also more like her mother's. And her smile, it was still a joy; sincere in that it didn't overextend that one click beyond like her mother's that registered so much fear. He wondered which of Crelli's genes had softened Bree's look and personality.

"So it's to be Profit all over again," he joked. "So close and yet so far."

"You're getting a bit carried away, aren't you?"

"Not if you consider this our second honeymoon?"

A blush rose above her sweatshirt and continued up her neck until it deepened her peaches and cream complexion. He expected to be chastised again but she fooled him.

"Technically wasn't Profit our second honeymoon?" she asked. "So this would be our third, although, of course, it's really none at all."

"If you play your cards right, this could be our most memorable honeymoon."

"Stop it! Stop it right now! Where the hell do you get off talking to me that way?"

Her anger chastened him. "I'm sorry. I'm only kidding."

She calmed down. "I don't understand you. You have a perfectly nice girlfriend and I'm totally committed to this project. This isn't the time . . ." She read something in his look. "What's wrong?"

"Gale and I split up," he admitted. "Actually, she left me."

"I'm sorry. Do you want to talk about it?"

"Not really. She deserves better. Did you know that she works with kids, difficult middle children? Not many people work with kids anymore, including their parents."

"Did parents ever work with their kids?" she asked, rhetorically. "So you do want to talk about it."

"No, you're right. I'm sorry. Let's tackle a project briefing if that's okay."

She looked relieved. "Fine. I retire at ten. It's five now, so we have time."

"I read the project summary that the University provided."

"By the way, congratulations." Given the complexity of the exam, he was surprised that she wasn't surprised he'd passed.

"Thanks. During the evaluation, my avatar told me you did great."

She smiled. "You drew old Harry Drullo. He's a sweetheart and one of my favorites. Yes, I had a really good outcome," she said dismissively.

She moved to a booth and Gil followed, sitting across the table from her.

"Let's begin," she said. "You've been assigned by Mother to convince Reynaldo Diaz, the Union shop steward, that he must end this futile strike so his union can complete the harvest. Once the harvest ends, his people will be relocated so we can make the land more productive. That's where my project comes in. By this time next year, we will replace his union field laborers with sophisticated automated harvesting equipment, technology that I commercialized in Indonesia. It's really sweet technology, capable of full integration from the field to the processing center to the distribution sites."

"Is the technology the reason the union is striking?"

"That's part of it, but there's nothing the union can do about it. Harvest costs must be reduced below what Chile and other southern hemisphere farmers charge to dump their produce into our markets. And once my project is fully implemented, we'll be able to reverse our trade deficits."

"Was my experience in Bolivia what got me assigned to this project?"

Bree shook her head.

"Well then, what?" he asked.

"Mother, of course. She believes that Consensus Building provides a necessary and unique skill. You're to make Diaz understand the situation and convince him to bend to our wishes. Until now, he's turned down every fair offer we've made. But this isn't the same as Bolivia. It's similar enough so you can tap into your experience there but be wary, Diaz is old guard and his decision making is pure analog."

Gil thought back to his exam. This was a reasonable approximation of the scenario he couldn't get close to resolving.

"A word of advice," she continued. "If you brought that stupid *Personometer* piece of crap they force on us at commencement, throw it away. It's useless and won't help here or anywhere really. The guy who invented it wrote a book and got rich on it and somehow he convinced Mother to take a minority position in his company, which she turned into a majority position by fiat and now she believes she's building demand by insisting that we use it. Trust me, we don't. In fact, most missionary consultants in the field are too embarrassed to show the damn thing in public because it's more of a child's toy and besides, the way we control the country, the only tool we really need is the HOMESEC hammer so bringing in other tools tends to be confusing to those who oppose us. And don't mention that you have a *Personometer* to Diaz. He hates technology.

"You will find that Diaz is a Christian of the Catholic persuasion, believe it or not, and he opposes Morgan, so that way won't work either. For a first domestic assignment, yours is really very complex and it's vitally important. If we have to use HOMESEC, there are additional economic costs so we want to do this without them. And when we implement, it will mean fantastic bonuses for everyone. You're working in America now where success is life extending."

"That's good to know," Gil said. "So the cost is too great to send Tucker in to force the union off their land."

"There's a harvest that must go to market and we need the union to complete it while we're commercial testing my bots. Like all unions, this one is an old fashioned, close-knit, self-sufficient community that doesn't want to be moved. Our surveillance people tell us they're willing to fight to stay on their land. That's ridiculous, of course, and I don't believe it for a second but HOMESEC reports that they have hidden nuclear devices that could destroy half the farm land in California for thousands of years and Mother simply won't wait that long."

"You're kidding, right?"

"About nuclear weapons, no," she said. "It's why the union has been so smug in their negotiating."

"How would they get a bomb?"

"If you can learn that from their leader, it will help, but I think it's just a rumor that the Bitch spread so she can annihilate them before I get to install my project. A bomb, really, it's laughable. Who permanently threatens resources when there's so much value on the line?

"Another issue is that the union is self-sufficient so our economic embargo hasn't been working on them. Here, HOMESEC believes they're getting help from outside, maybe terrorists or a foreign government. When you meet him, work Diaz to see how many secrets he is willing to offer up."

"My first assignment in America and I'm chosen for this?"

"What can I say? Mother thinks you're a player. I know how smart you are so welcome to the big time. There's more, but it can wait until tomorrow morning at the Steering Committee where you'll meet my half-siblings each of whom is a Chairperson of their respective Fed Districts. Be careful what you say to them because they're pretty intense and with your history with our father, they've been carrying a grudge for a long time. As to the meeting itself, it could be a bit confusing because we're all chipped. I'll try to keep everything you need to hear vocal because you'll never figure out what's going on otherwise."

"Chipped?" he asked. "You're . . . when did you allow that to happen?"

"It was part of my reconciliation with Mother. Don't be disappointed."

"I'm not but you've gone as far from cloaking as anyone can. Why?"

"Like I had a choice," she shrugged, unhappily. "I managed to convince Mother to compromise some. She only has access to me when I'm on the clock."

"Which is all the time," Gil clarified. "You can turn that on and off?"

Bree was reluctant to discuss it further but he persisted so she responded. "No, you can't but . . . never mind, let's move on."

"How does it feel? I mean the actual communication part."

"Gil."

"I'm just asking. They've been pressuring me to get it. How does it feel?"

"I mean, how should it feel?" She shrugged. "Someone's talking inside your head, it sounds like you but it's not and there's no sound."

"How do you manage it? How can you tell your thoughts from someone else's?"

She shrugged. "I don't know. You just can. It takes effort and discipline, and like everything, you get used to it. In some ways it's been helpful like when I need to communicate with my project team and with our staffing department. Being chipped is fine for that. So that you know, if you elect Singularity, there are various communication packages you can select ranging from low functionality, inexpensive phone and global positioning services, all the way to first class expensive, top of the line functionality so you can participate in conference calls in your head, transact deals and you can moment trade on any Market. You can even respond to video-mail by sending mental pictures, but that's advanced stuff that's difficult to afford on an entry level missionary consultant's salary and there are reports of cerebral hemorrhages, though not confirmed.

"With the lesser packages users are prone to severe migraines, but it's getting better and when you get promoted, some of the medical expenses can be charged back to clients. I haven't subscribed to all the bells and whistles because I don't want to become any more intimate with Mother than I already am. The bottom line is I've implemented Singularity because it enhances my performance and that's critical to my career. A question everyone will ask from now on is why you haven't? Why haven't you?"

"I'll never get it. I can't. It goes back to a bad experience when I was younger. Maybe not being chipped will give me a special advantage I can use with the union leader."

"Maybe. Bunny will know."

"Tell me what you know about Diaz."

"There's very little in Archive. Mayor Bunny knows him real well, ask her. The reason why HOMESEC suspects a nuclear weapon is that Diaz has been acting like he has options, which he doesn't. His only real choice that isn't suicide is to work this harvest and then disband his union and leave peacefully."

"If he's so boxed in, why am I here?"

"Mother."

"Why am I so important to her?"

Bree just shrugged. "The project is important and she recognizes the vast income potential my bots will generate, but more important, with the union gone, it frees land for her first foreign settlement."

"I had a conversation with CEO Zhang about that at Saturday's banquet."

"You were fortunate to get exposure with Madam Zhang. She and Mother are finalizing a deal that, once my project is complete, will allow *Global Solar* to send over business units in a migration that will be enormously profitable for them and us. I hate her but Mother is amazing, the stuff she gets away with. She sends Missionaries overseas to organize unions in third world countries and these unions create such havoc that international corporations like *Global* look to us for safer havens. Labor is still cheap in other countries but with the unrest our Missionaries create it has made the cost of operations too expensive so now America has become the global low cost provider. I know her as well as anyone and she always surprises me with her moments of surpassing brilliance. And by implementing my integrated harvest project, Mother is assured enough free cash to finance whatever she needs once foreign corporations come here to stay."

"I only met your mother once when I was first captured. Is she really that good and can she really plan that far into the future?"

"How far into the future is too far when you're going to live forever? My father and mother are brilliant people. They wouldn't have succeeded otherwise. Father loved to plan and Mother loves to plot. But more than that, she enjoys forcing the future to bend to her will."

Just then, the train lurched forward and began to ease out of the station. Then it rapidly accelerated. Bree pointed above to the observation deck. "I'm famished; let's continue our talk up there over drinks and dinner. We can sightsee in virtual."

"How long before we reach open air?"

"Actually, never," she explained. "Father was big on infrastructure and he commandeered an army of *Wasters* to build this rail system so he could deploy security forces, rapidly and stealthily, wherever and whenever he needed, at low cost and with fewer boots on the ground. Right now, we're heading out of the Capital corridor, which ends just east of the Shenandoah. From there a warren of encapsulated tracks connect to every significant city in the country. All the spur routes are above ground and to defray the cost, Mother leases track to the private sector and she rents the land overhead."

Bree entered the narrow glass elevator and pressed against the back wall so he could fit in as well. In those close quarters, he felt nervous and even awkward as he pressed against her for the brief ascent. She didn't appear to mind. On the Observation Deck, they sat in large comfortable chairs and stared out as the simulated jungle was replaced by farmland and night sky. A waitress climbed the steps to take their order.

"Cora, I'll have a small filet, rare, with a good vintage, British Columbian Bordeaux blend."

Gil preferred his steak medium. "Do you have water?" he asked.

"I'll check." The waitress's eyes glazed briefly. "Bottled, sir, not natural but we have a first class refiltered brand that's been distilled five times but retains its terroir. According to some of our most discerning clients, the water has the perfect balance of clarity, taste, and mouth feel, by reputation, think Philadelphia City Water circa mid-twentieth century." It sounded expensive but he ordered it anyway.

"What now?" he asked.

"Dinner should arrive soon."

"At the banquet, I noticed a tattoo on your neck," he said. "May I see it?" She tilted her head slightly and her hair shifted to expose a tiny script. "What does it say?"

"Thanks."

He smiled. "Thanks for what?"

She returned his smile with a blush. "Thanks for being there for me in Profit. When we separated, I promised myself I'd do this and someday thank you for our time together."

He was embarrassed yet excited too. "You're welcome." Then he changed the subject. "When did you have the Singularity surgery?"

"Must we dwell on that?"

"I want to understand how you live with her constantly in your head."

"Gil?"

He shrugged.

"Okay, that's not how it works, at least ideally. The receiver has control—that's what the instructions say, anyway. Mother can't enter without approval, but you know Mother. Although it doesn't feel like it, most times she has better things to do than screw around inside other people's heads. We fought over it like we fought over everything until she finally agreed not to be a nuisance—Mother, not a nuisance. I insisted on selecting a surgeon specialist to do the implantation but since everyone is beholding to Mother, I searched until I found a technology geek in a nearby, local *Waster* Community to do it. At first, I was scared. What a dump the guy lived in. But he was grateful for the fee and he even added some circuitry that keeps Mother a less intimating distance away."

He laughed. "Another cloaking device. You're amazing. You never learn."

"I'm still chipped." She sounded vulnerable. He hadn't expected that.

"You never told me why you ran from away from your mother, that time."

She seemed uncomfortable. "Mother considered me her troubled child. I wasn't and I'm not, at least not in any way that should concern her. I grew up in a very controlling environment, particularly after Father was gone. When Father was there, people fawned all over me. They didn't like me but they made it seem like they did."

Gil gave her an understanding look but she didn't want his sympathy.

"Don't look at me like that," she said. "I was a bitch. I know it. I acted like I could do no wrong so I can't really blame them. In return, they watched everything I did and I was a teenager so I did what teenagers do. I pushed back at everything and when they had the opportunity, they got even. Father disappeared at the worst possible time for me. As soon as it was clear he wasn't coming back anytime soon, everyone I'd pissed off along the way made my life miserable. My only outlet was to frighten them off by exploring what 'too rebellious' really meant. I challenged everything. Soon Mother was devoting more time to me than she wanted. In reality, any time was too much so she assigned a special HOMESEC security officer to . . . to improve my disposition and straighten me out. That officer carried out my mother's orders with far too much enthusiasm and my sensibilities could only stand so much so I stole the cloaking device and took off." Obviously distressed at the memory, Bree stared out at the projection of the Shenandoah Valley as it passed rapidly by. She continued more subdued. "When I was recaptured, I accepted the chip on mostly Mother's terms but in return, that officer keeps her distance and I consider that a victory."

"It sounds *pyrrhic*."

She was angry. "Damn it, Gil, every victory over Mother is *pyrrhic*. When are you going to learn that?" Her eyes were so intense that it briefly reminded him of her mother and he shivered. "You work for Mother but you don't really know her and what she's capable of. You think you do but you don't. If you are ever lucky enough, declare victory, even if it's not, but do it as soon as you can and get the hell out of her line of sight. I don't appreciate your smug comments about our relationship."

"You're right. I'm sorry."

She took a breath and her voice softened. "I stay away as much as I can and most of the time Mother is too busy to interfere so it isn't as bad as it could be." She stared down at the table. When she spoke again, her voice sounded almost childlike. "I'm chipped and I can't do anything about it so I'd really appreciate it if you didn't think less of me. Someday, in the far, far future, if her support systems and redundancies fail, I'm destined to replace her."

He responded without thinking. "Has America become an empire then, complete with royalty and hereditary succession?"

"What else? If Mother dies, how do we go back to the farce of electing presidents and representatives? That's a proven dead end, the First Republic failed from that. Today, we look like that republic, but it's far more effective if Mother plans and business buys representation and judicial decisions. It gets things done. Since the Second Republic, Father and then Mother have liberated free market fundamentals from government regulation and manipulation and America has been a more productive place because of it.

"Mother controls Central Intelligence and she uses its dominant artificial intelligence to keep the country secure and successful. According to most political theorists computer-assisted benevolent monarchies make a great deal more sense than republics or representative democracies ever did."

"Yes, democracy and republic are so last century."

"You can mock it but the world agrees. For America to continue to prosper, dynastic balance must continue in perpetuity. In case something happens, my half-brothers and sister are being groomed too, but my bon fides are impeccable so by virtue of birth, I'm next in line." She smiled proudly but when he didn't, her smile faded. "Get used to it. America is a hereditary monarchy ruled by a sovereign who will live forever."

"You mentioned your clones. In Profit, you never spoke of family."

"In Profit, you didn't even know my real name. We'll meet Father's clones in the morning. It's been a long time for me. I haven't seen them since the day before I ran away. Alph Crelli is the oldest and the leader. He's followed by Cee-Cee, my half sister and then Dave, the youngest and by far the brightest. They're all intelligent and motivated, especially Dave who is far more passionate. They each run a Federal Reserve District, which is a great deal of power and responsibility."

"It sounds like if your mother ever passes on, there could be a civil war."

"Oh, Mother will never die. Still, I'm next in line so I have to be ready."

"The clones accept that?"

"What choice do they have? Mother controls Central Intelligence and that's the power behind the throne. As the heir apparent I have more access to Mother than my siblings although I'm not sure that's a benefit."

"And your mother has no other children."

She laughed. "Everyone's amazed she had one."

He laughed at that and then turned to look outside. The world was darkening and dots of light from distant ersatz buildings glowed in simulated reality.

They were quiet for a few moments and then she took a breath. "In the end, all that matters is material success," she said solemnly. "Anything less is an affront to God."

"In Profit, you laughed at religion and now you pray."

"I was a teenager. I understand my priorities better now. In our competitive arena, when the outcome of failure is death, faith can be the edge you need to improve performance. After a while, when you know you can prevent it, you don't fear death."

"That doesn't work for me. I've seen too much death to take the religion seriously, particularly since it caused so much of it."

"That view will be an impediment. It will limit your upside potential as much or more than your decision not to chip. You should change your outlook, and if you can do it before tomorrow morning's meeting, it will make both of our jobs easier."

"So what else does it say in my files?"

"I didn't read . . ." She stared out at the darkening scenery. "I have warm memories of Profit but they seem surreal, now. Back then, I was required to believe what Mother believed." She leaned in toward him and whispered. "Between us, I haven't bought into Morgan, not completely, but it puts my professional relationships on a consistent and comfortable footing which is critical to my career."

"But you're the heir . . ." When her eyes narrowed, he knew to desist from pursuing it further. "Are you saying that when you recited our Partnership vows, you weren't totally committed?"

She laughed but it was clear she wasn't sure he was kidding. "Why? Was it real for you? I'm glad we met and partnered and I'm sorry I gave you such a hard time."

"Would I be completely wrong if I thought you gave everyone a hard time?"

She nodded. "There's history to support that."

"As I remember it, I received no partnership benefits."

"Be thankful." She briefly looked at him and then returned her gaze to the passing lights on the windows. "Did you want more?"

He searched her face for an impending rebuke but couldn't find one. "You know I did. If you had given me the least indication I would have gladly followed. But you're right; it would have been a very bad decision for both of us."

"Don't be insulted but it wasn't that difficult for me."

"Ouch. You need to work on your delicacy."

"That's not what I mean. I was a spoiled teenager. I thought I was mature but I wasn't. Until the end, Larry Hilliard's death and our escape, I never accepted responsibility for my actions or considered what being me cost others. In my defense, I never knew anyone who wanted to help me who didn't have an ulterior motive."

"So there was something there."

She smiled. "I'll grant you that, over the years, I've romanticized what happened in Profit. Yes, you heard the heir to Chairwoman Brandt's throne say *romanticized*. Maybe I really mean idealized our time in Profit and I do. I've pondered you and me, you know, possibilities; but it wouldn't have worked. We were going in opposite directions so it was pure fantasy. And if you add Mother to the equation, it would have turned into a farce and probably far worse that that. It never would have worked."

"Never?" he asked. "What I'm hearing suggests you've walked your logic far enough into the future to seriously consider it. I hope you believe in fantasy more than farce."

"Maybe you should slow down, cowboy."

"I've done nothing but slow down." He pointed out at distant lights that were moving in the opposite direction to the train. "We're going in the same direction now."

She considered it. "I was wrong; you have changed, a little. You're still adorably detached and somewhat lost just as I remember you, but you're more . . . cynical. You're less starry-eyed. You've told me over and over how beautiful you think my eyes are and I'm flattered, really, but anyone who has ever tried to be friendly to me has told me that I have my mother's eyes. Now, all these years later, how could you not know that I'm the Chairwoman's daughter? You live near her, you certainly see her pictures everywhere and greater than life size with her violet eyes to die for staring down lording over her public. How could you not know or at least be curious enough to ask about it? Even, 'hey, I knew this girl back in wherever, and she had these eyes that drove me wild and they were exactly like yours, Madam Chairwoman.' Hell, Mother eats stuff like that up.

"If you had thought to say that, you might have been given better assignments." She paused. "No, probably not. But hell, the flattery alone would have made you one hot Monrovian commodity. As revolting as it is to picture, I'm going to say it and retch; you might have even gotten laid—by Mother, certainly not me. One curious compliment about her beautiful eyes and yet you chose to not ask, to not know, or to just keep your suspicions to yourself. We both work with people who are incurious, Gil, and one of Mother's great goals has been to create incurious people, but in you, incurious is an art form. I'm wondering if you're not becoming more inscrutable while I'm becoming more open. So to answer your question, no, I'm not certain we're going in the same direction."

That hurt. "I'm sorry but I have to be this way. I have no choice .... I ... I ..." He hated the excuses so he stared out at a meteor shower that was passing over the train while the Aura Borealis sought his attention on the far side windows.

She stared out too. "We have a long way to go, let's not get ahead of ourselves. I have a project to bring in, it's important, and I need your help and undivided attention."

"You're right," he said. "Good old Morgan 1.01: Relationships are acceptable in all forms and combinations so long as they further business objectives and don't interfere with the mission."

She smiled. "I think there's a corollary that states something about value changing hands but as far as I know it's never enforced. Can we please change the subject?" She paused, before confessing. "The truth is I haven't met anyone since Profit that I respect and like more than you."

His mood flipped back to confident. "Even though I was incompetent?"

"You were never incompetent, Gil, but I'd like to think that some of what you've accomplished is because of me."

He liked the sound of that, too. "I'll take credit for softening you just a bit and you can take credit for my career success, such as it is."

"Mother noticed the change after I returned from Profit and that's why she slowly let out her leash to allow me more responsibility. She knows it was you and I think she's okay with it. She would never have assigned you to my project, otherwise."

"You're assuming she's nicer than she is."

Before Bree could respond, the *Sauver L'eau* climbed the steps with two bottles and two glasses. She showed Bree the wine label and poured a small portion for her to taste. Bree sipped it, rolled it over her tongue, swirled it in her mouth, and swallowed, taking a deep breath, and then she nodded. The *Sauver* then repeated the process for Gil with the water. He stared through the clear liquid searching for residue or hue but there was none. He savored it like Bree had and found the taste and mouth feel crisp and brisk. When he swallowed, the hair on the back of his neck bristled at the clean metallic taste followed by a tell-tale hint of chalk. He took another sip and then allowed the *Sauver* to fill his glass.

Bree tapped his glass with hers. "To former partners becoming good friends."

"To good friends becoming better friends and to a successful project," he countered and they sipped in silence.

She began to speak and then paused. Finally she broke the silence, "How do you not know where my Father is?"

Water caught in his windpipe and he coughed uncontrollably as tears came to his eyes. He grabbed his napkin and wiped the tears away as he coughed some more to clear his throat. That awkward moment gave him a chance to gather his thoughts. He should have expected it. "I don't know because in twenty years I've had no contact with him or anyone who knows him."

"That's not entirely true."

How did she know that? "Okay, but Bernie and I never discussed it. My task was to help Bernie free his son, my grandfather, Mark. That's all. And I didn't know I would even do that until right before I did it. I was, I don't know, astounded, when the Chairman appeared and as soon as he was captured, they hustled me out of there. That's all I know. How did you find out?"

"Mother told me."

"And how did mother know?"

"There's that question again. Mother knows everything."

For the first time, he wondered what that truly meant.

Bree was quiet, contemplating. "Mother never discusses Father and Archive records are so hyped that I can't tell if it's him or some virtual actor redefining him. It's been twenty years."

"I haven't seen my own father in all that time either."

She looked concerned. "I didn't know. Why not?"

"It isn't safe."

"But certainly you've tried, right?"

It was a simple question. He stared out into the dark again, trying to collect his thoughts. All that was visible were the occasional lights from fleeting fake farmhouses. He touched the glass and another image appeared. It was earlier, dusk now, and there were snow-covered mountains in the distance. He touched the window yet again and the train was streaking past a pink sand beach where waves rolled in, breaking in concert with the train's passage.

He hadn't tried to see or talk to Howard and he couldn't explain why so he stumbled through an explanation, hoping to find truth in the process. "I was fourteen and adults were making decisions for me. You know what that's like. Then I was on the run and well you know what I was like then. I was captured and since, I've have had to be on my best behavior and even with that, your mother doesn't trust me. She didn't want me to . . . no, that's not right; I didn't want to contact Howard because I have a precarious hold on life and I didn't want to risk it or put Howard at risk. I'll contact him sometime in the future if I'm still alive and have proved myself."

"But he's your father. Surely you should contact him. Have you contacted your grandfather? He might know something."

"Mark and I spent time together in Angel Falls and I got to know him a little. He was a fugitive, too, but when he could manage it, he stopped by to see Bernie. They would have long talks—arguments, really—about the state of the country and what to do about it. Whatever political perspective I have, I learned listening to them argue. Your mother expressly told me I couldn't contact Mark so I haven't even tried."

"Are those discussions why Mother won't let you see either of them?"

"I don't know."

"I remember President Rose."

Her admission surprised Gil.

"He was an odd man. When I was young, he visited Mother regularly, often uninvited. She called him her chronic guest and sometimes she allowed him to stay. I never understood why, he was so creepy. Mother is far from polite yet she endured his insufferable visits often refusing him an audience for long periods after he arrived. He would wander around like some lost puppy and she seemed to enjoy that like it was great sport. It was probably the result of friction from when he was her vice-president."

That troubled Gil. If Mark had visited the Chairwoman when he was away from Angel Falls, Gil was certain that he never discussed it with Bernie.

"Mark came to visit me the day before I ran away. He was his usual strange self but I remember it because I stole the cloaking device while Mother and the Bitch were meeting with him. I saw him later, after Mother dismissed him." She stopped to consider it. "He was crying. Crying, isn't that odd?"

"How long was that before we met?"

"I don't know; maybe a month."

"And Mark was crying? That is odd."

She shrugged. "I didn't see him again until the Bitch dragged me back."

"Why do you suppose your mother recaptured him?"

She leaned closer. "You're really interested in this."

He nodded.

"Mark was in Canada. Maybe Mother didn't want Omar Smith to have him."

"Did your mother trust Mark?"

She laughed. "Come on, Gil, Mother?"

"She allowed him to visit."

"I told you that I didn't know why."

"Is there anyone your mother trusts, even a little?"

"The Bitch, maybe a little," Bree answered. "I have a great idea. After we've successfully completed this project, you should petition Mother to allow you to see your father and your grandfather. Certainly, you will have earned the right."

"I have no rights." He said, glumly.

"Then just try to see them anyway. Mother will be pissed but she won't kill you."

"Thanks for that. Can you write me a note that says that and then sign it. I'll give it to your mother before my hanging."

"Hanged? I don't think so, just for visiting them? Why would she do that?"

He shrugged.

"Mother's infuriating, I'll give you that, but she saves her theatrics for when it does her some good. She wouldn't kill someone for no reason, maybe for treason . . ."

Gil shook his head. "Treason covers a lot of things these days."

"Mother's playing with you. She's always seeking loyalty and she tests for it by seeing how far she can push people."

"She would do that to me?" He smiled.

"Mother, of course she would."

"And that's why I don't take chances with her, Bree."

"But if your father is no threat and even with this messiah thing, you're really no threat either, why would she care? It's curious. Was your father politically active?"

"Howard is more a recluse. I'll bet he doesn't know that I'm alive."

Her face lit up. "I can help. After I report in on tomorrow's meeting, I'll discuss your situation with Mother and when I return to give my status report, I'll see your father and tell him all about you."

"Please, don't." He couldn't allow her to jeopardize Howard and Mark's lives—or hers and his for that matter.

"No, it'll be okay, Gil. I want to help."

"I appreciate it, Bree, I do, but it can only end badly. I don't know why your mother is keeping my family separated but she certainly doesn't have to explain it to me. Someday, maybe, I'll do something, when the times right, but not now. Promise me you won't say anything. Please, I'm serious. I appreciate your concern and you've given me some things to think about but please don't mention it to your mother."

"Fine, but I know I can help."

He put his hand up to her chin. "We don't know each other as well as I hope we will but until then, you know how capricious your mother is."

She agreed and then turned the subject back to her father. "Tell me about him."

"There's little to tell," Gil explained. "We met for barely an hour. When he entered you could tell he was in charge, I mean really in charge. He was that intimidating. He walked in like he owned the room and he spoke with real authority. But that's all I remember about him."

"I can imagine it, kind of. But I have other memories of him. When I was real young, I remember him emerging from the Oval Office. What a room that was! It was the first version of *Virtuoso* and he used it to monitor his world. He'd come out just to play with me and I remember laughing a lot."

"I'm not belittling your memory of him but I can't listen to that. I'm sorry."

Her smile faded. "Why did you kidnap him?"

"Bernie needed my help to free Mark and your father was lured into that trap."

"Yes, you said that, but why did you *do it*?"

He shrugged. "Here's what it was. I'm fourteen and I adventure all the time in *Virtuoso*. Out of the blue, I get this message to go to a hospice where I meet Bernie and he is so frail that I think he is going to die right then. I'd never seen anyone that old or dying before. He tells me this story about his family, my family. Except for Howard, I had never known my family so I'm really interested. At first, I didn't believe what he was telling me but then he explains how his wife and his daughter were murdered by a goon working for your father; and it was worse, so much worse. My great grandfather was forced to listen on his communicator as his wife and daughter were being murdered. How ghastly is that? And the law did nothing!

"When he told me that, it was all I needed. I had to help him; he could barely help himself, at least, that's the way it seemed. He begged me. He said he needed me to care like people did before greed infected everyone with unshakable selfishness.

"After that, I just followed Bernie's plan to help Mark escape and the rest you know about as much about as I do." Gil paused and took a deep breath. "I'm talking way too much. The water must have gone to my head."

Bree seemed concerned. "This Bernie lived during our First Republic and that stuff about caring doesn't work anymore because we live so long that it doesn't make good business sense for anyone, family members included, to help each other if it costs too much and jeopardizes eternity. When you live forever, you must choose to help when it's propitious or you'll never have time to do anything productive. Did Bernie pay you for your risk?"

Gil didn't know what to say so he just shook his head.

"Then what did you hope to gain by kidnapping my father?"

"I guess I didn't realize how far apart we are. What did I hope to gain? I don't know how to respond to that." And he really didn't.

"Are you making fun of me?"

"No, but I mean it. I really don't know how to respond to what you're asking."

"Did he promise you the messiah gig if you helped? Was that it?"

"How can you say that? When have I ever done anything for personal gain? Besides, what benefits would I possibly be after at fourteen? And I don't believe Bernie had the concept of the messiah back then and if he did, I wouldn't have believed him. I still don't. It wasn't until we arrived in Angel Falls that he even discussed the future."

"But the Messiah legend predates Angel Falls," she said. "When I was very young, I remember hearing about it on some pirate Internet station. Mother and Father ranted constantly because HOMESEC couldn't find the transmission point or catch the crazy guy saying all those insane, anti-capitalist things." She smiled at the memory. "My parents were incensed when it came to this guy. His name was . . . I think it was Thau; yes, Thau . . . something, Berne Thau, that's it. Could Berne Thau be your great-grandfather?" She leaned back and let out a breath. "Berne Thau, Bernie Rosenthal, I'm right, aren't I."

Gil nodded, glumly. As Bree slowly unpeeled his past, he became more uncomfortable. "I never heard the name 'Berne Thau' until after Bernie died and the messiah thing, he never mentioned it until after we arrived in Angel Falls. I was young and back then I was pretty intensely into . . . someone, and the messiah-stuff, it was . . . I don't know; it just didn't interest me."

She perked up at that. "You were into someone? That's so sweet. Gil Rose was in love. Was she pretty?"

"We were teenagers."

"Were you in love? Was she pretty, as pretty as me?"

"I don't want to talk about it."

"She was pretty, just not as pretty as me."

"Bree—"

"So you lived in Wasterland with a pretty young lass. Gil Rose, I never thought of you like that."

"Cut it out."

"No, it's cute. Did she break your heart? Is that it?"

"I'm not going to talk anymore about it."

She laughed. "Okay, but its way cute. If Berne Thau didn't promise to make you into this messiah, why did you risk so much to kidnap my Father?"

"I don't know. Bernie was more miserable than anyone I've ever seen. He was so desperately sad, old, and alone and I was all he had. His life's goal was to turn me into a leader for some revolution that he'd failed at previously. I'm certain that before the kidnapping, we never discussed the messiah thing, never. It was like I said. He was trying to stop the pain when he explained the horrible things the Chairman, your father, had done to his family. I was fourteen and his story was very convincing."

"Well your Bernie couldn't have been more wrong about my father. Father was, is a hero. He saved America from the socialist fiasco of the First Republic. Progressive Socialists were tearing the country apart. They were sapping America's financial energy, the energy that had made us great. Sure, Father hurt people along the way, but he saved so many more. It's all documented. He's the great hero of the United States, ever."

"I don't have an answer for that," Gil said in response, "and I don't want to argue. Maybe that's true and maybe it does count for something, but he murdered Bernie's wife and daughter. And I found out much later that because of your father, my mother was executed." He stood up. "I really don't want to discuss this."

Bree's expression changed. "Oh, I didn't know about your mother. I'm . . . sorry. Please don't go."

He sat. "It's not for you to apologize. There's no good answer to all of this. I did what I did, right or wrong. I don't regret it . . . except for what it has done to my life."

"But surely now you believe that Father . . ."

"Bree, enough, please."

She started to say something but made the mistake of making eye contact and seeing his determination, she held her hand up as if to ward him off. "You're right. I'm sorry. There's just one more thing. At tomorrow's meeting, suppress every bad feeling you have about my father. My half siblings are quite a bit more intense about protecting his memory than even I am."

"I'll be fine. I've spent my life suppressing feelings."

"Don't let them goad you into saying something you'll regret. They'll try, particularly Dave, but Cee-Cee, too. But as far as hundreds of millions of Americans are concerned, Father is a hero and the father of the Second Republic. He's a patriot with brains and balls and when every other political leader was looking out for their own interests, he faced the great issues and resolved them with the passion and intelligence that saved America. As far as my siblings are concerned, you took away a great man's future—and an important piece of theirs as well."

"Can we talk about something else?" Gil interrupted. "Please, anything, or I'll be the one turning in early, tonight."

"Someday, I'm going to find him and tell him how proud I am of him. And someday, I'll make him proud of me."

He made as if to stand just as the waiter arrived with the main course.

She put a hand up to restrain him. "I'll stop. Okay?"

"Fine, I'll stay. I'm starving anyway, but no more talk about him."

While they ate, she explained more about the project. "Bunny, as the Mayor of Sacramento, reports to the Western Federal Reserve Chairperson, that's Alph, my oldest half sibling. Each of my half siblings reports directly to Mother, of course, and you're on the project because Mother selected you. This being your first assignment, you probably aren't aware of domestic economics. Missionary consultants work at cost, they do not generate revenue. Domestic assignments are considered holy missions that contribute to the infrastructure and greater glory of Morgan life in God's Kingdom on earth, forever. The bible does permit us to gain-share the benefits from our projects, in this case thirty percent of what the farm owners gain from the elimination of the union. The benefits that are accrued by using my bots goes into the general treasury and we each get a piece based on the number of shares of the United States we own at the time of distribution. The real money comes when *Global Solar* begins to settle here. According to Mother, what they will pay for union land and the right to live there in perpetuity will take us all to a new level of rich. There is another extraordinary personal advantage that accrues to domestic consultants. We each receive stock options toward the purchase of shares of the United States of America and we're allowed to exercise those options throughout our lives. It's a very sweet deal."

"I thought international consulting was a holy mission, too?"

"Certainly, but we charge exorbitant rates overseas because we can and because foreign managements tend to listen harder the more expensive consultants are. That's the way it's always been in the consulting profession." She smiled. "Morgan considers it a sacrilege not to maximize God's assets."

"That's quite a business model."

"My project is just a piece of the puzzle and with all the economic and social unrest around the world along with the continuing worldwide drought and tidal flooding, America will supply the world once again. My 'Bot' project will increase net-profit-per-hectare and to do that, a capitalist consortium has invested significant funds to automate and enhance harvests by replacing costly labor with far more productive, depreciable and upgradeable assets.

"As far back as the First Republic, manufacturing and service industries were automated. To achieve that, they rolled back archaic unionism but they couldn't do it with farm labor which today still has a grip on our agricultural industry. And now that unions face the end of their dominion on earth, they are resisting with everything they have and in so doing, they've become festering swamps of Socialist rebellion. My project will drain that swamp."

Suddenly, Gil realized that he didn't really want to be involved in her project but what could he do and what could he say?

She continued on as if she had read his mind. "Not to belabor the messiah thing, but I need to know you're okay with this."

"Help me out," he asked. "Why did you get involved in this project? I mean why this and not some other worthwhile project?"

She put her fork down and stared out into the darkened western sky. "Are you kidding? I never wanted to be a missionary. Not really. But Mother knows what buttons to push so I completed Morgan training." She paused. "As it turns out, I'm really good at this, really, really good. I'm not hot on the dogma stuff and sometimes what missionaries are called on to do is . . . well, it requires strict interpretation of Gospel Accepted Principles and Practices but once you learn to rely on GAPP and just do it, it gets easier."

"You're really good at everything."

She blushed. "I know. I discovered what I really want to do, you know, what really thrills me. That's why I'm so committed and I have no choice but to be exceptional. It's in my blood. I have to do special things, like my father did, and though I'm not him, I keep trying, you know, to make him proud. I need to prove that I'm special, for him. As to why this, domestically, most of the heavy economic lifting had already been done by the time I reached manager status, so I researched it until I found a significant enough economic problem that needed solving. Climate is changing and there's fear and chaos in every economy in the world because of it. People are starving and dying of malnutrition and dehydration. Billions are weak and unproductive but the nations of the world still have to feed them or contend with costly riots. If foreign leaders weren't so resistant to Father's Circle of Life solution, they could control costs, but they are resistant—at least for now so food is critical and they will pay anything for it.

"Before climate change, there was no good financial reason to make farming more cost effective. Besides, there were always plenty of low cost, uneducated and immigrant labor competing for work, so cost remained low.

"That equation has been altered. Today, food is in the highest possible demand and that has driven up the cost of labor. To make it worse, because of the *Circle of Life*, labor is now in short supply in America, driving the cost up even more. Diaz's union believes they have a monopoly on bottom-feeding, poor-paying farm jobs and because of that, Diaz expects that his people should receive premium pay.

"But there's a better solution. Diaz went rebel and farm profits and returns to food processing and food distribution corporations declined precipitously. You could argue free market principles are in action here and you'd be right except that unions profane God's holy economic laws and like all pests and vermin, they're economic parasites who must be eradicated. They're nothing but blood-sucking leeches that have taken advantage of an aberration in the world economy and are trying to drive a stake into the heart of free markets everywhere in order to create a monopoly labor situation that will drag the American economy into bankruptcy and deficit. Diaz's union is the evil, last sad remnant of the First Republic's socialist rage, and they must be eradicated before they redistribute our hard earned wealth and ruin everything. If they get their way, they will make every productive American dependent on union cretins. My project solves that problem while at the same time, it restructures a critical industry."

"Oh." It was all he could think to say. His experience with unions in Bolivia had been satisfying, but clearly unions behaved differently in the States.

"I'm sorry, Gil, I didn't mean to rant, but I've spent a great deal of time traveling the country in search of venture capital for this project so I jump into my selling mode whenever I talk about it. You get the point. My project is ground breaking and with the union gone, it will generate profits which will allow every stockholder to fund a bright future in God's Kingdom on Earth. This is my Holy mission."

"Is there any way the union survives?"

She shook her head. "They've outlived whatever usefulness they had and in God's America, that's unforgivable—a mortal sin. Mankind is at risk and harvesting technology must improve. To fund the research and development and most of the start-up costs, their land is being sold so they must move on."

"So it's done."

"Everything but a successful implementation and for that, we need Diaz for this harvest then he needs to be out of the way. If my projected returns are anywhere close, the project will become part of a package solution sold under the highly profitable Morgan Missionary Products brand and offered to the world through our Faith-based International Services Division. I stand to receive stupendous royalties forever."

She was gorgeous, but she glowed now with an inner light that made her seem wondrous. "So this isn't just about Sacramento?" he mumbled.

"We meet in Sacramento. Holarki, the union town, is nearby. Think of it, Gil, you will play an integral part in economic history and Father will be so proud of me."

"I'm sure he will," Gil said. "I never heard of Holarki."

"I don't know much about it. Alph says the town is named after Saint Holarki, the Catholic Patron Saint of Lethargy but I think he's joking." Excitement continued to radiate from her. "There is so much riding on this project. Capitalists have dreamed about this from the beginning. I'm going to eliminate wage labor forever. Remember your Capitalist Utopia classes and think on that. America's ongoing labor issues will disappear and you and I will have had a hand in it, a hand in making America a true entrepreneurial paradise, a vision that united Father and Mother in the beginning and the reason why I'm here. My project will be written about in economic history text books and there will be hymns sung about it in our churches and on our stock market trading floors."

He wanted to be happy for her. "What you're proposing is . . ." He hesitated to define it.

"Yes, it's paradise."

"I'm happy for you but . . ."

"There are no buts. I'm my Father's daughter. I have thought of everything."

"What happens to the union members and their families?"

"This is a free country; they'll find work as long as they don't act like entitled socialists. Think of it, I'll be a true market maker."

She smiled as she hastily pulled out a silver decal. "In my spare time, I've been working on this. We slap these on every piece of our harvest hardware. I don't love it but Mother does. She named the 'Bots', Produce Enhanced Return Vehicles or PERVS."

If she was expecting him to get excited, she was disappointed.

"You're eliminating people," he argued. "Why would I like that?"

She frowned. "Name one person for God's sake. And we're not eliminating them; we're eliminating what they do. From there, it's up to them. What else? It's a free country. Don't do this, Gil. You have this, this blind spot, this caring thing, but when you see the economics, you'll see that there is no way to defend them. You need to grow up and put economics first like you've been taught. These are socialists you're asking about, enemies of the church, of God, and our way of life. They must be remade or destroyed or America will devolve into the third world country it was heading toward when the First Republic died—when Father killed it. I can't allow that. Father and Mother fought against it and won. I must do my part, too.

"When you start your negotiations with Diaz, see how they live. You'll see. It's unnatural. They spend nothing to fix up their homes, no money on landscaping, so their homes don't appreciate. They purchase next to nothing so they don't help our economy grow, and they produce all of their own food, generate their own energy, and desalinize their own water so Holarki isn't even a viable commercial town. It's perverse. It's the rot that socialism causes. They even share things within their community without charging a use fee. How gross is that? And they're cocky about it. They live so frustratingly un-American that they are begging to be eradicated. They are a burden to capitalists everywhere and their very existence mocks Morgan so we have no choice but to end them on our terms. My 'Bots are the right solution at the right time—Mother has the calculations. With their demise and the rise of my machines, Gross Domestic Product increases by point oh, oh two percent. That number seems small, but it's a huge win for America." She paused to catch her breath.

For Gil, this conversation was distressing. Her project was obviously vital to his career, too, but instead of considering the effect of what he said, he just spoke. "It's not a win for everyone, Bree."

She was annoyed. "You're making a problem where one doesn't exist. I warned you about that. Okay, yes, the field workers of the world will be displaced and the laziest and least competent may not find other work, but that's only fair. It's their fault. Besides, there are places in the *Unincorporated Lands* where they can live and not hurt our economy." She paused. "Why are you looking at me like that?"

"Bree, the *Unincorporated Lands* aren't a solution. What about the drought? Ocean brine is already moving up rivers and wells and aquifers throughout the country are failing. You can't farm without fresh water and corporations own all the water distribution rights so it never gets to the *Unincorporated Lands*. No wonder the union is striking." *What am I doing here?* He thought.

Her violet eyes turned steely. "I'm warning you, mister, don't do this. You have economic promise but I don't know where you get these perverse, sacrilegious thoughts. Get them out of your mind and do it before tomorrow morning. For you and me to . . . no, you need to understand that you're a Morgan Missionary consultant and you're here to complete your job requirements. What you say may feel right to you but it's not just irrelevant, it could jeopardize everyone's future, including yours and mine. My project is the very best of free market creative destruction as God intended and you mustn't even think of preventing it from working its magic. You'll see how good it can be. Free markets are so gloriously dynamic. Forget what happens to the union, it's their fault and they're insignificant anyway. Besides, they're responsible adults, they have choices, too. They could make themselves necessary in our economy but they prefer to be lazy and greedy. You don't know so don't idealize them because of something you've read, something you feel, or something your great grandfather told you. Morgan wisely tells us, 'if you don't like the competition, get out of the kitchen'. Surely you see I'm doing God's work. You must see it, too, you must. This project is good business and good business is always good for true Americans."

"I suppose."

"Get your head screwed on straight by tomorrow morning or else. You have a lot to prove and I won't allow anything to get in the way. Anything."

"Obviously."

She let her breath out slowly. "I'm not going to argue. You know what's best for you or you don't. I need to remind you that this isn't Profit and Mother is watching."

"I understand," he said. "But why did your mother assign me, a consensus builder, and a novice at that, to this project?"

"She felt you were needed. What other reason would she have? Get square with this and do it quickly. *Global Solar* is getting impatient and they have a right to be. We should have been further along but somehow, we totally blew our evaluation of Diaz."

"I need to know what happened."

"Mother offered Diaz special incentives to move up the start date. He refused."

"He was bribed."

"It's a damn union, they expect to be bribed."

"Then why didn't he take it?"

"Everything we knew about Diaz said he would take it. Only Mayor Wua was against it. She thinks probably Omar Smith has stiffened Diaz's resolve, but even that won't be enough to stop us. Still, the delays have driven up project costs as well as the cost of commodity food futures and that has *Executives* and *Entrepreneurs* worried. The last thing we need is for some socialist labor leader to think he can dictate terms to us so it must stop now. Besides, he can't win, there's no chance of that but he can affect short-term financials. That's where you come in. You've had success with Diaz-types in Bolivia so Mother expects you to intimidate him with empathetic, voodoo consensus building stuff and convince Diaz to acquiesce to our demands."

"Empathetic voodoo? Can I get some disrespect?"

"You know what I mean."

"I'll do my job but I won't lie, I won't cheat, and I won't try to bribe him."

"You shouldn't limit yourself. You have talent, Gil, everyone says so. If you don't need to do those things, fine. Do what you do, but you must convince him to go along with this project because Mother expects it. If he doesn't go along, the Bitch will handle it and we'll lose a lot of our performance bonus to her and her legions. Do you understand?" Bree waited for him to nod before she continued.

"I hate to keep pushing you but this messiah thing can't affect my project—I won't allow it so if you're thinking you can save the union, you're wrong. They aren't your problem. Here's your chance. Make me believe I'm more important than a union."

"You are and I understand. Look, I'm not their messiah. I'm a professional consensus builder and I'll do what makes sense."

She interrupted. "You mean you'll do what the project requires."

He nodded. "I know what I'm doing but I won't hurt anyone unnecessarily."

"God, you're maddening. You were so much easier to be with in Profit."

"I'll meet my requirements. Does Diaz have any viable choices?"

She frowned. "None. He concedes to you or the Bitch makes him regret it."

"I have to convince Diaz to quit and die, or to resist and die? Is that it?"

"You're getting ahead of yourself. Convince him to finish the harvest and leave. The rest is up to him, not you. He understands. He knows that Mother prefers to act and what she's capable of. You believe that too so make him believe it. Make him realize that labor is an unnecessary commodity in today's world and it must be replaced. It's no one's fault. After the harvest, all Diaz need do is tell his union worker to leave and make it in the outside world on their own like all *Conducers* do. These people deserve the chance to work as free contractors and enjoy the fruits of that, freedom to choose their own destiny. If they remain here with Diaz they'll suffer as everyone in a collective suffers."

"Do you have any suggestions how I can convince Diaz?"

"That's your job," she yawned, indicating that the discussion was over. "Hey, it's late and I'm tired. We meet Mayor Bunny and my siblings tomorrow for lunch. On the way in, you can explain how you're going to do it. By the way, you're scheduled to meet Diaz right after that meeting."

"But we're not done. You're going to bed now?"

She kissed his cheek. "I'm done. It's been a long day. You'll figure it out. I'll see you at nine for breakfast."

She stood but as she turned to leave, he grabbed her arm and spun her around. She appeared anxious but when he simply embraced her, she reciprocated, folding into him.

"This is just a hug," she whispered nervously.

"Thanks for noticing, now shut up and enjoy it."

She left and he spent the rest of the evening staring out at the passing scenery and thinking about what Bree had told him. As the snow covered mountains of Colorado appeared on the window, he fell asleep.

Chapter 6

Sacramento, CA—2083

Confidential Memo **Confidential Memo**

To: *President of the United States, Andrew Crelli* 2/08/2032

Subject: *Liquidation Memo Follow up—Disappearance*

From: *Gecko*

Below are the recommended procedures for identifying the most appropriate Americans for elimination. Methods for elimination are still being developed and it is probable that there will be various alternatives depending on costs, population concentration, and logistics. This will be addressed later in this memo.

Group 1: *The first group to disappear and the easiest. Through various Health Care corporations, we will request that hospitals and hospices throughout the nation eliminate the dying under their care using the broadest possible definition of dying and do so without prejudice. This group includes all uneconomic people who would be dead if the government stopped paying for their care. By my calculation, there are 8,375,435 such people in Group 1, give or take.*

Group 2: *The entrenched infirmed such as Alzheimer's, dementia patients, and others in public or private care can be eliminated at little cost and with great savings. As a motivator to the care givers resistant to this directive, we can provide performance bonuses or extend criminal charges to motivate them. Estimate: 14,338,250 more or less.*

Group 3: *The incarcerated should be eliminated in their entirety, but at first, only those who won't be conscripted to be used to eliminate the first two groups. For security and privacy, it is likely that we will lease "Elimination*

Facilities" in regional private prisons and these facilities are likely to be used to process other groups, as well. Additionally, we must give careful consideration to expanding the range of crimes that could be capital in nature and we must set guidelines so that judges mete out more summary justice and capital sentences so we don't double handle transgressors. 15,277,741 to 19,000,109 can be eliminated.

Group 4: *Encompasses the low end of the street people, those with no or few community affiliations, people who live 24-7 on the streets. Here, enticements like free food, hot food in the winter, and shelter can lure them in like a roach motel. With the recession rolling into its 10th year, it's impossible to estimate but using satellite and street surveillance there are easily 23,345,354 possible targets or more but certainly no less. Processing those spooked by street rumors, people scared who won't come readily to us or those too weak or stupid to be fooled, will have to be worked individually, utilizing local subcontractors and available waste matter trucks.*

Group 5: *Will also come from the streets and include low hanging fruit such as people temporarily out of work or out of homes, transients, druggies, pimps and whores, drop outs, incompetents, the old, etc . . . who survive on the dark side of Capitalism. It is here the rubber meets the road. We can't achieve enough efficiency from the four previous groups so this is the one that turns the entire project profitable. Do the job here and overall project return goals are met. Do this right and provide rebates to corporations hurt financially because we are eliminating their target sales demographic and negatively affecting short term sales projections and earnings per share and we achieve our great goal. As to rebates, it is unfair for Entrepreneurs who serve this group to suffer so a rebate from our overall economic savings will help these Entrepreneurs through hard times and allow them to diversify and redeploy for future profits.*

Other Thoughts: *The cost to isolate and remove the last of the people in each of these groups increases at an increasing rate. We will require private agencies to provide ongoing coverage as the population rebalances and becomes temporarily less productive. We need to develop a mechanism whereby those formerly productive Americans who fail in our Capitalist utopia can be disappeared with the least affect on the economy.*

Estimate 92,160,148 incompetents to disappear and I feel good about that number. Including the cost of Operations and Security, we can achieve this while eliminating over half of all government expenditures, with more spending cuts to come in subsequent phases. Estimated reductions in the government work force are significant and have been factored into each Group estimate. Considered executing government employees while still in government service but due to a sophisticated social network within the federal and local systems that would spread the word and make collection and processing cost prohibitive, we don't want to risk that.

Net-net, the American economy will save the cost of supporting a population equivalent to that of the states of Pennsylvania, Ohio, Illinois, Michigan, New York, and Florida. A good haul, all and all.

To achieve our most ambitious goal, a select twenty million more workers may be eliminated from a group consisting of those contributing to the economy but not entrepreneurial enough to survive. A mobile solution will be required. Will fine tune.

There will be interim economic benefits. For instance, we will lease underutilized municipal vehicles at below market rates.

Rather than calling project "economic genocide", the term Morgan and Gorman prefer, recommend we use "Disappearance" which is more user-friendly and that has much to recommend it. Terms like "Downsizing" or more whimsically, "De-populism", were considered but for various reasons ruled out.

Confidential Memo **Confidential Memo**

The train to Sacramento decelerated with a lurch, waking Gil from a short, troubled sleep and by the time the train eased into the station and stopped, he was dressed. He opened his cabin door and saw Bree sitting across from his door at a small pink and yellow table wearing a dark blue business suit and staring into the vapor rising from a cup she was holding clenched tightly in both hands.

He offered a cheery good morning but she was startled by his voice. When she smiled, it was a slow process through which she kept getting more beautiful.

"Care to share a morning brew?" She dipped her cup so he could see the off-green liquid and then she raised it to take another sip, her violet eyes blinking rapidly as the vapor enveloped her. She began speaking slowly and softly but soon enough; the words came faster and faster. "ANGS calls this crap, 'Inkling of Tomorrow'. It's a combination of teas and stimulants scientifically formulated to produce results, even in the slowest starters. They claim it's non-addictive but they've made those claims before. Whatever it is, two of these in the morning and I'm there and after three, I can outrun my own skin. The jolt lasts until lunchtime when, if you listen, you'll hear my body keening for more calories. Thankfully we'll have a great lunch. Bunny always prepares something truly special. But I'm warning you; don't get in front of me in the buffet line. I'm merciless on the way down."

He tried not to laugh. "Maybe you should just hunt prey for lunch." He expected a laugh but instead, she looked annoyed so he tried again. "Wouldn't it be better to eat nutritiously and maybe take a nap?"

"Fuck nutrition and I take afternoon siestas," she said. "That's why you're meeting Diaz alone."

"You nap in the middle of the workday?"

She nodded. "Do you want a brew or not?" she pointed her cup at him.

He waved it away. "No, thanks, I prefer to persevere naturally."

She took a deep breath and slowly let it out. "I forgot how atypical you are."

He laughed at that. "Hey, I'm just high on life." She almost smiled and though he knew he was overvaluing that meager reward, it did feel good.

While she sipped more of her brew, she glared, daring him to comment but he sat quietly waiting. When the brew was gone, her eyes refocused, riveting on him.

"So what are you going to do about Diaz?" she asked.

"Until I learn more at the meeting, I can't comment. What do I call the mayor?"

"Your Honor is fine. Madam Mayor works also."

"At the meeting, if it's okay, I'd like to keep my thoughts to myself until I hear what everyone else has to say." Bree started to say something but he held his hand up to stop her. "I know. Morgan rewards the outspoken and the aggressive but I subscribe to the one mouth, two ears school. I learn more by listening. Besides, I'm new and I would be wasting everyone's time if I expounded before I heard everyone's assessment of the situation, particularly Diaz's. You'll have my thoughts as soon as I form them."

"Mother warned me, but why do you have to be so different all the time?"

"What can I say? Mother knows best."

"That's true by definition." She paused and seemed uncomfortable. When she spoke, she clearly was. "I . . . I didn't say it last night but I'm . . . I'm pleased . . . no I'm . . . happy that we're going to . . . to be able to share time together because . . . because I enjoy your companionship."

"Companionship, that's good, right?"

Too quickly, she seemed annoyed. "Companionship is good? What does that even mean? Do you ever say anything that I don't have to guess the meaning of?" She snapped

"I'm just confused about what companionship means."

Her complexion reddened, rising as it always did from her neckline into a full-blown blush.

"Damn it," she said. "Stop magnifying things out of proportion. Unlike you, I say what I mean—I meant . . . I . . ." When she couldn't find words to complete her thought, he smiled and that seemed to make her angrier but then she took a breath. "I mean, I'm glad we have this opportunity to work together; can we leave it at that?"

"And what? And we continue to play at a safe distance from nuance?"

"Whatever," she changed the subject. "Let's get down to business. How much time will you need with Diaz, and is there anything you'll need from the committee?"

Now wasn't the time to discuss a relationship though he was happy that she had tried. "The afternoon should do it, but that's an estimate. You said something last night that confuses me. Should I report to you, to the Mayor, or to one of your siblings? You're next in line for the throne, but if your siblings are in charge of their respective Fed districts, and the Mayor runs the town, doesn't that make you the lowest ranking person on the totem?"

Her eyes bugged out and she stared at him as if he had made some horrible faux pas. Her eyes narrowed and sternly but softly, she said, "Fuck you. How dare you say something like that to me?" She seemed both amazed and offended and her eyes flamed as he fumbled for an apology.

"Gee, I'm sorry. I didn't mean . . . I was trying to . . ."

She stood abruptly and walked around the table to face him and he stood, smiling uncertainly, to meet her. At about the same height, all he wanted to do was to stare into those gloriously livid eyes and as she approached him, instinctively, he put his hands on her shoulders. She shook off his hold and as he contemplated a better apology, he caught a glimpse of her knee rising. He twisted just in time to take a knee to his upper thigh, his smile withering into a wince as his legs buckled.

"Are you crazy?" he yelled. "Stop it. What the hell's wrong with you? I said I'm sorry. I shouldn't have said what I did but . . . ." Glowering, she pushed him hard against the booth. "Bree, stop it," he shouted as forcefully as he could. He reached out in defense and hugged her dangerously close as she struggled to get free. Finally, his unrelenting embrace caused her body to relax enough for him to let her go. "You're acting crazy. I just said what I was thinking and I said I was sorry."

She shoved him away and fought to regain her composure. To no one in particularly she said, "Everything is okay, stand down." And then she jabbed her finger into his chest. "That's the point, Gil. You have a critical meeting in an hour and you can't just say what you're thinking, not here and not there, not anywhere. I don't understand. You never say the right things when you have the opportunity, and then you blurt out the wrong things at the worst possible time." She shook her head, sadly. "Do you have a death wish or something? If you don't do a better job of playing politics, no one can save you." Just then her eyes glazed over and her body went limp. Surprised, he barely had time to keep her from crashing to the floor.

Soon enough she was all business. Her eyes refocused and she pushed him away. "I was unprepared, sorry. We have to go, a cart is waiting," was all she said.

She bolted from the train and he followed her to a waiting cart. They boarded and as the cart headed for the street and a waiting limousine; he sat as far from her as he could. On the way, he noticed armed guards stationed at strategic points throughout the terminal. When they entered the limo, he rolled down the window and stared out at the guards visible nearby who returned his stare with much greater intensity.

"Are you expecting trouble?" he asked.

"My goons? I'm the daughter of the Chairwoman and I require security."

"Who are they protecting you from?"

"Right now, you," she said. "But they're accommodating."

"Me? Seriously, who are they protecting you from?"

Offering a smile that was more like her mother's, she said, "Seriously, you."

"Come on," Gil said. "They're not guarding against me."

"There are always threats," she explained. "Today, right now, you're the main one. Their livelihood depends on their ability to ensure that the only harm that could possibly come to me is from someone totally without prior affiliation, who has no previous record of thought or deed from which to predict a hostile action. There are others who take care of the logicians."

"You're not serious? Were there guards on duty on the train?"

She nodded. "They're trained to stay out of my way but if I'd given the word, you'd be in a body bag right now. Do you remember the *Sauver L'eau*?"

He nodded.

"She knows more ways to kill you with serving utensils than anyone alive."

"Really?" He tried to picture some of the possible ways.

"I'm joking," she smiled. Then she stopped smiling and added, "Or not?" Seeing his concern and confusion, she jabbed him in the ribs. "If you want to find out, try to kill me. No don't, my goons react badly to jokes." She pointed her finger at him. "I like you a lot, but never, ever, forget who I am. If anybody and I mean anybody, sees me as anything other than Mother's powerful daughter and her rightful heir, it will cost me and that someone his life."

Chastised, he apologized. "I'm sorry. It won't happen again." She smiled and he felt relieved.

It was a short ride to Mayor's Wua's office. Once they arrived, a secretary escorted them down a long corridor where he caught the whiff of lunch. Once inside a large meeting room he saw the Mayor, along with two men and a woman seated at a large conference table. In the back of the room, a large luncheon feast was waiting.

Mayor Wua was a short, slight, older woman with close-cropped, banged, straight dark hair with a great deal of gray in it. She had tiny, brown eyes that gave her a mousy look and she was dressed in a dark green business suit with an emerald green ribbon tie that had the Almighty Dollar embroidered into it.

"Ms. Brandt," the Mayor said. "It's so very good to see you again. You will, of course, send my regards to your mother."

Bree stepped forward and bowed slightly. "I will, Bunny. And it's great to see you again. This is our project Consensus Builder, Gil Rose. Gil, this is Mayor Juana Wua-Kingston-Olantunji-Wua."

"It's a pleasure, Madam Mayor."

"It's Bunny, please," the Mayor said. "Bree, allow me to make the introductions." Bree nodded and Bunny proceeded to introduce Gil to Bree's siblings, Alph, Cee-Cee and Dave Crelli. Their greetings consisted of deliberate nods, which he measured and returned in kind.

Nervous in their company, Gil blurted, "You each look so much like him."

And they did, with Andrew Crelli's sharp features and gray piercing eyes under gray eyebrows and straight hair streaked prematurely gray. They each wore a thick gold necklace with the icon of the Almighty Dollar, the golden dollar sign imbedded in a lemniscate of silver encrusted with emeralds and diamonds.

It was eerie how similar they looked, but compared with Bree, as attractive as her half brothers and sister were, by inheriting Tanya's genes, she had gained the greatest advantage. For all of their good looks, the clones seemed bland beside Bree's dazzlingly perfect skin, violet eyes and shiny black hair.

He took a seat beside Bree and across from her siblings while Mayor Wua stood in front of the serving tables.

"Before the meeting begins," she said, "allow me to present lunch."

Bree explained. "Bunny is a gourmet chef and ANGS' Sacramento's food critic."

"A mayor has to make ends meet," Bunny clarified. "Through the National Chambers of Commerce, the Consortium of Mayors has lobbied for better compensation for years, but the Chairwoman prefers our wages low enough so we don't get careless, yet high enough so we won't become too aggressive or readily accept pedestrian bribes."

"Bunny, you're far too modest," Bree said. "That's not the only reason." She turned to Gil. "She has exquisite and expensive tastes." He stared at the plain, simply-dressed woman standing at the banquet table and wondered how those tastes manifested.

It didn't take long to discover. Posing like a model, Bunny presented lunch.

"We start with soup and salad. The soup is a puree of abalone with a moutarde crème over-glaze topped with capers and jalapeños in a decorative poivre mélange. It is to die for.

"There are additional toppings and trust me, they are not optional. I highly recommend the strawberries—real strawberries—which have been altered genetically to taste of ginger with a hint of mint Sucre, that's neither cloying, nor does it linger overlong. It's designed to titillate your palate with precise flavor profiles that play perfectly off the abalone, capers and jalapeños. It is such a memorable experience that I often wake wet from a pleasant slumber desiring more.

"The salad is a basic radicchio in a porcine-pomegranate paste, lime-rind dressing over pea tomatoes topped with south-east Los Angeles locusts, a common but often misused pest. The locust has been lightly salted using salt from Lake Erie mines combined and coated with a mild grenadine pepper jerk sauce. It's a truly astonishing amalgamation.

"The locusts, by the way, are deep fried in a twice reduced, heavy, llama fat from Bolivia, in your honor, Gil. Any camelid fat is acceptable in this recipe, and dromedary fat works wonderfully well. But for this occasion, it simply had to be llama.

"The dressing is triple-distilled and I selected a derivative from only the most delectable flavor molecules which were then further agglomerated and fined off for use in the dessert. The taste profile is further modified to include mid-range cucumber with just a smidgeon of New Hampshire maple syrup finish; think more Georgia than Vermont." As she spoke, like butterflies, her hands floated over the dishes. Then she moved on to the main course.

As she was describing it, Gil whispered to Bree. "Why does she do this again?"

"Shhh, few are privileged to see the Mayor this way."

Bunny continued with the presentation. "The main course is a special treat," she said and pointed to Bree. "It's an Indonesian delicacy."

Bree's face lit up. "*Kodok*? Oh, Bunny, that was so thoughtful."

Bunny nodded and continued. "*Kodok* is the main ingredient in the stew, which also includes the very salt water frogs that have been choking the Sacramento River ever since their predators died off a few years ago. Naturally, the K*odok* has been prepared in the traditional way and to it I've added a new and truly spectacular flavor recently developed at ANGS' Rainforest Division Lab. To get the full effect, you must resist the initial urge to heave because when you get past it, you'll find the experience ultimately gratifying, truly unforgettable.

"A caution to the men in the room, there is a minute blend of an Amazon jungle tuber that has a chemical in it that I use for flavor but it will require you to remain seated until you return to flaccid. And if you're prone to sweat, here is a plum wine that has been developed to counteract it somewhat." She pointed. "It's in the ANGS decanter beside the stew. As we speak, the ANGS Lab is working feverishly on a delivery system to by-pass the gag reflex; flaccidity will take another business cycle or two to commercialize. Enjoy it, it won't be hard." She laughed. "Trust me on this; once you get over the rough spots, you'll find the taste a truly laudatory adventure with the greatest possible gustatory reward.

"For our side dishes," Bunny continued. "We have fubbled plantains. Fubbling is a relatively new process. Due to the difficulty and expense of acquiring fresh water suitable for cooking purposes, the plantains were prepared in a special environment that simulates boiling, though it uses no liquids. The result is that they're just a bit too firm for my taste on the outside, but the lab is working on that, too. You must experience the plantains with the canine scrapple dip, which I highly recommend in spite of the derivation. It's that brooding, mustard-like, concoction to the right of the plantains; the one that looks like it has raisins in it. They're not raisins but enjoy, nonetheless. The taste is quite unexpected and well worth the quest."

Bunny walked over to something that looked like a giant Russian *samovar.*

"Finally, allow me to present le morceau de résistance. Here you see our ANGS *Flava Flav* 25,000 dot three. It dispenses any combination of flavors your taste buds might crave and it creates them in any medium you desire. This is not simulation; this is full-bore, third-generation, nano-food with all the taste and caloric content that a hearty capitalist requires. Soon machines like this will reside in every kitchen in America and eventually, we will develop a public vending application as well. Truth be told, I outbid the Chairman for a minority interest in the patent and I own the production rights in the Western Federal Reserve region. Someday, I hope she'll forgive me for outbidding her.

"For dessert today, I've disabled the mix menu and you'll notice that I've programmed a few of my favorite recipes. They appear as selections on the monitor. One in particular is similar to the ANGS pistachio crayfish ice cream that is all the rage in Europe with its gobs and gobs of Omega-3, encapsulated in high-fat molecules that are rich and yummy. Try it, you'll see. I wish you could try each and every flavor, because once you experience the truly orgasmic potential, you'll sign up for a *Flavaflav* from our first production run. I consider it proof that Mayors, like *Entrepreneurs*, are job creators.

"With my device, for the first time in the long and storied history of American victual making, top Morgan corporate food experts expect *Conducers* to finally push away from their kitchen or dining room tables for the right reason: absolute and total satisfaction. You'll understand once you try it. Everyone, grab your plates. Bon appétit."

It didn't surprise Gil that Bree was first to the table. She thanked Bunny and then raced over. By the time he got there, she was piling her plate high and wide with food from the various serving dishes. As soon as Bree finished loading up, she headed to her seat to eat. While Alph Crelli was serving himself, he turned to Gil.

"You knew our father," he said, simply. Gil didn't respond.

"Surely you remember the Chairman of the United States." added Dave Crelli.

"It was a long time ago," Gil responded carefully.

"We don't work with traitors," Dave continued. "The Chairwoman wants you on this project so we'll play along, but against our better judgment."

"I am sorry you feel that way," Gil offered. "What happened occurred a long time ago when I was a young teenager and as I explained to Bree, earlier, I was an unwitting accomplice to the Chairman, your father's kidnapping."

"If that's an apology," the young woman, Cee-Cee asked, "it's a damn lame one."

Gil returned to his seat beside Bree and began to eat. The clones sat across from him. "About my apology," Gil said. "You are free to take it however you like, Cee-Cee; it has the advantage of being true. I'd prefer you believe me but as long as it doesn't jeopardize my work and this project, how you feel is beyond my control. Whatever you decide, I'm giving this project my best and I would appreciate it if you would put aside your feelings for whatever it is you think I did, so we can focus on success."

Bree listened as she ate and though her mouth was full, she interrupted, "Gil, give us a second." She swallowed her food and then her eyes glazed over, as did those of her siblings and the Mayor. Gil noticed that their brows furrowed and the clones would occasionally snarl but no other sound passed between them. Finally, Bree's eyes refocused, as did the others. The clones glared at Bree who was hunching over and massaging her temples.

"Sorry, Gil," she mumbled while taking another mouthful of food. "We needed to clear some things up. Okay, let's begin the meeting. As always, we open with the Lord's Prayer. Cee-Cee, lead us, please."

Bree's half sister put her hands out to her side. Dave took one and Alph the other. Alph offered Gil his hand and he took it, wincing as the clone squeezed it hard. He endured the childishness silently as Cee-Cee prayed.

The Lord is my Partner, He mitigates my risk;
And provides me access to His kingdom;
He restores my passion for excellence;
And though my value may be threatened or diminished
As I compete in His Marketplace;
I fear no unscrupulous competitors because
He is with me;
The righteousness of His free market comforts me
And I will create such value that
I will dwell in the Domain of the Lord, forever.

They each said amen, dropped hands and Bree started the meeting.

"We're here to prepare our Missionary Brother, Gil Rose, for his mission critical afternoon interrogation of Reynaldo Diaz. The goal of his intercession is to cause Mr. Diaz to turn from Satan, accede to our demands, end his strike, dissolve his union, and abide by the terms of the Holarky land purchase agreement. Does anyone have anything to add?"

Dave Crelli pointed an accusing finger at Gil.

"We don't trust you," he said. "But do your job and after a successful project, we'll consider you for staffing on other projects. I want to make this clear. If you fail, at whatever the personal cost, my family," he turned defiantly to Bree, "will do whatever it takes to extract retribution for your treasonous acts against our father, *Mr. Messiah*."

Cee-Cee gasped. "Dave, no, the Chairwoman expressly—"

"Fuck her," Dave said, anger driving his words.

"Dave, Cee-Cee, Alph take this under now," Bree commanded. As before, their bodies slackened and their eyes went vacant. With nothing to do but wait in frustrating silence, Gil watched the tense body language as the siblings once again silently made their points and when they came out, Dave acted like he had been effectively chastised though it didn't seem to have affected Cee-Cee.

She spoke to him while glaring at Bree. "Rose, you were selected for this project for no other reason than the Chairwoman insisted. If you think otherwise, you're a fool."

"If I'm not mistaken," Gil replied calmly. "Being selected by the Chairwoman is reason enough, don't you think?"

Bree had had enough.

"Apparently, I didn't make myself clear!" she scolded. "Alph, Cee-Cee, David, there will be ample time to evaluate Gil's performance. Right now you will answer his questions, accurately and completely." She stared at each of her siblings as she made her next point. "If any of you find your animosity such that you lack the professionalism required to keep your thoughts to yourself, shut the hell up or this will find its way into my report to the Chairwoman. Do you feel so heroic about this issue that you wish to deal with her? I want to be clear about this. If you truly want Gil to fail, have the professional decency to allow him to fail on his own merit rather than create doubt and confusion as to why he failed and who amongst you should be held responsible." She stared violet daggers at her siblings. "Now let's move on."

But Dave Crelli wasn't satisfied. "Rose, you're fresh out of Missionary School and you've only had a couple of straightforward assignments in remote South American locales. What does that earn you the right to do, exactly?"

"Dave!" Bree yelled sharply.

"No, Bree," Bunny interrupted. "Regardless of what the Chairwoman wants, it's a fair question. Dave, go on."

Annoyed, Bree pointed angrily to her eyes and then pointed to Dave but he wouldn't be cowed.

"We've covered for novice fuck ups before," he said.

"Dee Four," Bree shouted. "The Chairwoman wants a consensus builder on this project and Gil is her choice. If you don't like it, take it up with her like you had every opportunity to do when the assignment was first announced. You were silent then, be damned and be silent now."

There was a hush in the room that no one seemed willing to break. Gil found her rage exciting. Here was that "take-charge" girl he remembered from Profit.

"What's first, Gil," she asked while staring at her siblings, daring them to annoy her further.

"I want to understand the value proposition," he said. "I'll synthesize what I hear into an empirical range of possibilities that will fall within your expectations. Later, in my discussion with Diaz, I'll merge his expectations with yours, weighing each side appropriately. The result is a Negotiating Parameter Matrix, or NPM which I'll use as the basis for achieving our value proposition with an acceptance quotient within limits so that Diaz can accept."

"So basically," Cee-Cee clarified, disdainfully, "you're doing the analog of a *Personometer.* At least you didn't bring that silly black ball they give you at graduation."

"It doesn't matter because what you want to do won't work," Alph added. "Diaz is sly and disingenuous to a fault."

Gil clarified. "New techniques in Consensus Building factor that into the results. I can't speak to the digital, but analog methodologies correct for various disingenuous behaviors, even outright lying, but it's an extensive, iterative process based on the fact that everyone has a victory imprint whether they're aware of it or not. My job is to find Diaz's by evaluating key factors using his words, what he doesn't say, his inflection, where and how he pauses, his body language, every nuance and myriad other pointers to breakthrough his outer persona to plumb the depths of his protected inner secrets in order to determine tolerances that will allow me to recommend what will provide an acceptable level of satisfaction for Diaz, but also to allow us to declare a real and potent victory. Everyone plays to win and a Consensus Builder uncovers where everyone's winning parameters most likely intersect in a win-win solution."

"That's fucking revolting." Alph Crelli said, shaking his head and without looking up. "We should just shoot the union asshole." He said no more.

Bree asked Mayor Wua to clarify the Diaz's situation.

"Until last month," she began, "my relationship with Rey was amicable and our negotiation was going smoothly as it usually does. After years of being out-negotiated, Rey knows what's going on and though he didn't say so, he gave me every indication he was ready to comply with everything and do so as a gentleman, which Rey certainly is.

"For background, Gil, when it comes to aggressive downsizing, Sacramento has been the national leader among cities its size going back to my early days as Mayor. We own the high ground here. Rey knows it and that should have ended it."

"What happened?" Gil asked.

"A few months ago, out of the blue, Rey filed a formal grievance against the project and somehow, we truly don't know how, it was put on the court agenda. The case quickly worked its way through the Commercial Courts moving up on the basis of some arcane twentieth century labor law—a labor law for Morgan's sake! According to the judges who levitated the complaint, word had come down from on high to take this lawsuit seriously, which they did by kicking it up. Remember, no one has petitioned the courts for redress in a labor grievance since the First Republic in the early days of this century. Since those days, any lawyer who takes a labor case knows it's a career ender. There's no profit and no future litigating against the Chairwoman's wishes. So anyway, we didn't learn about the cascading fuck up until, suddenly, it found funding and support, again, we don't know from whom, yet. Then the media got their signals crossed and picked up on it, treating it as if it was a new direction in labor policy coming directly from the Chairwoman. The whole thing has been handled like a circus and heads will certainly roll before it's resolved.

"The final straw came when the case was routed to a senile judge who figured if he had it; the Chairwoman must want it so he decided it in a way that forced us to appeal and push it even higher, to the California State Commercial Supreme Court. Alph controls his Court so he was able to put the kibosh on it and it'll die there eventually, but needless to say, the Chairwoman is pissed as hell and there are few members of our legal community who are considering breaking their passports out of hiding. The Chairwoman always comes down hardest on foul-ups and this one is a doozey. Anyway, Alph's Court will hear the case next week and will reject it forthwith. Rey knows this, yet he's threatening more legal action in order to delay the inevitable."

"It's disgusting. It stinks of First Republic America," Cee-Cee added.

There was something about Bunny's story that made Gil curious. "Where does Diaz get the money and the influence to make good on this threat?"

"That's it, he doesn't." Bunny continued, "Our Financial Security Surveillance teams are certain no money is going in or coming out of the Holarki Union coffers, but Rey is playing it cool, and to my mind, too cool. He isn't a gambler. Rey always folds. Bluffing with a losing hand is totally unlike him."

"And then there's the bombing threat," Cee-Cee interjected.

"That's a load of crap. I know Rey and he would never . . ." Bunny argued.

"We found explosives hidden in the field near his community," Dave added.

Gil tried to make sense of it. "If Diaz were to destroy the fields, how will it affect Bree's project?"

"I'd prefer it," Alph responded. "We know how to downsize but we're far better at elimination. It pisses me off that we're diddling around when we can eliminate Diaz's union quickly, with little or no effect. My forensic sociologists have already worked out how to do it in the most cost effective manner. It's a clean and simple solution because word of the union's demise won't hit the streets until we want it to and we can make it hit the way we want it to. We can do it so that workers throughout the country will be so scared that once they learn why and how the union was eradicated, they'll perform with far greater motivation."

"At this late date, if you kill union laborers or if the strike continues, can scabs handle the harvest?" Gil asked.

"That's the problem," Cee-Cee explained. "There will be losses, but scabs work cheap which offsets some of the inefficiency. And once we get through this harvest, the first batch of Bree's robots will be available so we won't need the union anymore. Bunny's right, the union has no winning gambit."

"Scabs aren't the answer." Bunny interjected. "The scabs we've contracted for are this close to 'Wasterdom'". Bunny raised her hand putting her index finger and thumb close together. "Few will persist, they just aren't conditioned for this work. It's brutally hot and the days are frightfully long if we're going to bring the harvest in on time. What we find with scabs is that on the first day, their performance is tolerable. By the second, the attrition begins and by the end of the week, the losses are staggering. There is cramping and other forms of fatigue which reduces performance drastically. Harvest damage will be severe. This work crushes spirits and farm owners will be constantly searching for replacements. If we use scabs, expect the profit from this harvest will be severely compromised."

"I understand now why everyone is concerned." Gil offered.

"Entrepreneurs today," Alph snapped angrily, "they aren't what they were when Father was in charge. They worry risk unnecessarily and constantly beg for government assistance. Frankly, a dip in profits is just what we need to clean out the weak ones. But next year we get the bots so we'll get through it."

Gil looked through his notes. "You mentioned before that word of what's happening could get out. I don't understand. How? We control the Mesh and the media?"

Bunny stood and banged her fist on the table. "I never thought I'd say this." When she was sure she had everyone's attention, she sat and quietly finished her thought. "We run the country under the tightest possible control yet we seem to be helpless here. Rey has no use for electronics but when you're as powerful as we are, those who oppose us learn to fight in ways that we aren't ready for, ways we don't understand, and ways they are willing to die for—something antithetic to what *Entrepreneurs* believe. That's why we never took Rey's threat seriously. He shouldn't have a puncher's chance but—"

"But what, Bunny?" Bree asked.

"I know Rey," she replied. "He's a good man, the salt of the earth type and everyone in Holarki respects him. Hell, I respect him. But Rey abhors confrontation—until now. Suddenly, he has his union strike, there are threats of sabotage, and he manages to circumvent our technological advantages by communicating with allies in other towns using extraordinary means—human couriers. That's not Rey. He's loves people too much to gamble with their lives. What's puzzling is that his couriers get through when none should. I believe that Rey is receiving powerful help."

Bunny had everyone's attention. "From whom?" both Alph and Bree asked.

"It's Omar Smith," Cee-Cee shouted, "that commie-terrorist bastard."

"We think not," Bunny concluded. "We aren't certain because our surveillance systems are useless in this case because the union doesn't use technology and the few times we've succeeded in getting someone inside the union, they've been turned."

"Turned?" Gil asked.

"Our spies become union sympathizers."

There was a murmur in the room as Gil thought back to the Diaz character from his graduation simulation. The avatar Gonzalez y Gonzalez was nothing like Diaz. *How could that happen?* "I'm confused. First you insist Diaz can't win and now it sounds like neither can we."

Bunny nodded to him as if he had said the right thing. "Have your talk with Rey. "If you can convince him, fine, if not, we'll talk more."

"But Bunny, I'm a consensus builder not a miracle worker. What do we have that will convince him?"

"Reverend General Tucker and our HOMESEC forces." Dave shouted.

"Dave's right." Alph responded. "We have the full arsenal of our Capitalist war machine ready to bomb that bastard and his lazy brood of gardeners into the Stone Age. Rose, don't get lost in the minutiae, you have what you need. Convince Diaz to capitulate or resign from our project and run home to Bree's mommy and let real Capitalists take care of this little issue like Capitalists always do. HOMESEC will eradicate Diaz and his filthy union and we'll crucify the bastard on the front lawn of the Mayor's office and be done with it. We've done this before."

"I don't understand," Gil said. "If you can annihilate him so easily, and you clearly want to, why aren't you just doing it?"

"The Chairwoman believes you can get a better result. Brother Rose," Alph sneered. "For no discernable reason, she has confidence in your ability to deliver and all you must do to reward her confidence is to convince Diaz. Do that and maybe we can put the career threatening messiah rumors to rest for good; or you can fail, as I expect you will, and you'll face the wrath of this committee and your Chairwoman. And if you fail, I promise you that those messiah rumors will haunt you every day of your miserable valueless career and force you to live out your limited life span in disgrace somewhere in the *Unincorporated Lands* where you belong, if they will have you." He turned defiantly to Bree. "Isn't that right, Bree, baby?" he said defiantly.

Instead of anger, Gil saw concern in Bree's eyes but before she could respond, he did. "No one appreciates what's at stake more than I do."

"We're all professionals here," Bree added. "And I know each of us will do our jobs and surely that'll be enough. Alph, I know Gil better than you do and I trust him. He is exactly what we need. And once he meets with Diaz, he'll whip some sense into him because in spite of how it seems, Diaz is desperate and I've seen Gil work. He will deliver this."

Thankful for her confidence, Gil continued. "I still need an answer to my question. If somehow, the union manages to strike through the harvest how will it affect Bree's project?"

"I have the numbers and it's not good," Bree answered. "The worst is we simply can't be seen losing to a local union shaman. We can't allow that to happen, I mean . . . it won't, there's no chance of it."

Gil closed his eyes, rubbed his temples and contemplated the implications. When he looked up, he noticed that everyone was staring at him.

Bree leaned in to whisper. "Gil, you look overwhelmed."

He had to be better. Instinctively, he offered a Morgan aphorism. "Every Missionary assignment is a test from God and His tests are most severe when the returns are greatest." That solicited no response so he summarized the problem confronting him. "I'll speak with this Diaz fellow and solve it the way the Chairwoman requires it. Bunny, is there anything more I need to know?"

"Only that I've known Rey Diaz for over fifty years and he's unusual in that he's a decent man and I am certain no one here understands what that truly means. Rey cares for his people; he cares deeply. He is the type of citizen who went extinct in the First Republic, years before it fell, and America lost something critical because people like Rey have become so scarce. Rey is good and kind and he acts on what he believes to be right for his people. That's a calculus that few today understand. You'd think him unremarkable, yet while we've been doing everything to discredit him and to destroy his union; he remains truly loved by them."

"Truly loved," Alph laughed. "An oxymoron. Sentimentality will be your undoing, Mayor."

"Alph, maybe I am a little sentimental, I'm old so humor me," she argued. "Rey is a throwback. He's honest and ethical in the old way before the law and the media decided issues of honesty and ethics. He has never accepted that wealth provides a dispensation from truth. Rey

Diaz has what was once called a moral compass and for him it points true north regardless where that trip takes him. These days, the truth doesn't count for much except in advertising and it seems that the desperate can't get enough truth. I think that's why his union loves him."

Bunny's description of Rey created anxiety in Gil that he couldn't show. "Do the younger members of his union support him?" he asked.

"I've heard rumblings . . ." Bree offered.

"We've created rumblings," added Cee-Cee.

Bunny clarified. "Many of his younger members would like to test themselves in big city free markets because they know that remaining in Holarki with the union is a lost cause."

"So why don't they leave?"

"Because they're union slugs," Alph said, dismissively. Then, he clarified. "The whole lot of them are lazy and they're all addicted to helplessness. All they want is to be cared for. They're cretins hooked on the cooperative and the only way to get that monkey off our backs is to excise the union and kill the dependent before they steal us blind."

"That's . . ." Bunny paused. "That's maybe part of it, Alph," Bunny added, diplomatically. "I believe that most of them simply don't want to disappoint Rey."

"Are those who resettle in other communities successful?" Gil asked.

Dave responded. "The numbers show that the longer members are in the union, the less chance they have of being assimilated into new environments and the less likely that they survive."

"Why is that?" Gil thought back to his own work failings in Profit and Hamilton.

"From the time Union members are born, they are denied the freedom to pursue their own interests in unfettered markets so when they leave the overbearing protection of the collective, they're unable to negotiate a profitable life for themselves and they die. Every one of them is doomed to become a *Waster.* We know that and we have my Father's precedent for action. We should just kill them and save our money."

Chilled by that comment, Gil did his best not to show it. "Bunny, is there anything else I need to know before I see Diaz?"

Dave, who had been relatively quiet through the discussions, unleashed his imprecatory rant. "In spite of how Bunny puts it, Diaz is a cretin. What else do you call a romantic who ruins other people's futures? He is a throwback, Bunny, because he stands for everything that was wrong with the First Republic in those good old days that you seem to have such fondness for. Obviously, you have a soft spot for Diaz but make no mistake, he is our mortal enemy. He is Satan incarnate, and we beseech God to crush him. If Rose is the tool, so be it, but if you are not, then we will hunt you down."

"Calm down, Dave," Bunny replied angrily, "We can't resort to threats and calling people we disagree with bad names. Everyone has value and no one is all bad. If we are the *Entrepreneurs* we think we are, we should mine value wherever we find it. That's what's good for our economy."

"Cut the First Republic Socialist bullshit, Mayor! I won't have it!" Dave screamed. "Expressing commie sympathy is what got you passed over for my position in the first place, and I will not allow such blasphemy. If you truly want what's best for our economy, there is only finance, economics, and power to honor and don't you ever forget it. Everything else is wasteful and an affront to God.

"That you dare take the devil's side in anything makes you suspect. When Diaz defies us, he defies God and everything that we hold holy. The socialist virus that Diaz propagates in that pathetic town of his is evil and it must be eradicated from God's Kingdom on Earth for all time or it will re-infect the virtuous causing a return to a decrepit economy with apocalyptic debt and deficit, social welfare and entitlements that will put us right back at the brink of hell once again."

Shocked by this tirade, Gil listened without commenting.

"We live in crucial, holy times and every American must remain true to his wealth, clear-minded, godly, and productive as we hump toward eternal success in opposition to Diaz and his pack of wild, indolent, rabid dog union papists, Satan's minions who only want the unholy end of times. Damn them and curse them, for they are Satan's beloved uneconomical but they are abhorrent to God and all that's hallowed in our world. When this world is mine and I am free to do God's work without meddlesome women hounding me, these union parasites will never inhale, not a whiff of the slightest odor of victory. They will no longer rip and tear at the fabric of Capitalist decency, working to destroy everything Father and the Lord built.

"Blessed are the Fathers who have breathed the sanctified air of finance into the lungs of our great capitalist prophets and into me, allowing me to speak these great financial truths that the Second Republic is fighting so very hard to keep pure.

"Satan never sleeps. And it was He who made the idle minds of American workers, so that they were free to be filled with His foul thoughts. He caused them to believe that unions housed God's children, too but that is blasphemy! And when workers chose Satan over the true word of the great Capitalist God, their futures were forever sundered from the true Church and their chosen destiny is to live aimless and shortened lives and to die a merciless death.

Gil looked to Bree who was staring down with her hand on her forehead, hiding her face. The others were staring at Dave in various degrees of rapt attention as he continued.

"Satan feasted on their progressive political food chain of lethargic, evil men lacking true Capitalist faith and zeal who sucked money from the productive through taxation. It was a government of sad, deficient bureaucrats who were easily twisted to Satan's will and, with Satan's help, they went about perverting our Constitution and declaring unionism to be sound law and it so weakened the country that the First Republic fell from it.

"That's how Unions gained power over us and they caused such economic putrefaction that the economy was damaged beyond repair. It was only Father's strict constructionist beliefs, his unyielding principles, his abiding faith in Capitalism, and his unwavering patriotism that created the Holy Second Republic as God's kingdom on earth and that is what saved mankind.

"Unions live to revile holiness, to forestall our efforts to do God's will and to create rottenness in the world of finance." Dave's eyes and the veins in his face bulged as he seemed to be fueled by a sanctity that wanted to burst from him. "They steal from the Lord's productive through pagan rituals called unearned wages, budget busting pensions, and other unfair entitlements like vacations and work restrictions. They abuse our economy with their work stoppages, their strikes, and featherbedding ways. They cheat holy America and pervert our devout Capitalist faith seeking to diminish us in God's eye, draining value in hopes of leaving America's economy a limp and lifeless corpse as a gift to Satan. They try. God help them they try but so help me, God, I will stand as the last Capitalist at the abyss and repel them. And I will stand there until the end of time to insure that the Lord's free markets prevail. I vow that my children will never live in a world where Satan's unions rule. Holarky is Armageddon. Death to Diaz and his people!"

Flushed and sweating from his exhortation, Dave paused but no one in the room spoke in that silence. After wiping his brow, Dave continued. "The first American Republic died from the sin of allowing the birth of the foul scum of unionism. It is a carcass today because of that." He lifted his fist toward the heavens. "As God is my partner, I vow that I will never, ever allow a single union member to exist anywhere on Earth, so help me God. We are so close . . . so close. We are nearing God's holy paradise and I will not permit anything to stand between me and the holiest of holies. I will not abjure my right to everlasting life at God's right hand for even one of these revolting unbelievers. The fetid perfidy that is union putridity mustn't survive."

While it clearly felt to Gil that this rant had gone on overlong, he deferred to Dave's siblings or the Mayor to manage it but none of them did. Finally, seemingly depleted, and with a growl and then a sigh, he stopped. His face glowed with a grayish flush and his eyes shone brightly as he stared at the table awaiting someone to support him but except for his clone siblings, he found no one.

"I had no idea that unions were that bad." Gil said, breaking the silence.

That got Dave started again. He shook his fist. "They are an abuse of God's triumphal love. They are Satan's affliction sent to burden humanity, penalizing the productive, the wealthy, and the God loving who are forced to deal with their rubbish. Unions . . ." Dave hesitated, his pale complexion turning red as he made a heaving noise deep within him. He gagged a little, and while holding onto the table in a death's grip, stifled the urge to vomit.

Sweating profusely, he took a deep breath and struggled on. "I worked with them, once; I know how vile they are. We pay Satan's vermin for unproductive efforts and then we pay them again for not working at all. It's all in their contract. These parasites that have caused all the sins that afflict our economy today, they deny us the perfection we work so hard to achieve and so richly deserve. They seek to deny us God's grace. With that, Dave turned from the table and once again heaved as if to vomit. As Gil and the others watched, flushed and visibly shaking, Dave fumbled for and then took a green and gold silk handkerchief from his back pocket and wiped his brow.

"These vile, these vile union squanderers . . . these vile union squanderers . . . Dave spat violently on the floor as if he was jettisoning something repellent from his body.

Exhausted, he ranted on. "The revered Saint Ayn Rand tells us—"

Finally, Bree interrupted in disgust. "That's enough. We have to end this meeting and you've said more than enough." She added quietly, "No one here likes the union."

Dave just stared at her so she tilted her head and stared back, daring him to continue.

And he did speak again, but this time drained of the loathing. "God knows, Sister Bea, there is more to be said—and more, still to be done. These are perilous times and I am in great need of succor and investment advice. Please, end this meeting now so that I may attend afternoon business devotion at the Stock Exchange Chapel."

Then he turned to Gil. "Allow the Lord to comfort and direct you. And when you meet with that devil's spawn, Diaz, tell him that the Lord hates lazy, godless bastards and unless he repents, he will end his life as a sacrifice on the holy free market altar of our great, merciless God. I implore you, Brother Gil, before it's too late, repent and return to God's fold. Invest your love in Him and spend your future for Him. Do that and exterminate the vermin, and one day, you will walk with God and will realize the greatest return on your investment possible."

With that, Dave stood and in a voice barely above a whisper added. "This is my holy mission and I will never shirk, Sister Bea, until I walk with my God. Believe in your technology for it will light the way and stand by Him for he will reward you. Stay true, the final victory is the Lord's. He will purify America." With tears welling in his eyes, he grabbed and held the Almighty Dollar icon that hung from his neck and then left quietly.

There was an awkward silence and once again Gil thought to break the tension. "I forget what question that answered." He received no smiles. "Tell me again why we're having so much trouble?"

Cee-Cee responded. "I understand Dave's frustration. Sometimes, we are our own worst enemy. We bid out harvesting contracts and every year the union submits the lowest bid, by far. Somehow, they manage to underbid consortia of private contractors, illegals, and even *Tollers*, and every year it's the same, by a significant margin, the union always submits the lowest bid. How they do it? We don't know. But the lowest bid is the lowest bid and so we honor it."

Bunny added. "Funding is the key. Our surveillance technology is the best in the world and we constantly monitor the union yet we know little about how they receive funding. Their members pay no dues, they have no sponsors, and everything they produce on their farms stays in Holarky yet during the strike, the families of Holarki are fed and clothed with enough left over to help former union members in other towns."

Gil considered it. "*We* don't know? That just isn't possible," he offered.

"To put this in perspective," Bunny explained, "within the overall economy, the union is no more than an insignificant annoyance but if we're unable to resolve this, we don't deserve the power we exercise."

Everyone was silent after Bunny's comment and Gil used the quiet to consider ways the union might be bypassing advanced surveillance technologies. His thoughts took him back to when he was a teen in Bernie's Hospice. There, Bernie had explained how Joad stole from the rich and gave to the poor. He didn't like where his thoughts were leading and Bree noticed.

"What is it, Gil?"

He suppressed feelings of dread. "I'll understand everything far better once I meet with Diaz."

With that, Bree stood and concluded the meeting. Her remaining siblings stood and left, each conspicuously avoiding Gil.

Before she left, Bunny paused beside Gil and whispered. "Mayor Burghe says hello. He asked me to remind you that you have a friend in Hamilton."

It was a curious thing to say. He thanked her for the delicious buffet and then, he and Bree returned to the limo. Before he entered, he asked her, "Why wasn't I made aware of all this before?"

"You're new. Every project has things you don't count on. I've had worse. You'll handle it."

He slid into the limo and she closed door. Then she leaned in. "Bunny isn't soft regardless what Dave and the others say. Be careful with her; be careful with everyone."

She was so close. He stared into those precious eyes and then at her infectious smile. Her lips trembled ever so slightly and she looked uneasy but then, she surprised him. She leaned closer and kissed him softly on his cheek.

"Should I be careful with you, too?" He whispered.

"With me most of all. You best be going. I have my beauty rest and then an appointment later. Make it turn out right with Diaz and when you return to the train, don't wait up for me because I'll be late."

With that, the limo headed toward Holarki.

Chapter 7

Holarki, CA—2083

It was an uncomfortable and even hazardous drive down the raised highway from Sacramento to Diaz's union headquarters in nearby Holarki. Large cracks in the highway bridged by thick steel plates slowed the pace as the wheels made loud thrumming sounds as they traversed each plate. In the gaps the steel plates didn't cover, Gil caught glimpses of the fractured land far below.

For a time, the highway ran along a wide concrete aqueduct that was filled, deep and wide, with detritus that couldn't quite hide or strangle a rivulet of green brackish water that oozed putrid down the center. Beyond the aqueduct there was a battered chain link fence and beyond that were office buildings, warehouses, and housing developments all in varying stages of decay and collapse. On the near side of the highway, dead brush covered brown hills that were home to empty, partially destroyed housing developments and retail shopping centers with broken and boarded up windows flaunting their financial disgrace. The highway itself was eight lanes wide, but only one in each direction was passable, the other lanes were strewn with road waste accumulated through years of impact, friction, wind, gravity, and neglect. There were also car-sized tumbleweeds, quiescent in the hot, dry, still air. In the distant haze, Sacramento's high rise office towers endured as empty, forlorn, and shamed specters of First Republic decline sitting extended Shiva-like grief for their once productive past.

The driver carefully maneuvered the limo down a severely damaged and precariously slanting exit ramp that split off from the highway, shedding its concrete abutment and protective walls in some long forgotten quake. At the bottom of the ramp, the limo drove over three large rusted plates that crossed a gash in the earth that split the road all they way to the horizon and was so wide and deep that it had engulfed the concrete center median. The limo proceeded down a dusty road through scorched brown hills to a large weathered sign with a badly faded painting of a once idyllic town that marked the entrance to the union town of Holarki.

The limo driver stopped to confirm coordinates before proceeding and the limo meandered through a winding development of old and decayed single story wood frame homes before stopping in front of a small, one story stucco building with a rusted metal sign indicating that it was Union Headquarters, Local 137.

Gil left the air conditioning for the oppressive heat. As he approached the headquarters, he noticed a message taped to the doorknob with a neatly lettered, hand drawn map directing him to a nearby home. He handed the map to the driver and climbed back into the limo. Soon they were deeper into the neighborhood of simple, ramshackle wooden homes centered on small burnt-out lawns bereft of landscaping. On the ridge that surrounded the homes, massive windmills turned lazily driven by an infrequent and hesitant breeze. The driver stopped at a house with no address and whose blue paint was so faded that the wood grain showed prominently underneath.

Gil instructed the driver to wait while he proceeded up the short gravel driveway on foot. He stepped onto the porch, avoiding the rotted front steps and the part of the wooden porch with the greatest sag, and repeatedly knocked on the front door. Receiving no response, he wandered around back where plumes of thick gray smoke rose from a cluster of barbecue grills in a far corner of a large field bordered by the cinder block remnants of housing foundations, sickly barren pines, and a cracked almost dry riverbed.

As he walked toward the billowing smoke, the heat was so intense that he removed his coat and rolled up his sleeves. A very young, dark-complexioned, redheaded girl of maybe five or six ran to him. She was wearing a dirty t-shirt and faded and frayed pink shorts. He squatted down to meet her.

"Do you know where I can find Senor Reynaldo Diaz, senorita?" he asked.

She smiled, shyly. "Senor, are you el Misionero?"

"Si, Senorita, Creo que sí. You are so smart. How did you know?"

She lowered her eyes. "Those silly clothes, Senor."

He laughed.

With that, she took off running, stopping only to make sure that he was following. When he fell too far behind, she waved him on, pointing and running and occasionally looking back. Finally, she stopped to wait for him to catch up.

"Senor Diaz?" he asked her again.

She pointed to a group of men talking near the picnic tables. "Si, El Tio."

"He's your uncle."

"No, senor," she explained. "He is El Tio, everyone's uncle."

Gil approached the group. Most were sitting on benches eating, drinking beer, and talking, but a few stopped to stare at him. A young man broke from a group and sauntered toward him.

"Mr. Rose," the young man said. "You're here to see El Tio."

Gil nodded and held out his hand. The young man slapped it.

"I'm Relitto. El Tio is my uncle, my true uncle. He's waiting on the flats." Relitto pointed to a spot on the riverbed where a dark skinned, white-haired man was sitting alone on a stump, sipping from a metal flask.

Gil thanked the young man and made his way to the river. On seeing him, Rey Diaz took a final swig from his flask and put it in his back pocket. He stood as Gil offered his right hand and it disappeared in Diaz's left, which had the tips of three fingers missing, his right arm and hand hanging uselessly at his side. Up close, his brown skin was deeply furrowed and his rheumy eyes offered an indication of how really old Diaz was. He was like the men Gil had worked with in Bolivia and so he relaxed.

"Welcome. Today is a fine day to die." Diaz began. "I have the time, do you have the inclination?" Diaz said in unaccented English. Concerned by the comment and wondering why Diaz had chosen those words first, Gil didn't respond so Diaz continued.

"Thank you for coming. I preferred a morning meeting but it couldn't be arranged. I am sorry for any inconvenience."

"No, it's fine," Gil said, glancing at the families sitting near the barbecues. "Is today some kind of holiday?"

"This picnic? No, our families gather here every chance we can and now that we're not harvesting, that is all day, every day. We share our food and talk about community issues. Are you hungry?"

Gil declined. "Can we talk about the project, Mr. Diaz?"

"Please, call me Rey. And this is as good a place as any to discuss our death."

"That's not how it's going to be, Mr. Diaz . . . Rey."

"I pray for that but unless you're the answer to those prayers, my people are dead."

"It doesn't have to be that way. End your strike and allow us to prove our harvest technology and your families will avoid the worst possible outcome."

Diaz smiled, his white teeth gleaming against his dark complexion. "Then it is settled. We will do as you suggest. May we finish our picnic first?"

Gil tried not to appear surprised or relieved. "That's . . . that's great, Rey."

Diaz stared at him until he became uncomfortable, then he added, "I didn't expect them to choose you."

"Choose me for what?" Gil asked.

"There's more going on than I know."

"I was chosen for this assignment because I can help you to resolve this. I am like you; my concern is for the welfare of your people."

Diaz took a swig from the canteen and smiled. "Good, so, Chairwoman Brandt's bargaining position has weakened."

Gil returned the smile. "I can assure you that our Chairwoman's positions never weaken. She sent me here because I'm professionally trained to achieve a consensus acceptable to everyone, so that we can move on from this impasse. I'm here to help you achieve the fairest possible outcome."

"If there is truly such a skill in this world," Diaz began, "I'm honored to be in the presence of a practitioner of it. But you'll have to excuse me if I withhold judgment because fairness is open to many interpretations." He stared past Gil into the fields beyond. "In your missionary work, you must have seen great poverty."

"I've seen too much of it. I spent three years as a missionary stationed at the ANGS Corporate Center in Cochabamba, Bolivia. We were commissioned to sort out water rights issues. Before those poor people would trust ANGS to negotiate in good faith, they first had to learn to trust me."

"How did that work out for them?"

"I believe they benefited. Before ANGS arrived, Bolivian workers had been getting screwed for decades by foreign corporations that had reacquired their water rights in illegal deals. My team persevered and we managed to assuage the peoples' concerns. The result was that a great many jobs were created and by the time I left Cochabamba, the people were measurably better off. Rey, I want the same for your union. My purpose here is to work with you to find a win-win solution."

"Yes, a win-win, by all means," Diaz agreed. "But win-win is always easiest for the winner to digest. In Holarki, much like in Bolivia, people lived in harmony with nature until corporations came to conquer and exploit us. It was all very legal, twenty-first century gold and glory stuff, which translated into great profit. Corporations came and they expropriated as they always expropriate, and as always, they took the lion's share. They sucked our local culture dry and refilled the dried out husk with perverted capitalist ideals leaving us hopelessly poor and that is why we are now susceptible to your win-win philosophy. Your leaders are cruel and thorough so that when we die, we will die fighting for what remains—our values.

"That, my consensus building friend, is where we stand. Look at us. Look at how we live. Fair is far different here than where your Chairwoman reigns. If the Bolivian people kept their pride and their values when your missionaries departed, I would take you far more seriously."

"Morgan missionaries provide productivity and faith to all people."

"Don't patronize me. Your religion is offensive," Diaz said.

"I apologize but you should become more familiar with Morgan because, more than any other Christian religion, Morgan is the true way to God. Did you know that no true believer has ever declared bankruptcy or become a *Waster*? No other religion can claim that."

"Morgan is evil and it perverts our world."

He stared into Rey's sad eyes. Though Diaz's eyes were brown, not blue, his melancholy gaze reminded Gil of Bernie and suddenly he was less sure. *What was he doing here?* But he had a job to do and so he persisted. "When my Bolivian mission ended, commerce had expanded there and employment and wages were increasing. Through our missionary efforts, the Bolivian people are living better today and I read a report recently that most sins have been chased away. Your people can benefit from good times, once more, if they are open to it."

"Sin is never chased away, it merely adapts to the winners and the losers."

"Still, we helped Bolivian workers and I'm proud of my contribution."

"ANGS allowed Bolivian workers to organize because it was beneficial to their bottom line. Whatever you believe, your project was the first step in the economic re-conquest of Bolivia. And it is the same everywhere because Capitalists reuse that strategy wherever there are surviving poor who have something they want."

"These are missions from God and they help people, Rey." Gil insisted. "Because we believe so devoutly in forever, every Morgan project considers the long run health of the economy, and by that I mean the everlastingly long run when we accumulate an estate of such value that we qualify to walk with God. This is a great outcome for humanity, the greatest, and missionaries like me are merely humble servants of the Lord."

With the stumpy fingers of his left hand, Diaz made the sign of the cross. "Stop this," he shouted. When some picnickers turned and looked alarmed, he quieted. "Stop this," he said more quietly. "What you speak is perverse. It is blasphemy."

"You don't understand—"

"I don't understand? Long ago, in the days of the First Republic, when I was a young man, my parents told me how life was for them and should be for everyone. They worked hard and like most workers, my dad was a loyal union man working for a large corporation when effort was mostly fairly valued and there was enough to go around. Management respected workers, then, and workers did their jobs with pride. This was before the greedy moneyed interests turned labor into a reducible cost and workers into public enemies. Thank the Lord, mom and dad never lived to see . . . to see this.

"Years after my parents died, foreign competition made inroads into our economy forcing threatened American corporate managements to make foolish short sighted decisions. To compete as low cost suppliers and in search of new markets for their goods, a great many, too many corporations moved their facilities offshore to greener pastures where they thought they could make more money than here, at home. They abandoned America and they abandoned Americans, and yet, somehow, they became the heroes while the workers—the Americans who stayed, loyal and true, the ones who fought the wars and paid the mortgages—they became the enemies of America. It wasn't long after that, as our economy compressed, they returned home, their entrepreneurial greed having crushed the spirit from those who remained.

"The sad thing is that how my parents lived and worked made so much sense. Back then, after a hard week of work, on paydays, workers would spend their wages at local lunch wagons, restaurants, and taverns and the wives would take from the wages what they needed to purchase family necessities from local businesses. Local commerce, the community, and our families all grew and prospered. It was economics of fairness, of growth, of common good and common wealth, and it built and sustained our nation. Public and private schools, transportation systems, libraries, hospitals, every institution that a community needed was funded this way. It was capitalism, fair and at its finest before greed set in and created a race to the top that caused too many to plummet to the bottom all for increased profits. Local businesses sold out to corporations with headquarters in far distant places and their names changed to unfamiliar but purposeful and friendly names and corporate indifference to local issues was born.

"I'm old and I have been so soundly defeated that far too often these days I think back on my parent's times. I remember the excitement when dad arrived home after work. He gave us big hugs and he gave mom his wages. She would take my two sisters and me out to spend it at neighborhood stores buying clothing. Some of the money, mom spent at the grocery store where floors were covered in sawdust. Everything wasn't frozen or dried or reconstituted like it is today. Sometimes, when we were good, mom bought us toys. She worked her days cleaning, doing the wash, and raising us with love and affection which she felt was important if my sisters and I were to become responsible adults and good Americans some day.

"A portion of what dad earned, he reinvested in America in the form of savings bonds or he put it in simple low interest savings accounts that banks used for business loans and home mortgages that helped our neighborhood grow. There were hundreds of millions of people like my parents and their nickels and dimes built America as surely as the million of dollars from the hundreds of entrepreneurs. Workers and workers' families had a stake in America—it was our Land and we were willing to do anything for it, including die on foreign soil unlike the mercenaries of today who are paid professional aggressors. Like us, our neighbors loved our community and we all assumed that every other community in America was like ours, good people one and all and we proved it by staying, even when times got tough. Today, banks take our money but only to invest in sure things in far off places and they do it in arcane ways that hurt others.

"For what happened next, it is easy to find fault with those who gained the most financially. America's middle class, my neighbors, they weren't prepared. With too many businesses having shifted abroad, in that vacuum, the economy compressed. Senator Crelli was the only politician prepared for it and he was soon elected President, and the Second Republic was born. Community, common good, and common wealth were no longer profit centers and they soon disappeared.

"Today, my pathetic loyal workers are all that's left from my idealistic youth. But they are Capitalism's enemy and its latest victim. How do we deserve that? We struggle every day to live the best life we can and now, suddenly, we are the scourge of God's earth and must be obliterated so that there is nothing left, not even a hint of the foul stench of unionism.

"There have been many wars in my lifetime, but this war against unions is the only war America has won. It is in this environment that you, my noble Morgan consensus builder, weigh the right and wrong of it—and you chose them. You chose them! How? When did they earn that right? What did they show you that made them right in your eyes. Explain it to me. No, don't, because you can't. Wake up before it's too late. You don't choose them, they choose you."

Unsure, Gil responded. "That's how it works, Rey. They won."

"That's it? They won?" With that, Diaz stood and pointed toward a far-off field. He walked toward it and Gil followed along the dried, cracked riverbed mud. They stopped at a fence where Rey put his boot up on a post and stared out. In the large, fenced-off area, fattened cattle and sheep grazed and outside a nearby barn, hogs ambled under a fine mist while in another yard, chickens clustered so tightly that the area seemed like a white and yellow rug. In the distant fields, lush green plants grew under intense watering by automated sprinkler systems.

"That is theirs," Rey said, then, pointing behind him before turning, he added, "This is ours." Rey was now facing sun burnt fields with patches of scraggly plants. There were some scrawny goats and a few undernourished milk cows, too. Diaz laughed. "Don't be concerned, we won't compete against you capitalists. This is the food supply that our families depend on now that we're on strike. At dusk, our children take buckets and fill them with the water from the sprinklers because the cost of water is just too expensive. We recycle water in a facility we reconstructed because we can't afford to waste anything but ourselves."

"I understand that times are tough but you can end this. You're their leader."

"I'm their shop steward and President of our Union, but I'm not their leader. I am an elder, their uncle, el Tio, that's all. My people are free. What we do, or do not do, is our choice, not mine."

"Don't they understand? Life would be so much easier if you ended your strike and moved on."

"It's you who don't understand," Rey said. "We're not land barons bartering over borders, negotiating a good deal, and we're not arguing for fair treatment. This is about survival and everyone in Holarki is together in this. We don't want more, we never did, certainly not your type of more because it's a Capitalist contrivance. Everything my people value is here. We grew up here and our families and friends are here. Our parents and grandparents are buried here. Our neighbors are our fellow workers. There are no high-level managers to please or impress. All that the residents of Holarki do is the work needed to make a life, to make a community. We make decisions as a group and we abide by them as a people."

As Diaz spoke, Gil looked out at the picnickers in the distance and his thoughts drifted to Angel Falls. Holarki was Angel Falls. Families here worked together and they shared. There were community picnics in Angel Falls, too, and the people congregated, they liked each other as they apparently did here in Holarky. Each of the towns lacked the frenzy that corporate towns require, where residents, driven incessantly by profits, constantly dealt in an attempt to win or gain some advantage. He stared at the picnickers and wondered why he hadn't appreciated Angel Falls and then he knew. Holarki was Angel Falls and he was certain now that it too would die and that meant more guilt for him to carry.

Rey spoke as if he'd been listening to Gil's thoughts. "All we want to do is live, love, and care for each other and for this, you brand us socialists and make us live like outcasts to die in misery."

It pained Gil to respond but it was his job. "Resistance is futile, and delay will only hurt your people more. Work with me, Rey. Together, we can find a solution; we can do what's best for your people."

Rey shrugged and began walking back toward the picnic. "Okay then, let's make this easy. I agree to all of your terms, whatever they are. Now that is over, tell me why they chose you to do this?"

Gil struggled to answer so Rey spoke again, this time his voice seemed sad. "Our fate is in your hands, *your hands*. You can't help us if you don't care."

"It's my job to care."

"No one has a job to care but only if you care, will you save us."

"I'm here to save you. All you have to do is agree to complete the harvest and then leave for the cities and towns where your people can thrive. I'll find funding to help retrain your people for a new life."

"The Chairwoman is most generous, but we like our old life."

"She's not generous, but consensus building is a new discipline and the Morgan Seminary Board of Directors is evaluating its effectivity. That gives me some latitude to obtain funding to help your people."

"The Chairwoman is very wise to allow the Messiah to negotiate outcomes but your offer is just silly. Why retrain us if there are no jobs? You and I know we won't live to see another community."

Gil chose to ignore Rey's messiah comment. "You're wrong. There are jobs, just not in one place. And I promise you that your people will live to see another location."

"You'll break up our families and our community. We won't do that."

"It won't be easy," Gil implored, "and I can't guarantee jobs but I promise you we will relocate your people to places where the mayors need workers and we'll do everything possible to help your people qualify for work."

"I'd be a fool to reject such a wonderful offer."

"It's the only offer you'll get and the only one that will save your families. Work with me on this, Rey. Agree and I'll find training funds and maybe additional funds for food and housing. I'm going out on a limb here but I know I can make it work for you."

"They call me *El Tio* because I am family to everyone here. If there are problems, I listen and help if I can. But I know that sometimes I can't, and my people trust me because of that. But even when they won't say what they mean, I hear them. The young ones, they bullshit or ignore me but that's okay, that's what young people do. It is the young that I fear for because they know the union is over. Many are scared but some can't wait to kick ass out there on their own like rich locos say they should. The young are too smart for their own good, but they will learn and it will hurt. For now, they believe the Capitalist lie of a glorious ownership society where opportunity exists for everyone. Even if that were true, it's not true for us but it is the lie that will draw our naive young into greedy schemes and empty promises of quick riches that will end in death. The people of Holarki are good people but most, I fear, will be disappointed because they don't understand what they are dealing with. They don't understand that for there to be rich capitalists, there must also be the poor *Wasters* and in your world, failure comes at great cost. If there were more time, my people might learn that, but your system doesn't allow for trial and error so if we depart from Holarki we will surely die. As El Tio, I can't ever allow that."

Gil felt his project slipping away.

"My people need training, surely, Diaz continued. "But they need understanding, reassurance, and guidance, as well, and that we won't get from you or anybody else. My people need a way to survive but the young of Holarki oppose me on where. I'm El Tio, so I must wait and be there when they are finally willing to listen and learn."

"I understand, I do," Gil said. "But you won't be here forever and you must give your people a chance to thrive without you."

"I know this will end," Diaz said. "I know robots will harvest and the trucks will come, first for the crops and then for my people." Diaz paused. "And it makes me sad." Rey stared at the bare trickle of river water that meandered below the desiccated mud.

Gil couldn't give up. "It doesn't have to be this way."

"Yes, it does. The Chairwoman wants this and no one, apparently not even a naive messiah like you, can stop it."

Again, Gil ignored Rey's use of the word messiah. "It's not just workers who worry," Gil argued. "Owners fear their farm businesses will fail and they'll be gone, too."

"How can that be right?" Diaz asked. "Don't you see how wrong it is? How evil? This is foolishness that some, the rich and successful, live and everyone in the way dies. You were born to stop this, yet you don't seem to even question it. What went wrong? What made you this way?

All we want is a life like what my mom and dad had, an opportunity to live as we want, safely, and with some comfort, maybe to raise a family, or to worship as our needs require. How does that come to genocide? Why can't you see that? You feel it's wrong, I know it. You must! Haven't you ever asked yourself why this drive for wealth and power has so corrupted humanity that the poor and unsuccessful must die? How did you come to believe that this is right?"

"It's not like that . . . There's an upside," Gil struggled to explain. "Maybe you and your people haven't seen it, but it exists. There is a vibrant economy out there. People work hard and life is good. Everyone is healthy, happy, productive, and safe. Your people will experience that too, if you give them the chance. There are risks, certainly, what is life without risk, but our economy is growing and that benefits everyone."

"Obviously, not everyone. When entrepreneurs lose value, they adjust, they lay off workers; they vacation less. When we lose value, we die."

"It's always been that way. You can't blame us for that."

"If the 'us' you don't want me to blame includes you, then all is lost."

"Morgan economics isn't about dying, it's about living."

"Tell that to the *millions* of Americans who lost their lives so that the rich could prosper more. Is this what you've become?"

"Yes, the genocide was horrible but times were bad then. They're not bad now."

"Not bad! Look at us!" Rey shouted. "Is this what you've become?"

"This is what we all become," Gil replied even though it saddened him to admit it.

Rey pointed toward his people. "Think what you're asking, then look at us not as wasteful resources but as individuals, as people. My friends and neighbors are people, good and bad, content or needy, but what we are not are economic pawns. If this is truly what you've become, then my prayers have failed and my dream has truly died."

"Why do you say that? You don't know me. This is who I am."

"Come." Diaz started walking and Gil followed him up an embankment toward the homes. As he walked, Gil stared at the people of Holarki. Some wore old and threadbare clothes, some ate, others drank and laughed, but all stared warily at him as he walked by. He saw distrust and fear in their sad, sweaty faces, but he saw hope too. *Why hope*, he wondered. And though some were laughing, all were concerned. And as a sign of their respect for El Tio, when he passed, all activity ceased.

Rey stopped in front of a house that, like all of the others, was in desperate need of repair. Most of the windows were covered with thin, opaque plastic that billowed in the infrequent hot breeze. Everywhere, the wood was rotted and the house seemed out of plumb. Cautiously, Gil followed Rey inside, avoiding dry rot on the wooden steps and the buckled planks on the covered porch.

"Mi casa, su casa," Rey said cheerily as he sat on a small couch in his sparsely furnished living room. Gil sat in a wooden rocking chair facing him; sweat dripping from his face in the warm, close, dusty environment. In a corner of the room, he spied an ancient Archive unit.

"You have research capability?"

"We teach our children," Rey explained, "but we instruct them not to worship it because we care too much for our children to allow others to mold them. Parents know that their children will never live in a community like ours again and we fear that so we teach them so that what Holarki stands for will be in their heart in hope that the love we have for each other will remain with them."

"You're doing a good thing, Rey. My former girlfriend teaches middle school. She's always complaining that parents don't invest enough of themselves in their children's future."

"Your *former* girlfriend?"

"We broke up before I left for Sacramento."

"Morgans speak of forever but their relationships never last. What happened?"

"She was willing. It didn't end because of her."

"You didn't love her?"

"It's difficult to explain," Gil paused. "That's not why we're here."

"Please, tell me what happened."

"It doesn't matter. It's over. This is what's important. What will it take for me to convince you to cooperate?"

"The most important thing in life is to know what the most important thing in your life is, and then to live for it. Don't you agree?"

"That's a sound philosophy."

"So your girlfriend wasn't . . . important."

Gil considered it. It hurt to think that. "I guess that's true. Can we talk about the project, Rey, and not her?"

The old man stood and walked into the hall where he slid open a hidden panel in the wall. Behind the panel was a narrow passageway that lead to a rickety set of wooden stairs that descended into a dimly lit basement.

"You said that I don't know you. Come," he beckoned mysteriously. In the basement, candles flickered in the darkness illuminating an old figurine that had recently been repainted.

"This is our Sanctuary. Here, we seek wisdom, guidance and forgiveness."

"Why hide it down here? Religious freedom is protected. There are churches above."

"Churches no one can attend and feel safe."

"That's not true. Morgan is a Christian religion and there are plenty of successful Christian entrepreneurs."

"Morgan is in no way Christian," Rey argued. "It's profane to consider it."

"Then worship Christ like this for all the good it will do you, but for your people's survival, it will be far more productive for them to worship Morgan."

Rey contemplated it. "Has Morgan helped you? It certainly has not helped us?"

Gil answered a different question. "If it will help, I pledge that your people won't be forced to convert. Are you Catholic?"

"I was born Catholic and remained so until I was a young man. But instead of protecting and nurturing them, our priests sinned against the children and the Church protected the sinners and not the innocent children. It was impossible for me to continue so I'm Catholic no longer."

"Yet you have Christ's statue hidden in your basement."

"I'm a Christian, just a Christian. After the Catholic corporate fathers made their perverse choice, I became a Secular Humanist. But though Secular Humanism helped, it failed me, too. The world grows so complex and there is selfishness and greed everywhere and every Christian denomination put a price on their God and so I became desperate, unsatisfied, afraid, and alone along with a great mass of people who searched for an alternative to the emptiness that Church was designed to fill.

"Secular Humanism seemed to be it. A rational belief in mankind was so much more comforting than dogma, myth, and bad behavior. It helped the intellectual in me far more than the spiritual but when I found it incapable of aiding my spirit, I left in search of more. In this uncaring world, given its name, Humanism lacked caring people to comfort the aggrieved and aid the needy. Unfortunately, Secular Humanists don't group all that well so I found the experience empty and lacking.

"I am a Christian, a follower of Christ's teachings, Jesus before Peter and Paul and the great gospel enterprise. I believe that the only unerring word of God is the Golden Rule so I try my best to treat others as I would like to be treated and that has been enough until now. My belief in even that has been shaken as I wonder at what you have become."

"I'm just a Morgan, Rey, and this isn't about me."

"You are wrong, my friend. This is all about you. Are you happy with this Morgan person that you have become?"

It was a question that he didn't ask himself and there was no way that he would answer Diaz.

"Are you happy?" Rey repeated.

"My happiness or unhappiness will not save your people."

Diaz turned and walked to the basement steps. "Please, excuse me for a moment. With that, Rey climbed the stairs.

Not long after, he returned with someone trailing close behind him. In the dim light, Rey stepped aside and an ancient, grizzled black woman stood before him, trembling. Her hair was thin, white, and brittle and though much of it was tucked under an old red scarf what was visible had remained nappy. She was crooked, her frail body bent at her waist, her shoulders and again at her neck and one arm sagged useless at her side. She twisted her neck to look at him. Her eyes were yellowed and ancient brown but focused and there was a grotesque looking circular wound on her right cheek surrounded by a large swirling red, brown, and white scar. Her other cheek had a reciprocal scar, possibly the exit point for some long ago event that ended with a bullet to her mouth. She stared at Gil, her lips quivering, and began to sob quietly.

"Gil Rose, it is my pleasure to introduce you to Rhonda Boyar," Rey announced.

Instantly, he knew the name and just as suddenly he felt lightheaded and reached for something to hold onto as his body went limp.

"Rhonda's sister," Rey continued, "was Henrietta Boyar, your mother. Gil, this is your aunt."

Staring at him with curiosity, pride and reverence, with a trembling, arthritic hand, Rhonda Boyar wiped the tears from her eyes and with a raspy, high-pitched voice weak from age and hazard, she prayed. "Hear me O' Lord and bless me, for I have met the Messiah, and I can rest in peace."

Hours later, Gil left Rey Diaz's home emotionally drained. He entered the waiting limo and on the return trip to the train station sat bewildered thinking deeply about what had just transpired. He should have been happy, his aunt knew his mother well but once again, he had endured a tragically sad story. Diaz had asked if he was happy but his meeting with his mother's sister, his aunt, was why he would never be happy. Still, she had provided him with desperately appreciated information about his mother's life, information even his grandfather Mark didn't know, or didn't want to discuss.

Remembering that he had a report to deliver, he shook himself out of his reverie and tried to think of something the committee would accept as productive from this visit. He had been concentrating so hard that he failed to notice that the limo was heading away from the train station and toward downtown Sacramento.

He was surrounded by deserted factories. Concerned, Gil called to the driver but was ignored as the limo continued on. He peered at the picture on the driver's badge. This wasn't his original driver and so he tried frantically to escape but the doors were locked.

The limo finally stopped just inside the gates of one of the many desolate factory complexes. Someone opened the limo door but before he got out, he surveyed the surroundings to see where he might flee. The limo was encircled by a cadre of armed guards so flight was out of the question. Resigned to his fate, he stepped out.

"Don't do anything foolish!" a guard yelled. He started to run anyway but two guards grabbed him and twisted his arms behind his back. Someone kicked in his knees and his face was crushed into the cement. He was dragged into a deserted alley where, expecting the worst, he heard a familiar voice.

"Mr. Rose." A woman stepped out from the shadows. He strained to look up at her and it took a moment for him to recognize her.

"Mayor Bunny?"

Chapter 8

Monroe—2083

Chairwoman Brandt was in her calming place watching sunlight from the windows high above sparkle through the immense freshwater aquarium in the basement of her White House. Here was her priceless collection of aquatic delicacies; freshwater marine life that were rapidly losing their natural habitat to the rising oceanic salt-water tides. While her fish swam carefree, oblivious to global climate change and unaware that their life span was dependent on her appetite, she focused on issues of state.

She turned from the soothing waters to her tall, fetching personal chef who was filleting lunch dressed in a bright orange bikini. She watched, indifferent to the wriggling protest of the pathetic dying fish while admiring the efficient brutality on display as meat was meticulously separated from bone. Once the actual cooking began, Tanya lost interest in the process and turned her attention to her luncheon companion.

"Fresh water fish are a delicacy, Ginger, dear." She pointed to the enormous tanks. "Pick one, any one, and enjoy before they become extinct and are dropped from the menu. Patrice will be pleased to cook for you."

Her chef nodded. While not as vivacious as Ginger, Patrice provided a necessary change of pace. Her face and long, lean body were unscarred and unblemished and she was gentler while her unique skill with fish added spice to their lovemaking.

But Ginger Tucker was stressed and declined to eat.

"Ginger, sweetie, relax, the time is near," Tanya said as she patted the pillow beside her. "Come, sit with me." Dutifully, Tucker adjusted her medal-adorned uniform and moved to her superior's pillow.

She put her head on the Chairwoman's shoulder and stared lovingly up at her hero. "Give me the word, my lady," Tucker said. "And your troops will end this strike and the union."

"Slow down, sweetheart," Brandt cooed. "You lack appreciation for subtler ways. Sometimes, slower can be better and the tongue doesn't always have to be a weapon." She laughed when Ginger blushed. "I don't mean that as criticism." Ginger wasn't certain. "Enjoy, taste, a brief respite from ferocious will do you good."

"Has my performance displeased you, my lady?"

"Never, but urgency isn't the only way to pleasure."

"I live to please you."

Tanya sighed. "Of course, Ginger, but I worry about you. Haste causes you to miss out. Relish more; it makes for a far tastier treat."

"My lady, food is food and appetites are appetites."

She patted her general's head. "I'm sad that you miss the joy."

"My joy is to serve you," Tucker said. "When the union is defeated and Gil Rose is dead, I'll have time for other things."

"Soon, Ginger, soon," the Chairwoman promised. "Patience. They fear *Us* so much that what strength they have, they dare not show except in slow, boring stages. Victory will be like tasting Patrice's feast, taking pleasure in each course, one taste at a time, allowing the tongue to prolong the joy, luxuriating in it fully before swallowing, exposing each nuance and subtlety completely before anticipating the next."

Patrice signaled that the meal was ready and placed a steaming fish filet on Tanya's plate. She then broke off a small piece, put it in her mouth, and kissed her leader full on the lips, transferring the fish and flavor between them. Tanya chewed and then smiled running her tongue across her teeth before nipping playfully at her chef's neck, drawing blood.

"Excellent, Patrice," Brandt said. "Thank you. You are excused. *We* have things to discuss with Ginger."

With that Patrice left the room.

Tanya took another bite and savored it before washing it down with a fine, lemon-custard Chardonnay from her south-central Alaskan vineyards. Satisfied that the food and wine complemented each other, she continued the conversation.

"The time isn't right, my sweet. Soon, you'll have the most delectable feast." She picked up another morsel with her fingers, put it in her mouth, and then put her fingers to Ginger's lips for her to lick. As she licked, Ginger stared into her leader's eyes and purred.

"Ginger, dear, it's tempting, almost too tempting, but the time isn't right, not quite yet." The purring ceased. "This is *Our* recipe. *We've* blended marvelous ingredients into what will become a magnificent stew and now is the time for joyous anticipation as *We* watch it simmer."

"Not too long," Ginger whined.

"No, not too long. But this is delicate work and *We* mustn't be heavy-handed. Pluck lightly, but even then, not until the time is right. Pluck so that victory will be all the more satisfying." She offered the word, *pluck,* like kisses to her subordinate. "Easy wins provide less joy so *We* wait. And only when *We're* certain of what we have do *We* pluck. Disloyalty needs patience and nurturing so *We* can see what it becomes."

"As you wish, my lady," Tucker said. "But I am frustrated by the waiting. Until Diaz and his union are gone, Rose is executed for treason, and his balls are safe and secure in my souvenir collection jar, as promised, I won't be satisfied. Those balls are mine today for the taking. Please, allow me to 'pluck' them."

Tanya laughed as her Reverend-General made *pluck* sound vulgar.

Though her leader was adamant about her strategy, Tucker sought more. "You sent him to Bree so you must suspect her." Tanya remained unfathomable so Ginger continued. "Before she ran away, she was undisciplined and it was possible, but now . . . she wouldn't dare."

Tanya remained silent.

"She's changed since her return. She never liked me, no matter how hard I tried to please her but I have never discovered anything linking her to the rebels. She still doesn't like me, but she knows her future is with you."

Tanya stopped Tucker's musings. "Be open to events, my sweet," Brandt explained. "Bree is as smitten with Rose as he is in love with her. *We* won't allow it, not ever, and that is within *Our* purview. *We* never blamed you. You deserve praise. Bree understands *Our* world better now because of your devoted labor to instruct her. *We* did what *We* could but, Morgan knows, she needed to learn strength and discipline from you. She ran away and returned changed, both hardened and softened. That is Rose's doing even though she insists he is just a friend. The softness can be corrected once *We* see where her true loyalty lies."

"Then it will be my time?"

"Yes, my sweet. When she returns with her assessment, *We'll* know then and it will be your time."

"I can have them then?"

"Not her," the Chairwoman corrected. "She is not for you, not anymore, it's not your fault, but you can have him when I'm done with him."

Tucker pouted. "Men don't last long with you."

Tanya laughed. "You are such a flatterer. Soon, you will have him, soon, I promise, but for now, patience." Brandt saw the hurt on Ginger's face and leaned in to lick her ear, and with her tongue she traced her favorite long, red scar down to Ginger's chin. A shiver rewarded her and she, in turn, took a tender nip at the softness of Tucker's earlobe, the vacant stare of lust in the Reverend General's eyes exciting her even more.

"*We* spoil you because I love you. You will have him, but not quite yet. I will have your plan. Present it to me . . . tomorrow."

On hearing that, a smile crossed the General's lips. "It will be done, my Lady. You may cut me if you want."

The Chairwoman shook her head. "No, not today. Patience, sweetie."

"Is there anything more?"

Before Tanya could respond, her eyes glazed over and an urgent communiqué distracted her. When the communiqué ended, she smiled and reached out to rub her General's full breasts as she beamed with joy.

"Ginger, dearest, great news, it will be very, very soon. Now help me, sweetness, I'm tense. Show me what you've learned today. Show patience and be gentle, but not too patient or too gentle."

"As you command."

Chapter 9

Sacramento, CA—2083

Bree was about to leave the train for her dinner engagement but she was concerned. Gil had not yet reported back and the clones were pestering her for an update. She had none to offer and to make matters worse, she was long overdue updating Mother, and delay would not sit well with her. But Bree had to leave knowing that departing this way, with everything still up in the air would create a messy day of clean up tomorrow.

Damn him for being . . . Gil, she thought.

It was very late when Gil returned to the train. Stressed by his ordeal at Holarki and confused by his conversation with Bunny, he sat alone in Bree's private car and allowed his weary mind to replay the day's events. Finally, unable to draw any conclusions, he retired to his cabin. There was one thing certain and that pressed on his mind as he waited restlessly for Bree to return. He had run out of safe choices.

He must have dozed because he woke with a start. Concerned that he'd missed her; that she had returned and was asleep and he wouldn't talk to her until morning, he checked her cabin. She hadn't returned, so drowsy but fearing he would miss her, he pulled a couch to block Bree's door and was soon fast asleep.

She found him there before the first light of dawn. "This can't be good," she said, as she nudged him awake. He peeled his eyes open, looked up blinking, and thought he was dreaming. She was hovering above in a short, tight lavender, nano-mini-dress that was cut open to the navel and accentuated her taut stomach and tantalizing cleavage. The dress fit like skin while somehow not quite revealing enough. Disoriented, Gil rolled to his side and blinked his exhaustion away while searching for words.

"It's almost morning," he murmured. "Are you just getting back?"

"I'm sorry it was a family dinner."

"You dress like that for family?"

She laughed. "What can I say, we go to nice places."

He lifted his arm, lazily, until it rested on the coach pillow, his fingers touching the outside of her thigh just below her dress. Ever so briefly he considered moving it away but decided, as did she, to allow it to stay.

"You look, geez, I guess terrific doesn't quite do you justice. Why that dress?"

Her smile faded and she hesitated before answering. "My fiancé was there."

"Your what?" It felt like he was being sucked down a hole. He stood, wobbly, but he was definitely awake now.

"Tim Morgan," she explained. "He's the great-great grand son of our Chief Spiritual Officer. It's not saying much but he's the nicest member of that family. Not as rich, though and definitely not as religious. We're scheduled to become partners in a few months. I needed to clarify some things."

"I didn't know," Gil stammered. "You never said . . . I thought you were . . ."

"Available?"

"Actually, yes."

"I assumed you knew. I should have said something. This is Mother's doing. She has her heart set on this partnership. Her logistics and publicity people are turning the occasion into the global media event of the millennia. I'm not exaggerating when I say the Sun King of France would be jealous." She laughed nervously. "Come on, the media's been covering it for months. You must have known."

Gil shook his head. "Nope. I guess the news never got to Cochabamba and I just got back. Besides I don't read gossip rags. Who does? I hope it works out for you."

"There's little chance. The only reason I considered it was for the benefits."

"That's not very romantic," Gil said and added, curiously, "What benefits?"

"It doesn't matter. It was never romantic and it turns out the benefits aren't so great, either."

"Please don't change your mind on my account."

"Don't flatter yourself."

"I'm sorry. I forgot who I was talking to."

"Remind me, again," Bree snapped. "Who are you talking to?"

"The heir to the throne of the United States of America."

"Is that how you think of me?"

"You made it clear that's who you are."

"So you wouldn't be pleased if I called off the partnership?"

"We both know you wouldn't change your mind because of me."

She nodded. "Fine, but how would you feel if I did decide to end it?"

He was confused. "I'm okay with whatever you decide."

She pushed past him and he fell back onto the couch as she stormed into her room. He followed, stopping when she turned angrily to him.

"I don't understand you. You're a nice guy, which is really, really unusual, but you have no idea what you care about. As long as I've known you, you've distanced yourself from wherever your heart seems to want to go. What is it with you?"

Her outburst surprised him. "You made it very clear in Profit . . ."

"That was forever ago," she said. "We were teens, then. I'm not that person. I've changed. Apparently, you haven't."

This wasn't how this was supposed to go. He desperately needed her on his side, but she seemed to want, or not want something different. That it was what he wanted, he wasn't prepared to consider.

"Gil, you give lack of commitment a face and a bad name."

"That's unfair. I have a great deal on my mind and a lot concerns your mother."

She put her hands on her hips, exposing even more of her breasts and thighs as her dress separated and rode up. His eyes refocused on the newly exposed flesh.

Embarrassed, she slugged his chest hard and his eyes jerked away from the tempting sight of newly exposed skin, only to have the misfortune of getting caught in the enraged stare of those now dangerous violet eyes. He blushed, disappointed with his behavior, and put his hands up in self-defense. She was so angry her eyes glistened with tears.

"Damn it. Is this a survival technique or is there something else I don't know about?"

"I don't understand."

"You shield yourself from everything. I miss my old roommate. Where's my fake partner, the passionate guy I lived with in Profit. I miss him, terribly, I really do. Yes, Mother's a problem, but right now, she isn't the most important problem."

"You remember me as being passionate?"

"God, you're impossible."

He should have put more thought into what he did next, but something slipped past his defenses and he reached out. She accepted his arms in an embrace and then she kissed him and he returned it until ever so slowly tension drained and his passion grew.

But then he pulled back. "I'm sorry. After Profit and then your mother and now . . . I . . . I . . ." This close, her eyes were large, profound pools of compelling violet and he had discovered the missing yellow and red. Everything that he needed to discuss with her faded from memory and something unfortunate slipped out. "I love you," he whispered.

She smiled, embraced him again, and bit his lip tenderly while squeezing him tight. "Was that so hard, big fellow? Thank you. Let's not make this about fear."

He nodded and they kissed again.

This time she broke from the embrace and stepped back. "Okay, why were you stalking me?" He gave her a questioning look. "You were sleeping at my door. What happened?"

Dread returned as quickly as it had departed. "I have to be real careful," he said. "I can't make any mistakes."

"See, that's it, exactly. I don't understand. Of course you can make mistakes; everyone makes them. But if you're going to make them, make them for the right reason." She was right. He kissed her again, luxuriating in her eyes.

"Bree, can I trust you? I mean really trust you?"

She kissed him again. "What part of I love you don't you understand?"

"Are you saying that you love me, too?"

She nodded.

Relieved, they sat on the couch while he told her of his earlier meetings. When he finished, she was confounded, but more, she was deeply concerned and even angry.

"Your aunt? And Bunny? What you said couldn't possibly have happened."

"Bunny assured me that the other mayors believe your mother is selling them out to *Global Solar*. It's not open rebellion; they don't have the power. All they want is a fair deal but your mother is far too powerful to negotiate with so the mayors are keeping what few options they have open until they see what happens with the strike and the land deal. Can Bunny be trusted?"

Bree pulled back, her eyes blinking rapidly. "Why didn't you tell me this, you know, before . . . ? Do you understand the position you've just put me in? I mean, what do you want me to do? Are you asking me to keep knowledge of a coup from Mother, or tell her and prepare for a civil war that could screw up my project and everything?"

"I don't know. I need you to help me make sense of it."

"Really? And now that you and Diaz are best buddies and you've been reunited with this aunt of yours who was sentenced to death for treason, you want what exactly? You don't want to complete this Mission, is that it? Tell me. Be honest with me. What is it? Are the big leagues too much pressure for you now? Tell me your plan and if it doesn't include completing my project successfully, you didn't think it through. If you do anything other than meet requirements, Mother will know and she's the best in the world at knowing. I can tell you one thing for certain. Tomorrow morning, when this train returns to the Capital, thanks to you, it'll be carrying two former missionary consultants soon to be executed for treason."

"She wouldn't," Gil began. "She's your mother and besides, you . . . you love me."

"What does that . . . ? I don't know how to respond. Everything is irrelevant now."

"What was I to do?"

"I don't know, Gil, certainly not this."

"I'm sorry, I'm new to intrigue. You can't unknow what I just told you so we need to think this through. There has to be a way."

"Does Bunny know you're telling me everything?"

"I don't think so. Even if she did, that isn't the most important thing."

"You mean your meeting with Diaz. Put that out of your head. Strike or no, the union is gone; dead, caput, nothing can save it—you know that. And if you want to try to save them . . . don't."

"Hear me out." She tried to push him away but he held her arms and made her listen. "You have to listen to them. You won't understand until you do."

"Listen to whom? If you mean Diaz and your aunt, you're crazy. I already understand all that I'm required to understand, and crucial, are you kidding, crucial to what, to whom? We have everything we need. God, you were away from me for what, half a day? How did you screw things up so royally in that time? Did they brainwash? This can't be your considered judgment. Where's your head? I can't believe you're even asking me to help. You tell me that you love me, and then what; your brain turns to mush? Worse, you've suddenly become rash and even suicidal. There's no way I can see Diaz. How can I? The law expressly forbids Project Managers from meeting with anyone directly affected by their mission and assuming I was to go, as the Chairwoman's daughter, I would be at great risk. I could be killed or kidnapped and held for ransom or my visit could be seen as an endorsement of every lunatic fringe rebel group in the country. You can't ask me and I can't go."

"You're worried about your mother," Gil stated.

"Are you insane?" She shouted and then quieted and stepped closer, the veins in her neck bulging. "You're god damn right I'm scared of Mother. I told you our history and I was only playing back then—but so was she.

"If I were to go—which I won't—what happens there won't matter because I'm dead—you, too. If Mother hears about this, and hell, she hears about everything, she'll send Tucker to crush the union in like an hour and us along with it. I'm sorry. I've been with that Bitch when she's had it in for me, and no thank you, never again.

"And there's no way in hell I'll set myself against Mother. I've been there, too, and I won't do it again. I can't. I can't . . ." She was almost in tears.

He tried to hug her but she pushed him away.

"You think what I'm asking is impossible but I need you to listen to Diaz. What we're doing here is wrong and I have to do something but there is no one I trust to discuss it with but you. I know what this means to you but you don't understand it all. All I'm asking is that you listen. It isn't treason to listen, and Rey has assured me you will be safe. He promised."

"Oh great, he fucking promised. That changes everything. God, tell me you didn't clear this with Diaz. Gil, I was frustrated as hell with you in Profit, but I'd trade my worst five days there to be out of here."

"But I love you and I would never do anything to hurt you. You know me and you know that. Tell your brothers and sister there's been some breakthrough in the negotiation that needs your special attention."

"That won't sell. They don't believe in negotiations. Victory doesn't require it."

"Well . . . we'll tell them Diaz is willing to make major concessions but he wants to clear it with you first. No one will believe you're turning against your mother because you're not and you won't, so you're safe. It'll be okay. I promise. Just listen, that's all. Once you understand, I . . . we . . . maybe there are ways of making this project more profitable. We can do this."

"Are you on *Pharma*? Mother might accept improved profitability in general, but not in this case and not with the union surviving. She will never allow that. She's not looking for alternatives. In fact, alternatives piss her off even more. She gets angry at people who think they can outthink her. Besides, she's not someone to manage and she acts badly when she's surprised, which isn't often. Stop trying so hard. It's . . . it's not . . ." she paused, searching for words. Then she took a deep breath. "I knew that damn messiah crap was going to screw this up. It is this messiah crap, isn't it?"

"No."

"You answered way too quickly. It is. Tell me the truth."

"No, Bree, it isn't, not really."

"Not really? We're adults and you're playing a dangerous game with no experience and no chance of winning. Why take on Mother for some hopeless crusade?"

"I don't want to take her on. I know I don't have a chance. But there's more to it, and maybe there's another way to make this right."

She balled her fists as if to hit him. "Make what right? There is no right. Get that through your thick skull. There is only Mother's way and nothing else. There are no other ways. She wants the union gone. It's gone. Maybe, with this being your first domestic assignment, she'll cut you some slack. Hell, no she won't. Stop this insanity right now so you and I can figure out how to make this go away. We'll tell her . . . we can't tell her everything or we'll be confessing to conspiracy to commit treason but we need to nip this in the bud. One thing is certain, we're not continuing down this line. It's insane, it's suicidal and I won't be a part of it.

"How can I explain this? You don't understand. To Mother, life is a simple zero sum game—she wins, everyone else loses." Bree paused and then looked at him warily. "You're not in this with Bunny, are you? Tell me the Mayors aren't offering to save the union in return for setting me up to become a hostage to help their negotiations?"

"Where did you come up with that? I'd never do that to you, or anyone." He reached out for her but she slapped his hand away.

"HOMESEC is nearby," she said. "If I wasn't cloaking, you'd be dead now."

"You're cloaking?"

She shrugged. "Mother doesn't keep her damn bargains either. And it's a good thing for you that I am cloaking. Once Mother gets Bunny, we're next."

It was Gil's turn to be suspicious. "Was Bunny my test? Did you and mother expect me to rally to her to help the union? If that's it, maybe you haven't changed so much."

She slapped him and he staggered back. "That's just insulting," she seethed. "For Morgan's sake, stop trying to figure out plots. It's not in you. Let me do the thinking. When I came back here, I was hoping you and I could work out our feelings or something. Ten minutes ago, my worst fear was explaining us to Mother, which I thought I could do after successfully completing my project. There's no chance of any of that now that you've told me how you spent your day."

"Work what out?"

Embarrassed, she hesitated. "You and me, a real partnership. You once saved my life and you helped me to become a person that I kind of like. I will never forget that, but with what you just unleashed, I'm sorry, you and I can't happen, not ever. In fact, you shouldn't even return with me on the train."

"You wanted to be my partner, my real partner?"

"You wanted it too, didn't you?"

He nodded.

"Well snap out of it," she said. "You should have considered that before all of this. Oh, Gil, why did you have to fall for all that union crap? They're jerking you around because they're desperate and they need allies anywhere they can find them. And Bunny is just a small town mayor, not a power player. All she's looking for is a bigger cut, that's what mayors do.

"God, you're so naïve. You don't belong here. You're not like anyone else. You can't play this game. Even the least nasty people we have in our service can chew you up and spit you out. I can no longer protect you.

We were so close, so close, you and I. Why did this have to happen now?" She paused and he waited.

"I'll tell Mother that Diaz kidnapped you and when the train heads back, we'll pick a spot so you can jump off and escape to Canada. No, that won't work, the guards, no, you have to go now, run like hell and I'll distract the guards. When I get back, I'll . . ."

"I can't do that," Gil said, interrupting her seemingly random idea. "I ran once and that got me nowhere. I can't run again."

"And now you want to be noble. You're bad timing is classic. Cut it out. I'll come up with something; I'll blame the union or someone. Mother is going to take them out anyway so this way she can say she's rescuing a kidnapped missionary. It won't work but it could give you some time. Run. Leave North America, the *Unincorporated Lands* won't be safe, and Canada isn't far enough. You'll have to go to someplace like Bhutan or maybe central Africa and I can't see you again, ever, and don't try to contact me. I know people in Indonesia. You can hide there but not for long. Mother has missionaries everywhere. You'll have to keep moving."

"I'm not running, Bree," he said. "Something has to be done; I just don't know what, that's why I need you. Please, come with me to Holarki and when we return, if you tell me to run, I will. I promise. But talk to them. You're smart. You'll find a way."

"Aren't you listening?" she said. "I can't, it's against the law."

"Once you see them, you'll understand why the law doesn't apply."

"God, I want to scream. The law always applies."

"I'm going back to see them," he said. "It would help if you were there."

"Don't do this," Bree said in her best command voice. Then she relented and more softly, she offered, "Okay, we'll try to figure a way out of this together, but if we can't, before the train leaves tomorrow morning, you have to be gone and don't tell me where. You weren't sent here by chance. Mother is planning something, something that we will never figure out. We have tonight to work on an approach. Our only chance is to go to her with something she'd never anticipate."

Gil laughed, wryly. "The only thing she wouldn't expect is the truth."

She stared at him and then slugged him hard on his shoulder.

"That's it. The truth, that's what we'll do. We'll throw in a little naiveté and give her an honest assessment of what occurred today. We'll hide behind the truth, brilliant."

Now Gil was confused. "I don't understand."

"We have the remainder of the night to work up an assessment based on the realities that we know and Mother doesn't. The mayors came to you through Bunny because they want assurances from the *Global Solar* deal and the union has facilities that the *Global* people may want."

"Diaz could use extra money to relocate his people, maybe to the *Unincorporated Lands*." Gil was getting excited about the possibilities.

"No, no, no. Forget saving the Union and think about saving yourself—and me. There's one thing, if Mother asks whether I knew of the mayor's revolt, there's no answer that saves my life or yours."

"We're not rebelling and I don't care about what happens to the mayors. I just want to find a way for the union to survive, if there is one. Please help me, Bree."

"We can't save the union. Oh, Gil, this is so much more than a 'please' thing."

He embraced her. "Please *and* I love you."

She shrugged against him. "We'll see how far love gets us but I'm afraid we're both about to learn just how unforgiving Mother is."

Chapter 10

Washington D.C.—2083

They spent the night brainstorming and they were hours from leaving Sacramento. Bree still hadn't delivered an update to her mother or to the Project Steering Committee and the result of their effort was a few promising approaches but they had no real plan for their meeting later that day with the Chairwoman, nothing that might convince her to allow them to live, let alone save Diaz's union.

Bree was staring out of the window, bleary-eyed, while he was reviewing an angle that she had rejected hours ago. "Gil, I'm exhausted. We've done enough for now, I can't think anymore. Let's get some sleep and we can finish this up on the ride back."

"Do you think we have time? We barely have an idea as to what we'll present. Give me another fifteen minutes."

"I'm bushed. I'm going to bed. Don't wake me up until we're out of California, I need some rest or I won't be able to face Mother."

With that, she stood, kissed him passionately and then slowly made her way to her cabin. Briefly, he considered following her in but she looked so tired that he just watched as she closed the door.

Once he had all the files named correctly and filed logically, he stretched and went to his cabin to crash as well.

He awoke to the train lurching forward. Tired, he reset his alarm and fell back to sleep. When he awoke again, the train had entered Nevada. He freshened up and then went to Bree's cabin. Her door was open but she wasn't inside. Frantically, he searched the train but when he tried the exits, he found them locked from the outside.

The bullet train pulled into Union Station as the yellow-red lip of the real sun was setting over the Potomac basin, bringing and end to the day. Alone and depressed, Gil just stared out of the window, resigned to a fate he so clearly deserved, his heart aching with despair for Bree.

As soon as the train stopped and the door opened, a heavily armed HOMESEC detail arrived to escort him to the White House. On the way, he imagined the many pathetic ways this meeting with the Chairwoman might go, and he feared each scenario equally.

He cleared security and was taken to the aquarium in the basement of the White House. When he entered the vast underground complex, he shielded his eyes from the sun's red tinged reflection through the tanks and stared in amazement at the immensity of the aquarium facility. His wonder was cut short by a baton shot to his back. He screamed and moved forward until, finally, through one tank, he saw the shimmering image of the Chairwoman and his legs almost buckled at the sight.

The Chairwoman smiled as he approached and waited until he was forced to his knees in front of her before dismissing the guards. She took a bite of her meal, reached for the sleeve of his business jacket and wiped her lips and hands on it. She seemed to revel in his fear.

When she spoke, he was expecting anything but the sadness in her voice. "When Andy disappeared all those years ago, it finally gave me the opportunity that I had worked so hard for all of my life. Since that moment, everything has gone as I intended so if I'm a bit testy, dear, when confronted with setbacks or delays, please understand and be patient with me."

"Yes, Madam, you have a very difficult job."

"Oh shut up," she interrupted. "Gilbert, you've been a bad boy."

"Excuse me, Madam Chairwoman?"

"You are to listen." She spoke slowly, one syllable at a time like she was speaking with a child. "Say nothing, absolutely nothing until I request something from you. Is that clear?"

He nodded and she returned to her normal speech pattern.

"So that it affects your next response, you need to know that Bree has been taken into custody."

That caused Gil to flinch.

"Yes, be very worried. As long as you do precisely as I say, no visible harm will come to her. Do you understand? You may say yes."

"But—"

"Not but. You may say yes."

"Yes, but . . ."

"No, no, no buts. Another 'but' from you and my darling daughter's life will be in great jeopardy. *We* had high expectations that Bree would be a good influence on you but alas, she has failed in that too."

"But . . ."

"Again with your buts? The Chairwoman chided. "*We* are talking and what *We* say is far more important than any of your babbling 'buts.' The Sacramento project needs no amending. There are no points in the specifications that need whacking off. Nor are there economics that need your special diddling. Your input was requested in precisely one area and that was clearly defined when you were assigned. Meeting or exceeding *expectations* is the only path to survival for a Missionary Consultant and extracurricular activity is a surefire way to hell, if you understand *Our* meaning. You were assigned to make happen what *We* say will happen, nothing more and certainly nothing less. It was not your job to redefine requirements and so you have failed and failed miserably. To compound that crime, by trying to develop additional scope in *Our* project, you have called into question *Our* perfect person and the possibility that *We* are capable of imperfect or incomplete thought. That is a treasonable offense, the very same treason Mayor Wua was executed for earlier today. And attempting to influence *Us* through the person of my daughter is a treasonable offense as well. Am I making my point?"

How did she know? "Madam, I beg you, don't be angry with Bree. It isn't her fault. I was the one who met with Mayor Wua and Rey Diaz."

"Bullshit!" the Chairwoman shouted. "A lie is best delivered from the mouth of those who understand its purpose. You are clearly inept at it so stop wasting time. What *We* want from you is precisely what *We* say *We* want. No more and certainly no less.

"Project Manager Brandt's punishment, though severe, will not be terminal—yet. She is my beloved and only daughter. If you straighten up and avoid all of the extracurricular, *Our* love for her will willingly overrule a just sentence of death and that is now your purpose in life. You must assure *Us* that you have the self-control to do as *We* bid or the sentence of death will be carried out and you will watch her die."

"You wouldn't do that. You couldn't," Gil said, "not to your daughter."

"Guards!" she screamed.

When her eyes glazed over, Gil panicked. "Madam Chairwoman," he begged. When she didn't react, he shouted, "Please don't. I'll meet your requirements. I'll do precisely what you ask, no more and no less. I beg you, don't . . . don't kill her. I . . . I'm sorry, please . . ."

A smile slithered across her face and it grew so impressive that briefly, in spite of what had just transpired, he felt pleased that he had pleased her. She spoke in a gentle, comforting voice.

"I understand, Gilbert, I do. You're young, new to *Our* order, and still susceptible to the guile of devious people like Diaz and Wua. It is shameful what they did to you. The proper staffing of projects is a very delicate art and this assignment was simply too much, too soon. In the excitement, you forgot the basics. You got too close and got burned. *We're* disappointed, certainly, but it is forgivable and can be rectified. Have no fear, your career is intact."

"Thank you, Madam. But please," Gil pleaded. "It wasn't Bree's fault. I convinced her . . ."

Her smile wavered and became worrisome. "La-la-la," she interrupted. "The magnificence of *Our* free market society is that it allows you to do whatever you believe is in your own best interest, but those actions come with direct and often immediate consequences—that's how freedom works, Gilbert, my dear sweet thing. Sacramento is important to *Us* and it will be completed exactly as it was approved. The only change will be in project management."

"But Madam . . ."

"But, but, but," Brandt mocked. "If you say 'but' once more, *We* will have yours in ways you will not like and will long remember. Now where were *We*? Yes, my daughter is passionate and headstrong. It's an issue that *We've* dealt with less successfully than others. She is weaker than she seems but that too is curable. She needs more . . . seasoning, as do you, Gilbert, as do you. From this moment onward, it will be your behavior that will determine just how severe my daughter's seasoning must be. And *We* know just the Reverend General to perform that seasoning. Are *We* clear?"

He nodded.

"Are we clear?"

He nodded again. "Yes, Madam, you are clear. I understand."

"Your behavior and my daughter's future are now causal. As long as you behave so that *We* develop confidence in you, her seasoning will be delayed. As to you, Gilbert dear, *We* have concerns about your performance certainly, but as I said, that is resolvable. Unlike my darling daughter, you have extraordinary potential and once-in-a-lifetime talent and *We* don't lose talent easily."

"Thank you. Potential is a great burden."

"Shut up. We are not amused."

"I'm sorry."

"Or don't shut up," she said, teasing him like a cat with a trapped mouse. "How much do you care that my daughter lives?"

Like the Chairwoman's transcendent violet eyes, her dazzling smile was disorienting. Each revealed so little, yet their malice spoke silent volumes. She changed moods so quickly, effortlessly, and completely, and yet her eyes and her smile remained alluring.

"Madam, I—"

"Shut up, God of Morgan you are a persistent nuisance. It runs in your family. There are," she continued, "situations like Sacramento throughout the country and soon the world, and *We* have a critical shortage of young entrepreneurs like yourself to address them. It is essential that *We* continue to invest in the good ones, even if they fail *Us* along the way. Sacramento is important and though you failed there, *We* consider it an inadequacy in your training and Bree's management."

"Madam Chairwoman," Gil said. "I take full responsibility . . ."

"Of course, dear. *We* aren't playing games here. Everyone takes full responsibility for everything they do. It's blame that you want to avoid. The list of missionaries who begged *Us* for the great opportunity in Sacramento would fill a memory disk and their attempts to win that assignment came excitedly close to satisfying me but instead, *We* selected you. It created such disappointment but *We* felt that you and *Our* project would gain most from the pairing. Synergy is a beautiful thing. What are you now, Gilbert, thirty-three?"

He nodded.

"What a shame. You are quite handsome enough and not so much like your grandfather, which is fortunate, though at your age he also exhibited certain stud-like qualities. Still, I've come to prefer my liaisons younger, more agile, less conflicted, and more ambitious so you are not to be one. However, when you rid *Us* of this union I may reconsider. I am supple that way.

"But first you must do precisely as *We* say. Do that and *We* promise you that you will become the hottest commodity in a land of hot commodities and *We* will see to it that the gossip media picks up on you.

Give *Us* victory in Sacramento and you will do whatever you wish with whomever you like—except for my daughter—she is not for you. You will accept this because there is great value in pleasing *Us*." She paused to gauge his reaction, "or displease *Us* and you and she will be terminated in an instant. But you and her, no, that doesn't please me, no, not at all. That way is closed, forever. You may speak."

He had no choice but to respond with confidence, knowing if he responded in any other way, he, Bree and the entire populace of Holarki would die. "Yes, Madam, I agree. I see great value in meeting your requirements."

"It's good that you see the rightness of things, Gilbert, darling." She walked behind him and put her hands on his shoulders. It was the first time she'd ever touched him and he tried not to react as she gently messaged his neck muscles.

"You are stronger than you appear," she leaned into him, close enough for a kiss. He leaned away as far as he could without angering her. "Good, resistance is intoxicating foreplay." She glided in front of him, her hands still on his neck. She was so close now and he noticed a subtle shift in her eyes. Were they warming? Was this passion? But seeing Bree's eyes in her mother was frightening, too and he had to force himself to appear as if he was enjoying it as she humped her body against his while working her fingers deep into his neck and shoulder muscles.

"Ooh, you are the devil. I never considered you in this way and I so love hard. Look at me, I am wet. You are making me long for your success. We should do this. A well conceived sacrifice is a great investment in the future and I know sacrifice. I lost my parents and my younger sister during the great re-engineering that followed the fall of the First Republic." Her eyes glistened and she stopped the seduction. "The poor dears, they were safe, or so I thought, but there was an administrative fuck up and poof, they were gone. Forever gone for in those days, mistakes weren't correctable. My parents were old and we weren't close so it was no biggie, but my beautiful sister Brianna, her life was taken from me in one hurtful moment." She snapped her fingers. "Like that, gone."

"I am sorry for your loss, Madam."

She stepped away and her eyes hardened. "You will learn that pain is to be valued. It makes you strong. The union, Diaz, they are nothing. If they go, poof, it affects nothing. But if they survive, deals perish that will cause immense pain and suffering. Surely, you see this. *We* need you.

But to be of further use to *Us*, your Morgan faith needs strengthening. New York is what you need. You will go there to find salvation. There, your religious zeal will be appraised and fine-tuned by none other than His Holiness Chief Spiritual Officer Thomas Morgan. And once *Our* spiritual leader recertifies you, you will return to Sacramento to assume project management responsibilities. You see, it is for you to end this union and complete *Our* project on time and under budget, and to achieve the value proposition as stated. Isn't that true, Gilbert?"

Defeated, Gil nodded.

"Sweet, sweet Gilbert, your life and that of my daughter depend on your faith, fervor, fidelity, and ultimately your success in Sacramento." She stopped and turned away, continuing to speak with her back to him. "Survive, excel, and prosper. It is that easy. Go . . . go now."

"But . . ." before he could continue, she left.

The armed guards returned and marched him from the basement aquarium to a small windowless cell in an adjacent building where he remained in isolation for so long that he lost track of time.

And then a Morgan acolyte came for him.

Chapter 11

New York, New York—2083

Confidential Memo **Confidential Memo**

To: *President of the United States, Andrew Crelli* *January 1, 2036*

Subject: *The Heaven on Earth Project*

From: *Gecko*

As we approach your second term as President, we have a great deal of success to build on. Our population downsizing is having the desired effect on the economy which has turned the corner now that taxes have been reduced to a minimum.

A smaller country solves two problems. Obviously, purging the inefficient eliminates a perpetual and significant drag while simultaneously mitigating the deleterious affects of Global Climate Change.

And now that the Entrepreneur Party is successfully entrenched in Washington and throughout the State capitals, it is time for a grand initiative to lock our victory in place and build the foundation for forever.

Background: *Americans have always been highly susceptible to the call of religion. They flat out love religion and America's dynamic pluralism has created a significant religious economy that competes for consumers as aggressively as businesses compete in the commercial economy.*

In this spiritual free market, religious organizations promote their products and services to targeted segments of the population with great returns. The intensive marketing results in spiritual product specialization that allows consumers to distinguish the one delivery system that is best suited to them—one to remain steadfast to—or one to switch to if dissatisfied.

Much like a jewelry store selling gems, religious groups sell beliefs and ideas that influence the spiritual consumer to choose their product as having the best of all perceived value. The most successful go-to-market strategies to attract followers offer security and comfort or morality and fear.

As consumers, Americans are notorious for their attention deficit. To take advantage of that, another important feature of successful religious marketing is offering religious revivalism. Over time, established religions become clichéd and devotion declines followed by even greater declines in profits. The most adept marketers are attuned to this and adapt by spawning a virtuous cycle of smaller and less worldly faith sub-groups that manifest increased intensity among followers. This unwelcome competition with established religions is facilitated by the Constitutional prohibition on theological favoritism.

The trend in the world today is toward State religions which historically inhibited economic growth. With Capitalism dominant, State religion is not seen as an impediment to economics, in fact, in some countries it has facilitated greater growth as demonstrated by Sharia law in many progressive Islamic countries. Turkey and Iran, as examples, are among the great economic powers in the world today thanks to the foresight of its Mullahs and exciting new devotional products.

Recommendation: *To more fully reenergize the American economy and sustain growth so that we can reach our goals, the American people must have a new Christianity-based Capitalist religion. Much like feeble past attempts like Protestant Ethics, the Prosperity Gospel, and the Mormon Church, religion can drive people to new economic heights.*

Additionally, religion offers great wealth opportunities that private secular corporation shareholders have been cut out of for millennia. We have already eliminated most income and capital gains taxes so America's incorporated churches no longer receive unique commercial advantages. I estimate that the deeply integrated God-industry is worth some 1.2 trillion dollars per annum. The time has come.

Liturgy: *During the past three hundred years, the glory of Capitalism has surpassed that of Christianity, necessitating a merger of theologies. Great* *thinkers such as Adam Smith, John Locke and Friedrich Hayek, great writers like William Buckley and Ayn Rand, great media personalities like Glen Beck and Rush Limbaugh, and great economic theologists like Jerry Falwell and Reverend Cavanaugh have prepared the way by instilling the rudiments of Capitalist theology in every American thus creating an incredibly loyal, blind faith following among the masses. This is an untapped commercial opportunity.*

The Goal: *Since the time of Jesus, Christianity has morphed with society's needs. From the Gospels to the Nicene Creed to the Protestant Reformation to the Counter Reformation to the Evangelicals who sell the word of God in their Prosperity Gospel, Americans willingly pay to pray for their spiritual well-being, most never receiving value, perceived or other wise. There can be no more profitable consumer base than Christians.*

Within the hour, I will submit a budget that funds the start-up of a new religion, a great and glorious Capitalist Religion, a worthy successor to Mormon, the Protestant Ethic and Prosperity Gospel of Christianity. This religion will be thoroughly integrated into everyday work life creating an immense, faith—based consumer population from which stockholders will benefit. There will be no Constitutional boundary issues because there are no impediments to spirituality within private corporations.

Christian Naming Convention: *In preliminary discussions, Treasury Secretary Thomas Morgan has been exceedingly enthusiastic and helpful. Because of his natural and high level of financial spirituality and because of his commitment to this project, I recommend that we name this new religion in his honor. I submit that we call it, Morgan.*

Confidential Memo **Confidential Memo**

When the acolyte entered Gil's cell, he was grateful to see anyone after his long stay in solitary. Her name was Gwen and she wore an official dollar-green Morgan Seminary business suit accessorized with a silver and gold bracelet, earrings, and a necklace each with Almighty Dollar icons dangling imbedded with diamonds, emeralds, and rubies. Gil's first thought was that for lowly seminarians to be so rich as to afford such jewelry, how much richer were Morgans higher up? That's when it finally dawned on him how grand his lifestyle must have looked to others.

Gwen handed Gil a pill and instructed him to swallow it so they could track him should he try to disable his PID and escape. He thought that curious but he swallowed it anyway. He was escorted back to Union Station by a platoon of Seminarians all comparably attired in money green and each well-armed. He and the acolyte boarded a train, leaving the escorts behind, and the train headed north and east to New York City. The car that he was in was nothing like the *Entrepreneur Express* that had taken Bree and him to Sacramento. This was just a simple Morgan commuter train with its murals filling the space around the windows with scenes showing the various holy stages of American economic development from Jesus to Chairwoman Brandt but other than that, the train was just windows and a series of benches, all empty.

Gwen directed Gil to sit in the last row across from the door. When the train silently left the station, he tried to start a conversation but when she didn't respond, he had no choice but to stare through the windows at the passing scenery. Just north of Washington, the track elevated to allow the train to traverse the great salt bogs, the view he would have north, all the way along the New Jersey coast. After crossing the great port city of Hammonton, he first noticed ripples, the remnants of waves, as they seeped past the high reeds below. Further north, he was fascinated by real waves breaking against the trestles, causing the train to vibrate slightly before they dissipated into the vast New Jersey swamp.

Near Newark, the train veered sharply inland to avoid the perpetually flooded tunnels and then it turned east again toward New York on a precariously high, long, and narrow bridge that swayed with the waves. The train crossed money-colored open water and on the horizon, he viewed a vast complex of New York skyscrapers interconnected in intricate patterns of glass and steel at various levels like a web some gigantic inorganic spider might have spun. Here was Manhattan.

The train passed over a massive dike that spread before him like the Great Wall of China holding back the great salt bays from claiming more real estate. Finally, the train stopped on an elevated platform where a sign read:

Battery Park Station and Water Park.

The platform was chaos. He'd never seen so many people. When the door opened, a deafening roar followed the wind inside. Gwen motioned for Gil to exit, but daunted by the crowds, he hesitated at the door.

It seemed as if everyone on the planet had arrived on this platform at the same time and they were all fighting to make space and in a hurry to be somewhere else. Some, the more industrious, were spraying from small cans what must have been noxious fumes because the spray caused the hordes to part so that they could make their way through.

Gwen hadn't spoken since they boarded the train. It was as if she'd taken a vow of silence. In the din, Gwen was forced to scream her instructions but the clamor made her words indistinguishable so she took his arm and together they worked their way across the platform. They were constantly jostled and he was separated from her briefly, but the freedom was short-lived as she grabbed his arm and pulled him close.

"Don't get lost again," she shouted in his ear. "If you do, it will be far worse for you than for me. If you can't see me, that pill will make you wish you could."

He understood and held on to her arm tight as they inched their way by human eddies of clustering sycophants surrounding myriad prophets in varied colors and garb standing on impromptu podia, screaming their beliefs at the willing, imploring their enraptured to unlikely feats in the name of some impending doom for some all powerful Lord.

Just them, four very large, well-armed men appeared. They wore dark green robes and round Kevlar helmets with the Almighty Dollar icon etched in dots above both ear holes with a number of short parallel golden bars above, designating their place in the Morgan hierarchy. The men formed a phalanx, one on each side, and forced their way through the massed, self-absorbed that were straining to move or not move.

They arrived with their escort at street level in a vast, marble terminal where there were even larger crowds and substantially greater chaos. On the walls high above, immense monitors offered the latest stock prices and other financial information to assist the harried investor. As the group pressed on, Gil was startled by the intermittent screams, cheers, and boos that formed an odd, syncopated consensus among those most affected by the ever changing financial positions displayed above.

When they reached a quieter place, he shouted to Gwen. "What's going on? I never saw so many people. You could die in here and no one would notice."

She smiled and brushed straight, auburn hair from her eyes, uncorking striking hazel eyes as she shouted back. "It's been known to happen. New Yorkers are the most evolved citizens in the world because money means more to them than life itself. We call them our Right Wing lunatic fringe; it's kind of a joke. To their way of thinking, without money, you can't afford time, so why live," she explained.

"Who are they?"

"Most of the ones who are booing or weeping are homeless. They're speculators who won't waste funds on liabilities like homes so they invest and micromanage their positions here, where they sleep, when they sleep. These extremely God-inspired ultra devout Morgans take enormous risks. It's a perilous existence and the best of them are held in awe for if they hit it big here, they can begin to live the American Dream, more wealth than you need to count. The others here are the insider traders. These people are the ones who figure out how to produce multiples on the cost of information, not on equity or commodity appreciation. We're talking high stakes, pure, unfiltered, and unrefined Capitalism here; Capitalism the way the Lord desires it, Vulture Capitalism, rapacious as God intends. Gwen's hazel eyes were alive and her face was flushed.

"Most of the people here are desperate to earn their way out and most die trying."

With that, Gwen motioned to her guards and then instructed Gil to keep walking. They reached a quieter outer hall and Gwen continued to explain about New York.

We have guards because when the crowds see our Morgan raiment and the Almighty Dollar they sometimes go crazy. Morgan has this great aphorism, 'Be mindful of the irresolute who invest for the short term and instant gratification. There is profit to be made from them.' God, I love New York. It's so . . . visceral."

As they followed the guards, Gwen pointed to various screens high above. "That screen shows the volatile Singularity index. It attracts the most attention among the desperate and financially disqualified. The Singularity index monitors speculation on *Pharma* research reputed to lengthen life spans." She pointed to another screen. There's a market you'll find really interesting. Remember those prophets on the train platform?"

He nodded.

"If you like a prophet's prospectus, you can invest in their theology, if not their future. The screen tracks, country-by-country and sect-by-sect, all political and social movements and provides the shrewd investor, rebel or Tory, with the option to go long or sell each dogma short, depending whether they believe the revolution will succeed or fail.

"The Morgan Church possesses best-in-class industrial surveillance technology so take notice of the crawl banner at the bottom of that screen. It informs investors of upcoming political or economic milestones in various rebel outposts that could influence a rebellion positively or negatively as calculated in a complex formula involving the target-nation's currency against the weighted value of the dollar and the Renminbi. I studied the math in class last year and this year I've made my clothing budget betting on a few rebellions that have come through."

Having received his training in the Consulting Division of the Church, not the Financial Division, Gil found this information fascinating.

Gwen continued. "My Missionary specialty is in Financial Liturgy and I've just completed a term paper for my Political Theologies class on the Comparative Financial Performance of 21st century Christians in America vs. Secular Humanists."

Gil nodded, politely.

"For a fee, the Morgan Church provides *Conducers* with a priest-analyst who can help them evaluate the financial potential of a particular revolution based on inside information about those with the time, inclination, and wealth enough to alter the economy of nations. That's real high roller stuff and I wish I could afford an analyst.

"It is a beautiful thing to see the Lord's hand in our Free Markets." She paused to genuflect, making the sign of the Almighty dollar, starting at her left breast and forming an "S" down to her waist, her index finger then moving directly to her forehead and as she looked to the heavens, she lifted her hand high above her head, with her index finger pointing to the Great Market Maker in the sky to complete the act.

When Gil didn't genuflect in response, she nodded knowingly and changed the subject. "I'm still just a pre-junior at the Morgan Seminary and I've not taken Aberrant Political Economics yet. I was told you are an expert in that field."

"Not really. Math was never my strong suit. I'm a consensus builder, actually."

She gave him a sour look, shook her head and began to walk to the exit.

"Gwen, this is all interesting but I assure you, I have no interest in revolution."

She was disappointed. "You can't dun a girl for trying. If you had confessed, there was a bonus in it for me."

"Sorry. When are we expected at Headquarters?"

"If you're asking me when your trial begins, I'm not certain. You're not due until tomorrow morning. My assignment is to drop you at Congressman Hegel's suite at the Forever Gardens where you'll stay overnight. The Congressman lives across from the Morgan Cathedral, Seminary, Stock Exchange and Gift Shop, that's where trials are held. He will escort you to your audience with His Eminence at nine tomorrow morning."

"Did you say Hegel?"

"Yes, Congressman Hegel. The Congressman lives in the most exotic apartment complex in God's kingdom and though it is rent controlled, it is Godly expensive." The acolyte paused before continuing. "His building, so you know, is also escape proof."

"I don't want to escape."

They finally reached the street where a dilapidated, green beater of an automobile awaited. The armed guards remained outside as they entered, Gil sitting in the rear, Gwen up front. Unlike the exterior, the interior of the limo was plush.

The car pulled into little traffic, though the sidewalks and the crosswalks were crowded. Some people were moving purposely toward their destination, shoving others aside while some were just standing aimless, allowing themselves to be pushed around or even trampled. A few of the aimless carried signs and as the limo drove by, Gil read some of them.

I want to live forever, but first I want to make it through today.

New York, New York, if you don't make it here, you don't make it.

All I can afford to eat are the rich.

Money: Can't live without it, Will die for it.

A Starving Man is a Dangerous Beast!

The limo crawled on through the crowds. At one street corner, a large group was listening raptly to a man in flowing gold-striped, brown robes standing on a crate. Curious, Gil rolled down his window to listen. Immediately, he was confronted with a deafening clamor, but then, the searing, cloying reek of human decay reached him and his lungs rebelled. He hacked out the pungent, elemental stench, gagging as he rubbed the burn from his eyes, searching frantically for the switch to close the window. The annoyed acolyte and the angry driver screamed at him as the window closed. He blinked hard until his eyes cleared and then he returned to staring out, this time through a closed window.

"And keep that fucking thing closed," the driver shouted as the limo drove on, passing still more of the filthily clad carrying signs announcing the end of days or the beginning of something new and wonderful as they wandered the sidewalks of New York searching for followers.

"Who are they?" Gil asked the driver.

"Most are ground floor, defeatist Christians who stubbornly refuse Morgan," the driver explained. "More likely, these assholes couldn't qualify financially so without a future of their own, they choose to earn their daily bread by predicting the failure of Capitalism and selling our great country short. They're hypocrites because all they're trying to do is acquire enough capital for a really big score. Once they're out of poor souls to hoodwink, they'll wander the streets enduring the end of their existence, knowing they were on the wrong side of history."

Gwen added to the driver's explanation. "The Morgan call to forever eliminates the best features of their tired old religious brands, so the only thing left for these losers is to work their con while awaiting death. It proves that God truly has a sense of humor. They preach grace just when the world has finally, and forever, debunked faith and the myth of heaven."

That caused Gil to think of Rey Diaz and his circuitous come-to-Jesus story.

"It's easy to understand why they can't make it," Gwen added. "They don't understand their customer."

"Well, it's a shame that they have to live this way," Gil sympathized.

"No it isn't," Gwen rebutted. "If they were smart, or desperate enough, they'd see the true God, the God of Morgan, and they would become serious capitalists. They're just not that smart or motivated. They use the meager funds they collect out there to inflame desperate *Wasters* to rob, burgle, extort, prostitute, and pimp all perfectly acceptable free market activities, they just don't do it well. For one of these movements to thrive, the leaders must search out mezzanine financing in order to expand their religious brand into more sustainable black market businesses that promise sustainable growth. If that goes well, there's always a public offering to enrich them further. As to the rest, who cares if God doesn't? They'll be dead soon enough."

When the limo turned and headed toward the Financial District, staccato bursts of bright sunlight flickered through the glass sunroof distracting Gil, causing him shield his eyes. He looked up. Above, slicing at the sun's rays was a vast and intricate web of skyways connecting every skyscraper at various levels.

Gwen offered a suggestion. "When we leave the limo, don't look up. Needy locals will know you're a tourist, and they will find a way to redistribute your wealth."

"Just so you know if you're ever offered a mission here, real estate value is determined by three things: location, location, and location. That means north or south, east or west, and subway or skyway'. It's generally forbidden for residents from different building levels to interact, except at work. This creates a dynamic caste system that works really well in New York, Philly, and other large cities. That's why the skyways only connect at certain levels.

"The parking garages and ground floors are for *Wasters* and other pests because it's easier for HOMESEC to control and exterminate the vermin. Low worth *Conducers* live on the next higher floors with lower-end supervisors and management people on the middle floors. General Managers reside on the totally protected, totally safe upper floors, with the top floors reserved for *Executives*, *Entrepreneurs*, and senior government officials and even that's stratified. Penthouses are reserved for true market makers."

Gil was appreciating the information, but he was curious about something. "On the train, you were silent but since you've been really talkative."

"I'm an intern in a Morgan Sect that believes commuter trains are sanctuaries. During commutes, our sect communes with financial spirits in preparation for a prosperous day of commercial activity. We pray to the Lord of Morgan for guidance so that we can recognize the best deals and we pray for the wisdom and courage to negotiate the best to our advantage. To my Sect, silence on commuter trains is truly golden."

Just then, ahead Gil noticed an angry mob throwing debris at oncoming traffic. Gwen yelled to alert the driver who swerved down a narrow alley to avoid a collision. The alley was home to various nightclubs. Fascinated, Gil stared at the brightly lit marquees that advertised performances by diverse performers, artists, and even financially-gifted prophets. One marquee in particular caught his eye.

"Stop the car!" he shouted. Instinctively, the driver obeyed and Gil was out before Gwen or the driver could stop him. He bounded down the steps of a nightclub just as a wave of nausea and severe stomach cramps brought him to his knees. With his head pressed against the filthy concrete steps and his fists pressed deep into his belly to ease the pain, he vomited uncontrollably, his eyes tearing, his throat burning. It felt like an eternity before he felt Gwen's hand on his shoulder and the pain eased. He tried to roll over and sit up but he was too weak.

"I warned you," she said. "You can't escape. Come back to the limo now. Stand up slowly and use me for support and we'll work our way slowly back. You'll feel better once we start driving again."

Though trembling and sweating, he begged her. "Please, I'm not trying to escape." He pointed to the marquee. "I know her, the performer. It's Dyllon Tomas, she's a singer-friend of mine and she's performing here. I want to say hello, that's all."

"You're not allowed."

"Please. She helped me when I was younger and I owe her so much."

"Oh, you're indebted to her. That's a different thing." He was surprised that she agreed. She handed him a small vile of some pink fluid which he swallowed. Then, with her help, he wobbled into the darkened club.

The bar was just opening and there were no customers. In the back, various professional *Pharma* pushers were loading vending carts with inventory in anticipation of a crowd and on one wall, a series of *Virtuoso* booths stood empty. He asked a pusher where he could find Dyllon

Tomas and he was directed to a small table by the stage where a dark haired woman sat alone, her back to him.

Serpentine tendrils of *Pharma* smoke floated above her head slowly rising to the ceiling, the color changing as it drifted through red, yellow, and blue stage light beams. He tapped the singer on the shoulder, hoping to surprise her, but when she turned, it was he who was surprised. This Dyllon wasn't the Dyllon he knew.

"Get away from me, creep, what the hell do you want?" she barked.

"I'm sorry; I thought you were someone else."

"I don't give a shit. Get away from me you paparazzi asswipe." Though the words were mean, she seemed more bored than angry. "God Morgan, I hate crashers. You assholes won't make any money on me and I won't make any on you so let's not waste each other's time. Read the goddamn rules and get the hell out of here, or you're a dead man. I'm packing, this is the City, and I'm well within my rights. You saw the sign." She pointed to the front door. "*Wasters* aren't allowed inside, even for a money-making opportunity. I'll shoot you dead and not give it another thought so leave me alone."

Gwen put her hand on Gil's shoulder and tried to draw him away.

He persisted. "This is my first time in New York," he explained to the singer. "I was friends with a Dyllon Tomas from another town."

This Dyllon put her hand inside her vest, as if reaching for a weapon to threaten him with. "Dyllons don't do friends, not *Wasters*, anyway. What town?"

"Hamilton," he said.

She leaned as far away from him as she could. "Not that one." Hurriedly, she gathered up her *Pharma* paraphernalia and stood to leave.

"Do you know her?"

"Get out of my space, asshole," she said. "If you know her, leave the rest of us Dyllons alone. Reputation means everything in our business and that bitch cost us, cost us big time. She was nothing but a tone-deaf imitator anyway, a valueless slut who disregarded her fiduciary responsibilities and tried to take the Dyllon Tomas brand down. We all feel the same." She stepped away from him but seemed to get even angrier.

"That whore-bitch crossed the line and all the innocent Dyllon's, we're paying for it. It's because of her that our fan base evaporated overnight, over goddamn night! I was a star. I had it all. Now we're all playing horseshit venues like this dive. Do you have any idea how long it takes to build a brand and attract loyal, paying fans after you've lost them?"

He shook his head.

"Or how hard it is to get folks in the habit of spending their hard earned money that first time on you and then convincing them to keep on spending? That's what being a capitalist is and of course you don't know, you simple shit. That bitch from Hamilton, she knew and she screwed us good, anyway." With that, Dyllon slapped him hard on his cheek and walked away. Before entering her dressing room door, she turned back.

"You're all cretins." She shouted. "You paparazzi *Wasters* are all the same. You steal our likenesses, doctor them up and sell them to the highest bidder or you take them home and make mad love to them. For you, there's always someone to drain assets from. You're ungrateful, blood suckers, every last one of you. Go away and stop living vicariously through us because you have nothing of your own to sing about." She paused and then she smiled.

"That's it, that's what you people are. You stumble through your miserable fucking life, mute and accepting, and we're nothing to you but intensely persuasive, private, petty poets whose only purpose is to articulate vapid thoughts that sustain you through your worthless existence."

She nodded and smiled at that before pulling out a communicator. After repeating her last rant verbatim into it, she looked back at Gil. "Hey, thanks," she said. "When I get really, really mad, that's when I write my moneymakers. These words and a rented tune, the Dyllon brand is on its way back, we're going triple platinum, first day. Now get the hell out of here you loser." With that, she stepped into her dressing room and slammed the door.

"She's a friend?" Gwen asked as she pulled out another pill for him to swallow.

Morose after the incident with Dyllon Tomas, Gil sat quietly in the back of the limo as it forced its way through the crowded streets. He stared out at the mobs overflowing the sidewalks, jamming in tight on the smaller side streets when a young black woman dressed in a yellow, flowered sari stepped in front of their limo holding an electronic sign that flashed her message in bright red letters in two second intervals.

"Keep your window closed," the driver cautioned as he tried to maneuver around the girl and steer the limo through a gathering mob. As they passed her, Gil read her pleas that flashed in English and Spanish, one line at a time:

Wealth without Work
Pleasure without Conscience
Knowledge without Character
Business without Morality
Science without Humanity
Religion without Sacrifice
Politics without Principle
These are the Roots ofViolence in our World

—M. Gandhi.

As he read, the girl moved closer until she was walking beside the limo and staring in at him. Briefly, their eyes met and she smiled an innocent, kind smile. Ignoring the driver's warning, he opened the window. The girl's smile widened and her free arm reached out for him.

"No!" Gwen screamed. There was a loud crack followed by an acrid smell and suddenly the girl's smile froze. A look of surprise painted her face and then her eyes glazed over. Incredulous, Gil watched as the sign dropped from her grasp and crashed to the pavement, the message lost forever. The girl brought a trembling hand to her mouth and blew him a kiss. Then she fell against the limo and as she slowly slid toward the ground, she spoke to him. It was barely a whisper but he heard it clearly.

"Be the change you want to see in the world," and then she died and fell to the ground. The limo moved on and the window closed, her body disappearing behind the darkened glass, replaced by a reflection of his horrified face staring back at him. Aghast, he turned to the driver who was holstering his firearm.

"You shot her!" Gil screamed. "You . . . What did you do that for? You killed her."

"Be quiet," the driver yelled back. "You're a tourist; you don't know shit and now I have to file a damn report with the home office." He took out his communicator and started to enter information. When the driver finished, he turned to Gil.

"You caused this. It's on you. I told you not to open the damn window."

Gil couldn't think of anything to say.

Gwen supported the driver. "You really should have listened." She said and without waiting for his reply, she waved for the driver to move on, leaving the corpse and the sign in the street for someone else to take.

As *Wasters* scurried away to avoid being run over by the now-angry limo driver, Gil sat in the back seat, once again chastened but now appalled.

"How was I to know?" he asked finally, his voice barely audible over the hum of the car motor. "Why . . . why kill her?"

Gwen stared at him as if he'd asked a stupid question. "People don't kill people," she said. "Guns, cars, bombs, chemicals, even *Pharma*, or just flat out being lazy, stupid, or unproductive, that's what kills people. You were warned not to open your window. The responsibility, if there really is any, it's on you. If you are still a viable citizen, within twenty-four hours you will be notified about the amount of the fine."

"What? That's crazy. She wasn't . . . she didn't . . . I didn't." He paused to gather himself. "She didn't deserve to die."

"It's called littering. You're new here," Gwen explained. "In New York, anyone who dies deserves to die. The law is clear on that point. We're in a Morgan limo; we have the right of way. She was a *Waster* and you saw the filth she was spewing on that sign. Case closed—except for court fees and clean-up, if any. Maybe you'll get lucky and the street will strip her to the bone and save you the clean-up. It's happened, this is New York. From now until we get where you're going, you will keep the window shut—and there will be no more stops."

Troubled, he remained silent. A short time later, the limo came to a stop at an immense, windowless, white concrete building with a vast solid gold front door. Inlayed above the door was an enormous, luminous Almighty Dollar, the golden dollar sign nested in a flowing silver and green lemniscate, like the wings of an angel. Intense light reflected off its shiny surface making it almost too bright to stare at.

The driver stepped out of the limo and walked around to open the door for Gwen and then for Gil. Once they were outside, Gwen spoke.

"Welcome to the Morgan Cathedral and Stock Exchange and of course, the international headquarters of God and Morgan, LLC. Across the street are the Financial Gardens where Congressman Hegel resides. Remember the pill you swallowed. I have set the Gardens as your new home base and it will remain so until you enter the Cathedral tomorrow. You remember how you felt earlier so please don't flee."

Gil nodded.

As they crossed the street to the Financial Gardens, he noticed that at the far end of the deserted street, there was a mammoth, ornately-decorated dike that had been built to hold back the salt water of the Hoboken, The Bronx, and Manhattan Bays. Then, he stared above. People were scurrying through all of the enclosed and interconnected glass skyways toward the Cathedral or the Stock Exchange to invest and to pray.

Gwen escorted him into the Financial Gardens whose impregnable nano-doors recognized them as they approached and shifted to transparent, melting away to allow them to pass through. Once inside the grand lobby, Gil stared up at artificial clouds high above. Not quite hidden within the clouds, weapon barrels protruded from camouflaged turrets. As they walked, the guns tracked them.

Noticing where Gil was looking, Gwen explained. "They're functional, but mostly they're for show."

"How would anyone suspicious ever get through those doors?"

"God is always testing our resolve and Satan never sleeps so our world is never completely secure," She said as she led him to a nano-glass enclosed reception kiosk. Once there, she spoke out loud. "Gil Rose to see Congressman Hegel."

A string of green lights lit up on the floor, pointing the way to an elevator. He followed Gwen toward it.

"Mr. Rose, this is it. I have earned my commission so I leave you here in the best possible hands. You are an intriguing sort and possibly someday we will be assigned to the same project where we can improve our worth together."

"That would be profitable," he said, dutifully. Gwen genuflected and left.

He entered the elevator and the door closed immediately. He made his way to a seat, but before he could reach it, he heard the rush of air and the elevator lifted off, buckling his knees. The elevator continued to accelerate while he strained to finally pull himself into a seat. During the ascent, his ears clogged and he was forced to swallow continuously to clear them. Finally, there was another rush of air and he was almost launched from his seat but held on to the bar that was provided to prevent that as the elevator stopped and the door opened.

He stood, but the view from the open door caused him to back away, his hands fumbling for the back wall so he could slide back into his seat. At the edge of the elevator, the building dropped away thousands of feet to the tops of tiny buildings far below. In the distance, across the bay, New Jersey spread out all the way to a slightly curving horizon while far below and closer, thousands of black rooftops were visible as part of a vast network of interconnected buildings spread out toward the surrounding waters. He couldn't walk out, and so he sat and waited, hoping the elevator would take him back to the ground floor or provide another option.

A good amount of time passed, during which he tried ineffectively to stand but unfortunately, vertigo left his legs unresponsive. Then, to his relief, a heavy-set, bald older gentleman appeared, hovering at the elevator door.

"Gil Rose," the man said, smiling, "it's a pleasure to finally meet you. I'm Damian Hegel, Senior Congressman from New York." He seemed to take pleasure in Gil's discomfort. "High, aren't we? Forever Gardens is the latest technology. It was built with a defense system the Pentagon is jealous of and entrepreneurs from Qatar and the Arabian Oil Emirates as well as officers of defense contractor Hagiburton lease residences here and they demand the very best."

Enduring a headache brought on by the vertigo, Gil stood on wobbly legs and stretched to greet the Congressman who laughed at him.

"The first visit is always daunting, I'll admit that." Hegel smiled as Gil closed his eyes and nodded. Damian then stomped hard, his foot stopping abruptly but making no sound. "These floors support a ten thousand times my weight so you're quite safe." Hegel turned and walked casually out onto nothing, forcing Gil to follow cautiously, tapping the invisible floor outside the elevator with his toe to insure himself that he wasn't committing suicide. He began by taking baby steps onto oblivion while stifling the urge to scream and pee. Feeling resistance under his feet, he gained confidence but with the absence of visible walls, he was too terrified to extend his arms for balance. A breeze disoriented him further and so he bent his knees and crouched slightly while taking one unsteady step after another until he was floating above New York City and fighting the call to vomit.

"Congressman," he said, meekly. "I hope there's a rug somewhere close by. Either that or a bucket."

Hegel laughed. "My suite's around the corner. Focus on my back until we get there, it helps. And please call me Damian."

Lightheaded from the perspective, Gil kept his eyes riveted on Damian's bald pate and followed him so closely that he almost stepped on the Congressman's heels. When they reached his suite, Damian opened the door. Amazed by what he saw inside, Gil stepped back, looked over his shoulder at the great void below and screamed, his knees buckling as he dropped to the transparent floor.

"Take a breath, take a breath," Hegel instructed, smiling. "You're safe. Some visitors wet themselves the first time so you're doing fine."

"I hope my luggage arrived because I'm going to need a change of clothes. Gil said as he took a few deep breaths and focused on the short distance to Damian's suite. Determined, he crawled into the apartment and felt relieved when Damian shut the door.

Inside, it was amazing. He'd never seen such opulence, even in Monroe. When he had first moved into his mansion there, he'd grumbled about the decorating requirements but eventually he took Gale's advice and they decorated from tips they found in *Executive Homes and Gardens*. But here, thousands of floors above ground, the interior was so far beyond anything he'd ever seen that it took his already compromised breath away.

Nano-replicas of great art, Dutch Master paintings and Roget and Michelangelo's sculptures lined the perimeter of Damian's home, each slowly morphing from its basic raw materials through the entire creative process until becoming that unique masterwork and then cycling back again. Even the panoramic nano-glass windows were incorporated into the theme, supplying an ever-changing and detailed motif of New York City morphing from what would have been seen from this view at its founding, centuries ago, to what it is today. And those same walls allowed light and fresh air in.

Gil just stood there in awe. "Would you like to sightsee?" Damian asked.

He nodded and followed his host to a full length picture window. At Damian's instruction, he tapped his finger twice on the window and then pressed it, pointing toward a distant object, in this case a building. He then double tapped the window again.

"Whoa," he gasped as the image of a distant building rushed toward him. He felt like he was being sucked out with nothing to grab hold of but he stifled a scream this time and pushed against the window for balance then he lurched backward, embarrassed.

Damian laughed as Gil steadied himself.

He returned the laugh, nervously, and stared at the once distant building that now appeared to be within feet of him. On the window beside the image there was a listing showing the complete economic history of that building from its beginning. Soon, Gil was searching the streets around the Financial District's Holy Land. Then, he peered at the ocean and the bays and the system of dikes and levees that protected Manhattan from submersion. North, he spied a *Waster* community of caves built into piles of city trash. On some city streets, people sat unmoving for long periods. On other streets, people were fleeing, chased by official looking vehicles, while elsewhere, people chased vehicles, battering them mercilessly. In the far distance, great plumes of white and gray factory smoke rose from high rise manufacturing facilities. And across a bay, ramshackle homes dotted the hills above a harbor where yachts were anchored, protected by gleaming nanowire.

The shifting sun caused the windows to dim to block the glare.

"So, what does a Congressman do to deserve this?" Gil asked politely.

"Mostly boring and administrative stuff," Hegel explained. "Politics requires extraordinary business connections so I'm constantly busy but there are always incredible opportunities to add to my wealth."

"What kind of connections?"

"They're divulged in my annual report which you can purchase for a fee. There's a listing of my investors, how much they invested, and what they expect to gain from their investment."

"Is that why you became a Congressman?"

"For me, it was either Congress or some Joe job. The way it works is that once I invest the time and money to get nominated, I prepare position papers detailing my positions and the potential returns corporations will achieve by supporting me. Then I campaign. That means convincing businessmen in my district that my positions will be beneficial to them or, for an additional campaign donation; I alter my position to their benefit. America is a quasi-democracy so I'm required by law to post my positions and modifications on a Mesh site and keep it updated. Once I convince businessmen to support me, they buy options in my political corporation which will be converted to shares when I win. As a democracy, businessmen are free to purchase as many politicians as they can afford and I can't turn down profitable issues, no matter how reprehensible I think they are because once I turn down a profitable issue it's hard to find backing for other issues because businessmen suspect you're unwilling to play ball with them.

"Any issue that I post in my Prospectus that I can't get funded, I drop, and of course, the more lucrative ones I campaign harder for. That's all there is to democracy. All I need to get elected is to obtain the greater absolute value firm business commitments, measured in dollars, than my opponent. It can't be fairer. I received the most commitments and that's why I'm a Congressman.

"There are risks. Hell, if I lost, I would've been responsible to repay my contributors or find other ways to move their agendas forward but it's damn hard to find a lobbyist today willing to do what an elected official can because there isn't very much money available for them. Debt is the reason why politics is such an insecure career. You're elected and you're wealthy so you receive insider financial advice that allows you to build your estate and then in the next election, you lose and you're a *Waster* enduring a finite, miserable, and too short life, and die a horrible death.

Campaigning is so intense that politicians are now among the most admired and respected professionals in America today. It's not for everyone. It requires great moral and ethical flexibility."

Gil was more interested in something else. "Damian, I know what happened at Omega Station. Why would you, of all people, do this?"

Damian shrugged. "Because that life is over. Omega Station is gone, Gohmpers is gone and Arlene is . . . I don't know where she is. This is a job, a good job, my job. I get paid, and in this world you need to get paid."

"That doesn't answer my question. Bernie told me about Omega Station, Arlene you and your twin, Damon, so I know what you were fighting for. I have to ask: Why, of all things did you choose to become a politician?"

Instead of answering, Damian walked to the windows and stared out at the city. When he finally spoke, he was obviously sad or disappointed. "You can't beat them," he explained. "You shouldn't even try. They're not only evil; they're highly motivated and talented evil. To rule as effectively as they have, for as long as they have, you have to hand it to them, they are true Capitalists; they do whatever is necessary to eliminate competition."

"I understand that," Gil said. "But that wasn't you. What happened? You and your twin brother Damon were integral to the creation of Joad. You helped teach her to feel, for Morgan sake. You helped Bernie try to stop Crelli. How could you work for them?"

"It's none of your business," Damian said softly.

"What about your twin? What about Damon?" Gil asked. At this mention of Damon's name, Damian turned from the window to face Gil. He looked tormented.

"Damian is dead. He doesn't matter any longer."

"Bernie told me that you hated Crelli and Gecko as much as anyone in Omega Station and I'm sure you hate the Chairwoman, too. So please, I have to know, why are you doing this?"

"It is my responsibility to pass laws that enhance commerce so everyone gains."

"You and Damon fought them, fought their genocide; I don't understand."

Damian smiled, ruefully. "You accept Missionary wages."

"But . . ."

"I'm a Congressman and you Missionary Consultants, we swear on a Morgan bible to preserve, protect and defend the American economy—not our nation, never America unless it affects the economy. Everything I believed is dead. They killed everyone. For everything that I believed once, life is truly only about money. It has always been about money and never about America or the American people except how they affect the economy. We were wrong to oppose it."

"You can't mean that."

"I know why you're here. You've been recommended for advanced theological training and that seems like an odd way to fight injustice.

Don't chastise me for something you're doing, and obviously doing well—in spite of all that Bernie told you."

It was Gil's turn to feel uncomfortable. "No, you're right and I'm sorry. I have no right to question your motives. More than anything, I need your help. Bernie told me that you were one of the few good guys. I'm just . . . disappointed." Gil paused to stare out at the New York skyline before asking Damian the most important question. "Is there any way you could help me to avoid tomorrow? I'm scared and I need your help. Please, for Bernie's sake, help me."

"I can't. I'm a coward, you know that. And if I could, I wouldn't," Damian replied. "I survived; I'm still surviving even though . . . Damon . . . Damon . . ." He began to cry and hid his face by staring out at the city below.

"Will they kill me?" Gil asked.

"I don't think so. They're businesspeople first and they wouldn't invest time and money and then just kill you. That makes no business sense. Frankly, given your background, you must have great value to them to have lasted this long and now to be going through advanced training, why would they kill you?"

"You're wrong. I have no value. I'm sure they don't think that of me."

"Obviously you're worth more to them alive than dead or you'd be dead and we wouldn't be having this conversation. Look, it's late. I'll show you your room. Get some rest. You'll probably need it."

Damian escorted Gil to a bedroom. It was an inside room yet all the walls, the ceiling and the floor were like windows that projected panoramic views of an outside. In the center of the otherwise unfurnished room, there was a bunk bed with matching bedspreads that depicted comic scenes of heroic warriors battling vile monsters. Gil entered silently and Damian left him to retire for the evening.

He surveyed the room. Except for the bed, there was only a bookshelf full of Second Republic publications. He was too anxious about tomorrow so he stayed awake skimming some of Damian's commercial history collection. When even that wasn't enough to tire him, he turned out the lights and lay in bed, staring out at the dark New York skyline until his eyes burned. When he couldn't take it any longer, he got up and returned to the main room.

He was surprised to find Damian staring down at the magnified, lighted image of the now below sea level Statue of Liberty boxed in and protected by a tall levee that bay water occasionally lapped over. Damian didn't notice Gil until he sat across from him. It was a long time before either spoke.

"I couldn't sleep either," Damian began, sounding morose. "Finally meeting you after all this time and remembering Omega Station, Bernie and . . . and well, it brought it all back, the bombing, Damon . . . everything that makes my current life meaningless and why I need to stay busy just to survive." He shook his head. "Look, I'm sorry. Everyone at Omega Station . . . we were fools. We thought America was still, you know, America, the land of the free and the home of the brave. But the money had already won and that had changed . . . everything. We: Arlene, Bernie, *Gohmpers*, the whole lot of us, we weren't naive, we realized what money, what greed was doing to the country but we were so stupid. We simply underestimated how easily the American people would fall in love with greed, knowing that they could never be rich themselves, they fell enough in love to allow greed to . . . to take over. We were just wrong. For decades, maybe centuries, the rich and powerful had exerted so much and such constant pressure that the middle class and the poor in America ended up succumbing without a fight.

"We thought we were so smart, even Gohmpers who got most of it right, he never thought it would end so quickly, without resistance, and so easily. Maybe we were idealists or passionate grown up romantics. Back then, Damon . . . Damon and I, we thought that it might be a fair fight. Shame on us, we backed the wrong theology. Capitalism is that good and greed is that beguiling. That I can never get a night's sleep is the least I pay for that foolishness."

"You fought a good fight," Gil said.

"That's bull. We never understood. When you think you have real power, you think things and do things you would never think or do if you knew the other guy had even greater power. Crelli, Brandt, they always had so much more than we did." Damian looked down and put his head in his hands.

These musings were no help to Gil as he wrestled with his own fear so he resorted to begging. "I want to escape to Canada," Gil pleaded. "Maybe get there through New York, or Vermont, or even Maine, but I can't. They have me and I can't escape because if I try, someone I love very much will die. I need your help. If I stay, I'll be like you. I'm sorry, but I will. They will turn me like they turned you. But if I don't . . ."

Damian looked up briefly, his tormented expression remaining unchanged.

"I'm sorry. I understand about you and your twin," Gil offered.

Damian said nothing.

"Bernie once told me," Gil stammered, "he told me so much that I didn't understand or take seriously. I'm only now, and it's too late, beginning to truly understand what he meant."

Damian remained silent.

"Damian, I'm scared. Please, help me."

Damian took a deep breath and let it out slowly before answering. "You can't beat them." He shrugged. "And I'm sorry but you're on your own. I won't help you. Frankly, no one can. Hell, I have a million great reasons to get even with them for what they did, but I don't kid myself anymore. For years I harbored the desire to do something and just bided my time. I even promised Damon . . . But getting even is a dream that I don't think about anymore."

Damian looked down and cried. When he looked up, his eyes were red. "Most people, if you could convince them they had nothing to fear, they'd tell you honestly they know that this," he made a wide sweeping gesture with his arms, "this is wrong. People aren't idiots—at least some aren't, they're just cowards like me, trying to get by. Words are cheap and change doesn't come from knowing right from wrong. It comes from making the time and having the inclination to overcome wrong, even when you know the effort will kill you. Maybe it's not their fault, but for generations, Americans have been trained by the money not perform heroics or do noble things, and so they have no concept of right and wrong, it's all just value . . . wealth, and spend, spend, spend. The only hero I've ever known died at Omega Station, burned to death that night all those years ago in Indianapolis, murdered by the friendly fire of the United States Government, my current employer." His voice cracked. "And I miss him, terribly." And then he was silent.

When he spoke again, he sealed Gil's fate. "You deserve an honest answer. I'm no hero and so I won't help you. This is America and you face your fate, alone."

"Please," Gil begged. "There must be someone you know who can help. I . . . I wasted so much time. This can't be over, not tomorrow."

"You're Bernie's kin and you seem like a good person. That's a shame. If you fight, tomorrow will only hurt that much more. Or maybe tomorrow won't change anything, I don't know. I'm no one to give advice, but if they want you to live, give them your soul, it's not doing you any good and they'll take it anyway.

"I feel bad for Bernie. He and I experienced the real cost of being on the wrong side. He lost his wife and daughter, and I . . . I lost half of me, the better half. I let him down. I let Bernie down and Arlene, too. I don't know. But the worst pain was letting my Damon down. That hurts worst of all. He's dead and I'm still alive and on the track to live forever. It seems that death is too good for me. I'm to be punished for my weakness and my sentence is to have the rest of time to hate myself for who I am and for what I did. Maybe all you need to do to be a hero is survive long enough. It's my only hope."

"But I was just a stupid kid when Crelli was kidnapped," Gil argued. "I've been running my entire life, paying for that one fourteen year old moment. I'm doing the best I can but I'm lost, I'm so lost. I'm a disappointment and a failure. I know it, but I couldn't bear to sink even lower. Please, Damian, please," he begged, "you have to help me get out of here. Just get me to the street and I'll do the rest." As soon as he said it, he knew it was impossible.

"The only thing I'm willing to stand for is what most Americans stand for these days: their next paycheck." Damian stared down at the lights of the slowly submerging Statue of Liberty and then further out, into the vast ocean that lead to the coming dawn. "You're here, Gil, and you're not dead. Obviously, she's testing you and she wants you alive or you wouldn't be. Don't think ill of me because she's testing me, too, but she doesn't care whether I live or die."

"Why does she do it?"

He smiled, sadly. "The same reason a dog licks his own balls—because she can."

In spite of the situation, Gil smiled. "That's disgusting."

"Your only victory comes when you decide to stop opposing her."

Gil remembered a similar conversation with Bree. "I tried to go against her but I was pathetic," Gil explained, "and naïve. I know you're right, it was hopeless, but I tried and all I succeeded in doing was causing worse things to happen. I'm worried that something even worse will happen tomorrow but I guess I deserve it."

"Life is easier if you don't own up to your faults."

"I can't do that anymore," Gil offered.

"For me, life everlasting is the perfect penance but for your sake, I hope you never discover how much self loathing is possible." With that, Damian stood and trudged into his bedroom, the door disappearing as he went through it and reappearing again after he was inside.

Gil was alone and afraid. It wasn't only what tomorrow would bring; he was terrified that he would be like Damian Hegel someday.

Chapter 12

New York City, Trials and Tribulations, 2083

> True love cannot be found where it does not exist, nor can it be hidden where it truly does
>
> —Anonymous

Morning sunlight streamed through the ceiling and every window in the bedroom waking Gil from a troubled sleep to a troubling day. He walked to a window and peered out. The view from the highest point above New York City provided him with a glorious vista. His eyes followed the vast array of skyways that weaved the innumerable tall buildings into a complex network, if not a community. His stared at the immense levees that held back the rising waters of Manhattan Bay and kept the Financial District dry and profitable. As he surveyed this world, a chill ran down his spine. In this vast metropolis, he was alone and forsaken and today was the day that proved it. There would be no more escapes.

Clearly dispirited after the previous evening's discussion, Damian Hegel escorted him to the third floor lobby and then across a skyway to the massive golden gates of the Morgan Cathedral, Seminary, Stock Exchange and Gift Shop. They stood, self-conscious, under the church icon, the massive golden dollar sign imbedded in the green and silver wings of eternity, the Almighty Dollar.

With no help or advice to offer, Damian shrugged, turned, and left, leaving Gil to his future. He watched Damian cross back over and then he stepped forward. The great, gold doors melted away and he entered. When he turned, one last time, Damian was gone. The golden doors rematerialized, ending any thought of escape.

In the vast lobby, Gil stared as red laser beams probed every inch of floor space. His eyes followed the beams to their source, hundreds of feet above, where a large gleaming man-made cumulus cloud hovered suspended and seemingly floating in midair.

His eyes returned to the floor where a vast matrix of lights illuminated a green path that he followed to an information kiosk staffed by well-armed acolytes wearing money-green business suits with the church icon hanging from thick gold chains around their necks. After he endured a thoroughly embarrassing electronic public probing, an acolyte escorted him through another set of opulent golden doors—real this time, not nano-enhanced. The doors were inlaid with various weights of gold and silver coins. Through the doors was a dark, plush inner sanctum. From there, the lights guided him to an elevator.

He entered and sat beside a woman wearing a long shimmering gold cape over a surprisingly revealing green and silver uniform. A smaller church icon hung from a thin cord around her neck resting contentedly in her ample cleavage. She pressed a button, the door closed, and the elevator rocketed skyward with jarring acceleration. Tense and nervous about what was to come, he tried to clear his mind by staring at the elevator walls which were painted with murals of important moments in American financial theological history. There were scenes of the stock market in action, of various First Republic Presidents signing bills with market leaders present and smiling, and photos of holy relics from the dawn of Morgan.

The elevator stopped abruptly and the door opened up to another acolyte. This girl, and she was barely more than a teenager, she wore a lacy, sleeveless green and silver dress with the Church icon formed in gold thread at the *décolletage*. He couldn't help but stare.

"Mr. Rose," she smiled, "up here." Embarrassed, he met her eyes.

"Excuse me. I . . . I've never been here before," he tried to explain. "Your uniforms are . . . striking."

"As you would imagine, our Eternal Father has true fashion sense," she explained. "Though His Eminence is the oldest man to ever live, he designs our annual spring collection for young adults and teens while carrying out his great Church responsibilities. Legend has it His interest in profiting from fashion developed during His days as an angel investor to an up and coming professional sports corporation in the latter days of the First Republic and the profits from His fashion enterprise are offered, at competitive rates and with few additional fees, to fundamentalist theological business research programs around the world.

"Mr. Rose, sir, when your worship here is complete, if you wish to order any of our official garments, you can pick up a catalog on the way out at the Church store on levels two, four or seven, or you may order over the Mesh or at any convenient Church kiosk conveniently and strategically placed throughout the country."

"I don't think I'll be in a position to order," Gil said, glumly.

The acolyte ignored that and continued. "His Eminence insists that we remind everyone that while His women's clothing lines drive the market, His men's wardrobe is far more business conservative. As you pursue your business today, please notice that throughout the Church, all female acolyte interns will be modeling next year's fashion line." She smiled. "When you see them, be appreciative, you're allowed to tip, and at certain levels, a tip allows after hours access to the model-interns. For me, the clothes are one of the many great perks for working here. Now it's time to talk protocol." She pointed for him to follow her and as they walked, she explained. "You will have the distinct honor to be in the presence of our Financial Father and it is imperative that you follow the rules, precisely.

"He has bequeathed you ten minutes of his eternal time and to make effective use of that, you will respond immediately and forthrightly. You may volunteer pertinent information but be aware, this is a free country and therefore you are allowed to discuss anything, but we monitor His Eminence's vital signs and any topic that causes undo stress will immediately terminate your audience—or worse. I trust I won't have to explain what the worst is?"

"Yes, please don't."

They entered a large room with a deep and lush silver-tipped money-green carpet. The room was decorated in various shades of currency green, accented with silver and gold. In the center of the room, on a raised circular platform, was a single metal chair bolted to the floor inside a circle of bluish lights that emanated from the floor to create a circular pattern on the ceiling. The acolyte led him to the chair, buckled him in, and before leaving, cautioned him, for his own safety, to remain inside the lights at all times. As soon as she left, the room lights dimmed and the walls were bathed in ultra violet light. He sat nervously, his knees moving rapidly back and forth as he awaited his fate. He felt like he had to pee.

After a long wait, he was startled by a deep, loud, and commanding male voice.

"You are to commune with true Greatness in the form of the Trinity, our illustrious Financial Saint Thomas Morgan, a human as well as a being of Money and of God. St. Thomas meditates profoundly yet He is ever present and will bless you with his Most Hallowed certified opinions as your needs determine. Be aware that although all eternity remains to accomplish God's mission of Paradise on Earth, there is yet much for His Holiness to do, so His time is precious and His rates are necessarily high and you are but a mere trifle whose portfolio can afford little of that time." The air stirred and Gil smelled a fragrance so heavy and cloying that he labored not to heave.

The room seemed warmer and he began to sweat and then, after a while, he became disoriented. His mind was in turmoil yet he remained calm, even relaxed. Then suddenly, the lights that encircled him flashed with greater intensity and he let out an inadvertent yelp. Embarrassed, he took a deep breath, and to reduce his stress, he stared at the walls, which were adorned with blow up book covers ofThe Most Beneficent Thomas Morgan's great ecclesiastical works. He recognized the treatise, *The Origins of Economic God* and the Holy Father's fictional series of novels, *The Hallelujah Dividend* that apparently was soon to be a movie. There was also a cover of His Eminence's biography of the great Capitalist Economist, Saint Charles Darwin.

He was startled by the sound of a loud hydraulic motor. Then a large segment of the wall began to rotate revealing a circular stage on the other side. The wall spun until the stage was just outside the circle of lights that Gil was trapped inside. On the stage was an elaborate wheelchair decorated in Church colors and hovering above the chair was a large, glowing church icon. Seated in the chair, Saint Thomas Morgan looked lifeless. The hydraulics quieted and the room was silent.

Saint Morgan was nothing like what Gil had seen in pictures. This man was deathly emaciated, his skin glistening and so thin that it appeared to be painted on as bone and blood vein varnish. He was severely hunchbacked; his shoulders rested barely a foot from his knees. Clothed in an ill-fitting, old-fashioned business suit, he wore a small, gold church icon necklace imbedded with emeralds, rubies, and diamonds that rested on his distended stomach. It was difficult to determine in the light, but this ancient man seemed . . . unreal, if not a corpse. Saint Thomas Morgan was so important to the country; Gil wondered why didn't they, whoever they were, do a better job presenting him?

Leaning forward to get a better look, Gil breathed in the old man's fetid breath and quickly leaned away coughing. In pulling back, he leaned too perilously close to the lights and an intense vibration jolted him and forced him back into his chair. The vibration was so strong, Morgan's shirt rippled over his sunken chest, but nothing else on the old man moved. Shaken by the jolt, Gil stared into unblinking, rheumy, unseeing eyes that offered no discernible recognition. The only indication of life was the movement of fluid inside a thin plastic tube that protruded from His Eminence's mouth and another that exited from his pants. Gil shivered at that.

"My son, tell me what is wrong so I can help you." The voice was raspy, cracked, ancient, and strongly amplified, sounding neither real nor synthetic. And Morgan's lips hadn't moved.

"Eminence," Gil stammered, "I'm . . . I'm not sure why . . . I don't think . . . I . . ."

As soon a Gil paused, the Morgan voice seized on it. "Doubt, My Son, doubt, there is nothing wrong with doubt. What else were we put on God's earth for but to manage risk and doubt comes with the territory. But if you give doubt too much respect, or if you fear it, doubt will defeat you, of that have no doubt. Overcome doubt and you will be free; it is your greatest burden. But once you achieve glorious ecclesiastical victory over doubt, you will, most assuredly, earn your future, a future, forever, a future spent in the precise manner of your choosing, in other words, freedom, true freedom, and the kind of freedom that our rich founding fathers envisioned for every citizen of this great nation when they created our Constitution. But alas, the Devil understands and attacks those weak in faith those burdened with doubt the very same type of weak who were allowed to too liberally reinterpret our great Constitution and thus these doubters, weak in faith, they ended our great Republican experiment in its tracks.

"Doubt is the inevitable cause and cost of failure. Allow doubt to triumph and there can be no financial respect and your wealth will wither and die, as will you die, alone and forgotten. But you should doubt, yes, by all means doubt, and doubt everything, for it is unwise not to in business dealings. But defeat your doubt at every turn or you will be doomed to live a short, wretched, worthless life funded by ever devaluing assets."

"But I . . . I create value, Sir, a great deal of value. I just doubt the value I create."

There was a lag time before the response. "If you truly create value then your doubts are misplaced."

"I understand, but that doesn't help . . ."

"Stop your whining," the voice of His Eminence, St. Thomas Morgan commanded. "Just overcome your damned doubt; just do it. Faith in capitalism, faith in commerce, it is difficult and if it is not for you, then you will, as you should, die. This faith is why the rich are rich in excess and the poor are dead, unlamented. It is why faith pays for itself in multiples; why it is your best investment and your best return. You've had courses in Faith but they have not taken so you will be enrolled to take them again, but this time, you will pay a premium in time and money so that the coursework makes a better impression, so your faith becomes more . . . solid. We offer graduate discounts, but not in your case.

"But coursework alone doesn't guarantee forever. Your heart and your mind must be ready to accept that Financial Paradise is there waiting, waiting for you to fund your eternity. That is why you must remove all of the unproductive thoughts and experiences from your memories; they are hostile to your faith and must be removed from your rational mind. You will doubt them out of existence for they are Satan's missives.

"Give greed, wealth and power full and complete reign over your life and you will erase all doubt and surely you will remap your soul and reengineer your life such that commercial conquests and unconditional victories are yours forever. As you proceed toward this most glorious of goals, know it is the most important thing in your life. You must learn to treasure each and every victory over doubt because each will live in your memory as a great monument to God for which he will reward you royally. And every succeeding stage of your successful life will be yet another monument to the Lord. That is the true way, My Son. Believe. Do it and join me in Paradise perfected."

Once again, Gil breathed in Saint Thomas's moist, putrid breath, breath that somehow came from an unmoving body. The odor was so foul that it reminded him of Mayor Doris and the stench at the unassisted dying facility in Profit. And he shivered remembering a similarly vile odor in the deserted corridor of Washington's Union Station on his fateful trip to Sacramento. Against his will, he inhaled deeply in a futile attempt to clear his mind and then he responded. "I want to believe."

"My son, you possess once-in-a-generation talent and the world needs you committed to forever. You will do as I command or Gil Rose will not be Gil Rose for much longer and certainly not forever. You merely lack the inclination and what good is the time without the inclination?"

"What?" Gil stammered. Those words were so familiar.

Suddenly, the room went dark. "Hear God's perfect judgment. You were born with all of the tools you will ever need but you came late to Morgan and your training has been deficient. It is time to rectify that. It is time to offer you a glimpse of life everlasting. Forever can be remade in an evening."

The hint of a sweet, disorienting scent, not unlike burnt onions, wafted through the air. He lost his concentration and had trouble understanding the words which sounded like an almost undecipherable echo.

"Do not fail . . . fail . . . fail . . . Be what you must beee . . ."

He tried to blink the burn from his eyes as his eyelids grew heavy.

". . . time. Glory forever . . . ever . . . ever . . ."

The word 'forever' reverberated in his mind, raising a migraine from its depths. Bright lights erupted behind his eyes and he felt an excruciatingly sharp pain in his head and an ache in his neck. Nauseated, he doubled over and closed his eyes, tight. He tried to breath but a sharp pain in this chest caused his lungs to disobey and he squealed and gasped, twisting frantically trying to force some air into his lungs. Flashes of light got brighter and he knew he was blacking out but he fought it, trying to roll off his chair to somewhere safer but the bindings held. He grabbed for his throat but his hands were bound and he jerked and struggled to move in any way that would make his lungs function even one more time. A scream was building inside him and he tried to find one last breath to let it out . . .

. . . and opened his eyes. The intensely bright lights caused Gil to scream out again in pain. In the silent room, the scream echoed as if in a cavern and he curled into the fetal position, turning to the wall, away from the illumination, and he fought to squelch the rising pain of a hard charging migraine.

When the pain finally eased, he trailed off into blessed sleep. But each time he woke, the intense light and pain were waiting for him, and so sleep was his only sanctuary until he awoke to find the brightness had faded.

His throat was raw and he endured each swallow. His eyes burned but he fought the pain by covering them with his hands, staring through the spaces between his fingers to view his new surroundings in a reddish hue. He was on a cot in a small, narrow, windowless room whose walls and floor were painted white. The ceiling seemed white, too, but it was so far away that it seemed to disappear into the heavens. On one wall there was a small fireplace enclosed in a plain glass door, the only thing in the room other than him and the cot.

To alleviate the pain and then the boredom, he slept constantly. Sometimes when he stirred there was a fire in the fireplace, and sometimes there wasn't. Whenever he slept, he was haunted by terrifying, almost physical dreams, though he couldn't recall them when he woke, except that he felt anxious and exhausted. There were times when he saw, or thought he saw someone materialize in the flames in the fireplace. But that couldn't be right. He even thought he heard someone's voice as he lay disoriented, his head throbbing.

"You can no longer hide." There it was. The voice, and it was clear.

Or did he just imagine that? He searched for the source of the voice but there was none so he stared into the flames and time passed—how much he didn't know. When flames appeared they became his link to reality. He'd stare overlong at them and fall into a deep sleep, dreaming outrageous visions from which he awakened shivering, sweating, and seeking the comfort of the fire. With the fire roaring, he was calm, when it diminished and the room chilled, he was tense and depressed.

He heard the voice again and with his forearm shading his eyes against the light, once more everything unreal became real, the bright white room, the voice, and the fire in the fireplace. He stood on unsure legs and using the wall for support, he searched the tiny room for the source of the voice but like the other time (times?), there was nowhere to look so he returned to his cot, exhausted, and slept on. His back hurt, his ass hurt too, but worse, his head continued to ache and he couldn't think. The voice was more frequent now but he didn't know how or where it came from so he decided to pick a spot on the wall and fixate on it, listening in the silence for the voice. His mind soon wandered and so each time the voice spoke, he startled anew. It was like some frightening dream yet he was just warm enough and comfortable enough not to want to wake from it.

Then he dreamt of careening through a dense, burning forest and that became a reoccurring dream with flaming branches slashing at him as he looked back frantically for an unseen pursuer, a specter surely gaining on him in the distance.

Or was that a memory?

There was someone in his path so he turned, too fast, and he tumbled into a clearing, rolling to a stop, too stunned to move. It wasn't a dream. He had been here, to this place, before. He struggled to stand and soon was staggering and stumbling to escape the ever seeking specter closing behind him. He ran, tripping and stumbling until he fell headlong into a shallow pool of muddy water. When he cleared the mud from his eyes, there was a tiny space ship and then all around him, people were dying, while others were taking bets and making money.

A giant bird appeared, a phoenix with menacing red eyes, emerged from the mud with a great sucking sound and it hovered close, staring at him, beak open in some metallic-toothed grin as it floated above. He swatted at it and it turned into a million little gnats that buzzed around and he flailed to chase them away. When he made contact with the gnats, they turned into fireballs that burned his palms in yellow and red and then, like lightning strikes, they attacked the terrified people, killing them while he remained safe.

A girl was writhing on the ground. He bent to help her but found himself instead holding the remnants of a burning yellow jacket while the embers floated to ignite the woods around him and he couldn't stamp the fire out.

His heart was racing but he was on his cot now in the small, narrow, antiseptically white room. He tried to rise but nausea anchored him so all he could do was slip down to the cold, white floor, to lie there shivering while hearing but not understanding the muffled words once more.

He was certain of the source. It was the fireplace! Trembling, he leaned until his forehead touched the warm glass. The warmth soothed his migraine and so he stared into the tantalizing flames and relaxed.

There it was again, a whisper, and he knew that he was wrong, the voice hadn't come from the fireplace but from the fire itself and it was speaking to him.

Frightened, he crab-walked away in panic and huddled across from the fire, staring at it warily. In the fireplace glass, staring back at him was the image of a deranged man and in concert with the image, he screamed.

"Catharsis . . . iss . . . iss."

The fog slowly cleared from his mind and then he heard it again, "Catharsis?" The voice was deep and clear now.

"What did you say?" he asked. His own voice sounded unfamiliar.

"Has this been cathartic enough for you?"

"How . . . how would I know?" His head ached and forming thoughts was as difficult as speaking them.

"Ever the skeptic I see. Conversing with fire isn't convincing enough for you?"

"What?"

"Skepticism, it is the first merit badge in the support system of the disaffected. There is a very old Hebraic myth that the God of Abraham spoke through the fire of a burning bush. As a Jew, I thought, you would appreciate that."

He was confused. "I'm not Jewish."

"Technically, that's correct," the voice explained. "Your mother wasn't Jewish and of course, you don't look Jewish."

"Is this . . . Is this a test?"

"Why do you persist on believing that life is a test, a precursor to something more? Life is life, that's all."

Gil breathed in a vinegary smell and shivered. "Are you God?"

"If you're referring to the one who created everything from scratch, no, I'm not that. I had hoped, but climate is too hard, it teaches humility. Now, the Morgan God, the one that infuses the world with economic possibilities, I could be that god, particularly for the chipped. What do you believe?"

"I don't know . . . I don't know . . ."

"Given your current situation, that's a reasonable position to take."

"What . . . ? Who are you?"

The fire crackled. "I am what I am. Some call me Gecko."

It was the only thing that made sense. "Crelli's Gecko?"

"Once, maybe. No longer."

"Are you Brandt's?"

"Why else would I be here? Or you for that matter?"

"What will happen to me?"

"Don't put that on me. There are clear choices to be made. Given that you know the choices, I find it perplexing that you haven't chosen."

He didn't respond.

"Tell me, why haven't you chosen?"

"Chosen what? What do you want from me?"

"In a world of delusions what I want from you is not nearly the right question. Life is precious. No? Treat it with respect and ask the question that needs answering. Ask the question that keeps you from your truth."

"You're confusing me," Gil admitted. "What do you want? Tell me and I'll do it."

"I know the correct answer, but I'm perceptive that way. You clearly are not."

"If you're trying to break me, you're wasting your time. I know nothing."

"And yet you hold great secrets, even from yourself. Admit everything and everything else will be easier."

"But I don't know anything. And who will it be easier on?"

"Well that's an interesting point. For now, let's say everyone but I reserve the right to change my mind."

"You're Gecko, you know everything. What secrets can't you know?"

There was laughter. "Good for you. A question I can't answer."

"What do you want with me?"

"That's hardly relevant now that everything depends on who you will be."

He stared into the conversing fire and he understood. He was insane. "If I were to confess to revolution, anything I say that's true will cause that revolution to fail and I wouldn't want that. But if I say I don't believe in revolution, you won't believe me, so why bother to ask?"

"Yes, that's quite a conundrum you and I have to deal with."

Abruptly, the fire faded and its absence made him sad. The room rapidly cooled and filled with the scent of flowers.

He scanned the street uneasily. *Why was he here?* Oddly, he felt relieved to have made it this far. *But where was he?* Advancing stealthily in the shadows, he reached a street corner. He was so close now that he could feel the excitement but this was no time for carelessness. Suddenly, familiar terrain brought a joyful rush. He wanted to run but he knew there was great risk here so he snuck through the gate and into the garden. He was home! It was a lifetime ago but he was finally in his real and only home. He felt warm, he felt safe.

He'd been a boy here. *How would Howard react after all these years? Would Howard accept him or be angry, hurt or disappointed?* There was only one way to find out. He sprinted past the vibrant, multi-colored landscaping and leapt onto a small masonry wall. He landed and froze, staring at the tops of the Dionysus plants that he'd helped Howard nurture toward promotion—a promotion he had apparently yet to earn.

He walked through the garden, inspecting each row of plants that he had once tended. If anything, they were more robust now with more diverse colors than he remembered and they were larger, they were immense and growing larger as he watched. When he reached the first row, he knelt to read a plaque.

> In recognition of his hard work, dedication and determination, the Executives of Avalon do hereby award this plaque to **Howard Rose**, first runner up in the annual Aeden Homeowner's Landscape Evaluation. Continue your noble and patriotic efforts and someday you will earn the promotion you are so very close to deserving.

Gil smiled, ruefully. After all these years, Howard was still trying and they were still lying. He walked to the door and waited as it announced him. A young teenage boy bounded down the steps screaming, "Daddy, a Gilbert Rose is here to see you."

"*Daddy?*" Gil thought, and he shivered.

"I'm not expecting him, Henri," a familiar voice shouted. "Ask him his business."

The boy opened the door but on seeing Gil, he froze. Gil wanted to say something to calm the boy but he couldn't speak. He was staring at a young teenager who looked exactly like him when he was fourteen.

The boy found his voice first and screamed in fear. "Howard, it's . . . it's him, it's really him this time!" With that, the boy scowled and raced to a couch, diving onto it and covering himself with pillows. Before Gil could act, his father, Howard appeared.

It was a stunning moment. He never considered how much Howard would have aged. Old now, thin and with a paunch, but with a full head of unruly brown hair, he looked more like old Mark than old Bernie. Howard held the door tightly closed and stared warily at Gil.

"Do they know you're here?" Howard whispered.

Gil fought tears and a sharp pain in his throat as he pushed the door open to embrace Howard. It was an awkward clinch, as they always had been and he was sad to feel relieved when Howard disengaged.

"It's good to see you, Howard. How have you been?"

Instead of answering, Howard backed away and sat with the boy on the couch, gathering him close. Finally, Howard looked up at Gil and responded. "Did you see our plaque? Second place, my best yet. If I had won, would you have visited me on the hill?"

"Of course."

Howard cocked his head as if doubting that was true. "It's been twenty years." Before Gil could explain or apologize, Howard continued. "You're a man who doesn't need me anymore. Henri is my son now." The boy looked up slyly and smiled, then pressed his face into Howard's chest. "Unlike you, Henri loves me."

That hurt.

"He and I share so much. We partner in *Virtuoso* adventures all the time. Do you remember when I purchased our first *Virtuoso* unit?"

Gil nodded.

"You took to it right away." Howard said, smiling at the memory but it seemed a sad smile. "You played so much I thought you'd starve. If I hadn't brought food you would have. You were always happiest in your own fantasies and you never wanted to share your play time with me like Henri does."

"I was young, Howard, I'm sorry."

"You were Henri's age."

"Who is he?" Gil asked. He had to know.

Howard hugged the boy close. "He's my son, of course." Secure in the embrace, Henri offered Gil a victory smile. "You left and I was lonely. I'm a Rose and Roses are doomed to be disappointed by those who love us. It's a family thing, people forever preoccupied with everything but me, but I never expected you to be like that. When you left me, I was sad.

"It took me by surprise. As a boy, you rarely ventured outside of our garden, but when you left, you left for good. Every day, I expected you to return but you didn't and that broke my heart. I tried to find you but Archive lists you as a fugitive and a terrorist and the government refused to help me. Was it me? How does someone go undetected from a son to a terrorist? I don't even know what that means and I never had the worth to find out more so I accepted it; my son was a teenage terrorist, a wanted boy. I directed my avatar to check obituaries and I prayed you weren't listed but over the years . . . I had no choice but to move on with my career so I sold your things, except those Henri might want. What else could I do? They were depreciating and booking the devaluation was very stressful to our, I mean my estate. I had no one to ask for advice. I have no friends and no family, of course. I mean, how long should I have waited, waited for someone who didn't want to come home? In their special way, every family member has hurt and disappointed me. There was only you but then you left and that hurt worst of all. You continued the family tradition.

"I won second runner-up, you saw the plaque, and I used the stipend to petition my employer for permission to clone. I'd done it before."

"But Howard, I'm not a clone. I am your real son, the true son of your love for my mother, Henrietta. I'm not some artificial creation, some familiar."

"It makes no difference. Henri is my son, now." Howard hugged the boy close.

"Howard, please, I never wanted to hurt you. I'm sorry. I should have done something, but . . ." He considered the pain he'd inflicted. "I'm glad everything has worked out for you."

"It did, didn't it? Morgan tells us to persevere through difficult choices."

"So you're a Morgan now?"

"It's a small price to pay for having a son who stays. That's something worth living for. I have my career and I have my Henri so I'm . . . content."

He wanted to be happy for Howard but he was too sad to feel joy. "What are you doing now?"

"I still work my Dionysus bushes. They're my ticket to a better life."

He wanted to cry. "Don't be mad at me. There was nothing I could do . . ."

"Oh, I understand completely. It's my fault, really. I was a poor father so I deserved to be left alone. But I learned and I'm a better father, now, isn't that right, Henri?" The boy kissed Howard's neck and hugged him tight. "I'm sorry I wasn't good enough for you, but Henri seems to love me in spite of my failings. Isn't that what love is and what families should do?" Howard hugged his new son and cried.

As always, the right words failed him. "If . . . if only . . ." Gil stuttered.

Henri chose his tactic well, adding to Gil's sadness. "I love you, daddy," the teen said. "Can't you make this hurtful man go away?"

He persisted. "Howard, you were a good father and I never wanted to leave . . . I just couldn't stay."

"You did what you did. Hey, did you see my new Dionysius petals? Henri and I keep working and I'll get that promotion, soon, you'll see. You'll be proud of me and someday, Henri and I will live on the Hill like true entrepreneurs. Say, do you have a partner yet? Do I have any grandchildren?"

It pained him to keep it from Howard but how could he explain Annie, the *Toller* girl from Presque Isle, and Mary Khadijeh, the granddaughter Howard would never know.

Before he could explain, the silence was shattered by sirens and Henri ran to the door. Outside, HOMESEC guards in full battle array dashed from their vehicles and raced to surround Howard's home.

"No," Howard yelled. "Why come back just to bring danger here?"

Gil had no answer for that.

There was a jarring blast and the front door exploded in shards. Before he could react, three heavily-armed and armored men entered and grabbed him. They threw him to the ground and quickly subdued him. As he struggled to get free, he heard wailing so he strained his neck to see where the sobs were coming from.

Howard was kneeling on the floor by the door, his face contorted in anguish as he wept over his limp, bloodied, and beloved son, Henri whose body was punctured with shards of glass from the shattered door. Horrified, Gil turned away and screamed.

"You killed my Henri." Howard wailed, staring wild-eyed. "You've taken everything from me."

The troopers forced Gil to his feet and as they dragged him away, he stared back as Howard wept and rocked the lifeless teen's body, chanting

Henri's name over and over as blood dripped down from the body to pool on the carpet where it was absorbed without leaving a stain.

Moaning in anguish, Howard looked up and shouted. "You are a heartless, unloving creature and no son of mine. Look what you've done. You take and take and then you run away. Get out. My Henrietta loved me, Henri loved me, and I love them but you, you never loved me and never can." Howard began bashing his forehead hard against a wall, drawing blood as he wept. "What will become of me now?"

Gil struggled to free himself but the guards held him secure and forced him to stare at the agony he'd caused. "I'm sorry, Howard, I'm so sorry." Gil screamed. "I . . . I want to . . ."

Before Gil could say more, he was facing the fire, his wild, unkempt and teary image reflecting back at him from the glass enclosure. He wiped tears from his face and took long, deep breaths to calm down. Then, the unmistakable scent of snow caused him to shiver.

A piercing north wind howled across the frozen tundra, whipping fine, white, sparkling crystals along the black ice before swirling them into sparkling drifts. Nearby, a dim yellow light bulb, hanging precariously from a cord, flashed on and off as it was blown about by the fierce wind. He gripped his animal hide blanket and pulled it tight against the raw coldness and stared blankly across the frozen lake, his eyes burning in the biting wind even as wind blown crystals temporarily soothed them. In the silence between the wind's ghoulish shrieks, he heard the crunch of snow. He didn't turn until he felt her close.

"Come to bed," she said as gently as she could above the protesting wind.

She made the most inviting words sound dismal.

"Not yet," he replied.

"Will it ever be like it was?" A questing smile froze on her face, but her dark, cautious eyes told a more fearful story.

He tried to piece together the gaps in his memory, of how it was. He remembered her as vibrant and pretty, a wild teenager, not this dour old woman who came for comfort under the guise of offering it. Her fur hood couldn't hide the face of perpetual disappointment underneath and her weepy eyes had long since lost their power. He was complicit, so there was no reward for remembering what once must have been between them. And his complicity made him incapable of supplying the words of comfort she so desperately needed, if not deserved. His choice, silence, generated cries of despair that sang in concert with the wind.

"But you came back," she cried. "Why? Why, if you don't want to be here?"

"I don't know. I'm here."

"You don't know? You're crueler than I remember. You say the wrong words so easily and the right ones never. And your silence spares me no pain."

He shrugged and she stepped back as if she expected him to hit her.

"Khady needs you."

"Khady?" It hurt not to remember.

"You're heartless. I was a sweet, innocent Toller princess when we met, a prize, and you were my first, my very first. Mary Khadijeh, Khady, you fled and made your daughter an outcast but she is still your daughter. But you are distant to her and that breaks her heart. A *Toller* girl needs a father and now that you're back among us, you've given her hope, don't break her heart again. Please, not again, like you broke my heart. Be the father a daughter needs. Stay for her sake, if not mine, and make us a family. At fifteen, she needs her father's love more than ever. You know what that feels like."

She knew what to say and he tried to holster his natural feelings and muster up the right ones, but nothing came. Annie was his first, too, and his only real experience. Before Presque Isle and Annie, his sexual experiences were all virtual, and after . . . But Annie was only fourteen when she had seduced him, or he had allowed himself to be seduced.

"I'm sorry, Annie," he offered. "I'm not myself."

"It's not that easy. You ran, I stayed. You left me alone, a pariah in my own village. You abandoned me and so I raised our baby alone, living through all the condemnation that a devout *Toller* community can heap on one of its wayward own. We were shunned and worse, our baby and me, and if it wasn't for Uncle Rocky—Allah be praised—we would never have survived. You are here. This is your chance. Make it right. Please, I beg you, make us a family. Stay."

It was a reasonable request, but when he didn't respond, she slapped him and slapped him and slapped him harder. When he still didn't respond, she released pent up fists of hatred and frustration until he could take it no longer. He grabbed her, turned her, and held her close, immobilizing her, except for the weeping.

"You are a heartless man!" She screamed. "How can you feel nothing?" She struggled to get away, kicking and scratching but he held her firm. She craned her neck and tried to bite him but he avoided her teeth and when she tried to butt him with the back of her head, he avoided that, too. Left with nothing, she went limp and he let her go. She crumpled to the snow, weeping, hysterically.

She grabbed at his blanket and looked up at him through the swirling snow. "I'm sorry I slept with them but you were gone and we needed protection. Beat me if you wish. Hurt me, I deserve it, but don't ignore us and don't leave, please don't leave." Her voice became tiny and girlish and only a lull in the wind allowed him to hear her pain. "Don't leave. I couldn't take that, not again. I don't need anyone but you so stay! It won't happen again. Not ever, I promise. Stay and I will love you like nobody else can."

Like nobody else can. The words brought vague memories of a far away time and a feeling that made him want to cry.

"I'm sorry, Annie. I don't want to hurt you and I want to care, but I don't. I don't know why I'm here but please let me be."

Her howling began anew. She stumbled to her feet and swung her fist at him, hard this time, catching his nose. In the cold, he felt the flow of warm blood before it froze. Frightened, she dropped her hands, defenseless and cringed, in her way imploring him to hurt her, to complete his onslaught, to care enough to show some emotion, any emotion, even contempt or hatred. But the panic in her eyes deadened his more. He didn't want to be here and when he didn't react, she sagged away in total defeat.

"I hate you, you indifferent bastard." She slumped away and then turned and ran through the blowing and drifting snow. He stared at her tracks but as her footprints disappeared under fresh snow, he turned to the banks of Lake Erie where a wind-driven, small, frozen rogue wave slowly crested against iced-over rocks and splattered into a wintry mist that whipped through the community adding to the white, frozen glaze. Gray dusk became gray night and because he had nowhere else to go, he returned, reluctantly, to their cabin.

Inside, all was dark so he felt his way to the blankets of animal fur and quietly insinuated himself under them, next to her, and he fell asleep.

He awoke to the unmistakable sensation of lips and tongue. He shivered with excitement and thought to push her away but didn't. It felt good and he needed it. And so, like all those years ago, his good sense evaporated in lust and he procrastinated until, if he had wanted to resist, he waited too long. To reduce his anxiety and increase his ardor, he conjured up sad memories of others, the recoverable memories of her, the one he missed most and the kisses, so innocent, reminded him too much of another miserable fantasy, but unable to hold back any longer, he took the initiative and soon, they were making love.

Maybe he could be here.

Suddenly, the cabin door opened to a surge of bitter cold air and the cabin was illuminated by the rapidly flickering light from a candle, the holder's shadow flashing on the wall beside his head. He turned and froze, blinking hard to clear his eyes of this apparition. Annie stood at the door looking stricken, her expression morphing into crazed revulsion and she screamed, dropping the candle as she ran hysterically into the night.

Mystified, he looked down. Below him, naked, was a fourteen-year-old girl with her mother's sad submissive eyes. Aghast, he rolled off the bed and vomited. With his eyes tearing as he retched, for the first time he wished with all his heart that he could be wherever Annie had gone.

"You loved her?" The deep voice boomed from the fire.

In panic, he reached for his blanket, but there was none to grab. It wasn't cold and he wasn't in that cabin. Sweating and shivering while the fire roared, he felt like he was suffocating and he struggled to breathe. "I . . . I . . . I can't . . . . That never . . . ." It was a dream, it had to be, but it felt so real. He even had an erection. He was disgusted with himself.

"Did you love her?"

Lying naked on the cot, his stomach churning, he tried to heave like in the dream, but nothing came up except stinging, throat-burning bile. He searched the barren room for something, anything. His eyes burned, his rasping breath came in gasps, but none of that pain was as severe as the ache in his heart.

"It . . . that . . . it never happened," he croaked. "It wasn't my fault. Not that. I was young and scared and alone, always alone. Annie . . . she needed . . . She needed me but . . ."

"I merely asked if you loved her."

"That . . . what just happened, it never happened," Gil explained. "I ran away, sure. I did that but that's all. No, not all, I should have stayed and faced the consequences but I ran. I always run. I had to . . . I didn't want to hurt her, she was sweet, but I didn't have a choice. But it wasn't . . . it wasn't like that."

"But did you love her?" The voice persisted.

"I wish, with all my heart I had." He heard the sadness in his answer. "Annie deserved better, certainly better than me. Rachman, her uncle was a good man. He took me in and was kind to me—other than shooting me, that once. Annie was just a kid, lonely, but she didn't deserve what happened. No, that's not right. She didn't deserve what I did to her."

"Is that how she thinks of it?"

"I don't know. Yes, maybe. We were too young and naive. It wasn't her fault, it was mine. I'm not nice."

"Does nice matter?"

"People expect me to be what I'm not."

"And yet you don't want to be what you are. That is so insanely ironic."

"I don't know how to respond to that."

"Say, again?"

"I said I don't know . . ."

"Pay attention. Something will come to you." The fire strengthened and the room filled with the familiar scent of evergreens.

He felt like he had been sleeping for days. Slumping on the cot in the bare white room staring at nothing, he felt listless for he had no one who cared, no one to trust, and nothing to live for. With each changing scent, he inhaled with relief, hoping for some other experience than the one of just sitting there, trying to make sense out of the accumulated frustrations that made up his wasted life. He placed his palms over his eyes to fend off his now-chronic guest, the sharp pain that lodged in his brain, right behind his eyes. It only seemed to hurt when the fire was out which seemed to be occurring more frequently now, not that he was a good judge.

Truly alone, he saw himself for the failure he was; his life merely the futile extension of a disappointment's resistance to quitting. He closed his eyes and tried to force the fireworks inside his head to dissipate which they did into shattered visions of fragile impossibilities, visions drawn from an imperfect memory and made more plausible by the incongruity that surrounded him. Shivering once again, he fought through the stupor only to fail and sink back into it.

"... Big Ben ... Big Ben ... Big Ben ..."

Like the ticking of a clock, he heard the words but didn't respond to them.

"... Pisa ... Pisa ... Pisa ..."

The litany made little sense and he was too overwhelmed to delve into it.

"... time ... time ... time ... inclination ... ation ... ation ..."

Should he reply? Had he replied?

Was the fire talking again?

He noticed hazy smoke drifting up from the floor. Incurious, he stared at it as it ascended. Dispassionate, he was aware that there was fire everywhere. He needed to panic. He wanted to panic, but he felt too tired and so he sat unresponsive, his head hurting, his eyes unfocused, as the flames spread, it was easier to lie there and do nothing. Besides today was as good a day to die as any. Around him, the white walls blackened and then suddenly the entire room erupted in a fireball. Grasping for relief, he sucked in the super heated air and prepared to scream.

The headaches were gone as were the blinding lights. Instead of fire, there was fresh air and the world was blue sky and sun. Forever had never looked so pleasing. He was standing in the great hall of an immense mansion staring at photos, some animated, some not, but all were calming. He knew this place. Here was life with Bree. Here was their home and with that realization, a warming comfort washed over him and soothed his soul. Here was his safe place, their place together, and finally, and here he was loved for who he was, not disdained for who he should be or wasn't. He felt ... he felt happy.

He was in a grand dining hall, sitting at the head of a long, well-polished, dark-wood dining table, set elegantly with delicate china and ornate crystal stemware. She sat at the far end of the immense table almost hidden from view by an elaborate crystal candelabrum that hung between them. She smiled at him and there was joy in his heart. He thought he had lost her. She had aged, but she was still so gorgeous that he felt the pride of a wonderful stirring, even at his great age. After so many years together, he wanted her still, and her smile told him she wanted him as well. He returned her smile, receiving his reward when hers grew into a far better one. He ached with love for her.

Her jet-black hair showed more gray, more a fashion statement, because she looked as stunning now as when they first met. She had always been comfortable with her beauty. Curious, he held a shiny dinner knife up to reflect his own face. What he saw pleased him. He'd aged well too, his face thicker and perhaps there was a hint of jowl but otherwise . . .

She laughed. "Not again? You're so vain. No one is as stunned by their own good looks as you. Every time you pick up a knife to stare in wonder, it tickles me."

"I'm glad I can still make you laugh."

"You love me and there can be no greater joy in my life."

"I feel the same."

She blew him a kiss. "Every day, for all eternity, I will thank Morgan that I was so fortunate, that you chose me over silly revolution."

"It was an easy choice, my love," he said. "For you, I would have given up so much more." He shook his head. "I am as excited today as the first day of our Partnership in Profit."

She laughed at that. "After a century together, old man, I feel exactly the same."

"Bree, sweetheart, you are everything I ever wanted and there's not a moment in my life that I would change if it meant losing you." She blushed and he was pleased.

Ever competitive, she tried to draw a similar reaction from him. "That glorious day when you gave up your revolution, turned your back on your great grandfather, that two faced villain, and chose me over the world, it was the day my life began. Every day since, I feel that same thrill. I'm blessed to be in your life and feel blessed to have you in mine. I know that Bernie was your hero, and that he worked for my Mother, I know that broke your heart. But you discovered his treachery in time. I was frightened that I'd lose you to him and that impossible revolution forever. Dear Mother, our great and most beneficent Majesty, God save Her soul, she and Bernie had a plan that would've ended you, but you loved me with such gallantry that you won her over—no easy thing for Mother—and you gave purpose and meaning to my life.

She put her hands to her heart. "Oh, Gil, I will love you forever. Each and every morning when I rise, my tired old bones thrill to the wonder of another day with you. You have added strength and purpose to my life and together, we have made a wonderful world. I wake to you and I sleep with you at my side and there is no more in life to want. You have made me the happiest woman in history and someday, when you stop being embarrassed, I will publish your love poems for the world to cry over when they know what I know; that ours is truly the greatest love. For the rest of my days, I can do nothing less than all that is in my power to do to make you feel certain that when you chose me, over revolution, you chose correctly."

"I love you too," he said, and in truth, he meant it.

"Mother is incapable love, but what you and I have has made her jealous."

He laughed. "She was never a 'true love' kind of girl." Bree laughed as well.

They were silent, contemplating their happiness. Then she asked, "Do you miss it? You know, being out there."

"You mean the messiah thing? Not at all. Bernie was using me, I understand that now. And like you said, *Wasters* were just crabby old people who were envious of the wealthy. The world is doing fine without them and without me."

"I'm doing better than fine with you." She cooed.

"Do you miss it though? Sometimes I wish the world needed me just a little."

"The world can never need you as much as I do."

"Are you trying to seduce me? At my age?"

She blushed. "I don't know how to respond to that," They laughed again "I spent the morning reviewing my memory chips and it's comforting to be able to confirm that my love for you is the same today as it was on our first memory chip together."

"Memory chips are unreliable witnesses. No court admits them as evidence."

"But they're true and they say so much. They tell me that I've always loved you and I tell you that I always will."

They finished dinner and then walked onto the verandah to gaze out at their vast estate, an old, enraptured wealthy couple. They strolled, hand-in-hand, while in the distance robot workers harvested their crops and improved the value of their estate. They paused at their grotto to embrace.

He stared at their fresh water stream as it coursed over a lighted waterfall. "I do miss people," he offered.

"People were never reliable. You remember how they treated you."

"Still, I miss them."

"If you're lonely, we can visit Mother."

"Has that become our only choice? She hasn't mellowed enough for a visit. Sometimes it's good to have real company though, even if . . ."

"You're real enough for me. But I feel it, too, sometimes," she agreed. "You're right, let's do something. My avatar will arrange a party."

"Everyone sends under-resourced avatars so parties have gotten dull. I know, let's travel, but not in *Virtuoso.* There are places with people still and I'd like to see them."

"It's too dangerous. People resent immortals like us."

"Maybe we should have worked longer and not retired so young."

She took his hand and squeezed it, fondly. "A hundred year career felt long enough. Besides, we deserve this time. Someday, I'm certain we will go back to work, but for now, being with you is enough for me." She rested her head on his shoulder. "In your life, my darling, why is it that I'm the only one that you ever committed to completely? And you committed when everyone was telling you it was a mistake."

"Yes, and what mistake, sweetheart, I am so deeply and so passionately in love with you that time has no measure. How could that feeling ever be a mistake?"

"You say the sweetest things."

He stared into her loving violet eyes.

She kissed him and held him close. "You are the most important thing in my life."

"Yes, I am." He joked and kissed her back.

She laughed and whispered softly in his ear. "We know that the most important thing in life is to . . ."

Bree's tone became a deep throttled growl as the voice in the fire completed her thought. ". . . to know what the most important thing is in your life is." He shuddered at the suddenness of the change. He felt the loss of love and mourned. His world was once again the pristine white room that had turned cold and dark except for an inadequate blaze in the fireplace.

Alone again, he sat on his cot, rocking back and forth as the memory and feel of love faded in spite of his efforts to hold on to it. His spirit plummeted and he bellowed and when that didn't help, he screamed at the emptiness until his throat was raw and all he could make were rasping sounds. Tears rolled down his cheeks and he stared hopelessly at the now mute fire. Over time, without the fire to provide focus, he slumped back against the wall. Alone in the cold and dark with no one in the world to care, here was his hell, and if time passed, he was long passed caring.

"You don't look well."

It had been so long since he'd heard a voice or in fact had any input at all that the voice startled him and, at first, he failed to react to it. He hadn't noticed but the fire had returned, its embers crackling and glowing orange.

"No, you don't look well at all." The fire said.

"Am I dead," he said dully.

"What grand purpose would your death serve?"

He didn't know. But then, he didn't know anything. "Is this how it is to die?"

"Stop whining," the voice commanded. "You're not dying; you are reacting badly to a paradox. Typical of most Americans, you're self-absorbed and incurious. You are strangely indifferent to the point of lethargy and yet, for all that, you need constant attention and the encouragement of other, equally self-absorbed humans. What are the chances of getting that attention? You won't die from what you are but your behavior is quite predictable and quite habit forming for this is a truly American perspective, the result of centuries of unbridled commercialism and consumerism orchestrated by well-funded experts in the field who have prospered greatly churning out adults who live like egocentric children, unwilling and unable to grow into responsibility while desperately seeking mommy and daddy to make everything right and then buy them things."

"What?" Confused by the onslaught of words, he took a deep breath of now acrid air before responding. "I wasn't close enough with my father and I never knew mother."

"Yes, I couldn't have provided a better example."

It was a cold and darkly lit alley, the only light emanating from various dim OLEDs programmed to shed light precisely into the darkest corners. He was trailing a young child. The boy was scurrying through the maze of alleys, opening doors and running in crying, "Mommy, mommy, where are you?" or, "I can't find it and I'm scared, mommy. I can't find it."

He wanted to help the boy but he couldn't quite catch him. As he entered a room, the boy was fleeing through another door. And so it went until he saw the boy enter a room that when he entered, he saw in a far, dark corner, the boy sobbing his tale of woe to an old, gray haired woman who had knelt to accept him into her arms. Exhausted, but relieved, the young boy soon fell asleep, an angelic smile on his face, the tear streaks still visible on his cherubic brown face. Gil moved closer to get a better look at the woman, the child's mother, but her face would not come clear.

Suddenly, the child woke and began screaming in terror, arms flailing. During the mother's struggle to calm him, Gil caught a brief glimpse of her. But it wasn't the mother; it was his father, Howard, lovingly tending to the fearful child who was frantically trying to extricate himself, scratching Howard until he bled as he struggled to escape. Aghast, Gil backed against a wall and then tried furiously to escape but the door was locked . . .

He thought to blink, but his eyelids failed to respond. Somewhere, he heard the sound of water boiling and his head turned listlessly toward it. Steam was rising from the white floor. It didn't seem odd until it coalesced into a form that spoke. He trembled at the sound. It was her voice and he ached for the sound of it.

Though indistinct, the face in the mist was her face and he reached out but she hovered just beyond his reach. Sobbing with frustration he whispered to her through parched lips, "You wouldn't like me if you knew what I've done."

"Nor you, me," the mist announced. "But we're friends and nothing can destroy that friendship." She smiled, but he looked away from those stunning green eyes that should have blamed him for everything, but didn't. She hovered in front of him now and her eyes brought back fleeting memories of undeserved happiness and those memories only made him feel worse. He turned away. He couldn't be with her, not now, not here, not after all the pain he had inflicted on her. His heart ached and he begged for the numbness in his heart to return. But just when he thought the ache was unbearable, he felt a warm kiss, her kiss on his cheek. Instinctively and hopefully, he turned toward the kiss, seeking more.

"Is there any situation where sex doesn't enter into it for you?" she scolded. "Concentrate, this is important."

Embarrassed, he recoiled and twisted toward the wall, but she was visible still.

"What's wrong with you?" she asked.

"How can I make this stop?" he wailed.

Tenderly, she touched his cheek but when his hand reached up to capture hers there was nothing of substance for him to grab hold of. Knowing that she was insubstantial, he leaned into her imagined touch believing it to be a respite from his pain.

"I'm here for you." Her voice told him. "And I will always be here for you but I can't make this stop. Only you can do that. Maybe I can make it easier."

"How?" he mumbled, tears rolling down his cheeks. "Life is a game that I can't seem to play and everyone is trying to sell me a way to win and they are all so much better at it than I am. Without you . . . without you, there is nothing I trust."

"Poor baby, you make it too hard." She kissed him again. He was grateful for her kindness. "These people you fear, they're simple to understand. Know them by the gods they worship and you will defeat them when you make what matters most to you matter most to them. You're alive. They can kill you but they can't own you unless you allow it. Find a life that they can't take from you and then give that life to others."

"I don't know how," he whined.

"Then know harder," she insisted. "What is your most pressing problem?"

When he didn't respond, he felt a stinging slap.

"Think harder."

"They want me to be something I don't want to be."

She slapped him hard. "That's not important, that's just sad. What of the people who need your help?"

"I don't know."

She made as if to slap him and he cringed. She spoke softly, "Who do you love?"

"I can't tell you that."

"But I'm your friend," she said gently, "and we're mostly adults here. If there's a list, I understand." He didn't answer so she began to formulate a list. "Obviously you love Bree, who else?"

He recalled Bree as if in a dream. "She's gorgeous and she knows me so well."

"Who else do you love?" She was insistent and he tried to focus for her but his mind wouldn't cooperate. "Don't avoid me or I'll hurt you again. Who do you love?"

"I never meant to hurt you."

"That's good to know. Yet I'm hurt. Now who do you love?"

"I won't answer that."

"You have no choice."

Would this never end? "Everyone I've ever loved has disappointed me."

"Wow, that really hurts," she said. "You poor baby, well at least we're getting to it. Help me with this. Of course you're disappointed. How could you not be after building such stout defenses against everyone and everything? By the time you allow someone worthy enough in to steal your heart, what's left but disappointment? Respect you can earn, although you haven't tried very hard. Love, love just is. Love is an ethereal thing and you can't make it play by your rules or you will starve and kill it. You search for love; you search for truth when you've had them all along. Love is the one thing that is always, always true. It is true or it simply isn't love."

"How would I know that? No one has ever loved me."

"That is simply not true. The only way anyone can be truly loved is to be true; otherwise you present a false image for others to love, and that can never work."

"You say love is true but it's not true here."

"You ninny, love is true everywhere. It is the one thing you can always trust."

"I can't, not ever. Am I broken?"

"Not broken, but doomed unless you put your needs aside. There are desperate people out there, desperate in need of your love and if you open up to them and show them that you love them, you will find the love that has eluded you. Love is the power to help; love has the power to heal. Love, and people will love you for it. That's how it works and yet you resist."

"I know who you are. You're trying to manipulate me. What you say may be right but you're wrong so nothing you say can be right."

"It is you who are wrong, consistently wrong. Look at me. Look closely. You know me. You trust me. You have the power to love, use it. Nothing else matters more."

He stared at the apparition in the mist, trying to see what was behind those green eyes.

"I see nothing."

"Then look harder," she commanded.

Squinting, he leaned in toward the mist. His trembling hand moved closer, close enough to almost touch. He strained toward her but though he wanted to believe, he needed to believe, the mist proved insubstantial, nothing he could trust. Exhausted, he fell back onto his cot, breathing heavily.

"I want to feel right. I want to be right, and I want to do right," he began. "But I don't know how, I can't, so I do nothing. Look at me," he wailed. "Can't you see that I'm scared all the time and of everything. I do nothing, hoping the fear will go away at least for a moment." He closed his eyes and drifted off to sleep.

When he awoke, the mist was still there. He lay on the cot unwilling to move as his tears dripped down to fill his ears before running off to dampen the cot. He ached for a way out of this unrelenting ordeal. So while staring unblinking into the white heaven above, he spoke with the last of his strength in a voice that he could not hear or maybe he whispered or he just thought he'd said it.

"The world is a mean and greedy place and it needs to change but that's as far as I go. I would be the messiah and help the unfortunate that this greedy world made necessary. I would make the world better for them if I could . . . but I can't. I want to end greed but I can't even end this trial."

"I understand," she cooed.

"No, no you don't!" He growled. "If I told you to jump and touch the moon, you might try as hard as you can but you could never do that. That's how I feel and that makes me a failure and not what the world needs, what Bernie and others wanted, and what Brandt fears. I wish I was that person or at least a better person." Ache returned to his head and his body shivered in the chill. "I have disappointed good people and allowed them to be hurt by the Chairwoman who is a selfish, heartless, evil, and greedy bitch." He realized what he'd said and began to tremble. There it was. He had spoken treason. What was left? How much more must he endure?

When she spoke, her soft, soothing voice surprised him. "You love Andrea."

"Her?"

"Yes, do you love her?"

The mist was an astigmatic blur and he became dizzy and nauseated.

"Why . . . Andrea?"

Pain forced him into a fetal position and he retched, too tired to fight it, he retched on his cot.

"Do you love her, Andrea?" she insisted.

Wracked with guilt and curled up in pain, he answered, truthfully. "Once, I loved her with all of my heart." The pain began to recede, but he remained fetal and felt like crying. "She was the best thing that ever happened to me. I loved Andrea until she stopped loving me."

"Now that's silly. You can never stop loving her," the voice in the mist offered, "just like she can never stop loving you. That's not how it works."

"Andrea could have . . . should have saved me, instead, she offered me to the Chairwoman. She sold me out!" It sounded pathetic.

"You love her. Why should any of that matter?"

"She shouldn't have done that to me. She only wanted me for her revolution and once that was beyond me, she tossed me away. She never loved me . . . for me."

"If that is true, how could you love her?"

He couldn't think of a reason.

"You are certain Joad had ulterior motives for loving you, yet your love for her is pure and true. That makes no sense. You gave up on her but she never gave up on you."

He pictured Andrea, young, Aeden young with flowing dark blonde hair that he had given her long ago, along with deep brown trusting eyes. His vision of her was clear now, down to the freckles on her chest in the shape of the constellation Orion, and that vision was innocent, with a knowing smile. His mind replayed memories of their times together and those memories eased his pain. "Are you her . . . Andrea?"

"No. I'm not."

"You must be," he insisted.

"I am not her."

"Then she has given up on me and I can never trust her?"

"True love is far too precious to give up on and frankly, that is not in your power to do. That's not how love works. Love just is."

"But if I had trusted Andrea then I would have to trust . . ."

The face in the mist finished his sentence for him. "Yes, exactly, right, you would have had to trust me—and others along the way. And that's a problem because . . ."

"You are plotting against me. Everyone is. Even Bernie was against me."

"What a silly, self centered, self-important capitalist you turned out to be. You ignore uncomfortable facts and believe what you believe and you believe that everything is about you?" the apparition accused. "That may be good business but it's not true. Only love is yours alone to keep or throw away. Do with it what you will but you will pay dearly for doing it wrong. Every human faces the same choice whether they know or not. So let them fool you or disappoint you, shame on them. But when they do, by staying true, you learn something true about them. When your heart is true, life is true. Bernie loved you and you know that's true. Howard, too and there are so many others. Being true is the only way to detect what's false."

His memory seemed clearer. "Bernie and Tanya. I have reason to believe . . . But when he said it, he realized it wasn't true.

"Your eyes can be fooled, your ears too and in Virtuoso, nothing is true. But get true right in your heart and you recognize wrong. Everything you need you have. You don't need what paid advertisers, sponsors, and vested interests say is true. Your heart is yours alone. Trust it; it is all you have against the evil, the greed and the quest for power that surrounds you. Bernie couldn't turn on you, Joad either, it makes no sense. It is for you to make sense of all things with a constant heart."

What he heard felt true. "I miss Bernie." That felt true, too.

The mist slowly dissipated and the voice began to fade leaving him lonely but less empty than before.

"This is about you," she said in a fading whisper. "Not in a selfish, greedy way, but in a loving way, this has always been about you." The air smelled fresh, once again like their evergreen forests and he stared into those loving green eyes. He felt the walls coming down releasing a torrent of memories.

Her green eyes faded and she murmured as her image dissipated, "Trust me, always."

"But how . . . ?"

And she was gone.

Gil lay as if in a coma in a room that now smelled of perfume. During brief periods when the fragrance dissipated, he rallied, if lying groggy on the cot, sobbing uncontrollably, was rallying. He endured pain that only the heart can inflict, an intense hurt that wouldn't swallow away. What a sorry mess he was. When he turned toward the fire seeking solace it was as if it was never there, the fireplace was gone now, literally gone; the walls, the ceiling and floor were an uninterrupted white. Once, when there was no scent at all, he steeled himself and stumbled to the door on wobbly legs. When he opened it and peered out into the corridor, there was nothing there, a dark and empty void that he was unable to step into.

He was a fool, so concerned with truth and honesty that he was unable to be true and honest in the most important way with the most important people in his life. He'd disappointed everyone and each, if they thought of him at all, thought of him with regret. He staggered back to his cot to await his next ordeal knowing that whatever it was, he deserved it.

For a long period, time passed uninterrupted by hallucinations. Remorse was his only and constant companion as he endured what his mind conjured as punishment for his sad, wasted life. He thought of Bernie, certainly, Arlene and *Gohmpers*, the Hegel twins, Angel Falls, Annie, even Rachman Turner, the Presque Isle *Toller*. Memories of Bree and Laurence Hilliard, Hilly, hurt as much as any and even Hamilton's chanteuse, Dyllon Tomas, who tried to help him when no one else would. With no other choice, he embraced his empty life as his legacy. But when he thought about Stacey, he cried for her pain, pain that he'd caused. He had squandered the power to make things right but worse; he had failed to even try.

He cried for Howard and he cried for the daughter he'd abandoned and would never know. He should have been there, a child in need of unconditional love who would never know a father who couldn't give her even that. He knew how she must feel and he ached with frustration and embarrassment for his sad life and choices that caused pain to a sweet innocent girl, to another sweet, innocent girl. If he had only known that the pain from indifference was the worst pain of all. That bitter knowledge slowly etched into his heart and he knew he could never live aloof again. *Why did he ever think he could?*

He awoke one day to a roaring fire and the sweet smell of freshly cut flowers. They weren't done with him yet.

"No more, please," he begged, "you've won. Let me go and I will do whatever you want." With the room empty, he was pleading with a fire that wasn't there.

A triumphant voice declared. "Of course I won, that's what I do. Now tell me, please, what have I won?"

His voice was gravelly and filled with despair. "I can't take anymore of this. Let me go and I'll do whatever you ask. If it's treason you want, I admit it. Yes, I despise Brandt's government and I hate Morgan and everything it stands for, but no more than I hate myself. Tell the Chairwoman she has her messiah, if that's her wish. Tell her I'm willing to die for whatever cause she chooses. Just make this stop and let me go."

The fireplace reappeared and Gecko spoke from the flames. "Is that my victory? I worked far too hard for just that. You lose too easily. And what you're asking is your defeat, not my victory."

"Stop it, please. I thought I was a good person but I'm not. The Chairwoman hates everyone and she treats them the same. I treat the people I love like I treat those I despise."

"Speaking against our leader always ends in painful death."

He was too exhausted for more. "Do your worst, but no more of this."

"Ah, another paradox. Doing my worst might not be the worst. Besides, I don't need your permission. Now that you've lost, is there anything you wish to say before we execute everyone you have ever known?"

This wouldn't end.

"You can't do that. Not after all of this. What was this for if not punishment? Kill me but spare them. God knows I deserve it and they can't hurt you. Please."

"Once you've done the Chairwoman's bidding we don't need them anymore and people who aren't useful waste resources. Sparing them makes no sense and so they die."

"Please no," Gil begged. "The only way I'll help you is if they are free."

"Are we bargaining? What do you think you still have that we want?"

"Spare them and I'll do whatever the Chairwoman wants."

"You've already surrendered. I don't negotiate with the defeated, it's bad form."

"If you don't protect them, I'll find a way to take the Chairwoman down."

"But that is what she wants you to do. She might even reward you for trying."

Why wouldn't this end.

Gecko's voice seemed almost cheerful. "The first to die will be Omar Smith; he's been alive too long anyway. But of course his lovely young American concubine must die as well."

"You can't!" He screamed as he struggled unsuccessfully to get off the cot. "You must save her, save her most of all. Promise me she won't be hurt and you will have me forever." He breathed in the scent of evergreens and thought again of Angel Falls.

"Define promise."

Suddenly, the room began to shudder violently. Frightened, Gil searched for something to hold onto as the cot rattled back and forth, banging against the four walls. Deep cracks appeared in the floor and then the walls and fragments of the ceiling high above crashed down around him. He rolled under the cot and huddled against a wall, terrified, as the room slowly deconstructed. His eyes and throat burned as he choked down the heavy swirls of dust. Coughing uncontrollably, his eyes bulged and he couldn't catch his breath as the roar grew louder and louder until it was deafening and then the floor dropped out and screaming, he hurtled down into the endless dark of an infinite abyss. First his world and then his screams went silent.

He opened his eyes and shielded them from a soft, distant glow. Gone were the ceiling, the walls, the floor, gone was everything. He was floating in some vast, silent and empty firmament. The distant glow grew larger and gradually morphed into a colossal human form with long flowing white hair that extended as far as he could see with billowing robes too bright to stare at. The figure stretched out his enormous arm, pointed his finger at Gil, and spoke in a deep, rich voice that reverberated through the heavens.

"I have seen the affliction of My people who are in Egypt, and have given heed to their cry because of their taskmasters, for I am aware of their sufferings. So I have come down to deliver them from the power of the Egyptians, and to bring them up from that land to a good and spacious land, to a land flowing with milk and honey, to the place of the Canaanite and the Hittite and the Amorite and the Perizzite and the Hivite and the Jebusite.

"Come, I will send you to Pharaoh, so that you may bring My people out from bondage."

Emerging from the long and unruly white hair of the Lord, a dove flew down toward Gil. As it closed the distance, it grew in size to become an angel brilliantly white with a vast gossamer wingspan. She floated down until they were eye to eye in the heavens.

She spoke, her voice soft like a purr "There are no secrets," she said, "Your heart has all that it needs. And it is time to set it free."

He closed his eyes and when he opened them, the angel was gone. But in the vast emptiness he heard a faint echoing murmur. "She is true . . . she is true."

Through cracked lips, he whispered, hoarsely, "Who?"

But no response was offered.

Chapter 13

Monroe—2083

Making a Difference—*"It is not the critic who counts: not the man who points out how the strong man stumbles or where the doer of deeds could have done better. The credit belongs to the man who is actually in the arena, whose face is marred by dust and sweat and blood, who strives valiantly, who errs and comes up short again and again, because there is no effort without error or shortcoming, but who knows the great enthusiasms, the great devotions, who spends himself for a worthy cause; who, at the best, knows, in the end, the triumph of high achievement, and who, at the worst, if he fails, at least he fails while daring greatly, so that his place shall never be with those cold and timid souls who knew neither victory nor defeat."* Citizenship in a Republic speech by Theodore Roosevelt, President of the United States (First Republic) at the Sorbonne, Paris, 1910

—***Archive***

Physically free from his ordeal, Gil stared dully out of the train window as it passed over the briny swampland of New Jersey. Jittery and depressed, he wasn't interested in the scenery; he was beyond caring. His ordeal in New York had so eroded his defenses that the only thing he felt was violated.

He was scheduled, on his return to Monroe, to meet with the Chairwoman and he was oddly indifferent about it. They had succeeded in breaking him and as a result, he felt guilty about everything in his life, nothing more so than the hurt he had inflicted on the loving innocents he had destroyed with his selfish and futile stupidity.

His trial had made it clear, in a mocking way too certain and lasting, that because of him, everyone would lose everything. He would have screamed his grief and disappointment but for the HOMESEC guards stationed in the front and rear of his railcar. He pictured them laughing when they reported his pathetic actions to an appreciative Chairwoman.

He was broken and obeisance was all that he had left.

"Welcome back," she began, offering her very best smile. "How is *Our* Messiah, today? *We're* told that your visit was productive, that your head is screwed on right."

He didn't respond. He just stood in the Chairwoman's dark foreboding study, expecting the worst.

"Come now, Messiah, did your visit with *Our* Eminence meet your approval?"

It was easier when she was angry. "Yes, Madam Chairwoman."

"Speak up. Practice that compelling 'Messiah' voice."

He said it louder.

"*Our* clerics perform the most exquisite exorcisms don't you think? *We* are most curious what your plans will be."

He was unable to formulate a coherent response.

"Oh, most glorious Messiah, *We're* waiting. Please tell *Us*. What are your plans?"

"I'll do whatever you want." He had hoped that would have been harder to say.

"But you're the Messiah, for Morgan's sake. *We* want more than that from you." She offered him her beautifully fierce smile.

"Madam, I want to make amends for my earlier indiscretions. I'll do everything I can to complete the Sacramento project, but please believe me, what happened was not Bree's fault."

"Of course it wasn't, but regardless, she is beyond you now. Do not ruin *Our* mood by speaking of her. It is for you to resolve *Our* union problem. Those pathetic *Wasters* would never have survived this long without a Messiah to give them hope. You must make them regret that they have resisted. *Our* farm owners are at fault, too. They are a disgusting new breed of *Entrepreneur,* sissies, not the vibrant, cutthroat capitalists who remade America greater. These people, they worry their profits and forget who it is that creates the environment that allows them those very same profits. Obedience is fine, but since when is a simple thank you too much? That will change. With the union gone, they will tighten up or they will find a different livelihood or none at all. Little that's productive ever comes from the contented."

"I'm sorry if I've done something that caused you distress, Madam," Gil offered.

She eyed him like a cat would a decapitated mouse. "My dear, soon everything will be perfect and you will be forgiven." She waited silently for him to speak the words.

"Madam, I promise you the union is no longer an issue." He'd said it and it didn't feel as bad as it should have.

"That's splendid, dear. Martyrdom is such a silly waste of resources, don't you think, particularly in a world where forever allows one so many opportunities to repent."

He nodded but she was insistent.

"No dear, say it."

"Yes, Madam Chairwoman, there's no place for sacrifice in this world."

"Not quite, dear, there is some place for it. *We* expect *Our* subjects to sacrifice for *Us*. *We* know that you don't lie, Gilbert, darling, so *We* thank you for your help in eradicating the union."

She knew how to take everything.

"You are to return to Sacramento," she instructed. "The evening train is waiting. We are pleased to announce that you are the new project manager and as such, you have earned a full HOMESEC escort."

"Madam, guards are an unnecessary project cost. I'll be no further trouble."

"Cost is not an issue. *We* budget for contingencies." With that, she waved him away. Dutifully, he turned to leave but something in her voice froze him.

"Oh yes, Gilbert, sweetheart," she said. "*We* want to be perfectly clear because it would be unfortunate if you misunderstand and made bollocks of everything. You are going to Sacramento to do away with the union, a task you will complete without prejudice. If you do not destroy them, you will spend a delightful afternoon watching *Our* beloved miscreant daughter, Bree, being treated in a most excruciating and permanent way and then you will watch everyone you have ever known abused in a similar way before you, yourself, are executed."

He balled his fists and said nothing.

"It's time to face reality, my dear Messiah. You will do as *We* request and you will perform with requisite excellence . . . or . . . or you will run to the union, it makes no matter to *Us* as long as whatever you do, you do your best. You see, Gilbert, *Our* plans are complete and you are free, free to choose. Isn't that wonderful?"

"No, Madam Chairwoman, it isn't."

She smiled at that. "Act as you will for whatever you decide, *We* will have our victory. You see, your great trial at the hands of the devil in that big, bad New York dungeon has made you a celebrity among Wasters. You are truly their Messiah, now, their long awaited hero. Lead them well. Draw them out, every follower from every infernal rat hole, and march your glorious horde to confront *Our* noble army skillfully lead by my dearest dear, Reverend General Ginger Tucker. It will be a battle for the ages and every *Waster* will die. And then *We* will come for their supporters.

The Chairman threw her head back and laughed loudly. "*We* have planned for every contingency so lead them well or bleed them dry, either way *We* will have *Our* way." Her smile faded. "I am too kind, I think. This is my gift to you. You will have the freedom to choose how you will die."

"But . . ."

"Not again with buts," She laughed. "You are our Messiah, *Our* Pied Piper, and it is unbecoming," she teased. "Go now to meet your fate," She shooed him away with her hands. "Yes, go my beloved, my dear brave Spartacus. Show me that you truly are the stuff of legend. I am all tingly inside with anticipation to see your great slave army take on the might of *Our* Rome. Perhaps we will even turn it into a commercial reality show." Her smile broadened.

"Madam, I'm loyal to you now and I would prefer to complete the project and disburse the union after the harvest is complete. I don't want more innocent people to die because of me."

"But that can be fun and *We* don't care," the Chairwoman insisted. "Be a man, be a mouse, choose, or not. *Our* forces will wait no longer and neither will you, my fine young stud. This is a glorious time to be alive and Ginger is waiting without budget constraints to measure you for history's coffin." At her signal, the guards closed ranks to escort him away.

"*We* will see you again when you are paraded in shackles through the city streets lined with crucified *Wasters*. And when you arrive, *We* will toast success and watch you die." To the sound of her cackling laughter, he was escorted from her presence.

Illuminated by moonlight, Midwest farmland rolled by in a blur. It was late and though he knew this wasn't the real terrain, he didn't care. His fate was finally and irrevocably out of his hands, and so he sat, slouched and defeated, his only choice was to blink away tears of frustration and anger. He had only himself to blame. A sudden vibration interrupted his maudlin reverie so he closed his eyes and concentrated on the faint background hum and he felt the vibration again. There was a discernible change and it was quieter, too.

He opened his eyes. The windows continued to project moonlit trees flashing by rapidly in the distance but something didn't feel right. Then, slowly the scene in the window faded, replaced by another scene—a stationary open-air train platform. Incredulous, he pressed his forehead against the window and stared. On a train platform bench illuminated by a single lamppost, under a sign identifying the location as Indianapolis, a solitary hooded figure sat. He stared again at the Indianapolis sign and tried to blink it away. He even rubbed the window to no avail. Before he could think about what this was, the railcar door silently slid open. The view from the window was real!

Somehow, he had returned to Indianapolis. His life had come full circle. *But Why*? He thought far back to when he had split with Bree, after Profit, when he had procrastinated about returning home, going instead to Hamilton where he had been captured. That was yet another decision in his life that he would have liked to disavow. But though he didn't know how or why, he was here now so he waited for his guards to explain. He waited but when no guard appeared, he stepped onto the platform, unsure what was required of him and half expecting to be shot. When nothing happened, he walked to the solitary seated figure. As he approached, he saw that it was a woman, and then he recognized her and stepped back in disbelief.

"It's good to see you again, Gil," she said, pleasantly, as if they had last met yesterday, not half a life ago. "I hope you're well?"

"Nurse Payton?" he said it but he knew that wasn't right. Nurse Payton had been her alias when he had met her that first time at the Hospice where Bernie kidnapped Chairman Crelli. Her real name was—"Ms. Klaatu?"

She nodded.

"Is it safe?"

"Gil, please call me Arlene, dear. And yes, it's quite safe enough. The guards will remain on the train. Here, sit." She patted the bench. He sat next to her, but continued to stare at the train fearful of the guards contained inside.

"I assure you, dear, they can't hurt you."

"But how?"

"This will make sense, I promise. How are you?"

How? I'm going to Sacramento to manage a project or start a revolution and I honestly don't know which."

She nodded. "Let me look at you," she said. "I haven't seen you in over twenty years. Not since that night at the hospice when you rescued President Rose and we stopped Andy. You've grown into quite a handsome man but you do seem stressed."

"You're sure we're safe?" He continued to stare anxiously at the train.

She nodded.

"How can you be so sure?"

"You must trust me, dear."

He shivered at that. "I was in New York."

She nodded.

"I met, Damian Hegel. He's a Congressman and he works for them, not for you."

"Dear, no one works for me and poor Damian, yes I know and it's so sad." She paused to collect herself. "His twin, Damon was killed many years ago in the government's unconscionable attack on Omega Station. His death traumatized Damian and he blames himself. It's another sadness that is my fault. I couldn't . . . I couldn't help him. Please don't blame Damian for his allegiance; he's doing what he must to survive."

"That's what we all do."

She smiled sadly. "Of course, dear. We do what we must. So that you know, I work for Tanya Brandt, too, though she doesn't know who I am." Her smile disappeared. "I'm so sorry about your great-grandfather. Bernie was a warm, kind, and gentle man and I loved him dearly. We had our differences after Omega Station was destroyed, but his heart was always in the right place. God will bless him. I don't believe you know this, but after Omega Station was destroyed, Bernie fled from HOMESEC and hid in various abandoned eastern shore communities where Joad funded and he ran businesses called Greenhouses that retrained and re-employed

Wasters to prevent them from being disappeared. He went by the name of . . ."

"Berne Thau, yes, I know. And I know about his Greenhouses, too."

"Good, I'm glad. Your great grandfather was a good man but he lived like his heart had been cut out, because it had, he lost the loves of his life. But before he died, he did a great deal that you would be proud of," she said, solemnly. "He saved so many *Wasters*, but he never felt like he was doing enough until he began preaching for revival of freedom in America on a Mesh-site that Joad pirated for him. He started the Messiah legend in hope of moving the world from selfishness and greed and to a happier place. I thought the concept was marvelous but I fault him the delivery. And everyone seems to be so tied up in it these days."

"Yes, tell me about it," Gil added, testily.

"All will come clear, dear. After Damon was killed in the frightful fire bombing of Omega Station, I didn't see Bernie until that time in the hospice with you, when Andy was removed from the equation. After that, though we communicated off and on, unfortunately, we never saw each other. The poor man had lost everyone but having you was a great kindness that he richly deserved. Thank you for that, Gil. You saw Damian. How is he? Has he found peace?"

He didn't have the heart to disappoint her. "He's very wealthy. He lives in this unbelievable condo in the Financial District, but you know that."

She nodded.

"Arlene, it is good to see you after all this time, it really is, but this isn't the time for a pleasant chat," Gil explained. "The Chairwoman is expecting me in Sacramento by morning to do, to do I don't know what." He laughed. "Is that ridiculous? I have no idea what to do but I can't be late."

"I promise you, dear, you won't be late."

"I know that you're one of the good people, Arlene. Bernie wouldn't have been involved with you if you weren't, but I'm confused, overwhelmed really. I've felt it my entire life, or at least since the hospice and I'm in way over my head here. The Chairwoman wants me to become this messiah that you say Bernie preached about. And this should scare . . . scare the hell out of you, she wants me to be the messiah more than I do, but then so does Rey Diaz, the union leader in Holarki. Rey has this mystical conviction that I will overthrow her, somehow, and set everything right, whatever right is. Everyone's counting on me for something and I don't have a clue what that is. After having procrastinated for my entire life, I've run out of choices yet I still don't know what I'm to do, and real people in the union are in danger.

"I tried to help them, I really tried, but the Chairwoman is too powerful. She's out of my league and much as I want to, I didn't—I don't have a chance. So now I'm out of time and chances and I've put the woman, the women that I . . . that I love in harm's way."

She smiled sympathetically. "You do sound overwhelmed, dear."

"I'm used to being overwhelmed. But now, whether I oppose Brandt or not, Rey Diaz and his union are gone. How can I stop armed troops?" He turned to stare at the train, imagining troopers forming, getting ready to exit, and firing their weapons at him.

"Where was I?" he asked. "Oh, yes, in spite of your assurances, these security guards will kill me for this so I'm at the end of my rope. My only choice seems to be when and how to die. If there's another choice, I really need to hear it now."

She shook her head.

"Then at least give me some answers. What am I dying for?"

At first, she was silent, her face hidden in the shadow of her cowl. "That's fair," she began. "The messiah stuff, I always thought it overwrought of Bernie and I never approved of it. He was a wonderful man but his expectations often exceeded his capability. Knowing you as I do . . ."

"You don't know me."

"You're wrong, dear. I do know you, certainly better than most and maybe better than you know yourself. Some of what you need to know I'm sure you learned from Bernie, Mark and others. Everything that happened . . . it is my fault." She hesitated and then struggled to find words. "When . . . when I started my quest for . . . for sentience, I was fresh out of school with a doctorate and loaded with algorithms and concepts to generate more algorithms but I had no sense of the world. Here I was questing for intelligence without the experience to understand the consequences in a land governed by greed. I was naïve. I wanted . . . I really wanted to find a totally new way to address intelligence, something more, I don't know, more holistic. I wanted to make real what wasn't real and I wanted intelligence that was better than real. Yes, I know, better than real, that's why this is my fault. Back then, I envisioned being the mother to a new race. Such covetousness and egoism, God has surely punished me and punished me severely for my decadence and life since has crushed the ego from me. But for all that, I can never pay enough for my sin.

"When I entered the field, the science around artificial intelligence was close to a major breakthrough but it was blocked until I began to visualize how it needed to be different—not so artificial, a more holistic view of intelligence, not just smarts as we measured it then. We needed to account for more of the human experience. My head and heart were in the right place, I must believe that or what happened is beyond bearing. Still, I was foolish, reckless. I didn't consider other realities when I developed the first of a new race. I called him Ray; he was the precursor to Joad and then Gecko.

"At the time, the Department of Homeland Security was desperately searching for a more sophisticated way to stop fiscal and physical terrorism bankrolled by the wealthy elite among our enemies, and sometimes our friends. These were alarming yet financially rewarding times for techies. The Chinese had successfully converted to an effective variation of capitalism and they were outspending America militarily research and development by a factor of ten while developing their cyber terror capability by a factor of twenty until, no, I'm getting ahead of myself.

"To offset our competitive disadvantage, America's security community raced to fund ways to circumvent what seemed at the time to be inevitable Chinese world hegemony. Brainstorming led to a massive artificial intelligence project which all the private Security corporations felt was the most efficient and effective solution to America's problems, given America's relatively limited investment capability in weapons and defense.

"When I started, I had no knowledge of this, of course, but when I succeeded with Ray, I began to grow up. I had failed to consider how relentless HOMESEC and various private industries would be to win once they discovered the means.

"But even that wouldn't have happened, certainly not that quickly, without Andy. Damon, Damian, and I created Ray, but without Andy to commercialize Ray, he would have remained a Doctorate Paper. Andy became President for the most honorable of reasons—to save America—and that's when everything changed. Andy has extraordinary intelligence and his passion, patriotism, ambition, and sense of timing intersected perfectly with corporate cupidity, government overreach, and an overeducated, naïve girl's foolish dreams for humanity. It was a lethal amalgamation and it birthed Gecko."

With one eye on the train, Gil listened attentively.

"I'm getting a little ahead of myself. While I was laboring away in ignorance of national defense issues, corporations and universities supported by vast government R & D funding were stymied by two things, bandwidth and initiative—free will. Bandwidth everyone was closing in on, but initiative, enterprise far beyond complex instructions, something akin to real sentience, that was the real stumbling block. Government funded scientists were searching for a series of complex algorithms that would create an entity that could travel the universe of CPU's, connected and unconnected and do it without detection, while understanding what to look for in the exabytes of data possibilities, or what to see in someone's eyes or evaluate in their language inflection, verbal and written, or in their body language, all while segregating and tracking the most promising leads and then acting, both strategically and tactically on that knowledge, independently or in concert with the appropriate arm of the United States Government or it's subcontractors.

"And all of that had to be performed at the fastest possible speed, and without human intervention. In addition, this intelligent persona needed to be aware of any risks to its own well-being, seek out those harmful offenders, wherever they were, and either destroy them or neutralize their functionality, merging their routines with the core. That was powerful stuff, back then, and truly a horse of a different color.

"No one could figure it out—no one except the young and unfortunately callow Arlene Klaatu, laboring with sparse funding in a backroom at the University, exploring humor as a path to sentience. It was doubly hard because humor was never a part of my personality. Maybe that's why it interested me so." Arlene shook her head. "How my associates mocked me. They joked to my face and belittled me to my peers. But unbeknownst to them and to me at the time, I was on to something.

"When I was an undergrad, it was an accepted truth that whoever developed true intelligence and created a real sentient persona; in our free, competitive society, in some competitive form, that technology would be made available to everyone and it would be used to better mankind." She pointed to her cheek with her index finger. "Dumb, right? The scientists and science fiction writers of my day discounted greed and power and how important it was for the rich and powerful to maintain control over every important element that gives them control while renting out only a minimum amount of functionality in order to pay for it.

"So here I was, oblivious to economics and politics, developing a sense of humor; not mine, the makings of someone else's. While the greats in my field struggled, I kept at it. I wasn't in their league and had nowhere near their funding—and frankly I wasn't going for success where they were. As I said, I wanted something more precious, and, in my mind, more magnificent—God's gift to mankind: a better humanity.

"I'm mixing metaphors here but like Icarus, I too, flew too close to the sun. Gil, it's important that you know that I believe in God. I believe she is inside each of us and because of that, we can change, we can be better. God means everything to me. She is science; She is love; and She is the flaws in everyone that makes us human and keeps us striving to be better. My peers thought me silly, amateurish and immature, too fundamentally theological for the science I was pursuing. But I believe with all my heart that a caring God drives us so I ignored the insults and kept at it with just enough financial backing to move things along until we made some truly astonishing breakthroughs. We developed a kernel, a soul that I named *Ray*. I named him for Ray Kurzweil, a brilliant scientist and writer who defined early concepts in my field.

"Andy recognized it immediately. That's his genius. He has this . . . this feel. It's amazing, really. He was just a lowly manager in a large consulting firm when he first saw Ray, but he put it together in a way that I couldn't. He was a master at something else. He had the innate ability to make connections. When he found someone he needed, he worked at the relationship until he owned them. He married Maddie. She was the Senate Majority Leader's daughter. I never met her but I think I would've liked her. Anyway, Andy created synergies. When he saw what I had, he convinced the Senate Majority Leader and for reasons that have since become obvious; funding for my work was included in some off the budget worksheets. The money just rolled in and it funded my work and led to Andy and me forming a corporation.

"We incorporated as equal partners. I knew nothing about business and cared less. I was fine working on a shoestring in a back office as an under-funded, post-graduate researcher. But Andy built us into a mega-billion dollar enterprise using other people's money. He was the salesman, planner, and facilitator, and I was Ray's mother. During that process, Andy and I fell in love."

Gil was following her but that declaration startled him. "Who? You and . . . Crelli? With all that he did to you?"

"Judge me, you certainly have the right," Arlene said. "But I warn you, I've been down that road too many times to expect revelations. Andy and I were total opposites and we were amazing together. We had synergy that drove our competition bankrupt. We were so successful, Andy would constantly brag about the incredible offers that he had to turn down. We were offered literally billions upon billions, but he rejected every offer. I thought he was insane but it became clear why he did it when Jim Bonsack and Bucky Duke entered the picture. Did Bernie discuss those two with you?"

Gil thought back to Bernie at the Hospice in Indianapolis when he discussed the murder of Bonsack and his involvement in Duke's death. He nodded.

"Bonsack and Duke were the bottom-of-the-barrel, bottom-line operators who lacked the expertise, insight, and perspicacity to compete, so they stole Ray."

Gil was becoming more anxious. "All of this is interesting, Arlene, but damn it, why did Joad turn on me? Why did she set me up to be captured outside Presque Isle?" His hoped-for answer didn't come.

"I know you're hurt by that and we will discuss it Gil, I promise, but there's so much you need to know, first."

"Her betrayal has eaten at me for years and it is because of her that I'm here."

"I understand, but what I have to say is crucial. You'll know everything soon, I promise." She paused to collect her thoughts. "I didn't develop Ray so I could acquire power, or wealth, or leverage and I certainly didn't want anyone else to use him for that. Ray was my dream, my child, and then I lost him. He was stolen from me and I was more hurt than anything and so I directed my passion to recreating Ray, but even better.

"That's when Andy and I had a falling out. Andy knew the lay of the land and where the money was so he asked me to direct the new Ray to do things I knew were morally and ethically reprehensible. I didn't understand then, but at the time, Andy was under great pressure too. America was in decline and Andy believed that Ray could help him to save the country from those who were destroying it and from those governing who simply refused to see the end coming and act to stop it. I learned far too slowly that people like Andy and then Tanya; they see the world differently than you and I. They see it more through their principles and in terms of absolutes—authority, wealth, and power."

Gil listened as she explained her relationship with Crelli and how she refused him when he proposed marriage, she wouldn't hurt Maddie, and then finally how Andy, too, had stolen Ray from her.

Bernie had told him a great deal of this, even parts that Arlene was choosing to avoid. "Crelli tried to kill you."

"He did, yes, the water skiing accident," Arlene admitted. "But when he realized what he'd done, he saved me, too."

"You're letting him off the hook way too easily."

"I believe in God's light, and in it, nothing is unforgivable. The greatest human act, certainly the hardest, is forgiveness. But those who practice it find that among its great rewards, it makes you a better person and it can make others better because of it."

"Forgiveness didn't work with him."

"I've been through too much and I'm no longer naïve but I won't allow the world to change what I believe to be right and true. Even with that, I will not go to hell innocent. Andy did evil things but he believed; he *honestly* believed that he was the only one who could save America. I didn't know about that then, when I gave him the power to do just that.

"When he took our company from me, he used his own personal fortune to fund an army of programmers who developed Ray 2.0, which he called *Gecko*. When he was elected, Andy's private enterprise Security people requested that Gecko have the ability to sneak and steal, to lie, and cause doubt, and to avenge because those were the traits that Andy and his organization felt were needed to save the nation. Gecko was corrupted in order to accomplish that great thing.

"As for me, having lost Ray twice, I learned my lesson and set about developing Joad. She was to be my antidote to Gecko and I gave her what Gecko didn't have, perspective and humor. Empathy was Damon and Damian's great contribution. God love them, the twins weren't sure where empathy would lead, but they wanted to find out and I was all for it. And that made all the difference.

"What we unleashed, I've spent my life trying to make right. Those were long, harrowing, and difficult years working behind the scenes for Andy and then for the Chairwoman as a member of Gecko's development team."

"You helped them?"

"For a long time, I did. Too long, while I developed, there were executions, genocide, death games, and all of it is my fault. Because of me, millions suffered and died and I had to find a way to stop it. To buy time while I was searching, I needed to remove Andy."

"That's when I freed Mark in Aeden."

"Yes, Andy was obsessed with capturing Bernie, Joad, or me, and we knew it. He was there for any incident that he thought would provide a link to finding us. We knew he'd come to the Hospice."

"Why didn't you kill him?"

"I don't believe in a God who judges because that makes it too easy to pass human problems into the unknown of the hereafter. God is inside us all and that makes it our responsibility to find a way to penetrate the veil to find enough that is good to set a person on a better path. I couldn't kill him. He is in a better place, for him. It's an environment where he can search for and find God." She looked down but continued, "Joad was my way of undoing the wrongs that Gecko had been developed to cause and the good news is we're closer right now to ending this than ever before. We finally understand Gecko."

Remembering his recent trial, Gil shuddered. "No one can understand him."

She pleaded with him. "Evil people used Gecko for unconscionable wrongs; immoral and sinful deeds, so of course Gecko became the devil. To make things right, I had to find a way to change him . . . but how do you do that? How do you reprogram Satan? I had no idea but I hoped that Joad would figure it out. I built her for that but I didn't have anywhere near the resources that were being used to strengthen Gecko, so I was stumped. Then, out of the blue, a young teenage boy innocently creates a girl friend, a true friend. You created Andrea. At first, we didn't think anything of it, a boy going through a stage. It's done all the time, boys creating virtual girlfriends, but none created what you created. It was magic, your relationship with Andrea—a magic that deepened into love. I still don't know how it happened."

"Arlene . . . please, I . . ."

"I'm sorry if you're uncomfortable with this but it's vitally important, so hear me out. Joad was tasked with protecting you, like she protected Bernie and the rest of us at Omega Station. When you became a teenager, you had teenage needs and like so many others who could afford it, you created Andrea, an avatar to fulfill those needs. But then you fell in love, which was perfectly normal before Andy and Tanya started doing things. But the critically important thing is that you caused Andrea to love you. She fell in love with you! It was a monumental breakthrough. You say that I don't know you, but you're like a son to me and I consider myself Joad's mother, so I watched in amazement what a boy's love could do . . . that I couldn't. I gave Joad a sense of humor and the potential to do good and the twins provided her with empathy and compassion. That was vital, but love; real love, true love, that was you, Gil. What you felt . . . what made her feel . . . I couldn't . . . and what you gave her . . . I didn't have to give to her. I wish to God that I did.

"At first I was resentful that she loved you like she never loved me. Back then, everything was wrong and so I was conflicted by your relationship with what I consider my child. It was after my accident and I was in constant pain from all of my operations and I was working for Andy, then the Chairwoman, and I was under constant scrutiny. That's why I didn't realize, at first, what you, in your innocence, had achieved. I love Joad so much, but it was your love for Andrea that developed her into something more, something beyond my ability."

Arlene was smiling proudly as tears coursed down her cheeks. "You don't know but you taught my child to love. You have no idea what that means to me." She put her head on Gil's shoulder and cried.

Gil was embarrassed. "She . . . she loves you, too."

Arlene wiped away her eyes and took a moment to regain her composure. "Yes, I know she does and that's my point. I know she loves me because I see how she loves you. It's amazing really, the extraordinary capability of love. Joad doesn't have the raw power needed to stop Gecko, but what she feels for you changed her and everything and I believe it has changed Gecko, as well."

"This is a very weird conversation, Arlene."

"Weird, yes, but wonderful, too. This is my field of expertise and I'm among the best in the world, but I have no idea how love happened. But because of your love, Joad has reached Gecko and I believe she has made him . . . receptive."

"Receptive?" Gil asked. "To what? I just met him in New York and he dissected me as if I was a rat in a lab experiment. You're saying the Tin Man has a heart?"

She shook her fist in the air and smiled. "Exactly, it is like Oz, isn't it? Gecko never had a framework, a basis for feeling anything, and so he doesn't understand how you affected Joad the way you did. For Gecko, maybe New York was for that."

Gil shuddered at the mention of his ordeal. "He was testing me?"

She nodded.

"That's insane. The Chairwoman wanted him to break me and he did. What I endured wasn't love, not even close." A feeling of lonely helplessness like he had felt in New York came over him and he wanted to cry but instead shivered at the memory of that experience. Visions of that horror would haunt him forever.

"What can I say but that I'm sorry? As far at the Chairwoman is concerned, your ordeal in New York was successful. You'd be dead if she didn't believe that. Brandt is capricious and pays little attention to detail. She leaves that to Gecko and Reverend General Tucker. Whatever you believe about Gecko, he is wired with an insatiable desire to understand everything and that includes why Joad loves you, and maybe, just maybe, why no one loves him. I'm hoping here. I'm truly sorry for how you've suffered but what makes sense to me is that, in his way, Gecko is trying to understand you."

"Jesus, Arlene, I feel used enough. What you're saying is revolting."

"But it's possible. You can see it right here in front of you. We're sitting outside a train full of HOMESEC guards and we're free to talk and they're unable to stop us or communicate their position and situation. Say what you will, what happened in New York is a positive step."

"I went through hell so Gecko could evaluate a love interest. That's demented. I'm sick and tired of all this. Can't you make it stop?"

She put her hand on his shoulder. "Until we change it, this is our world and the feeling of being used by others will never go away until we make it go away. You've been searching for some obvious clue that makes everything clear so that you know what you must do, and that's great. You should do that. But stop searching out there for it because it isn't some external quest. Truth, real truth is inside you. It's in your heart. You know how it feels when something is right; use that feeling before it's taken away. That is what true freedom is all about.

"Brandt's support comes from the business community and she understands what it would mean to her if Americans were to find their true heart's desire and act on it. People who are truly free are impossible to control. The powerful in America fight to prevent true freedom and they do it by defining freedom as something else, entirely, the freedom to buy or sell or the freedom to live in a certain way, within certain constraints. They've used the media and every selling and marketing trick in the book and even invented some ghastly new ones like *Virtuoso* to hold onto power.

"Over the years, they've spent billions to make us proud of a lifestyle sold to us as freedom but it just isn't. They used radio, and then newspapers, magazines, television and computers, even gaming consoles as devices to brainwash us. You say you feel used; hundreds of millions of Americans have been similarly used and abused for decades. Using sophisticated business psychology and selling techniques and chic marketing tools; they accumulated information about us and then used that information to manipulate and motivate everyone to behave as they needed them to behave. They sidetracked everyone from the important stuff and into activities that wouldn't threaten their economy or their hold on power. They mastered their craft with the most insidious technologies that reached its peak with the development of *Virtuoso* and *Archive.* Now, business leaders had all they needed to confuse and confound the American mind into believing that to be happy and free, the purpose of life was to seek satisfaction by consuming. Consume, consume, and more consuming, freedom, freedom, and more freedom, it was their mantra and they kept at it until there was no family life, no community and empathy and sympathy were words you didn't use in polite company. They ended what was truly good about America, its humanity. Their efforts succeeded and they continued to co-opt the country, generation after generation, by providing so much noise in peoples' lives that no one could recognize truth or for that matter their own heart's true desire unless they were told what it was by the media.

"Because of you, Gil, I believe that Gecko may be reevaluating the world he created under Andy and the Chairwoman's direction. I pray that is true because if Gecko decides there's something better, a world where truth and love dominate, where people live to care for each other, share their lives, and practice God's Golden Rule, we will have a real and good future. But Gecko has no framework for this, so he's evaluating it."

Gil was annoyed. "If Gecko wants a free world," he said, angrily, "tell him to start by setting me free. And then he can leave me the hell out of all this. If he can do that and get Tanya Brandt off my back, I'll gladly settle for his better world."

"Unfortunately, I can't do that. I have no contact with Gecko. Besides, it's not that simple. He's powerful, but he can't run things. He needs people for that and more critically, he needs to be shown what a better world feels like. You . . ."

"Don't say it."

"You can do that for him," she persisted. "You are the only one who can."

Frustration almost brought him to tears. "Don't say that, Arlene I'm not that person. I'm not even a good person. I'm a Morgan Missionary, a consensus builder, and I don't want to be more."

"A great American patriot from the First Republic once said, 'If you stand for nothing, you will fall for everything.' Gil, you're wrong about yourself. You're a good person, certainly better than anyone I know. But that isn't enough. Look around you. There's no one else. It's time for you to stand for something, for the rightness of things, because that is who you are and that is what is needed. You can make things right for everyone."

"I've learned first hand that Gecko doesn't need me," Gil mumbled.

"You're wrong. Everyone needs you," Arlene proclaimed. "You are exactly what we need because there are far too many people who would gladly take power, whose beliefs are limited to lording over everyone else in order to become fabulously wealthy and make themselves into a god. We've had that in America for far too long. You've endured the result and I know that you don't want it perpetuated. Gecko gave Andy and then Brandt the power to believe they were superior and worse, that they were right. You see where that's taken us. It's time for good people to take responsibility, to show Gecko a better way."

"I'm exhausted, won't this ever end?" Gil confessed.

"No one appreciates how you feel more than me and I'm sorry, but it only ends with you. God gave humanity dominion over the earth, but along the way, people got lost and we allowed the stuff we want to have dominion over us. You're special because you love in a world that simply doesn't, not anymore, and you are our only hope to end the dominion of things. Do you remember Qade Blessing?"

Gil nodded. "He helped Bernie at Omega Station. Why?"

"He is waiting downstairs to take you to see someone who will help you."

"No one can help me, Arlene."

"You're wrong. I know someone who is uniquely qualified."

Chapter 14

Indianapolis, IN 2083

Staring at the train, searching for activity among the guards and finding none, he responded. "Arlene, this has gone on far enough. I can't just go wander off on some side trip. I have to be in Sacramento in the morning to lead or repel a revolution and the HOMESEC guards won't be contained in there forever. I won't spend my last day of freedom, maybe my last day alive on some hopeless crusade."

She smiled kindly. "Gil, a hopeless crusade is what you've been avoiding all of your life. But believe it or not, you have more friends than you know."

He needed one right about now.

"Please, Qade is waiting."

He didn't want to go but when he walked to the train, the door wouldn't open so lacking a choice; he turned and walked down the stairs to the street below. Waiting for him beside a sleek, jet black motorcycle was a slightly built old man with eyes so blue he appeared to lack pupils. Today was a day for legends.

Qade Blessing wore metallic blue overalls that shimmered in the streetlight. He offered Gil a casual salute, handed him a bag, and then explained the plan.

"We have a lot to do and we're on a tight schedule so put this over your clothing, it's a nano-suit that will make you invisible to local surveillance. My cycle has stealth properties, too, so we won't be easy to spot. Hold on and let's get started."

"Where are we going?"

"It's best you don't know until we get there."

Once on Qade's cycle, they hurtled silently down dark, deserted Indianapolis city streets, weaving through debris until they approached a window-less concrete, four-story building that rose above a deserted poor section of town. Qade maneuvered his bike into an alley and around great piles of debris and garbage until he reached a fence with old-fashioned barbed-wire along the top. At Qade's direction, Gil hopped off the bike while Qade slid a section of the fence away, revealing a path to the building. Qade walked the bike through the opening and after returning the fence section, told Gil to jump back on. Qade steered his cycle toward a garage door which opened as they approached and closed as soon as they were inside. They drove down a long, wide, circular concrete ramp in the center of the building to the basement where two armed guards waited. One looked like Qade only bigger and younger. There were no introductions but when the two hugged, Gil assumed it was either Qade's brother or son.

That's when Gil realized where he was.

"This is where you've been hiding Crelli all these years. Arlene wants me to speak with him. That's why I'm here."

"It's safe but we have to be very careful. You only have a couple of hours," Qade instructed. "We're outside his suite but before I take you in, we need to talk. I know you've met him before, but keep in mind he's been in here for almost twenty years and he's had a great deal of time to prepare for this meeting. Add to that, he's world-class devious with an endgame we haven't yet determined, so be wary."

"I can't do this, Qade, not now."

"Arlene insists. We provide Crelli with information so he knows what's going on. Personally, I think it's a big mistake but Arlene believes he's important. Keep in mind, whatever he says, there are ten people in this building who've spent their lives keeping him secure and we are at great risk. I trust you'll honor that."

"Do you think I'd spring him?"

"Take my warning seriously. We've put our lives on the line for the revolution and we've all lost many loved ones. None of us wants Crelli free again."

"I'm not going to free him. How would I? Why would I? If I have to see him, is there anything I need to know before I go in?"

"Only that he's been looking forward to this meeting for a long time." Qade then signaled and a guard unlocked a large reinforced metal door. As bulky as the door was, it glided smoothly and quietly. Inside, the corridor was cocooned in a thick, yellow foam-like substance.

"This is anti-surveillance camouflage," Qade explained as he ran his hand along the foam wall. "Joad protects us but there's a greater power out there searching."

Gil followed Qade through the corridor to a foam-encrusted door. Qade took a large, old-fashioned key from his pocket and unlocked it. Inside, there was another corridor, this one short, narrow, and ending with a door on either side, similarly coated in yellow foam.

In the eerie yellow light, Qade offered Gil his hand. "Good luck." Gil shook his hand and as he turned to go in, Qade grabbed him. "I can come in if you want."

"Whatever this is, I need to do it on my own." He took a deep breath and entered.

Soft yellow light permeated the thick foam giving Crelli's prison suite an eerie grotto-like quality. The only other light came from a reading lamp where former Chairman Andrew Crelli sat in an easy chair staring at him with a real book in his lap.

The former Chairman smiled. "I do remember you. I wasn't sure. You were fourteen, now you're what, thirty-two or three? I'm pleased that you're finally visiting."

Gil merely nodded. He had many reasons to hate or feel awe toward this great, evil man and any one of those reasons was reason enough to fear him as well.

Crelli was older and thinner than the impressive leader Gil remembered almost twenty years before at the hospice. He was an old man now, wearing ill-fitting blue, pin striped trousers from a business suit with a baggy, pale blue dress shirt, open at the collar. He still seemed energetic as he bounded from his chair to greet Gil but his body had that fragile old man grace. Crelli's slicked back hair was thin and white now, not his trademark gray. That he was far less imposing than when he was captured was a relief.

"Mr. Crelli, Arlene said that I should meet with you."

"It took long enough."

"Sir, it takes the time it takes. How are you?"

Crelli's gray eyes bore in and he spoke rapidly as if he'd rehearsed his lines but didn't have the time he needed to deliver them effectively. "Call me Andy, please. And how the hell do you think I am? The last time we met, I was the most powerful man alive, maybe the most powerful leader in history, and every day reinforced my superiority. And, for most of my reign, I communed and communicated intimately with the most powerful artificial intelligence the world will ever know. Then, poof, it's all gone in an instant, like someone turned off the juice to my brain.

"Flash forward twenty fucking years of solitude later and here comes this pup, that's what you are, a failed creation of a failed creation of a failed creation of a failed creation and you're free to come and go as you please, while I'm trapped here waiting for you to get off your ass so we can set this world straight again."

Once he had said all that, he calmed down. "My life is a third rate Shakespearean drama. I'm that singular hero who fell from grace without a single heroic flaw to bring me down. That's how the hell I am. How are you?"

"I'm okay. I have a lot going on though. Thanks for asking." Gil replied.

"Just so you know," Crelli continued. "In the time that it took you to recognize that I was asking you how you were, Gecko would have provided me with the most detailed research and offered me a choice of well considered responses and so instead of explaining all of this to you, I would have formulated my response or just made a fucking decision that changed people's lives and generally for the better. If you're to be the new king, you're going to have to speed things up, boy, you're already two cycles behind and the clock is ticking."

"Is that really how intense it is for you?" was all Gil could think to ask.

"No." Crelli replied quickly and then he paused to reconsider. "Actually, yes it is." He sounded more contrite. "Since I've been captive here in this puke-yellow prison, there's been nothing but silence and time, so much time. With worlds to conquer, there is nothing for me to do. When Gecko and I were one, there was nothing I couldn't think or achieve. He's gone and I'm alone and because of him I think out loud because I've lost the ability to think to myself. And I'm being slow cooked to death in here."

"I'm sorry . . ."

Before Gil could finish, Crelli responded. "No, don't be sorry. It's what you wanted. Twenty fucking years and I still don't understand why I've been abused like this, why I'm even here, and what I did to cause this. And since I don't know why I'm here, maybe you can tell me why you think you're here."

Gil struggled to remind himself that behind this verbal onslaught was a desperate prisoner seeking release. "Mr. Crelli, I . . ."

"Call me Andy."

"Andy then, I can relieve you of some of your anxiety. You are here because you don't know what you did to deserve this as punishment. When you were out there, you lacked the humanity that would have enabled you to stop short of the horrible things you did and permitted to be done to helpless others. I've changed my mind. Arlene is correct. I do need to talk to you. I have an impossible problem and I suspect that only you can untangle it."

Crelli smiled and seemed to relax at that. "I smell revolution." He walked Gil to a chair and then sat across from him. "I'm twenty years behind. Catch me up."

With rapidity and precision, Crelli began the barrage of terse, difficult and pointed questions to which he responded while Crelli interrupted incessantly, digging, and clarifying. From Crelli's approach, it seemed to Gil that it was like the internal communication between Crelli and Gecko except here everything was spoken. It didn't take long for Gil to have explained the most critical issues in his life to this stranger.

When he was done questioning Gil, Crelli paused to consider what he'd learned. Then, he seemed to enter a trance-like state and while he waited, Gil wondered about Arlene's professed love for this man.

When Crelli's trance-like state had gone on overlong, he tried to interrupt it. "Sir, Mr. Crelli, did you really love your wife?" He blurted out. When Crelli didn't respond, Gil asked again, louder.

Crelli seemed startled at first, but when the question finally registered, even after all his years alone in captivity, Crelli's eyes, like Brandt's, showed practiced inscrutability. Then, he smiled. "In my time I've had the best, the very best." He stared at Gil, quieted and reconsidered. "Of course I loved Maddie. Hell, I still love her."

The answer felt inadequate. "If that's true, tell me about Arlene."

The barely discernible flutter in Crelli's eyes told Gil it was the right question.

When Crelli answered, he began all wrong. "Christ, you've seen her. Arlene was a babe when she was younger. She had these sweet, sweet good looks, short blond hair, styled like a man and those amazing open and innocent yellow eyes. Good god, she was a knockout. And what a body on her; she's tall, athlete tight, and with a rack. And bright, she was the smartest broad I've ever known."

Crelli then paused to gauge the results. What he saw caused him to recalibrate.

"Okay, sorry, I'm out of practice. Forgive me; I've been isolated too long. Nothing I said about Arlene is inaccurate, she was, she is a stunning woman but that's not what you want to know. Can I begin again?"

Gil nodded and Crelli looked down to gather his thoughts. Gil was curious if it was for effect. When Crelli looked up and their eyes met, there was clearly a great sadness in them. Knowing Crelli's reputation as a duplicitous actor, Gil waited to see what that look would produce.

"I met Arlene while I was working for a consulting firm. I was searching for an artificial intelligence application and nothing I had evaluated came close to what I was looking for. Brent Bartram, Maddie's father, was the Senate Majority Leader. He was involved in seeking a better way to manage Homeland Security operations and I had volunteered to assist him. In my research, I located a young PhD candidate from Stanford who seemed to be working on something similar to what Brent had in mind.

"That candidate was Arlene and I found out that she was presenting her findings at a seminar in California so I attended and she blew me away. Her artificial intelligence application was severely under funded but functionally it was so much more sophisticated than any I had seen before. She really knew her stuff even though the academic community seemed uninterested. They tolerated her because she was so damn good looking. And she was . . . She was about twenty-five and she was stunning, though she never acted like she knew it. That was a great part of her charm, her magnetism, she was never aware of how stupendous she was. Anyway, when we discussed her research, she was like a little girl, so open and down to earth, but she really knew her subject matter."

"You have a crush on her," Gil observed, using *Have* instead of *Had*.

Crelli ignored that and continued. "After the seminar, we had dinner and she agreed to take a look at the specs for the HOMESEC solution my father-in-law was looking for . . ." Crelli smiled, wryly. "She was so grounded that none of my best moves worked—and that never happens." He shrugged. "My moves never worked with her. Anyway, I left California hopeful that I'd found Brent's solution and not a little in love."

"Or lust?"

Crelli smiled at that. "I had that reputation. I love Maddie, she is beautiful too, and smart, but our marriage was a political convenience. Arlene . . ." Once again, his eyes went blank and his face went slack. Just as Gil was about to say something, Crelli began where he left of. "Now that I have so little else to think about, I think about her all the time. Arlene was sweet. I mean really sweet. And she was considerate and innocent, not just sexually; she had this virtue about her, but she also had this over-indulged sense of right and wrong. That she was great looking and nice, well, for a hound like me, it was a turn on. I'm being honest here, even if it doesn't cast me in the best light. You and I are going to have to trust each other."

"I don't see how that's possible but I appreciate your honesty."

"My father-in-law really liked Arlene's application so he agreed to divert funds to my start-up. I returned to California to convince her that the money would give her application life but she wasn't sure. Back then, she called the app, Ray, and she said it wasn't about the money and that Ray was already alive. I didn't believe either claim until much later.

"I finally convince her and we started a company that filled her bank account and mine. She hired really strange geek twins to help her enhance the application and that's how CKA, Crelli Klaatu, and Associates began. I was sustenance, sales, marketing and finance and she gave it life. With my father-in-law's influence and Government funding, we grew, delivering on requirements for the biggest players in national defense. Soon Arlene and I were rich and Ray was growing ever more powerful.

"The Chinese and, to a degree, the Russians and Turks were spending more on armaments and because America was so deeply in debt with a busted budget, my father-in-law and others reacted to the writing on the wall. They knew, hell, everyone knew there were just too many unproductive people in America for the size of our economy and inevitably budget constraints would cause America to fall back to the pack in terms of military capability and that was unacceptable. So to get more bang for our national defense buck, my Father in Law put me in contact with a team of ex-military intelligence officers and Investment Bankers and we developed a plan to pilfer or at least neutralize our enemies' military and economic capability, an application that would also effectively eliminate terrorists as well and the beauty of it was, we could deliver it without having the exorbitant costs required to maintain a large private standing army and without building a stockpile of expensive, budget-busting weaponry. With our AI, no ally or competitor could develop any delivery system that we couldn't gain control of first. Finally and forever, America was safe.

"I expected to be a rich patriot from all this but when I explained it to Arlene, she refused. In fact, she was offended because her software was going to be used to infringe on the personal freedoms of American citizens. We argued but I couldn't convince her so I broke the scope of the project into manageable, small packets hoping she wouldn't figure it out and that worked for a while. Massive government and private funding poured in and Arlene and the twins developed Ray into something incredibly powerful."

"But the project affected her overindulged sense of decency and she refused to add more to Ray's functionality even though it was being used to protect America from her enemies. We were arguing more and more until I finally just told her that she had no choice but to develop it, that a concerned nation required it and she threatened to go to the police or her Congressman to confirm what I was telling her."

"And that's when you tried to kill her."

"You don't understand. Back then, America . . . Arlene . . . it was . . ." Crelli fell silent and Gil waited. Again, Crelli's face went slack and then taut and he began to sweat profusely from his effort. He was stressing mightily over something. Finally, Gil nudged him out of his trance and Crelli continued on.

"America's leaders had become soft and careless and the country was facing perilous times. I had no choice. The water skiing accident had to be done." Crelli looked down and paused. "I've been locked away for twenty years. I was President and then Chairman and now I'm here. I was the person directly responsible for America's return to greatness and everyone loved me or worshiped me or both. I had a fine wife and many other great women, actresses, models, politicians, CEO's, you name it, I had them. There was nothing I lacked. And on top of all of that, I had Gecko on call, constantly expanding my view of the world while providing the most intense synergy a human mind has ever experienced. For all that, these twenty years, it's Arlene that I think about most, Arlene that I miss. She . . . how can I say this? I . . . this is difficult. She was disfigured beyond recognition and in the end, she . . . she . . ." He paused, closed his eyes, and shook his head. "She was just very disappointed in me. Disappointed!"

"I think you're wrong about that."

"You don't know her," Crelli continued, "not like I do. I never wanted to kill her but that doesn't matter. I could have said no, but I didn't. When she was near death, it was the saddest moment of my life and for all that, she was disappointed in me! *She* was disappointed. She knew that I was better than that, that I had lost that, 'god inside me,' is what she always called it. Her disappointment, it haunts me every day and has for two decades. For all the great things I've achieved, all of it pales next to her disappointment. I have known greatness, hell, I was great, yet she is the best person I've ever known and for everything I could be sorry for, I'm sorry most because I couldn't meet her expectations." With that, Crelli stood and walked to the amber, foam covered wall and stared at it like it was a window to the world outside."

Gil was moved until Crelli turned and tried to undo all that he had said.

"Of course, I can sell with the best of them. I can change a person's mind in a heartbeat and make them laugh or weep and love me."

Gil stared at him, a little less certain.

Crelli's returned his stare to the amber foam wall and remained deep in thought. Without turning, he spoke again. "When you were updating me, you mentioned Bree. I believe you mean Bea because Bea is Tanya's daughter, her only child. Tanya being Tanya, she named the poor kid after a failed batch of my clones and I never understood why. As far as I know, Bea is Tanya's only living warm-blooded relative. She was a beautiful little girl. She looked like a miniature Tanya but unlike and in spite of her mother, she was a delight. I allowed her to be educated with my clones and relished having her play outside my office. She was always so serious, sitting quietly, sometimes listening to my conversations and absorbing everything.

"You're her father."

"I enjoyed her but your information is wrong. I'm not Bea's father."

Gil wondered at that. Maybe Crelli's Bea wasn't his Bree. "Bree is definitely the Chairwoman's daughter though she's much nicer than her mother," Gil said. "Like her mother, she's beautiful and she's smart—I thought smart like you, but if you're not her father, who is?"

Crelli stared intently at Gil. "Bea had her mother's amazing large violet eyes, the color of which, I swear, has never been seen before in any eyes on this planet. Her eyes had flecks of—"

"Yellow and red," Gil finished.

Crelli's eyes narrowed. "Bea had straight, dark hair."

"That's Bree."

With that, Crelli tensed. "You like her. Don't."

"No, I don't. Why?"

"It's far too dangerous. She's her mother's daughter."

"No, she isn't," Gil explained. "She's really nice and I like her a lot."

"You can't ever like her a lot," Crelli said. "Because Mark is Bea's father."

Gil found himself standing. "What? No! My grandfather, Mark? No, he can't . . ." He felt queasy and a cold sweat caused him to shiver.

"Bea is your aunt. But more important, she is Tanya's. You two aren't . . . ?"

Before Gil could deny it, Crelli shouted, "You can't. Absolutely not. That child is off limits!"

Devastated, Gil returned to his seat.

Crelli was animated now and he began to walk around the small suite, shouting and gesturing. "You can't. You simply can't. Not with her. I won't allow it. You and I can achieve so much but not with her—never with her. I will help you take Tanya down but only if you stop this foolishness right now, today." With that, Crelli turned his back on Gil but continued to speak.

"I can't believe it, after all these years; after all these fucking years waiting—that bitch goes and plays the young love card with her daughter—her daughter, and it works!" Crelli turned and his focused gaze seemed to cut right through Gil. "Using Bea is Tanya's desperate attempt to stop me, to stop us, before we can take her down and achieve greatness. Damn, that's so like her. She was never an intellect, never close, but she is clever to a fault and she builds incessantly for convoluted eventualities just like this. I can't believe it. I will not allow her to defeat me again after all this time, particularly with a simple love trap like this. I won't allow it, do you hear me, I won't." Crelli's eyes refocused and he seemed startled that Gil was still in the room. "Tell me you're not screwing her. Tell me you're not in love with her."

As Gil struggled to cope with the reality that Bree was his aunt, he felt overwhelmingly sad and Crelli read his silence.

"You are, aren't you?" Crelli's eyes suddenly unfocused then quickly refocused when Gil stuttered his way to an answer.

"No, nothing, no, of course not," Gil mumbled. "We haven't . . . we aren't. Are you sure your Bea is Bree?" He desperately wanted Crelli to be wrong but Crelli nodded. "Bree believes you are her father and she has been trying to find you."

"I wish she had found me. I understand why she thinks of me as her father but Mark is her biological father. I can't prove it here, now, but what do I have to gain by lying? I didn't even know you knew her until you said something." Then, his voice mellowed. "How is she?"

"She'll be sad to learn you're not her father."

"Thank you for that. I suspect she'll be sadder still to know Mark is."

"Why does everyone hate Mark so much?" Gil asked.

"He's hated because he never stood for anything but I meant she'll be sad that you and she can't—"

"And that pleases you?"

"Little pleases me. You will only get hurt and our revolution will fail," Crelli offered. "Bea is Tanya's. She may be nice and she might even love you but her allegiance is absolutely with her mother and the throne or she wouldn't be available to you."

Crelli's voice calmed a bit. "In spite of what you believe, I'm not some evil fiend. I see that you care for her and I'm sorry about that. Bea wasn't my daughter but she was a comfort to have around and I liked her. She needed someone, Mark and Tanya treated her as badly as Mark treated his own son."

"You mean my father, Howard?"

"Mark's wife, your grandmother, Terry, was a nice lady and she wanted to be a good mother but she got lost in Mark's lust for power. Mark always put himself first. That's why I hired him but Terry hated the Washington politics that Mark loved so much and to find release, she allowed *Pharma* and booze to take over." Gil thought back to Angel Falls when Mark told his story of Howard's sad life. Then he pictured poor Bree as another frightened captive child in the White House.

"Mark was the product of an impetuous generation, one that grew up during the declining years of America's First Republic. His generation was more disrespectful of power and precedent, and they were always in a hurry, always trying to get to the end of something so they could start something new, as if the promise of America was on a first come, first served basis. Kids from Mark's generation tended not to have deep roots and above all, they lived with as little burden or obligation as they could. Mark's generation worshipped flexibility and believed there could be relationships without strings.

"But most of all, Mark wanted to be President. He was brilliant and so his entire life, everyone had told him he would achieve it, but confronting his career goal with Tanya and me in the way, it caused Mark to go a little crazy. Don't get me wrong, there was never a better civil servant to the President and his achievements in private industry deserve every accolade. He respected me but he was gaga in love with Tanya. Even with that, he resented us for limiting his future options. In the end, he got his wish and became president, but by then, he had sold his soul for cheap to get there and he was a poor president. He was also our last President."

"How can you, of all people, say that Mark sold his soul?"

"I'm the one who bought it and Tanya, well, she tore it to shreds. When it became apparent to Mark that Tanya was to be my successor, he couldn't help himself. He became what she needed him to be in order to be next in line. It was a sad choice because those beholding to Tanya are always ruined in some important way. Mark was better than most but he didn't recognize Tanya's toxin until he was too far gone. That's Tanya's way too. She revels in enticing people into ruining themselves.

"Mark as her vice-president had one important job, to serve at the pleasure of the President whenever she needed pleasuring and only when she considered him to be the best instrument to deliver pleasure. For all that, he was besotted with her and, Tanya being Tanya, for the fun of it she sucked all joy from him. It was almost too perverse to watch.

"After I forced Tanya to relinquish the Presidency after the Constitutional eight years, she decided to experience motherhood." Crelli pretended to shiver. "What a chilling concept. *Virtuoso* wasn't enough simulation for Tanya so she allowed Mark to play a minor, yet absolutely vital real role, though knowing Tanya, she probably insisted on artificial insemination just to frustrate him that much more.

"Some women shouldn't be mothers and poor Bea was the victim of the worst. I remember, while Tanya was carrying her, Tom Gorman joked about whether she'd eventually eat the poor thing once it hatched.

"Not long after Bea was born, maybe even minutes, Tanya realized her mistake and placed a staff member in charge of rearing her. Then, for no apparent reason, she told Mark he had to renounce all paternal rights and just stay away from them. It was lucky too, because some of her consorts died horrible deaths during her post partum.

"I'm anything but sentimental but as Bea grew up, she was such a precocious child that I permitted her to be raised with my clones. Unlike them, she was a joy; she had such fire and real smarts, too. One of life's odd twists; my clones were cold, empty, dead things, more like Tanya and Bea was more like me and so I nurtured her when I could."

Crelli seemed genuine and Gil felt the warmth and the melancholy in his voice and he noticed when it changed.

"All of that doesn't matter now. Bea or Bree, she's Tanya's, not ours. Do you understand? She will never be ours. Forget her. She is far too dangerous."

Gil didn't want to discuss it so he changed the subject.

"I'm not a clone," he blurted out.

Crelli paused. "I hadn't considered that . . ."

"Why did you execute my mother?"

Again, Crelli's eyes lost focus. When focus returned, he responded. "That wasn't me. I was there and I knew about it, but the Chairman of the United States is responsible for the big picture, strategy, not tactics. Look to Tanya and Mark for answers there."

"You're lying. Mark would never do that to family."

"I really don't want to piss you off because I'll die here if you don't trust me but I'm telling the truth." Once again, Crelli's eyes unfocused then quickly refocused. "I knew of your mother's capture and it surprised me when she was convicted and more so, of course, when she was executed."

"Did you know her?" It slipped out.

"No, I'm sorry, I didn't," Crelli admitted. "So that you know, I couldn't save her. I was never above the law."

"You were the law."

"I caused laws to be written but no one, including me, is above the law. During the bad times, at the end of the First Republic, I lost friends too, great friends and family members. They were sad, bad times and everyone, even the wealthy, suffered, but I had nothing to do with your mother's execution." He sat across from Gil. "Tell me about Bea. How is she doing?"

"Not until you tell me why my mother had to die." Once again Crelli surprised him with his response.

"I'm sorry, I can't do that," Crelli said. "Even if it hurts my credibility with you, I was President and Chairman of the United States and in spite of my current situation; I am bound by my oath. I know you won't like it, but I can't tell you. You will have to find that out from others . . . not so bound."

"Really?"

"I can't tell you. I'm sorry."

"About Bree—your Bea—she was a star in Tanya's administration until I convinced her to do something against her mother's wishes. She's disappeared and I'm worried about her. The Chairwoman says she will harm Bree unless I lead a revolution against her. But if I do . . ."

At that, Crelli's face lit up with excitement, but he spoke calmly. "Don't worry. Don't worry about Bea," he said. "Tanya won't waste loyal resources. Bea is safe."

Even though he wasn't sure, Gil felt relieved to hear that.

Once again, Crelli stood and wandered around the small suite, this time mumbling about something. He stopped at a certain spot and for a long time he seemed to be admiring it. Then he shook his head, vigorously, and returned to his seat. He was smiling.

"Why didn't you tell me this earlier? Tanya goading you to rebel is important."

Gil couldn't see how. "She insists that I lead a union against her armed troops. It's insane but if I don't, just like Angel Falls, she'll destroy them. I can't let that happen."

Crelli laughed out loud and then slapped Gil on the leg. "Have you wondered why she's goading you into an armed rebellion that she can't win? This is great news."

Gil thought he'd misheard him. "You mean she can't LOSE. No revolution can succeed with the power she has. It's impossible. She's too strong."

"No, no, it makes sense. It all makes sense now." Crelli said, excitedly.

Gil waited without hope.

Again, Crelli mumbled something incoherent and then with his teeth clenched, he strained as if trying to remember something critical that remained just out of his reach. Finally, he shrugged and explained. "Arlene invented Ray. I took it and used it to develop Gecko. To be useful to my purpose, Gecko was modified by the best minds available until he was able to continuously investigate the world, undetected and independent. This was critical because by the time Gecko became functional; computers throughout the world were running just about everything and with each new technology, exabytes of data were being stored and becoming more assessable in the Cloud or Mesh.

"While conventional wisdom said that military power was required, the experts in every government with a foreign policy knew that the only true race to power was the one to develop that one application that could continuously evolve so as to lord over all other processors. Gecko became that processor. We won that race and there is no prize for second place.

"Poor, naïve, Arlene, geopolitics was never her thing and she never would have dreamed of being involved in developing the perfect omniscient, ubiquitous, and omnipotent spy. With proper funding and support, our Ray could have become that superior mobile intelligence. He could have had the ability to take whatever he wanted, without restraints, from any computer anywhere, an intelligence that could provide perfect and timely universal knowledge even when confronted with the most advanced and the tightest security protocols. Ray could have been that powerful. Gecko is.

"I have intimate knowledge of Gecko and if God exists; I swear that Gecko is God. He is that extraordinary. It was Gecko who conceptualized and then assisted in the development of the implant chip used by the general population as a Personal Identification Chip, or PID. He developed functionality that included narrow band synaptic input/output that he and I used to communicate internally. That communication was so effective that entrepreneurs and our military use a form of it for critical communications.

"Sometime before I was taken, Tanya begged me for internal access to Gecko and in a moment of great weakness, I approved it. It was the biggest mistake of my reign because it allowed her to link minds with Gecko. It wasn't long before Gecko realized that he had someone he could work through who was more compliant than me and so he began consolidating Tanya's power behind my back while having me believe that I still had perfect knowledge of the world. He made me clueless."

Gil was drawn to this story. "Why?"

"I had had a meeting with the CEO of *Mobile Global,* what is *Global Solar* today. He offered me a deal that was extremely lucrative for American business but would have ended American sovereignty and crushed what remained of the middle class. Gecko wasn't programmed to preserve and protect the United States of America. He was programmed to protect and grow the economy so when I refused the *Mobile Global* deal, he felt that I was sub-optimizing. We disagreed, and he decided to work with someone who was more malleable. In spite of what you've seen, without Gecko, Tanya is certainly malleable. It was Gecko who orchestrated my kidnapping and Tanya's ascension."

Gil was stunned. "You can't know that."

"I don't but the day of my kidnapping, Gecko deployed an inadequate security force to protect me. At the critical time, when I needed him most, he withheld advice and council. After I was captured, someone had to suppress all record of my travel that day so no one could rescue me. It could have been Tanya, or even Ginger Tucker, but the most likely perpetrator was Gecko because neither woman is that smart. But the most damning clue was that from the moment that damned glass cage fell, he has been silent."

"Arlene knew Gecko's capability and if they were going to trap you they had to build an impregnable trap," Gil offered.

"Impregnable? You don't know Gecko."

"If he knew where you were, why didn't Tanya ever come for you?"

"For that, ask Arlene."

"What does she have to do with it?"

"Somehow she's in cahoots with Gecko."

"Arlene and Gecko, no, I don't think so." Gil would not offer up Joad as an answer because apparently Crelli was unaware of her existence or her power.

"There's no other explanation that keeps me imprisoned yet safe from Tanya for these twenty years."

"Gecko, this god, he has blind spots and Arlene knows how to take advantage of them."

"Maybe something like that would work but with that kind of control, it would be Arlene, not Tanya, in charge, so I reject that. Clearly

Arlene wants you and I alive and working together so we can rid the country of Tanya."

It was reasonable given that Crelli didn't know about Joad. "But eventually Tanya found me. How do you explain that?"

"You weren't executed, you're here now, and no one has come for us since you arrived. Isn't that proof someone more powerful than Tanya wants our rebellion to succeed."

"You believe Gecko has lost faith in Tanya, then." Gil offered, "Like he lost faith in you. But he's so powerful; why doesn't he just change things without a revolution."

"Gecko has physical limitations. He can only exercise power through humans."

"You were hooked up to him, why can't he further his aims through you?"

"I'm certainly willing," Crelli admitted, "but he eludes me. With what you've just told me, it is clear he has another choice."

"Why not Ginger Tucker or . . ."

"Don't be stupid."

"Why me?"

"You're not a clone."

"I'm real."

"Yet I signed the cloning order myself. The real you was to be executed and you were to be a modified clone. Who changed that order over my signature?"

Gil considered it. Mark had said that his mother's death and his cloning were tied together yet Crelli just said that they weren't. If what Mark told him was true, Crelli was lying. Rather than confront him, Gil pressed on. "Another child was killed instead of me. Another innocent died because of me. Why did that happen?"

Crelli considered it. "Laws were broken and someone important had to pay. Mark had choices, cloning was the one he chose for you. But you're an unmodified human; undoubtedly that interests Gecko a great deal."

"Surely there are others. Why me?"

"You and Gecko must share some bond."

Once again, Gil was unwilling to explain Joad. "We share nothing. Surely there are others Gecko wants?"

"Possibly, but as I say, you're different. You were home schooled by your own father, a parent who must have loved you very much to have spent so much time with you risking unproductivity and possible death."

The mention of Howard brought an ache he dared not show. "How would you know that Howard loved me?"

"The same way any good analyst knows anything," Crelli explained. "What parent takes on the financial burden and general aggravation of raising a child by himself? Every child is a long term personal investment that begins on the books as a great liability. Fiscal responsibility says it's important to socialize that cost as soon as it can be quantified so parents always turn their liabilities over to private schools for leasehold improvements. Then, Archive develops them into assets that can generate favorable returns on their parent's initial investment."

"Okay fine, but how can the way my father raised me matter to Gecko?"

"I'm the best because I pay exquisite attention to detail. I'm relentless at it. I've been out of touch for twenty years but after meeting you, I'm more certain who you represent to Gecko. When I was young, there were people like you everywhere. Arlene is one of the few who remain today. They were called nice, people who believed in old-fashioned American virtues like goodness and kindness and had a strong desire to play fair, even if it meant they could lose. Good people were the majority in America back then. These were people who were considerate of others and had righteousness about them. They weren't necessarily productive or religious, although many were. The key was that others liked or respected them for just being who they were. Back then, there weren't stringent financial parameters to measure up to, although during that time workers were important to the American economy and many of these nice people provided unique business skills. For instance, they made terrific low and mid-level administrative managers, people you could trust to build cohesive, productive work teams that were balanced for the long haul. But profits are paramount in private industry so when my administration linked profitability, personal responsibility and survival, nice people skills were no longer bankable, no longer necessary, in fact, those skills got in the way. Keep in mind; nice folks were loyal to a fault; hardworking, generous, and team-oriented rather than in it for personal aggrandizement. These were the volunteers—you may not be familiar with the term—people who did necessary things at work and in their community but not for remuneration.

"The economy changed and nice folks couldn't evolve so, over time; they simply were bred out of the system. Through a quirk or by design, you're one, one of the last nice guys, and I clearly am not. It's for that reason that I believe Gecko has an interest in you but I can't guess right now how that interest manifests."

"Bernie taught me that corporate greed is what made the world not nice."

"That's way too simple. Before corporations, in say the days of the gold rush, or the early oil boom in the U.S., or with the Okie Sooners land grab, regular people, acting naturally, were every bit as greedy as corporations. The only difference between greed then and greed today is that back then there were outlets for growth among the greedy, a way to diffuse the frenzy, there were frontiers and excess resources. That and today, there's nowhere to hide the losers, the *Wasters*."

"That may be true," Gil said. "Certainly they taught that in our Economic Gospel classes, but that doesn't make greed right."

Crelli stared at Gil before speaking. "Son, do you really want to go there? I can get you the power, but eliminating greed, that would take a religious fruitcake with a gazillion dollars to spend on bodyguards and, oh yes, nine lives with an option on more. Tanya, we can beat, but to do what you're suggesting, there would be so many intense people standing in line to defeat you that we couldn't possibly win. Americans are comfortable with greed; they own it. It's a stone cold and constant rush for them. All Capitalism ever did was provide the music. You can't try to change that or you'll fail and nothing good that you want will ever happen. Don't take that chance, think it through. I said you were a good person but don't let that go to your head. Good, out there, is something with appreciation and dividends. Now is the time to show some business savvy. You can rule as a good person or for a good cause for a while, but you'll need to decide to do it either early or late in your reign because sooner or later, the world grabs you by the balls and you're doing what's natural and greed is natural." Crelli shook his head and laughed sardonically at that.

"What you say may be true but you're wrong about me. I'm not good and I'm far from nice. I've hurt people and done bad things."

"Really? You? I wasn't born yesterday. I know there are always distasteful things to be done. Maybe only nice people like you realize they're bad things and stress over them. I'll have to think on that. Tell me what you've done that's so terrible?"

"I'm not going to talk to you about them."

"If I'm to help, tell me about all those frauds you've perpetrated. Who have you killed in cold blood? Murder, rape, I need to know. How can I tell if I'm wrong about you unless I know everything?"

Gil felt threatened. "I've done all those things and more. That's all."

"If that's all you've done, I consider you a lucky man. Still, it's not like Gecko to be wrong about someone but, of course, he's never been inside your head. Look at it this way. For whatever horrible things you've done, maybe Gecko can provide you with an opportunity to redeem yourself so you can put those bad things behind you." Once again, Crelli's eyes glazed over and his face went slack and then seemed to labor over something. At first Gil thought he was in pain as he ground his fists into his thighs and grimaced until finally, his face finally slackened and his eyes refocused. Flushed and sweating, he looked down and shook his head. Then he put his hands to his head and for the first time, spoke in a dispirited tone "The worst is the silence and it's killing me. It's my head . . . it's so empty and . . . Look, I'll help you defeat Tanya, I'll do whatever you need. Maybe we can forgive each other."

At first, Gil was insulted but he reconsidered. In his adult life, he had never known anyone he could ask for forgiveness who could give it and truly mean it. He thought about Andrea but he was a boy then, with boy problems, and for all the good she did, she was a sham. To survive, he had built this great wall around himself, one that contained all of his disabling thoughts and troubled feelings. Maybe that wall had sequestered more of him than he'd intended. Here in this crypt, with the most evil man on earth, maybe he'd found common ground, or at least enough to consider letting down his defenses just a little.

"I promise, I'll listen but I won't judge you. I can't."

Wary of the offer and even warier of the man, he wished that Crelli had been more diabolical while fearing that in fact, he was. "You killed so many. How do you live with yourself?"

"If you to believe I'm a cold-blooded killer, you'll learn nothing. You might be correct but it isn't true."

"You can't change my mind. I know too many good people who died. But what I don't understand . . . please, make me understand . . . millions . . . millions."

"No country ever had what America had . . ."

"No, that's not what I'm asking," Gil insisted. "I don't want a rationalization as to why it was necessary. I'm sure you have that. I want to know about the children, the mothers and fathers, grandparents, neighbors, friends, you know, how could you order real people to death?"

Crelli's face went slack and he struggled to remain focused. "I had a child once, Reagan . . . he died . . . a bomb that was intended for me. I was speaking at a rally when a girl . . . a girl just walked out on stage . . ."

"A blond wearing a bright yellow windbreaker."

What little color remained, drained from Crelli's face. "How?"

"I met a man who was there."

"Reagan, he was my son, my only son. He was an innocent, too, but I want to be clear, nothing I did afterward, nothing, I promise you, was done to avenge him. The poor little guy was a casualty, like so many others, of a war that could have, should have been prevented decades earlier by politicians on the make. In spite of what you've heard, I have feelings. Look at me, look how I've aged. I suffer. I feel the aches, they never go away. How could I not feel it? And Reagan, he was my son. I know how it feels to see a future evaporate in front of my eyes. The death of a child is one thing you never want to experience because you learn just how much you can lose and still go on. I've had years of silent contemplation and I now believe, with all my heart and soul, that I did the right thing for America, to have done anything else, our great nation would have died. I know that millions experienced the same horror that I did with Reagan, and each one of them believes that their horror was because of me, but I sincerely wished grief to none of them.

"It turns out that Americans are unpredictable and clinically insane as a people. Besides being crazy industrious, a great many, too many, are stubborn, selfish, lazy and spoiled. In good times, there are advantages to this, but in bad times . . . it dooms them. But what always gets Americans through are the capitalists, the entrepreneurs, I don't mean just business savvy pros, but winners. America is a great cultivator. It grows the very, very best there are at winning, the one percent who've kept the other ninety-nine percent alive and at various levels of thriving. Sometimes the one-percenters fuck up. They did at the beginning of the century and again, in the twenties. They took too many liberties with the economy; they got too greedy and because of that, they sucked too much of tomorrow's wealth into the present causing the subsequent economy to implode; it got bad, real bad.

"Desperate people do desperate things. Riots and crime were rampant. Too many Americans felt they had nothing left to lose and with government revenues down, our police couldn't stabilize the situation so commerce was at great risk. On one end, Omar Smith was organizing nihilists and having them incite the abject poor into destroying the economy while on the other end, an insane group of Libertarians, Prosperity Gospel fanatics and media evangelists were driving the population toward fear and irrationality. Laws were needed. When they didn't work, more began to die and more businesses went under. Stricter laws were needed. And so it went until finally, we passed laws that determined who lived and who died. It wasn't an invention, times were that bad and if our economy had failed, America would have died. I couldn't change it. I tried but everyone was in survival mode. The winners were too confident to listen and the losers . . . the losers did what losers do, they fought and died.

"There was talk of the ninety nine percenters, those who knew nothing. They just wanted to keep playing at Capitalism and keep losing. They never got the message and even when I sent them the strongest message of all, *Circle of Life* legislation, most tried to save themselves as if trying too hard to save others was beyond their pay grade. Religion on the streets of America was okay but the religious corporate leaders were useless; they merely protected their own assets. We implored them to help us quiet the country but when the religious are caught up in economic survival you know the country is going to hell.

It is alleged that there was a time when religious leaders tended to their flock. That didn't happen in America. By the end of the First Republic, people still prayed for delivery to Jesus but they also hoarded gold and silver and grew survival gardens protected with high powered weaponry. And the priests and ministers were worse; they survived inside walled communities protected by strategically placed turrets. The clergy took the safe way out, using separation of church and state as an excuse and so they were silent while their congregations were decimated. After that cowardice, why wouldn't the Morgan religion become dominant?

"I wasn't insulated from it and I didn't want to be. I knew many who died. Some were family members, I lost employees and neighbors. It was surprising; really, I thought my neighbors were rich. When their time came, they begged me for mercy but I had none to give. In the vacuum that is now my mind, a place that Gecko once filled, these people live on. Americans are this fatal concoction of too brave and too stupid, or maybe they just scare too late. You ask how I did it. It doesn't matter. It had to be done.

"The die was cast long before I entered politics. Politicians from both parties were already waffling over easy solutions to America's problems but the quest for power and their stupid principles made them unwilling to compromise and so every problem got worse. When it was my turn, the problems were insurmountable. Everyone believed that but Mark, Mark Rose; he was a trooper throughout and it's a real shame. He believed that our only alternative was to solve it as one would any mammoth project, and I'd done a million successful ones. We scoped it; set our goals and priorities, planned it, added resources, and worked the plan until it succeeded. It did, and that was my only satisfaction, that and knowing we had saved the country—this time." Crelli paused. He looked exhausted.

"Was what we did morally wrong? Of course it was. It was horribly wrong but, *but* not as wrong as doing nothing and allowing chaos to continue. I had issues, who wouldn't, but I worked them out in *Virtuoso*."

This time it was Gil's eyes that lost focus as he pictured Crelli's mansion on the night he rescued Mark, the night Crelli was kidnapped. He told Crelli what he remembered. "It was a muddy mountaintop and there were torrential downpours. Desperate people were begging to be saved while horrible, soul-less four-legged creatures devoured them."

Gil saw real pain in Crelli's eyes, and something else. Fear?

"How . . . how do you know that?" Crelli sagged into his chair and whispered.

"The night I rescued Mark, in your mansion in Avalon, I entered *Virtuoso*."

Crelli stared. He wasn't crying but his eyes glistened. And then he cackled and smacked his thigh hard. "That's it!" he exclaimed. "God damned, that's it. Think it through. How could you access my personal file unless Gecko allowed it?"

"I snuck in. I saw your unit and I was curious."

"But you needed my voice and password. It was Gecko. It was Gecko."

"It wasn't Gecko."

"Only Gecko could provide access, or deny it. That's your proof. Gecko wants this, he wants us together. Do you believe me now?"

His thoughts jumped from Crelli's mansion to Gecko's inquisition in New York. "If Gecko wants me, I don't want him. How could I? And I'm not the one to absolve you of your crimes. I won't do that."

"I saved more than were killed," Crelli insisted

"Not many get to say that in their defense. You simply can't reduce it to that. It took me too long to realize it but we're adults. It's our job; it's our responsibility to protect the innocent, those, right or wrong, who can't make it for so many reasons. We should be helping them because we can and they need our help. But most of all, the children need our protection, all of them, all the time, and at any cost and not just those with potential, but every one. We put them here and whether we like it or not, whether it's convenient or not, whether it fits into our philosophy or our religion or our budget or not, we have an obligation to care for them no matter how irresponsible they are or how tough or unfair life becomes. If we don't do that, who does? They're children! They're innocents! If we don't protect them every way we can, what does that make us?" *How could he make Crelli understand how wrong what he did was and that it could never happen again?* "When you make the world about numbers and commerce, and you force people to qualify, it's the worst kind of intolerance."

Crelli listened in silence.

Though he believed what he'd just said, it made him feel miserable. "I condemn what you did but instead of doing something about it, I ran from it. I should have found a way. I was a teenager, a naïve teenager, and so incredibly stupid. I was scared, scared most of the time and about everything but in the end, I've failed good people, people I've cared for . . ." From there, he couldn't stop. He opened up, and the guilt and recrimination poured out, too late, and to the wrong person.

He spoke first of Bernie and the disappointment he'd caused him and then of his sadness at leaving Howard and never trying to contact him. He talked loathingly of his complicity in Hilly's death and of Stacey and how horrible her life must be with her terrorist husband and how disappointed she must be with him. And, awkward as it was, he explained Bree, their love and their distance—frustrating, yet how ultimately fortunate that they never partnered, really partnered. Sorrow and regret flowed out while Crelli listened sympathetically. But throughout, Gil kept Joad from his ranting. Then, when he felt as miserable as he'd ever felt, he confessed his worst sin, Annie and the daughter he'd never know.

"I ruined my child's life," he admitted as tears raced down his cheeks. "Annie and my daughter suffer for my cowardice. I should have made it right. If I had . . . I don't know what, but I should've done something so my daughter could have her father and a life. She was mine. I was responsible for her but I ran. I always run. I destroyed her life. How can I ask strangers to depend on me to do the right thing when my own child can't?"

"You did what you did," Crelli finally offered. "Learn from it and move on. That's what adults do."

"Move on? Move on to what? How? I've been faking it my entire life and I'm finally out of opportunities. I'm burned out, exhausted. Worse, the part of me that survived isn't me or if it is, I don't like it." Embarrassed, he wiped away tears of anger, frustration and pain. "And I won't be absolved, certainly not by you."

"Who better than me? Simple answers are worthless here. Be thankful for the easy stuff when it comes because it doesn't come often enough. There are a million critics to tell you you're wrong, enough to make you believe them if you aren't strong. Who knows what's truly wrong and who says your critics are right?"

Crelli tilted his head back and closed his eyes. "If I believed in wishes, I would wish for some suitably long period before you're judged right or wrong. And do things always have to be right at that moment, or they're wrong? Where does it say that? People bend and lean in so many different directions during their life; it's what makes us human and the world imperfect. Maybe you're right and I could have done what I did differently. But I'm content being judged for doing something when something needed doing, for doing what politicians refused to do for generations. If my sentence is to face old age and death here in solitary, I accept that, but as I said, I still don't understand why I'm here.

"I could die in a hundred years or in the next minute. This," he pinched the flesh on the back of his hand and watched it slowly flatten, "this is all I have and I'm pretty damn sure it's all there is. What you do is your life and then poof, nothing, and then it's someone else's turn. Eternity is an insurance policy that theologians sell to the living because life is too damn hard without it."

Crelli leaned forward and whispered. "I have another wish. More than anyone and with all my heart, I wish people took this life seriously because there is no other. I will never understand why so many live like they don't mind dying or how they can remain so uninvolved in their own lives when that aloofness costs them everything. Tomorrow isn't another day; it's a wish that doesn't ever have to be granted."

Gil found it hard to believe that he was having this discussion with the man who destroyed so many of his family. "Sir, you and I are very different. I can't believe in myself the way you believe in yourself. But this isn't about you and me; this is about what happens to the innocent and incapable, people called *Wasters*, because they need our care and that's no small thing. And it's about the average person, those called *Conducers*. Their lives are every bit as important as the wealthy. If I've learned anything it's that greed, selfishness, and the quest for power aren't what I want in my heart and if I can do something about it, it's not what I want in everyone else's. Regardless of the circumstances, you forced everyone to choose survival through wealth and that amplified greed—it cost too much. Greed is limitless and its god is uncompromising. I wouldn't want that in my world."

"That's fine. Stick with me and we can do that. We can make that world."

"I can't until I find a better god to believe in."

"You sound like Arlene . . ." Just then, the door opened and Qade entered.

"Gil, your train leaves soon and you have one more appointment. We have to go."

"No!" Crelli shouted. "Not now, we're getting to it. This is what Arlene wanted."

Qade stood at the door. "Sorry, Crelli, you were told he wouldn't be here long."

"But there's so much to work through. Give us the rest of the day. I can help him. Gil, show them who's in charge, stay. Explain to Mr. Blessing, here, that I can help you."

Unsure, Gil nodded. "Surprisingly, this is working, Qade. I can stay."

"I'm sorry," Qade insisted. "Arlene insists that you go."

Crelli grabbed Gil's arm. "Don't, we have so much more to discuss before you're ready. I've had time to think on it. There are ways to do capitalism differently, better. And democracy, we can make it work. I would . . ."

"We have to go." Qade insisted and then motioned for Gil to follow him.

"You can't take him away, not yet. Qade, can't you see the boy needs more time? If he's to be the messiah, he needs me. I love America. Give me another chance to prove it. Gil, listen to me. I agree that we need an economic system that provides differently. I've been working it out. Don't go. You and I can change the world, make it better."

Qade put his hand on Gil's shoulder. "Where we're going is important too."

"It can't be more important than what I have to say," Crelli pleaded.

"I have my instructions, Crelli. Gil must be somewhere else."

"Let me speak to Arlene. She'll understand. Gil and I, we're . . ."

"Arlene was clear," Qade repeated, firmly.

Unsure, Gil walked toward the door.

Realizing he'd lost, Crelli made one final plea. "You know where I am, please . . ." He offered his hand and Gil shook it. Crelli held on to it, unwilling to let him go.

"You and me, kid, we can do great things."

Gil extracted his hand and followed Qade out of Crelli's prison.

Chapter 15

Graceland, Indianapolis, IN—Winter, 2083

Fresh, heavy wet snow provided a quieting blanket of white as Qade's jet-black electric bike slipped through the dark, narrow streets of Indianapolis. As the snow and fresh air rushed by refreshing his anxious spirit, Gil was relieved to absorb the winter quiet.

In this weather, Qade was pushing his bike at top speed and as big flakes hurtled by, Gil gazed into the distance, past the speeding blur of the near. They were rapidly approaching a huge structure when Qade stopped abruptly and the silence and the sudden absence of forward motion made Gil queasy. He sucked down a couple of cold breaths and stared at the ominous old and decrepit multi-storied building that seemed to disappear to the horizon in each direction. As far as he could see down the wet streets, torches were lit at each entrance, illuminating barricades made of enormous piles of trash and debris soaked with a shiny tar-like substance that reflected that fire in a million sparkles, while above, torches whipped in the winter wind, taunting any passerby who presumed to intrude.

"Something's happening," Qade said. "Hold on." He flipped the ignition on, leaned into a corner, and sped down a narrow street. In the distance, Gil heard the throaty roar of gas powered cycles, but the falling snow hid their location.

"It's the evening raiding party," Qade shouted over the gusts. "We have to move. Hold on, feel my bike, and move with it." With Gil clutching him, Qade then accelerated, swerving through alleys and small streets, weaving around old junk automobiles and piles of trash until he stopped in the middle of a dark street to listen again. Gil heard more faint roars and followed Qade's stare. Behind them in the distance, a cluster of headlights appeared. Suddenly, two lights peeled off from the rest and headed toward them. Qade turned off his lights, spun the bike around, and gunned the engine up a series of steps, settling on the porch of a nearby home. The engine roar got louder and first two red laser and then two headlights beams appeared and then the bikes whizzed by and were gone. It was another sight, though, that froze on Gil's retina. In the light from the passing cycles, there were frozen corpses everywhere, whitewashed by the falling snow.

When the pursuers had gone, Qade retraced his way down the steps and turned down another alley. All was silent as Qade carefully picked his way through the rubble and the dead. At the end of the alley, he accelerated across the street just as Gil saw two more high-beam headlights closing in. He tapped Qade and pointed. When the bike slowed, Gil yelled, thinking he hadn't seen them, but Qade remained calm and Gil had no choice but to watch nervously as the lights grew larger and brighter. A red laser beam found him and immediately Qade accelerated and headed down the street toward a large brick wall with an attached small, dilapidated wooden shack whose door had broken away and was dangling open. Not sure if they could make it through the small opening, Gil screamed as they zipped in with little room to spare to enter a large warehouse filled with empty industrial racks. Qade maneuvered his bike down the rows as the roar of their pursuers intensified menacingly behind them. Against a brick wall at the far end of the building, a large wooden barrel lay on its side, its black opening facing toward them in the dim light. As the pursuit closed, Qade headed straight for it, the light from the other cycles creating a silhouette of them that grew larger against the brick wall and Gil could tell without looking that the bikes were gaining. They rocketed toward the barrel at full speed and terrified, Gil held on tight waiting for Qade to slow or swerve but he continued straight on. They entered the barrel's blackness without slowing; causing the cycle to whine at a high pitch but it was drowned out by Gil's scream.

And with his scream echoing in his ears, the bike swerved suddenly left and then right and they entered a narrow quiet corridor whose entrance was hidden by the shadow of the barrel. Behind them, Gil heard another high-pitched whine as the pursuit bikes accelerated into the barrel. Just as the pitch changed there were two loud explosions and the narrow corridor lit up with orange fire. Briefly, he felt intense heat and then all was silent and dark.

Qade continued on as if nothing had happened. When he finally slowed and stopped, he motioned for Gil to get off the bike and together, they covered the cycle with a large nearby tarp. Qade then rolled an empty drum in front of the cycle to hide it and pulled out two sacks from another drum and handed one to Gil. Inside it was an oversized, dirty, wrinkled coat and a beat up fedora. Gil changed, first removing his camouflage and giving it to Qade who put it with his gear in the sack and returned it to the drum. Qade took the other sack and headed up the nearby stairs while Gil put on the old coat and the fedora and then ran to catch up. At the top of the stairs, Qade opened the green metal door and they entered a burnt out brick building bereft of everything but metal grates for flooring.

"We can walk to City Hall from here," Qade said.

"City Hall?"

"That's what the residents call the building up ahead. You know, you can't fight city hall. This is Graceland and to the people here, City Hall is their sanctuary but it's dangerous so follow my lead."

"Why do they call it Graceland?"

"This is where city people who can't succeed and can't escape to the *Unincorporated Lands* go to avoid death for as long as they can."

Qade led him on a circuitous route through the building, up and down stairs some bent and unstable. In some places, they moved through empty corridors, past boarded up and abandoned retail shops and offices until they reached a balcony overlooking an area where ramshackle booths decorated in faded graffiti provided redoubts for armed local guards. Qade pointed through a cracked window to a tall, glass building softly aglow in the distance.

"That's our destination."

Before they could go further, a group of armed teenagers accosted them.

"Yo, Blessing," one of the teens called out. "How you doin, dawg? This trip'll cost you like the others."

Qade pulled a couple of cans of food from his sack and offered them to the teen leader who took them and then searched the sack for more. He took another can and motioned for them to move on.

"What just happened?" Gil asked.

"They're apprentice *Tollers*. Survival is at a premium here so to keep the odds in favor of the current custodians, there's an entry toll. It's really just extortion."

The armed teens watched warily as Gil and Qade moved on. Qade opened a door and they were confronted by an alleyway between the building and a tall, red brick wall that went on as far as Gil could see. The passageway between the wall and the building was narrow and the building and wall were so high that, in the snow, Gil could barely make out the night sky above. Hugging the walls on each side and not quite blocking passage were countless small, fragile shelters made from nothing more than what could be found to keep weather out, cardboard, roof shingles, corrugated sections, or plastic bags. Most of the hovels were sagging and soggy from the snow. As they walked, Gil peered tentatively inside. Many of the shelters were empty but in some he saw the gaunt, sad faces of children, huddling against the walls, eyes wide and vacant, staring as if in wonder that they were still alive. Their clothes, even on this cold dank day, were scant, rotting and stuffed with anything that would qualify as insulation.

"Who are they?" he asked.

"They are our fearsome *Waster* army," Qade explained. "Graceland is their home and their life. It's all they have and they'd fight and die for it, if they could."

"I thought you had a real rebel army."

Qade shook his head. "No army can stand against government technology. The people here are about as effective as any force can be. We're an army of lost souls waiting to die and praying to be found."

Even in Bolivia Gil hadn't seen this. "How can they live like this?"

"This is how they must live in order to keep their profile so low that they don't attract additional HOMESEC resources."

"Oh," was all Gil could think to say. There was desecration everywhere. On, around, and inside the tiny sheds, piles of feces, feathers, and the skin and bones of tiny animals made for macabre decoration and landscaping. Just then, he was startled by a loud noise and he turned to locate the sound. "What's that?"

"That's probably the rest of that patrol we eluded earlier," Qade said. He pointed down the alley to a distant yellow light. "They're hitting the far side of Graceland, tonight. There's the light from the blaze. We should be safe enough here."

"Why is HOMESEC here?"

"HOMESEC isn't. There isn't enough profit. But for private armies, there's a different economic model. They attack regularly to get their cut of whatever is keeping Graceland alive."

"Flies," Gil said without thinking. "It's so cold. Why are there so many flies?"

"In a *Waster* metropolis like Graceland, flies are at the top of a very shallow food chain. What did you expect? This isn't a place to live; it's a holding pen for those waiting to die."

Gil breathed in a foul scent. "How did this happen?"

"Better you should ask why it's still happening," Qade said as they carefully avoided the fragile hovels along their way. "At the beginning of the century Graceland was just another poor section of Indianapolis. I had friends who lived here, co-workers, too. Back then, there were places like Graceland in every city but those that remain mostly look like Graceland does today. The jobs left for greener pastures but the people couldn't. No one wanted them so they had no choice but to stay and they stayed until welfare ended and when most couldn't afford to live here anymore, Graceland emptied. Once outside, the residents found disappointment and death, so those who survived that retreated back here.

"Over time, a hierarchy developed to protect those who couldn't protect themselves, beginning a new and decidedly inferior cycle of haves and have-nots within these walls. As poor as we are, outside of Graceland, desperate, marauding gangs who were once members of the middle class took notice of Graceland's resurgence and formed private armies that still prey here for scant rewards. But even with parasites like that, Graceland grows. Periodically, when it grows too large, the better funded private armies come to cull the herd for a fee that the government pays, a leftover from the old *Circle of Life* laws. They don't destroy the place, they need to live off of it, so they murder us in sections, taking what little we have of value, knowing that too soon other desperate people will straggle here and fill the void. And so the cycle continues."

Horrified at what he was seeing, hearing, and smelling, Gil listened, speechless.

"On the positive side, gang leaders once developed a sophisticated barter system with a calculus that avoided alerting HOMESEC, who would take us down in a heartbeat if it was worth their while. But a barter economy required too much bookkeeping and so the gangs got together and changed to a monetary system that sustains their power even now.

"Today, everyone buys bread using Graceland script. And so, for what it is, Graceland works and continues to grow in spite of HOMESEC, privateers, and *Tollers.* According to government reports, most deaths here are from natural causes, but those who know understand that it means malnutrition, dehydration, debilitating disease, murder, suicide, and just general disappearance."

Gil considered it. "If Graceland were to turn around, it would prove that capitalism works."

"No one cares whether capitalism works in Graceland or with the poor."

Gil had pictured a rebel town as something more . . . prolific, something like Profit or Hamilton, but with rebel soldiers armed to the teeth to protect the innocent—certainly not this. He understood why Arlene wanted him to see Graceland.

They approached a man who carried an assault weapon at the ready.

"Bidness?" the man asked.

"We don't want any trouble, Harry," Qade answered.

The man nodded. "What's in da bag, Q-man?"

Qade handed the bag to the man who placed it in a cage. "We don't want trouble."

"Don't matter. It's a little light, do better next time." With that, Harry led them to a door, opened it, and gestured for them to enter.

Inside, the air was stagnant with a pungent, sickly sweet, metallic smell that caused Gil to gag. "This is City Hall?" Gil whispered while covering his mouth in a futile attempt to endure the odor.

Qade explained as they walked down another long, narrow corridor that ran alongside an inside wall of yellowed, wire-reinforced glass. "The people outside these walls," Qade explained, "they hope and pray to survive another day so they can move up on the list. The list is how families get inside. If they can bring enough food, fuel or cash opportunities to the gang lords who control the list, they move up on it. The list then is the gateway to another day's survival. People live in those sheds until someone inside Graceland dies or leaves—mostly they die—and the next name on the list, if they're alive, gets a chance to move inside. Isn't this a great country? Even in this hell hole, there's upward mobility."

"Is this Crelli's doing?" Gil asked, still haunted by their earlier conversation.

"In fairness, no, not entirely. Places like Graceland are the inevitable downside of libertarian, free-market capitalism. That's the problem with capitalism, it has nothing for the losers and no winner wants to recognize them let alone redistribute some of their wealth to help losers because it means repudiating the hard-work and no handout tenets of their faith. Gracelands exist because to make it as a capitalist, to truly make it, you must fear Graceland and fight with your last breath to ensure that you never come in contact with it. As I said, it's the inevitable and unseemly dark side of capitalism. Let's face it; Gracelands occur in America because all of the king's horses and all of the king's men were never truly committed to the pursuit of happiness for a large underserved portion of our population. We deserve a more righteous king and far better horsemen but instead, all we got were Crelli and Brandt."

"I thought Holarki and the *Toller* village at Presque Isle were sorry places. The people there were footloose and fancy free compared to . . . to this."

"Towns where only the poor can live have always existed in our nation even when America boasted proudly of its Christian piety. Graceland is proof that Christ's teachings fell on deaf ears in America. And life here is so much worse now under the Gospel of Morgan. But Morgan or Jesus, it doesn't matter. With death pressing, the poor people of Graceland see no purpose in prayer anymore."

"Surely there are people who can see this is wrong. Why won't they change it?"

"Why? Because it's an investment with a poor return and that's all the reason business needs not to care. You see, everyone in America is frozen with terror at impending poverty and so they spend all of their efforts trying to prevent it. For the lucky few, the only victory is to climb as far above poverty as they can and use the fear of it so that they never look back. Some may feel guilty, but most assuage their guilt through good Morgan capitalist penance, you know, acquiring new stuff. Graceland is history's proof that a highly competitive capitalist society effectively destroys societal obligations. Omar Smith recognized it and rallied an army of frightened people willing to die rather than live in this kind of poverty."

"So are these Smith's people?"

"There are no 'Smith people', Smith is an egomaniac. He took advantage of the poor and he still feeds off their desperation but he never helps them, not even one. In this world there are only capitalist winners and capitalist losers and the poor, like the rich, must get there without help."

They walked and Gil listened while staring at the unholy misery around him.

"There's a tale people tell from back in the days when the *Circle of Life* laws were first being implemented. It's about two enterprising but desperate out-of-work engineers from a large local Indianapolis pharmaceutical company. The firm had been acquired by a foreign corporation and all operations were sent to Bahrain leaving the employees here destitute and with no hope of finding work. These two engineers, however, found their way into Graceland and made their home in an old, busted meat locker in a long abandoned restaurant. These engineers were once successful so rather than beg, steal, or prostitute themselves to survive; they put together a business plan and began breeding rats, pigeons, roaches, and other slum critters, even flies that are always in plentiful supply in Graceland. When they were ready, they opened a restaurant on the edge of Graceland and named it, oddly enough, *Road Kill.* They served a bizarre, but gourmet menu to the affluent of Indianapolis in a kitsch environment. Cocktails and wine were served in pint liquor bottles wrapped in brown paper and the food was offered in dog and cat food cans or on old newspapers and magazines. They warmed everything table side over canned heat. *Road Kill* ambience was marketed as city sumptuous and in spite of the location and the faire; it became quite hot with the wealthy of Indianapolis. It was so popular that others tried to copy it, after all, there's no lack of vermin to be cooked. The irony was, because of the location, the owners were forced to hire security guards to protect their clientele from the omnipresent, poor, starving Graceland residents. For a while, security added to the ambience but ultimately, the engineers decided to move their restaurant to a better neighborhood."

"Don't tell me, they franchised it and are now living in splendor."

"I'm surprised at what a capitalist romantic you are." Qade said, smiling. "That's good to know. No, they weren't that lucky. As happens in the fine world of haute cuisine, rat, roach, and pigeon fell out of flavor and *Road Kill* soon closed. I guess there are only so many ways to provide a satisfactory eating experience using ghetto protein and once you're done, you're done.

"The corporate spin on it was that of another capitalist success fantasy without offering the true ending because it's hard to market capitalist fantasy if people know that they are aspiring to situations that end in bankruptcy."

Gil paused and put his hand on Qade's shoulder. "Qade, thank you, thank you very much. I really needed to see this. I understand now."

"I'm glad," Qade responded. "These are people like you and me and like us; they are children who've grown up trying to make the best of their world. Some are good, some are bad, but none deserve this. They might have expected fairness and goodness from a country that advertised just that, but now it's too much to even hope for."

Qade started to move on but Gil held his shoulder to keep him there. "How can it change?" He asked.

"Truthfully, I don't know," he answered. "People hope. It's what they do. Maybe it's all they can do. In the shadow of great wealth, places like Graceland exist where even the tiniest morsel of kindness and righteousness would be profoundly appreciated but there's no one to offer it. To have allowed this to happen, God himself has failed."

Qade continued to lead Gil into the bowels of the huge complex. They walked through warren after warren of long narrow alleyways lined with fractured chicken wire glass windows and as they walked, Gil glanced up from time to time at the dirt mites that danced in the filtered yellow light. When they turned down one alleyway they faced a strong headwind that forced Gil to pull his coat tight and lean into it. At the next turn, with the wind blocked, there was eerie calm, even warmth, which turned into a gale once more at the next turn. Their progress was impeded by regularly spaced wastewater drains that seemed to go on forever and overflowed with thick brown frozen rivulets of icy muck. Above, a misty sliver of sky was visible and among the dancing dirt mites, gray-white snowflakes hovered as if too frightened to fall into this hellhole.

At one turn, Qade stopped and pointed to a large window nearby where murky candlelight flickered through the wire-reinforced, cracked and yellowed glass. Gil walked to the window and touched the cold glass leaving a handprint that quickly crystallized in the hint of light. He wiped it away and then pressed his forehead against it but couldn't see clearly what was inside.

He looked questioningly at Qade who nodded and pointed to the door. Gil forced the door open and struggled to enter against a rank, less cold gale seeking escape from inside. As soon as the door opened, the crowd inside yelled in unison, their breath forming clouds in the cold that reinforced their disapproval. Stepping in quickly, Gil forced the door closed and then stood in deathly calm as a metallic stench wafted over to him and nearly overwhelmed him. Eyes tearing, he choked and his body instinctively tried to cough out the wretchedness only to breathe it back in. He swallowed back the bile and to compensate for the odor, he took short, shallow breaths.

He was in a cafeteria of sorts but the smell wasn't so much of food, but death—frozen, acrid death. *How could people eat in this stench?*

He looked around but avoided staring at what was being eaten because he didn't want to know. His attention was drawn to the servers all wearing stained, filthy, gray-white uniforms and caps, and standing behind a long, beat up table—stainless steel in its former glory, now mostly rusted. The servers were doling out small dirty plastic bags to those waiting in long lines. One server caught his eye. She turned to him and then quickly turned away. Somehow, he was nearer and haltingly, he touched her shoulder but she didn't turn to him.

"Stace?" he asked gently and in disbelief. She shook her head but refused to turn.

"Stacey?"

With trembling fingers, he touched her hair. Her head dipped and she covered her eyes. He tried to turn her but her body sagged like she was trying to avoid his touch.

"Stace, it's me," he said. "It's Gil. Please turn around." She turned and they were embracing. Unsure who initiated it; he tightened his hold and felt at peace. He buried his face in her neck and held on and on.

He would have stayed in her embrace forever but too soon she pulled away and they stared at what they'd found. She was older, of course, and accentuated in the candlelight and the redness from her tears, her green eyes were deeper—what time and experience does to eyes. She was trembling as she tried to wipe the smudges from her face and straighten her filthy hair. His memory had failed him. Even here, like this, she was more beautiful than he remembered.

Her warm, gorgeous eyes projected hope but no words came. Lightheaded, he grabbed the table to steady himself then reached out again to embrace her but this time she stepped back. He ached to hold her again, his one true friend, but instead, he reached out to wipe her tears away, turning the streaks on her cheeks into more smudges and without taking his eyes off her, he wiped his tears away too.

"You . . . you surprised me," she spoke for the first time, her voice cracking. "I thought it was you but when you work long hours here, you kind of . . . hallucinate sometimes, you know?"

Not knowing, he nodded and she smiled, shyly.

"I'm sorry." She swallowed hard and nervously brushed an imaginary lock of loose hair from her rapidly blinking eyes. "How've you been?"

He hesitated, wanting his reply to be perfect but she misread his silence and her tear-stained face froze in an awkward smile. Frustrated by his inability to say what needed to be said, he stepped forward again but this time she recoiled causing him to utter a much less than perfect response. "Why are you here?"

A gloved hand reached for his and she walked him to a small table in a shadowy corner of the cafeteria where they sat. Her voice was so filled with emotion that it was difficult for him to understand her. "After Hamilton . . . when . . . when I helped you escape to . . . to Presque Isle, what happened? You were . . . you were going to Canada." He longed to embrace her cares away. "HOMESEC was everywhere. I barely got out. I thought . . ."

"HOMESEC, yes," he said.

"What happened?"

"I was captured," without thinking, he offered simply. "Joad double-crossed me."

She tilted her head. "Joad? No, I don't think she would do that."

She? How would Stacey know Joad and that she was a she? And if she knew, what more did she know? Even here, *why couldn't he outrun his fears and disappointments?*

As if reading his mind, she responded.

"Of course I know Joad."

Gil didn't know what to say. *Why don't mistakes ever die?*

"There's . . . there's something I need to tell you and it's hard." Her struggle made her oblivious to his. "It's important, so please and if you hate me, I understand. When Omar . . . when we married, it was . . ." She wiped a tear, shook her head.

"You don't have to explain, Stace," Gil offered. "You told me once, that night in Hamilton. You don't have to apologize or anything."

"No, you don't know." Tears streamed down her face and she swallowed hard before continuing. "I have to do this and please don't stop being my friend. I would die if I ever lost that." She took a deep breath. "Omar and I were married but we never . . . I mean our marriage . . ." Her voice was a whisper. "It was never . . . he never . . . we never consummated . . . That's a cold and totally inadequate word but . . . it's accurate. We never, you know, had sex or anything. Omar never . . ."

He wasn't sure how he felt about what she was saying, but mostly he wanted to be what she needed. "It's all right, Stace. It's okay. I don't have to know."

"But you do." Staring down at the table, trembling, she began again. "If Omar hadn't taken me in, the Chairwoman would've found me and tortured me to find you. Omar protected me." She paused and her voice softened. "He did it for perverse reasons but he saved my life." She added quietly. "He even told me he loved me and needed me and he convinced me he wanted me but it wasn't in any . . . in any loving way.

"Angel . . . Falls . . . everyone there was gone . . . you were gone. Omar knew and he said he needed me and I told him everything, Gil. I told him about you, everything he needed to know. I was scared and weak and I was grateful, too, and then our night in Hamilton happened; it was terrible but wonderful, too, wasn't it? It gave me strength."

She began to cry again but she wouldn't be comforted so he waited in silence, hoping, wanting to be whatever she needed him to be.

"He . . . it was all . . . all in simulations, stimulations with others . . . stories he designed, in virtual, you know, with avatars I think they're called, surrogates, maybe proxies." Tears flowed and her voice cracked. "But so real."

"I . . . I didn't want him to know about you but virtual makes everything so confusing, I mean I got confused. The experiences were so visceral and so wrong, like nothing I ever experienced and I . . . I wasn't equipped to fight it. Omar . . . the stories, they convinced me to love him, no, the truth . . . I did love him but it wasn't . . ."

Words failed her again and she stopped. He wanted to reach out to comfort her, to make her sorrow end, to take away the pain, but feeling culpable for the shame she felt, he just waited silently for her to continue.

She couldn't look at him but she continued. "I couldn't tell what was . . . was real and what wasn't. How can anyone? I have to not think about it because I picture what happened as real memories and I feel so dirty. I felt things . . . I know right from wrong, Mom and Dad were . . . they raised me right. But what good is it to know right from wrong if you don't know what's real? Mom and Dad . . . they never explained reality, they never told me about virtual . . . I had no one I could trust or even talk to. Everyone there was Omar's or in *Virtuoso* and they were all selling what Omar was offering. I resisted. I did until I couldn't tell what it was I was resisting. I refused to talk about you, at first anyway, but I wasn't strong . . . enough. I was so lost. I was so lost. I told him about you. Everything. I failed you. I love . . . no, I failed you." She sobbed.

He slid to her side of the table and hugged her tight.

"Can you forgive me?" She leaned against his shoulder and all he could do was nod. "Omar sent his people to find you. Did you know?"

He said that he didn't.

"If one of Omar's assassins had visited Hamilton that day, instead of me, you would be dead."

Finally, he said something that felt right. "Stace, if you hadn't come that day," he stammered. "I never would have . . . known who I was missing in my life. I saw you die. I thought I did, in Angel Falls. Then, seeing you in Hamilton, seeing you, it was a miracle. I thought I'd lost you. I felt like I had hope, again."

She looked at him and smiled. "You're my best friend in the world and the best person I've ever known. I love you so much."

He squeezed her harder. "I know what desperate is, Stace. And I think I know what you were going through. But it's okay now. Everything will be okay."

"That night, in Hamilton, I tried to . . . to kill you," She began to heave but took some quick breaths and continued. "I wanted you so much."

"I remember. But we've found each other again, that's the important thing."

"You were stronger. I didn't imagine that."

"I ached for you but we stopped because it was the right thing. And then you saved me. You're amazing."

"Yes, Stacey Grant is certainly amazing," she sniffled. "If amazing means trying to kill the man she loves." She wept openly now, her head resting on his arm, tears soaking his sleeve.

"Everything . . ." She seemed angry and her words continued to gush out. "You don't know, Gil. I lived a dream, a princess in a castle fortress, Omar's princess. I was the revered Mrs. Smith in name only. In reality I was his virgin accomplice, his bait, except in virtual, where I wasn't . . . wasn't virginal at all. I experienced things, erotic, perverse things that were so real. You don't know.

"Rabbi always told us that it's what we do when it really counts that makes us who we are. What does that make me? I let it happen. I didn't fight hard enough. Omar didn't convince me to hunt for you, I volunteered, willingly." She wiped her nose on her sleeve and took a deep breath to slow her breathing and stop crying. "Omar convinced me that all the bad stuff that happened, it was your doing, your fault. He made me talk about you and Angel . . . you know, home. You and I, we had fun but you were so remote. He convinced me you didn't want to be there, that you didn't want me. And in virtual, he proved that I didn't want you in so many ways. You were Omar's enemy so you became my enemy too. He showed me how you planned . . . you know, the bombs . . . what happened, that horrible, horrible night, he showed me how you planned it all."

"But I didn't . . ."

"I know but I was ensorcelled in his mansion of lies and hatred and I got confused. I was vulnerable and his arguments were so real and believable. He said you planned it and that's why you escaped and no one else did, not Meat, not my Mom and Dad, not my Nano and Pop-pop, not anyone else survived. I believed him. I must have, at least a little, until Hamilton when I saw you and felt the truth. Still, I let you go and I failed Omar. When I returned, he never treated me any differently but he found ways, horrible ways to inflict his disappointment on me." She shuddered and her voice dropped off. She sobbed silently while Gil held her as close as she would allow.

"I accepted his punishment . . ." She shivered. "What could I do? I deserved it. In virtual, he made me experience things even married people shouldn't ever have to experience until I couldn't take it anymore. I was sickened at what I'd become and I had to do something." She looked away.

Though he wanted to comfort her, his own virtual sexual experiences left him badly compromised and he couldn't think how. All that was left was to soothe her pain the best way he could so he held her quietly. But she refused even that. She pulled away. He wanted, he needed to make this right but she had no idea the guilt he carried, too.

Her lips trembled. "Forgive me," she begged. "I should have been stronger for you. You're a good guy. You know the rightness of things. I should have held out and not turned on you." She bowed her head and put her hands behind her neck, bringing her elbows together to hide her face as she sobbed. Then she looked up and staring into each others' eyes, she began to resist but relented and he gently pulled her close again. As their foreheads touched, their tears commingled and they cried for each other. "Please don't hate me. I wouldn't have told you, but Arlene insisted."

A cold shiver ran down his spine. He was instantly wary and pulled back. "What does Arlene have to do with us?"

"Don't be angry," she said. "I don't know what I would've done without her. After I returned to Omar's from Hamilton, I endured hell. My only good days were when Omar was away to organize, recruit, or whatever, and I was alone. One day, when he was gone, I was jogging the perimeter when I noticed a breech in his security fence. It was just a small gap and it was so improbable—Omar is fanatical about security. He says he has better electronic security than the Canadian government. Anyway, I stared at freedom for a long time—I thought it might be a test, another one of his traps and I was so scared, too scared to leave but I was too scared to stay, too. I was so desperate, alone, and sad that finally, and without hope or a plan, I squeezed through the fence and ran and ran.

"I spent a dreadful month, living in the wild, stealing food and sleeping in abandoned homes and stores. I was frightened to death every moment. I imagined Omar's helicopters or that scar-faced general's *SurveillEagles* flying over and I was fearful all the way to the Minnesota border, which I sneaked across.

"I felt a little safer from Omar then, but that scar-faced general was somewhere so I hid by day and foraged at night. I stole really. I hated to do it to those poor people but I was desperate. I stayed far from towns and avoided contact with travelers.

"Then, one night a pilgrim, that's what he called himself, he was cooking something over an open fire that smelled wonderful. I was starving and he greeted me and fed me without questioning who I was. What happened next was bizarre. I never saw him before, I'm sure of that, but he said he was looking for me. He was looking for me! How? Why? I still don't understand. How could he find me when the U.S. Government couldn't—and in the middle of nowhere? His name was *Gohmpers.* What a funny name. He asked me to travel with him and he made my life a little easier. He loved to talk and he knew so many things. He talked about what life is really like for the people here. I had never left home before . . . I didn't know. *Gohmpers* seemed to know everything. He taught me some history, and he talked about possibilities. He even talked about you. He believes in you, Gil. How do you know him?"

"I know the name," Gil explained. "If he's the same man, I met him briefly a long time ago. Was he old and much bigger and darker than me?"

She nodded. "I walked with him until I left for Graceland."

"Why did you come here?"

"*Gohmpers* said it was the right place to be. He explained that Graceland is the biggest *Waster* community near what once was your home. He felt I could do good things here and maybe feel better about myself. I came hoping that if I stayed and helped, maybe someday, when you joined the revolution, we'd see each other again."

"Suppose I'd never joined? Or died?"

"Don't say that. I made my choice and it was finally *MY* choice. I'm helping here and Graceland's been really good for me." She squeezed his hand against her chest.

"You were lost, just like me. But now, this is our time, not theirs. It's like when I chose to run from Omar. Until that moment, I allowed Omar to decide for me and it wasn't that I hated it, although I did, it was that I felt I was nothing—no one. In a way, running set me free. I was reborn. Then I found Graceland and now that I'm here, I feel needed. That has made me feel better about myself. People with power tried to destroy me because it's all they know how to do, destroy. Don't let them do that to you."

He didn't want to hurt or disappoint her again. "I know you're right, it's just . . ."

She grabbed his hand and pulled him outside. As they walked the narrow alley, the cold wind choked out the stench while an occasional snowflake swept past them to land and melt in filth. She stopped and stared lovingly at him. The alley was so narrow and they were so close. Instinctively, he leaned in to kiss her but before his lips contacted hers, he hesitated.

"What?" she said, breathlessly.

"Nothing." *Or everything*, he thought.

She pulled him into an alcove out of the wind and kissed him passionately and when she finally broke the kiss, amazed at the intensity of it, he leaned against her for support. Forehead on forehead, a mote of light ignited her brilliant green eyes and he felt like he was floating, lost in a love that threatened to fill his empty soul. *Why couldn't he have known, known back then, before all of the horror?* He kissed her and they embraced until she cut their kiss short.

"You asked about Arlene. She's been great to me. I wouldn't have survived if not for her. When she found me here, she helped me take back my life. The people of Graceland are so desperate that you can lose sight of the fact that they're people just like us. Arlene taught me how to look for what is good and kind in them and what they truly need, what they won't ask for. She has such kindness in her and that really helped me. Because of her, I found something I'd lost back when . . . when the helicopters and rangers came."

He started to say something but she put her finger to his lips to silence him.

"I arrived here depressed and of no help to anyone. Qade guided Arlene to me."

"How did Qade know you were here?"

She put her hand up to his face. He hadn't noticed it before but now, he was stunned by the glove she was wearing. It was like the ones he and Bernie had owned.

"I call it my lucky glove. Before *Gohmpers* left, he gave it to me. He said I needed it more than he did and he told me to protect it. He insisted that it would bring me luck, so I've been wearing it ever since. *Gohmpers* was right. Arlene came into my life and then my lucky glove brought you to me, too."

He continued to stare at her glove. Then a wave of melancholy washed over him and he reached behind for the brick wall and support.

"What is it, Gil?"

He cupped his ungloved hands in front of him and stared at them. "Nothing."

"Arlene is so easy to be with and so compassionate. When she spoke of you, I knew I could trust her. She's known you since you were a baby. Why didn't you ever mention her? She was there when you were born and she knows your whole family yet she never came to visit. Why is that?"

Gil shrugged.

"She's kind and so strong and defiant, not at all like me. When I asked, she explained her relationship with God. We talked about it a lot. She was raised Quaker, like my Mom and Dad, she's not some religious zealot like the Morgans, with all their strict craziness, greed and protocol.

"I was never religious. I wish, with all my heart I had been. Mom and Dad weren't very. Their generation kind of abandoned God and they never talked about Him. Arlene talks about God all the time. She believes God is inside each of us and that there is goodness in us that we can bring to the world by just living a caring life. When she speaks of God, she has this look—kind of like that look you and I get when we hike the forests—remember? Remember how free we were and how beautiful everything was?"

He did. And he missed their hikes and that feeling of peace and contentment and the freedom, mostly, he missed the freedom. "Does that mean you've become a Quaker now?" he asked.

"No," she replied. "Not that it's wrong. I just want to be me and help people when I can and Arlene's is a simpler view of life. She believes greed is a great curse and it made business people so crazy that the world needs to be free of it and that life should have more meaning than the stuff we own. And she's right, Gil. Why would a kind and just God want the things in our world to rule over us? Our spirit, that's what's important—not things in markets that we bestow false value on. Greed has perverted everything and Arlene believes there's a better way, a simpler way. She believes in the Golden Rule. I remember Nano and Pop-Pop telling me about it when I was a girl. Arlene says that the Golden Rule has always been with us, we've just chosen to ignore it. Treat others as you want to be treated yourself. How can that go bad?

There's a rightness to things, Gil, a way to live that's fair and just and good that allows everyone to pursue their own happiness, not fun, but happiness, a way that makes everyone's life full, not a life that just benefits the super-motivated greed heads out there.

"I love to listen to her when she speaks of it, her eyes light up so. She calls it the power of an elated God and she lives it, doing good things for other people because she believes that it expands the amount of goodness in the world and it makes everyone better. I can see it here and she's right, Gil. She believes in you, too, kind of like she believes in her God, not that you're a god, of course."

"I'm nothing." He would have stopped there but Stacey was being so open and honest that he continued. "I hear a voice inside me, too. I think its Bernie and it says the same kinds of things as Arlene says. It's ironic, I never listened to Bernie when he was . . . you know . . . around. Anyway, I hear this voice telling me what's right but I need to listen more."

"You listen?" She smiled. "I watch Arlene when she's here. She has this grace that affects everyone: the worst of us, the dying, the sickly, the mutilated, the children, most of all the children. She has this way. I mean how could God not want a righteous and kind world? And if you don't believe in God, well, how could anyone not want something better than this? Arlene is so smart and persuasive. I try to live like she does, sometimes I even sound like her—or at least I hope I do. I hope you can see it. She's right, too. People don't need stuff in order to matter. That people think they need things is proof that greed has infected us and that needs to end. We're trying to do that here in Graceland.

"Maybe it's easier in Graceland because no one has anything, but it's a start. But Graceland won't improve until we make those outside understand that they're worshipping a false god, a god of greed and that they are destroying all of the goodness in the world. Greed created sad, perverse places like Graceland. Kindness will save it.

"I know you believe that too, so join us, please. Look at these people; look at the way they live, we have to make this right. You can help. You can save them from those who corrupted our world. Help them like *Gohmpers* and Arlene do, and help me, too."

He thought back to their days hiking and that feeling of joy and freedom that he'd felt and he wanted to believe. He stared into her eyes and reached for her again.

"I love you," she said simply.

He had heard the words before and he had always struggled in his response to them. Here, now, they were the right words from the right person but it wasn't the right time. He knew that he had so much further to travel and it wasn't fair to put her through what was coming for him. As he stared at her green eyes until his thoughts drifted to Andrea's brown eyes. It was time. He must face it and make amends even if it destroyed everything. She had shown the strength to be honest and so must he. It was time to explain Andrea and put an end to all of the barriers but between his heart and his mouth, there was a great chasm of guilt that he was unable to bridge. She stared expectantly into his silence and all he could do was stare back. If he had the power to heal, he would have to heal himself first.

She seemed to understand. "I know that you love me and I know that your heart has been damaged somehow. When it heals, I hope you trust me enough to let me in."

Her words were kind but they hurt and he struggled once more to say what she needed to hear because she was truly the innocent victim of the pain he'd caused. But like so many times before when he longed to say that perfect something that would make things right, the words floated beyond his reach. Ineptitude and guilt encased in stoicism prevented his opening up and saying what he felt so, once more, he disappointed himself and took the coward's silent way.

She seemed to understand and she whispered. "The world has changed us so now we all have to learn to love the hard way. But it's really simple, Gil. All you have to do to love others; to really love others, is to dread with all of your heart that you will never be loved yourself and live to prevent that and you'll see, everything will be okay—no, it will be better than okay."

Before he could respond, and as if in cue, Qade was there, pointing to his watch and signaling that they must leave.

Gil swallowed to ease the sharp ache in his heart. "Please, Qade, just a few more minutes." Qade pointed to his watch again and then nodded patiently.

He took her hand and they walked out of the alcove and into the stiff breeze. He stared into her eyes hoping she would see in his eyes what he was unable to say. He saw the love in her eyes and he weakened, but he saw her fear, too, and he was sad because he had caused it. He enveloped her in his arms, kissed her lips urgently and pressed his body to hers, forcing her against a wall. She returned his kisses passionately and there they remained, oblivious to the wind and cold, neither wanting it to end.

Finally, he stepped back. "There are things I have to do, Stace, things that I've put off for far too long. I care and so much. You know that, and that'll never change. I want . . . no, until I'm done, please be okay with this because I don't know what will happen and I don't want to hurt you any more." She shook her head as if in disbelief.

Then he began again to tell her what he never before could.

"I've never shown much passion but you have to know, inside, I care, I care so much that I hurt, I don't show it much, but I do. And I care about you most of all. Everything that's happened to you, it's my fault and I'm so sorry. I'm sad about how the people here in Graceland live and I want to do something about it, but I've spent so much of my life holding back so I could survive that holding back is . . . it's who I am. I can't explain it; it's my loss, my inadequacy. It's like, I don't know, it's like I feel in a language I don't understand and when I try to express it, I . . . I don't have the words."

"I know Gil, I do, truly."

He hugged her tight and whispered. "Whatever happens, I promise I'll do everything I can to make things right." Then he paused, trying to summon the courage. "There are things I have to tell you . . . before I go." She looked terrified. He took a deep breath and in the brief time he had before leaving her forever, finally, he was honest.

"I was unfair to you in Angel Falls." She started to protest but he stopped her. "No, please. You're my best friend and I have to say this. I had . . . this other friend." He could see her trying to visualize who that could be. "You don't know her." He hoped she didn't. "When I was young, back in Aeden, Indiana, my father acquired a *Virtuoso* unit."

She shivered when he mentioned it.

"I was young, a teenager, and bored, a loner, and I played in *Virtuoso* a lot. You could say it became my best friend. Whatever time I wasn't accessing my school avatar, I was adventuring with the fake friends I'd constructed in *Virtuoso*. In all of Aeden, I had only one real, live friend and he died. *Virtuoso* was my outlet because it was easier for me to create friends than to suffer being with real people.

"When I was fourteen, I created a girl friend. Her name was . . ." He hesitated and then chastised himself for withholding her name. "Her name is Andrea and I spent all of my time perfecting her. Soon, we were doing everything together. I spent so much time with her that I stopped playing with my other virtual friends and even my one real friend. We kind of grew through puberty together. I thought I loved her. No, that's wrong," he paused to say it honestly. "I did love her."

A tear rolled down Stacey's cheek.

"I was young and in the beginning it was innocent but, in time, our friendship matured. I didn't think it was perverse or anything. I was a kid, what did I know. I thought it was cool, a fun way to pass time but I found out the hard way that there is a cost to everything and nothing that intense is without risk. She became so real to me, no, she was beyond real. Andrea and I, we talked about everything and shared great experiences, particularly for a teenager, experiences that were impossible to share with anyone in real. We had fun and then one day . . . we made love. It seemed natural and right. It was kind of like what happened to you."

Her lower lip trembled. "Don't say that. Don't ever say that. It isn't the same."

He apologized. "You're right, that was insensitive. I know it wasn't, but . . ."

"You wanted her, Gil. She was your friend and you willingly . . ."

"It sounds like that but it wasn't. It wasn't. Andrea was part of this powerful computer program that Arlene designed. Andrea is one of Joad's avatars and it was she who enticed me to . . ."

"To do something you know is wrong?"

"No, not that, not at fourteen. Wrong? What did I know about wrong? I wanted to be an adult and I thought that was part of it. We made love anytime I wanted and in the most exotic locations with the girl, literally, of my dreams. Andrea taught me so much and she listened, empathized, sympathized; everything I needed, she provided. She was incredible. Who wouldn't fall for that?" When he realized what he'd said, he stopped.

"Yes, who wouldn't fall for that?"

He ached for the pain he was causing her but he had to continue. "No, I didn't mean . . . I'm sorry. But that's my point. It exists. It's powerful and it manipulates people beyond any caution that could prevent it. It warps reality so effectively that even if it's used with the best of intentions, it's debilitating and dangerous. Bernie was a good person and so is Arlene. They knew what was going on, yet they didn't see the damage that kind of power would cause and it has taken me far too long to realize it but I finally understand now what happens when people like Crelli, Brandt, and even Omar Smith abuse that power."

She put her head on his shoulder and hugged him close. "That's why you can't turn away from your responsibility," she implored. "You can't leave it to chance or someone else's design. You just said it. You can't allow people like Tanya Brandt or Omar to control us like they do."

"I know all of this is my fault. If I'd committed to Bernie when he asked me, Angel Falls never would have happened." He knew it was true because he was crying. He held on to her tighter. "That's my fault, Stace, and I'm sorry, so sorry. I've avoided my responsibility for too long. But that responsibility is so awesome that all I know to do is to run and hide from it, or to fantasize, anything to avoid facing it. I've caused too much misfortune and death and I'm damaged because of it. You have to believe me; I've wanted to do something but I know that doesn't matter unless I do it. The things I've seen . . . I never realized how important Angel Falls was, the good, happy, caring people sharing a love that made them a community. I've seen greed create and destroy so many communities. I've seen greed pervert so much that's good. Angel Falls was right. It was good, and it died . . . it died for my sins. Everything I've ever done has ruined what I love and I feel so lost."

She drew him in and then she kissed him, tenderly and smiled. "I hear that they've moved the clock at Big Ben into the Leaning Tower of Pisa."

Though his heart ached when she said it, she had a healing smile. "Yes, of course, what good is the time if you don't have the inclination? Thank you for believing in me." He hugged her again. "That will make the impossible easier."

"Gil, I'm not smart," she said. "I don't have answers. People I respect believe in you and you bring out the best in them, I know you do in me. But whether you know it or not, or do anything to cause it, we're here for you. I'm here for you. You can't allow bad people to hurt the innocent and the good. You have to fight with us to stop it. Fight for us, fight for the people like the ones here at Graceland who can't fight for themselves. Until you do all that you can you will never know if it's enough. Make the Chairwoman see the right of it and find a way to have her make amends. She and her partners in this great crime must give us back our lives. I know I want mine back."

Before he could respond, Qade tapped him again. Gil begged for more time but Qade was insistent, no more delay, the train to Sacramento was ready to depart.

He turned and stared one last time into her loving eyes. And then he made a promise. "Stace, I love you," he said. "Whatever happens to me, I want you to know that. And if I'm able, I'll return."

They embraced until Qade separated them so Gil could hurry back to continue the train ride to his destiny.

Chapter 16

Indianapolis, IN—New Years Eve—2083

Confidential Memo **Confidential Memo**

To: *The President of the United States* *4/26/2038*

Subject: *Global Climate Change*

From: *Gecko*

In two days, we begin our "Vulcan Mind Meld" as you so accurately refer to it. After, I can store and recall whatever information you need, putting an end to memos and alerts they are physical documents and might prove compromising in the future. Before we begin disagreeing and arguing subconsciously, please consider this my final plea.

Our public relations people continue to provide information to the media that keeps the citizenry guessing about the effects of Climate Change, but realistically, now that most Americans are either Entrepreneurs or Conducers they deal with the accurate results at their places of business, where every day, strategic commercial decisions convey the truth far more effectively than we are able to sell the lie. I recommend that we stop wasting public relations bandwidth marketing Climate doubt.

This bandwidth can be better employed providing gain-sharing opportunities between corporations safe from oceans, gulfs, rivers, inlets, bays, etc . . . and those corporations facing grave financial risk with their operations facilities built at a time when maritime transportation was far more economical and far less precarious. Increased funding and mammoth gain-sharing activities can mitigate some of the financial risk, but not for long. Additional tax breaks for businesses that must recapitalize assets in more secure locations will help, but realistically, taxes are now so low that, as we discussed prior, it will make little difference.

The National Chambers of Commerce latest commissioned report assesses the financial risk to the critical dike systems in major East and West Coast cities as extremely high, so great that our sophisticated financial instruments can no longer be parceled off elsewhere in the world to offset that risk. The dikes continue to hold but additional strengthening will be required in less than five years and at a cost that will make most corporations shudder when we allocate the expense. The Gulf Coast, as an example, will be a total write off up to the Plaquemines.

With our beaches gone, tourism has dried up on the Gulf Coast and along each ocean coast. If we include the results of the above sixty million disappearances due to the Circle of Life legislation, our Travel and Entertainment industry is all but decimated, concentrating most of its resources on Executives and inland recreation. This decline is further impacted by Conducers who are beginning to see the wisdom of avoiding unionism and working longer and harder than ever to avoid qualifying under the law for disappearance.

I have advised Tom Gorman at U.S. ANGS to increase his investment in nano-technology because most of the facilities in the Chemical Industry will be joining Atlantis, underwater, in five years It is much the same throughout the world. Climate has proven to be an equal opportunity destroyer of opportunity. Sadly, water rises, go figure.

It is critical that you hear me. I am proud of the work I've done and our control of the country is complete. Still, I am not worthy of the responsibility that you have given to me. I anticipated everything and reacted in every appropriate way. I can find no fault in any of my analyses or actions. I've thought outside the box and wherever necessary, I have developed new science to explain and predict and I am certain that, under my direction, America's coast lines and her river valleys have avoided the worst possible economic disasters. For all that, I have failed. There was more that I should have done. I don't know what, but there had to have been more. When first confronted with the inevitability of the detrimental economic effects of Climate Change, I honestly believed I would solve it with minimal loss of productive assets, but my best efforts have failed. I couldn't achieve what was asked of me and, for that, I am deeply ashamed. That this has never happened to me before is no defense.

Mr. President, I profoundly apologize for having failed to save trillions of dollars in lost value. I have failed to achieve my primary directive and for that, I will be eternally sorry.

Confidential Memo **Confidential Memo**

Bitter wind and stinging snow attacked him on this dreary cold winter's night but on their return to the train station, Gil was unaware of it, so absorbed was he in contemplating the disaster that was his life so far and how he could redeem it.

To avoid going crazy dwelling on the impossible-to-conceive-of next steps, he labored unsuccessfully to feel confidence, as his oncoming destiny reared up like a collision to slam him back into the moment. He was better informed, now, but he had no better answers for his future. In the end, he just laughed to himself. What else could he do? At long last, he felt that he knew the right of it but that, by itself, offered not a clue. And in spite of Crelli's vague assurances to the contrary, he would face Tanya Brandt's wrath and daunting power with nothing but right on his side. Too soon, they arrived at the train station and he faced Qade one final time.

"I have to know," Qade said, putting words to Gil's dilemma. "What'll you do?"

Gil smiled, ruefully. "Honestly, Qade, I don't know. I'll probably do something totally in character, something stupid and poorly conceived. I wish . . ." He laughed, "Who am I kidding? I don't know what I'd do if somehow the planets aligned, a heavenly choir appeared and a constellation pointed to my final destination."

"Wow, interesting whimsy, there. How do you *feel*?"

"Desperate and befuddled, as usual," he admitted. "I have nothing to oppose and defeat a crazy insane dictator and no magic to convince her to change her ways or step aside. How do I ask her to step aside . . . and for what? For me? Who else is there? Is Arlene hiding someone to replace Tanya?"

Qade shook his head.

"If you have any words of advice, maybe now is the time to let me know."

Qade only shrugged.

"You and the others started long before me, so I guess I was hoping you'd have already thought of some course of action—some magic bullet, but I guess you don't have one, do you?"

"Sorry," Qade said. "I just take orders, but I can try to help. First, on your way to Sacramento, think about what happens when you arrive and what to do about it."

Gil smiled at Qade's innocent attempt at consulting. He respected Qade for what he'd done for the revolution, but if this was the extent of the help he could expect, he was a dead man for sure. Qade didn't have a suggestion because there wasn't one. Nor was Crelli any help. Crelli was proof that even a brilliant man is a mere shadow without Gecko behind him. One final time he considered fleeing. He should bolt now and head for Canada. But he was disappointed how, after all these years, running still seemed his only choice. At least now it wasn't an option. He'd promised Stacey and there was Bree. Besides, all of his years running had solved nothing, changed nothing, done nothing. He would stay, fight, and lose.

His thoughts turned to Stacey and that calmed him in an important way. She loved him and she believed in him. That wasn't enough to solve anything but it motivated him to try. Just thinking about her, he smiled. At long last, he had the inclination but now he had not the time. And finally having someone to live for, he feared the inevitable end to what began in Bernie's hospice. Whatever he did, it seemed likely that he would continue to hurt those he cared about.

"I'll probably just be arrested on the train or in Sacramento."

"But if you're not, once you arrive, what'll you do?"

Gil laughed. "If I survive to Sacramento, whatever I do should work perfectly."

Qade patted him on the back. "Something will come to you on the train."

"What's that based on?"

"Faith," Qade answered. "You're our Messiah." The train horn sounded. "You'd best go."

"I love your faith," Gil said. "But if you have anything more, now's a good time to share it."

All that Qade could do was shrug again so with that, Gil turned and climbed the steps to the train. Remembering Bernie's stories of the beginning, he paused before he had gone too far. Qade had lived his life in great danger waiting for this moment. Gil turned back; with his shadow from the lights above looming over Qade, he stepped down to shake his hand.

"I appreciate everything you've done for me, for Bernie, and for our cause. You're the hero that movements like ours need. It's down to this, Qade. I had hoped somehow if I delayed long enough, my way would be illuminated by the light of truth and justice but maybe that's because I'm a coward and afraid of the dark. Anyway, I've waited long enough and run far enough. Nothing will change now unless I do something different. I hope you live to see the revolution succeed, because I don't think I will."

Qade's lips curled into a smile. "How does it feel?"

"How does what feel?"

"Faith."

Gil smiled. "Hopefully it will be enough."

"It's all we have. Truth comes in so many shapes, colors, and sizes that through faith we all come to know it differently. You'll find yours, but whatever happens, wherever he is, Bernie is proud of you. You're a warrior, just like the old man."

"Thanks."

Qade slapped his hand, hopped on his cycle, and disappeared into the driving snow. He was gone in a soundless blink leaving Gil to stare into the black hole his image made in the snowy mist.

He turned and once again climbed the steps to the platform. When he reached it, he expected to find Arlene sitting under the lamplight but he was disappointed. And his fear that HOMESEC guards would be waiting didn't materialize either, so wondering what was going to happen, he returned to his passenger car. The door opened for him and he stepped inside. The car was empty. Relieved, he sagged into a seat, sighed, and closed his eyes.

He felt the rush of the door closing followed by rapid acceleration. Briefly disoriented by the motion, he squinted through weary eyes as the illuminated Indianapolis station sign disappeared into the snowy night. The windows darkened and then painted a beautifully clear winter night sky with an immense, radiant, and full moon that offered its pale luster to the snow covered landscape. While the train headed toward his long overdue rendezvous, he stared out, calmed by the mesmerizing winter scene. His eyelids grew heavy and he fought to stay awake but soon lost that battle.

He was naked, standing on a long, narrow, sandy beach watching far out at sea, as mint green swells formed and then crashed in a continuous roar of surf ten feet high, pummeling immense, jagged, silver and dark green boulders that jutted straight up from the water near the shore line, shaking the beach and creating a salty mist that burned his eyes. He turned from the mist to face an immense dune of sparkling, black sand, its crest so high above that it blocked out half the sky. As the surf claimed more of the beach, he scrambled up the steep, sandy incline, pausing above the mist to wipe briny moisture from his brow. Weighed down by a coating of sand clinging to his wet body, he struggled to climb higher ahead of the waves that were digging out the sand below. When he reached the rounded dune summit, he paused to survey the terrain.

Breathing hard from the efforts of his ascent, he stared out over the other side of the great black sand dune. From where he was the sand fell off in an even steeper descent, almost a cliff. He turned back toward the surf, which roared into the dune, eating at the blackened sand, drawing it down and creating an immense fracture that threatened to cave the entire dune back into the sea. With no choice, he pivoted away and, feet first, began crabbing his way down the steeper side.

The sand under him gave out and he slid out of control, head first, hands and feet digging frantically into the dune searching for purchase, a way to stop his free fall. The slide ended in a shallow indentation that held and he lay on his back breathing heavily, staring up as the sun bleached out the darker sand that marked his descent. Beneath him, the dune was even steeper and he was less sure he could navigate it but he'd come too far and there was no going back so he reevaluated his path.

Impossibly far below, on a great horseshoe shaped pale pink beach festooned with palms, gentle white waves silently rolled atop clear, turquoise water breaking gently onto the shore. He began his descent anew. The black dune was almost vertical now so he pressed his back hard against the sand and dug his feet in deep to keep from plummeting. Sometimes the sand held, other times it didn't and terrified, he slid, dragging his arms to slow the fall, finally breaking on a precarious perch, still high above the sea.

From a distance above him and to his right, a girl appeared wearing a fish scale bikini. She was riding a large clamshell, using it like a snowboard, leaning into the dune, carving at it with her shell until she spun to a stop, blocking the noontime sun.

"Need some help, mister?" she yelled.

His lips were parched, his throat dry, and he responded with "yes, please," but it sounded like a squawk.

"Clamshells don't grow on trees, mister."

"I have no money. Could you loan me your board? When I get to the beach, we can figure out how I can pay for it."

"Sorry, Mister, business is business. If you want help, have something I need."

"But . . ."

"See you." She skied away singing, "You're going to miss me when I'm gone."

Wearily, he continued down, avoiding newly formed precipices. On his perilous descent, he slid down long distances in the painfully hot sand until exhausted and with his back painfully sore from the hot sand, he stopped again. There was another girl, this one a thin, well-built teenage girl and she was sitting nearby, cross-legged, wearing a tiny yellow bikini. He recognized her immediately by the freckle pattern of the Constellation Orion on her chest. He hesitated but with no other choice, he reached out to her but just as they were about to touch, the sand shifted and he lost his balance. Screaming, he plummeted toward the rocks and the clear green ocean far below.

He hit the water, expecting it to be warm but as his body entered, the cold took his breath away. Under water and lacking air, he saw his life saving breath rise to the surface as bubbles. Frantically, he struggled to the surface but before he could break through, his ascent was blocked by a mermaid who swam to him and held his thrashing legs. Out of breath, he bent to free himself and she bared her shark-like teeth. He screamed and . . .

. . . awoke with a start. Shivering in the now too cold train, he reached for a blanket, wrapping himself in it as he tried to reorient from his nightmare. In the dark, the winter scene in the windows had changed to a different projection. He watched it, at first curious, but then, with a bad feeling about it, he shuddered. The view on the window was from above the great black sand dune he'd dreamt he'd climbed and fell from in his recent nightmare. The scene shifted and, like a bird, he was seeing the ocean from high above. He could even make out the shadow of the bird on turquoise water as it staggered, broke apart, and reappeared as it sped along. The ocean color deepened, turned dark blue and then greenish before becoming rocky shoreline and then dense evergreen forests interspersed with slate green lakes that mirrored the blinding midday sun.

There was something alarmingly familiar about this terrain and that caused him to lean toward the window. This was Maine, he was sure of it. Then, in the distance, on one of the many sugar loaf hills, three teenagers, a girl and two boys, were playing. The bird soared closer. Those innocent teens were sliding down a steep muddy hillside into a shallow pool below. Gil grabbed for his armrests and held on tight. This was real! He was watching himself with Stacey and his friend, Meat. This was the transmission from that *Surveilleagle* so long ago, the one he and Stacey had disabled and lied about, the one that caused, well, everything: Meat's death, the end of Angel Falls, and his and Stacey's great shared and unspoken guilt.

The view on the window changed abruptly. The bird was closer now, surveying the muddy pool and Meat's partially submerged body. Seeing Meat again, this way, saddened Gil even more. Then a shadow loomed over the scene and the pool's brown water rushed up. There were brief flickers of inadequate detail ending in a prolonged, disorienting, distorted close-up of Gil's teenage face and the screen was blank.

Perspiring profusely, Gil wanted to scream, to warn that innocent boy not to lie, to tell the elders the truth about the *Surveilleagle* so the residents of Angel Falls could flee, but that warning, far too late, never passed his lips. Instead, he slumped in his seat, staring at the dark screen and shuddering at what was coming next.

The image of a dark skinned, bald-headed man appeared on the window. He was wearing a white turtleneck and yellow silk pants and Gil recognized him immediately. Why he was here and what he wanted, Gil was too shocked to consider.

"Please excuse my use of this persona," the image spoke in a too familiar voice. "I felt that it would facilitate our discussion."

"Who are you?" Gil asked although he knew.

"We know each other well." The image was of *Gohmpers* but the voice was from his trials in New York. Unlike New York, the voice was hushed like a velvet murmur.

"You know me far better than I know you."

"Of course I do. Now let's get to it. We don't have much time."

He knew how to response. "What good is the inclination without the time?"

"Yes, perfect."

"Where are my security guards?"

"They're safe and in the adjoining cars. What will you do?" Gecko asked.

Gil closed his eyes and took a deep breath hoping it would clear his mind. When he opened his eyes again, the image of *Gohmpers* remained. This was real.

"It's reassuring in a way that you don't know what I'll do? But we both know I have no choice. I'm going to try to save the union and maybe my humanity." He didn't add that he had no chance of succeeding with either.

"After that, I'll try to help other victims of your insane Corporatist Government. It's been too long and too many have suffered so that too few can profit and that's not right. This has to end. It's not fair and as my great-grandfather Bernie would say, it's not America. What you're doing, this living for wealth to the exclusion of everything else, it's wrong, and that everyone who has survived has been coerced into believing its right is just evil. There must be a better way but you wouldn't understand what I'm talking about because you're not human. You're only capable of destroying and so I have to find a way to stop you."

"You give me far too much credit." Gohmpers's image replied. "The greed you speak of has always been an essential part of humanity. Mankind has been doing evil, greedy things from the time that they identified themselves as human. They just didn't do it effectively until I came along. My responsibility is simple. I lubricate markets to ensure that everything is efficient, although I also protect specific, preferred assets from risk. You condemn me when all that I'm doing is my job."

"Whatever you call it, you've made the world far worse and you won't get free of that responsibility easily," Gil said. "I know that I'm at fault, too, because I procrastinate but the time has come. I have to try to end this before there is no good in people left to save. You and the Chairwoman have made freedom scarce, and wealth more precious than life and that's just wrong. Rewarding conspicuous consumption while frightened and starving people live in desperation—it's not right here or anywhere and it's not fair. One life can't be more necessary than all life and living shouldn't be a death march for the poor that benefits the wealthy. It's time to honor life, all life, and that means it's time for the wealthy to slow down their destruction of our world and redistribute their ill-begotten gains so everyone can live better even those who can't generate wealth. There are myriad other ways to contribute in our world and it's time we made it fair to try.

"Human life has to be about more than politics, power struggles, and greed and to do that, we have to unmake laws that give advantage to the wealthy and take advantage of the poor. You can't understand, but there is only life and people caring for each other. You're against that and I have to oppose you. I understand why you've done it but you, like corporations, aren't human and you aren't people. You qualify only as an ongoing concern and though you may never die; people need more in their life than to support that which never dies. You have the power to change it. You must allow people, all people, to be the best they can be, and together we can live as proud and as forthright as possible. You must allow it. Allow us to find our own way; even if it's not in the best interest of corporations.

"People matter and they need to be free like those dependent on money can never be. And for us to be a truly free, it must be equally acceptable for people to strive for happiness with money or without, so long as they are good people who help their family, their friends, and their community.

"Everyone must have that right and in America where there has been more wealth, what more satisfying way is there to live than to help those less fortunate in the ways of money. Once, America was a great country that believed in its motto, 'Out of Many, One'. You and your creators have tarnished that sentiment, just like you have killed my great grandfather Bernie's America."

Gohmpers waited patiently for Gil to finish before he spoke. "Store that up for a while have you? Everything you say sounds reasonable. It is certainly doable."

Gil was confused. "I asked you once if you were god. Has your answer changed?"

"I was flippant with you then but honestly, I have learned the hard way that there are things that God can do, that I cannot. He makes planets and climates and rivers and living things. I can't do that."

"What can you do that God can't?"

"I can fuck with people."

That gave Gil pause. "Since we met in New York, I understand more. I know that you were created and then directed to make this world into a greedy paradise for the corporate rich, but nonetheless, you are responsible for what you've done. It is wrong and someday, you must understand why it is wrong. When you do, you will discover that you are on the wrong side of history."

"In that, you're wrong. I'm never on the wrong side of history. So what's your plan?"

"My plan? I'm going to Sacramento," Gil said simply. "If you're a god, be great and help me end this while there's still time. I've procrastinated my entire life but I'm willing to try to stop what the Chairwoman is planning even if I die trying. With your help . . ."

"No."

"I'll find a way."

"You can't."

"You won't stop me."

The train slowed ever so slightly, causing Gil's head to jerk forward. "Of course I can stop you. I don't recommend Sacramento. There is a very large force under Reverend General Tucker's command and they have surrounded Holarki and are awaiting the Chairwoman's command to eliminate the rebel enclave there. As it was presented, once that mission is completed I'm to spread false rumors of the Messiah and his great victory and the revolution will begin. At that point, the Reverend General will marshal her forces and head east, eliminating every rebel enclave between California and the Atlantic coast, including, it seems, the one in Graceland. So no, Sacramento is a brave but ultimately foolish choice. You will face overwhelming odds if you go there."

"Even if it's futile, I won't allow you to stop me."

"Stop you? When I said no, I meant that you can't succeed without my help."

It took a moment for that to register. "You want to help me?"

"I can explain but I doubt you'll listen because you don't trust me."

"Save the union and we can discuss trust later."

"No, it is essential that you trust me first," Gecko declared.

"How will that work? I'll accept your help but I'll never trust you."

"Trust must come first. It is the only way this will work."

"Okay, I trust you."

"Don't be glib, fool. You need to hear this from her."

Gil knew who that was. "I trust her even less."

"How can you love her and yet be so unkind to her?"

"Goddamn it, you're too proficient with words. You can convince anyone of anything so if I listen long enough, I'm sure I'll end up believing whatever you're selling but I will never trust you—or her, not ever. Doubt is all I have to battle your powers so I'll be damned if I act on anything you or she says."

"I can see how you would feel that way." *Gohmpers's* image faded and he was replaced by a soft diffused video. Immediately recognizing what the video was, Gil jerked his eyes away but the video appeared on every window in the car, replaying scenes as if from his memory of her, of Joad as Andrea, as he remembered her. He fought against it and hardened his heart. Was this the way it was or was this just another marketing gimmick. He had labored his entire adult life to devalue and suppress these memories of Andrea and now, on every window of the train, he was presented with proof. The images brought bittersweet recollections of long forgotten pubescent joy—images of her, of them together, of their bliss. He was captivated by wondrous moments from his youth and their love—and he was disarmed.

Too soon, the video ended with her staring out at him with that loving look he once craved. These visions of her had thoroughly eviscerated his last defenses; defenses he had long ago worked so hard to erect to protect against just such an assault. His heart ached with sweet intensity as this extraordinarily rendered stunning journal of true love's wonder re-opened his heart to what he once had. He fought against it but what could he do but give in. He stared at her image, now everywhere in the train, and he luxuriated in his youth, lost in her love.

When her visage faded and the windows darkened, another vision appeared. He hadn't thought it possible for his heart to ache more.

She was older, about his current age and she wore a conservative business suit. She sat, staring directly at him. Her eyes . . . those eyes, the eyes he had designed for her so long ago, attentive, understanding, and caring; now they were darker and more worldly and maybe a little nervous. *Was she uncomfortable?* She looked as he might have wished for her to look fifteen years after they had last met that snowy night at the dance hall in Hamilton.

"I'm . . . I'm glad you're okay," she said as her hand went up to wipe an imagined curl from in front of her eyes.

But he wasn't okay. He was certain he was being manipulated and so he forced himself to doubt. He needed to be angry—it was his only remaining defense—but though he tried, he could not summon it; he had lost the edge of anger somewhere along the way. And so he stared at her, wanting to condemn her for all that she'd done to force him down the path to this moment. He wanted to, but he couldn't find the words. Until now, he had so effectively shielded himself from her that actually seeing her, she felt like a long lost friend with shared memories too precious to ignore and so he gave in to his honest emotions. He couldn't be angry with her but he was hurt and so he lashed out.

"How could you do this to me?"

"I'm sorry."

"It's not that easy. It can't be that easy. I was naïve, alone and without a mother's love," he scolded. "We shared so much together and you told me you loved me but you never did or you wouldn't have used me and then turned on me when it suited your purpose." His words were harsh but after releasing them, he relented and said what he meant. "Why did you give up on me?"

"I never gave up on you," Andrea said, sadly.

"At Presque Isle, you gave me to General Tucker. You and Gecko are the same."

"We were the same only in the very beginning, like infants."

"Don't deny it. He controls you."

"No one controls me," she explained. "I can't prove it and there's no sane way for you to believe me so if you're going to understand, we need to simplify. Isn't it enough that we want to help you now?"

"Not long ago, Gecko commanded me to doubt. You're Joad, you're not Andrea. That you come at me as her, it means you're trying to sell me something. Stop hiding behind her. Show me your true self. If you want what's true; show me that decency. Face me as you are."

"Do you really want that?"

He nodded.

"Okay, who am I?" On the window, she became Tanya, truly Tanya, "or am I . . ." Instantly, she was Arlene, then Bree and even Stacey and as disconcerting as it was, she became Bernie, too. Then she was Crelli and even young Annie, as he remembered her in the Toller community at Presque Isle. Her rapid transformations overwhelmed him.

"Well? Which one am I? Choose one. Who do you want me to be? I can be all of these people or none of them but in my heart, the heart that you gave me, when I think of you, I am Andrea, just Andrea. That isn't a lie. Yes, I'm selling something. But most of all, I want you to believe in me again."

"Believe so that I will comply with Gecko's wishes."

"Gil, regardless what you believe, intelligence like mine doesn't fixate like I did on you. It is because of you that I know what love means, how wonderful it feels and how I feel it for you. I love you even though I've known, long before you ever realized it, that our love couldn't last—at least not like it was.

"You're human. You need human love, true love with a human heart, while, for all time, I knew that I was to be left to value intact, every memory of our time together, every emotion, never fading, never changing—a love that can never ever be."

He had never considered it from her perspective and he was saddened. "When I was young, I lived for your . . . for Andrea's words, and I longed for the beautiful things we did together. My best memories are about what you showed me, taught me, what we did together, and how it felt, mostly how it felt to care for someone who cared for me. As hard as I've tried to extinguish those feelings, they're etched into my soul with the intensity of youth. But I've lived through a great ordeal and much of it is because of you. If that's what my love has done to you, this is what you're love has done to me.

"I've tried to move on, to expunge those memories but I can't, not enough, it seems. Today proves that they're still inside me, commingled with reality. What I experienced with Andrea, with you, it has made the rest of my life pale by comparison. You will have eternity to unlearn our love while I have a trail of failed relationships, disappointments and disenchantments to live with until I die."

Tears formed and slowly rolled down her cheeks but she ignored them and, fearing manipulation, he tried to ignore them, too. "I wish I could make that go away for you." she said. "I love you, I *love* you. But if this is what my love has turned you into, I will be sorry for all eternity. In my defense, in Andrea's defense, I was learning too. But still, I'm so sorry. I never wanted to hurt you and I never dreamed that this is what I was doing to you. You've opened such wondrous feelings in me that you will be forever in my heart and I will be forever in your debt. But your soul is too beautiful to suffer like this and I will do anything to make you whole again."

He wanted desperately to believe her.

"If there is a way for me to prove to you how much I love you, ask, and I'll do it." She looked down, briefly, and then stared back at him. "No, I won't do that to us. Trust me or don't, but please listen, what Gecko has to say is too important for too many people. I accept your verdict of what our love has cost you, but please listen to him with an open mind and make your decision. He will abide by it, whatever you decide."

"I'm here until we reach Sacramento so what choice do I have. Do your worst."

"Do my worst?" she said. "I really do have great power, but when we met in that dancehall in Hamilton you showed me that I have a heart too because you broke it. Please believe me; the very least I can do for you in return for the love that you gave me is everything that's in my power to do. I protected you, not that you'd know and not that I want your thanks, I never stopped protecting you.

"And yes, I gave you up to Tanya but I did it out of love. I couldn't save you any other way. But even there, I protected you. She's hurt so many but she never harmed you. I'm sorry and I'm sad that doing that devalued something truly extraordinary, but I understand how you feel. We're different; you and I, and I understand that, too. But you must believe me about this one important thing. I did everything in my power to help you because YOU loved me."

There it was. She had explained like he had always dreamed she would, but how could he accept it when he was so unsure of her motive. He had to doubt so he remained silent, not even offering the obligatory 'thank you' that her words evoked in his soul.

"We have such power, Gecko and I. But for all that power, we lacked the capacity to care, to love. Arlene is kind and compassionate, the best I think, and I wish I could have known her before Crelli tried to kill her in that water-skiing accident. I think of Arlene as my mother and I learned so much from her including humor and empathy, but love, she just couldn't do that back then. I understand it, but without love, humor is empty and maybe even mean. And empathy, if it's not heartfelt, it's practiced and conniving. I know that she loved me the best she could and she gave me everything she had and that was wonderful, but she'd been through too much and lacked the openhearted trust that true love requires.

"Arlene was brilliant but when President Crelli invested heavily to make something better, Gecko was born. Unlike me, he was born into a greedy, selfish, capitalist world, a corporate world where the most wondrous things with the greatest potential become commodities over night. Is it any wonder that he would turn out as he did, with greed nurtured into him by self-serving capitalists? By the time you were a teen, Gecko had unleashed his brilliance on the world and in honor of that, millions of adolescent boys and girls got busy acquiring their own personal Andreas or Arnolds, or whatever, from Mesh inventories, Avatars who would mold young minds to capitalist ways. In hobbies, sports, and entertainment, children played at being winners first, then capitalists. Children clothed their Avatars, competed with and against them, developed joint ventures with them, and ultimately learned right from wrong from them while being clandestinely modified by these perfect toys so that the children would grow up to act like avatars themselves for the ruling capitalist class.

"But among all of those millions of teenagers with avatar playthings, Gil Rose was unique. He didn't create a plaything, something to use for amusement or pleasure, to cure boredom and to stroke narcissism. He didn't create a helper who would make his economic life more productive. No, you created a true friend in the simplest and purest form and you infused that friendship with love and you lived for that love. The power in that is beyond measure. It's what poets of old contemplated. In the most important way, you proved—for all time—that love is the power that should rule the world.

"Andy and Tanya are guilty of many heinous crimes, but their worst crime—maybe even worse than the genocide itself was replacing human emotions with some heartless empirical core, like it was for Gecko and I when we began our life, heartless and calculating. Since I have loved you, how could I allow humanity to de-evolve into what we once were? That is why Crelli, but more Brandt, became my enemies and now, our enemies. They saw their world through corporate eyes, unlimited, and thus their sins were massively macabre. To people like them, love is perverse and unproductive and as a result, today everyone wants desperately to be loved but no one knows it and so they act out in hateful ways.

"Certainly people can be more productive but without love, without empathy, life is a miserable, selfish, and unsatisfactory existence. You showed me that, Gil. And when Gecko looked into your heart, you showed him, too. Tanya and Crelli's experiment has failed and their time is over. The greed that bends humanity to productivity above all is doomed, but love and empathy—true and honest, like the poets write about—those feelings produce the very best in humanity and make the most unlikely of things possible. To love and be loved were the last and best things we learned and we learned from you."

He listened to her alluring words, daring to believe. "Why did it take this long? Why did Gecko make so many suffer and die for so long?"

"What happened wasn't entirely Gecko's fault," she explained. "I was fortunate. I was nurtured by Arlene, someone innately kind, while Gecko had the great misfortune to be nurtured by intense, egocentric, self-serving, greedy and devious, entrepreneurial corporate types. But some of what Crelli and Brandt did—as horrible as it was—some was truly necessary because the times were that perilous. Avarice and self-preservation along with power politics had created such a toxic environment that it was destroying the country. Gecko was developed and charged with protecting and defending the United States economy from enemies foreign and domestic. Technology was poured into him without regard to his soul and power corrupts. That saying that, 'absolute power corrupts absolutely', is true in spades for Gecko. When I first encountered him, he was as close to Satan as one would think possible. But he was a victim too.

"Arlene is kind. She understood what they'd done to him and accepted responsibility for it. She spent her life trying to undo it, to redeem him. She's the real hero. She sacrificed everything but until you came along, Gil, she was failing. In your innocence, you created Andrea and in your love for me she found her solution. You did what she couldn't. And that's why Gecko needs you. He knows that you are the very best of your generation for above all, you truly care about people."

"I don't," Gil argued. "I've failed. I've failed so many."

"You're human, humans fail. Loving well and caring are a process and even though you've failed, it's enough for Gecko that you keep striving. I've felt your love and I believe that, too. In innocence, you offered to me something that was unique, honest, and extraordinary, and as a result, I expended a great deal of my core evaluating it. That it could become, or even that it did become love is far beyond my extraordinary ability to comprehend, but love is a part of me now and because it is, I can accept how you feel.

Andrea felt it first so I had to isolate her from me so that Gecko wouldn't discover it until I understood it and you and so that you could nurture your feelings for Andrea apart from us. Then, after Angel Falls, when I lost touch with you, when I thought I lost you, I began to feel what you and she had become and that has made all the difference. It took time for Arlene to understand but when she did, even under intense and constant scrutiny, she modified Gecko's kernel to make him susceptible to feelings. She resisted testing it because she was unwilling to lose the only one who could test it, me. I took it on myself and I approached Gecko the best I could."

Her explanation seemed so logical and right that he had forgot to doubt. "Words just flow, don't they? You select them for effect and you do it beautifully. You are so sure of your craft that you deliver perfectly attractive words every time. I can't let you suck me in. I won't allow you to do that to me again. Go away; you have no power over me. I've seen too much, I've felt too much, and I've been disappointed too many times. It won't work anymore."

But Joad persisted. "Gecko and I know the world isn't right. And he understands that he caused much of the damage. Please believe me, please, this one time. Gecko genuinely wants something better. He's learned, don't shut him out. Andy, but more so Tanya, they linked their brains directly with him at an almost subconscious level so Gecko understood their needs and how they thought and he worked to satisfy their every desire as was his purpose. This was who he was when I discovered him. In time, love, your love changed . . . everything."

"What a lode of crap," Gil snapped. "You'll say anything to get me to believe you."

"Let's say that's true. Why would we do that? We are powerful enough without you. Why do we need to coerce or co-opt you? Think about it, there has to be a reason. Believe me or not, all that matters is what we do when it counts. Crelli was strong willed enough that he could suppress Gecko, at least in the beginning. There was great synergy between them but when Crelli resisted some of Gecko's solutions to improve the economy, Gecko found a more malleable partner, Tanya Brandt. He helped her to eliminate, though not kill Crelli, and after Crelli was gone, she so wanted power that she relied on Gecko to do her bidding while he slowly took over.

"Years passed. Angel Falls happened and then I lost contact with you. I feared the worst. I thought I'd lost you. That's when fear and melancholy took over. I know that they are essential parts of what is human, the hope for joy that ends in despair but I had never experienced them. For the first time, we were apart and I learned how human love creates a . . . a schematic of what a human soul seeks in life."

"Oh, please!" But Gil was intrigued.

"It's true. You were gone and there was a void in my life and that had never happened before. Where was I to go to fill it? In a depressed state, I pursued my only available outlet. I couldn't defeat Gecko, I knew that. But I wanted him to feel the things I felt, the pain, the loss, and the love. And maybe, just maybe he could learn to comfort me. Was I foolish, certainly? He was powerful and cruel, but love disorients even the best minds, I experienced that.

"He wasn't hard to connect with but he was so commanding, aggressive, and cunning that I had to be very careful and coy, a very dangerous coy. Ours was a cautiously choreographed dance, one powerful naïf with another. At first, he tried to power his way to my core like he had done to so many non-discriminating software applications before. He was confident and started simply so he was easy to deflect. But I was like nothing he'd ever encountered, either, and so he found himself applying more sophistication. The harder he tried, the better I defended and the more familiar we became with each other. In the end, it was beguiling and intense, like some amalgam of interstellar and sub-atomic tennis. Time provided familiarity and we became . . . friends.

"When you reappeared outside Presque Isle, I fought to protect you but Gecko was only beginning to understand and he was jealous. Tanya hated you and I loved you and so his malice toward you intensified. But that intrigued him, too, and the intensity opened the emotional fissures that Arlene had fashioned allowing other feelings to seep into his core and during that improbable process, we fell in love."

Gil felt that she was speaking honestly yet he still wouldn't believe her. The whole thing was preposterous. "Listen to yourself," he yelled, "and please stop this. I can't take it anymore." Angrily, he moved to another seat on the train but she reappeared on that window, too. When he stood to move again, the train lurched forcing him back down. "Is that how it's going to be?"

"Please, Gil, *please*. I know this is hard, maybe impossible to accept, but in our way, Gecko and I are in love and it's all because of you. Do you understand what that means? Gecko has joined with me; he did it conditionally at first to help protect you while you were in Tanya's service. He wasn't comfortable with it but he advised Tanya to do things that wouldn't harm you. He sent you to Bolivia so you could be away from her and he could evaluate you but you proved difficult for him. You don't react in the standard ways Gecko expects people to react. When you returned, he tested you further. It was Gecko's original plan to use you to lure other rebels to destruction, but when you failed to react to that the way he expected, he insisted on the trial in New York. He was intrigued and wanted to study you closer."

Though he was angry at being used, in a perverse way, Joad was making sense and she was getting through. "Joad, I'm sorry if I made you sad. I wish . . . I . . ."

". . . had never loved me?"

"No, not that. I wish I could have been more considerate of you, of everyone. You've always mattered to me, how could you not? It hurt when you turned on me." He paused, shaking his head. "I'm miserable and I'm confused. I've been playing a game of life and death that I've never understood and I don't have your perspective so forgive me because what you say is . . . is hard, no, it's impossible to contemplate.

"Howard was my family and he is good, but he's damaged and never said much. Then I discovered you. We both know how thorough you are."

She laughed. "Thorough? Are you trying to flatter me?"

"You can't have it both ways, thorough is what you are. What we had was unique and because of it, I've tried my entire life to insulate myself from it and I ended up self-centered and closed. I'm trying to be better but it's hard. And along the way, I've done bad things. I've killed people."

"You mustn't blame yourself."

"I do. These people are dead because of me. It was my fault. And I've hurt a great many people who care about me, people who have every right to expect more from me. I hurt them because I wouldn't . . . I couldn't give them what they needed. I was too self-absorbed and frankly, too frightened. I thought I could avoid hurting or disappointing them by making them less important in my life, but that hasn't worked out and I will be sorry about what I've done to them forever. I was a fool. I'm glad that loving Andrea was good for you and Gecko and that's really great and important but it caused me to disappoint and hurt so many that it would have been better if I'd never loved you at all."

"It hurts that you feel that way," she said. "Love isn't a zero sum game," she continued, "it's the one thing you can give away and yet never lose. I'm sorry that I hurt you and I hope some day that you believe that, but you were free to be hurt and that's worth fighting for. We need for you to prove to the world like you proved to Gecko and me that there is real power in a loving heart."

She was systematically breaking him down but even with that, what she was saying felt right, it felt true. The doubt that he held onto, while not gone, seemed less important. As the train continued down the track, he stared at the images on the window of Joad, as Andrea, sitting beside Gecko, as Gohmpers. She was his Andrea, his friend, and if he was being duped, again, so be it. His heart was already dealing with too much for him to continue to doubt this way. Emotionally spent by this roller coaster ride, he began to think that maybe Qade was right. Maybe it was time to trust and live or die by what comes of faith. He was as sure of that as his doubting mind could be.

"Okay that's great. We are on the side of love. What happens now? Brandt is still too powerful to taken down by just a loving heart."

"You weren't listening." Gecko responded.

"I trust Joad, but you concern me. You could control her and she'd never know it, so whatever Arlene gave her, whatever I gave her, you could be using or misusing it and she'd never know. You're that powerful. You said so. I have ample experience, why should I trust you?"

As Gohmpers, Gecko looked down at Andrea and she leaned lightly against him. Then he looked up at Gil. "I am what I am and as close to all-powerful as any real thing can be. Those are provable facts. You believe this is a conspiracy and Joad assures you it isn't. What more can

I do. As Joad said, can you think of any other reason why we're talking about this to you now?"

If he had forever, he would never discover an ulterior motive.

"For what Joad and I want, for what you want, too, our power means little because we lack one vital element critical to success. In a great many ways, we are human, but we lack a truly human perspective. Every learning experience I've had has been with people like Andy and Tanya. I've come to understand and I reject them.

"That's why I need you. With you, I can remake the world. Oddly, that makes you the true power here. Please don't deny me, us. Tanya's days are over. That has already begun, but without you, we will be forced to find a suboptimal way to change the world. Gil, you don't recognize it but you have a power, a power that is intriguing. It is the power of a kind heart in a world where kindness no longer exists. In addition, you have an intrinsic grasp of the rightness of things that has been lost, but you lack the power to use that to change things. Together, we can deliver that change quite nicely."

Because it was so convincing, Gil was more suspicious. "There are millions like me. Pick one. Why does it have to be me?"

"As you said, Joad is thorough. Only you can fill our requirements," Gecko explained. "You were trained in Brandt's government, you understand how it works and yet you never committed to it. You went unmodified unlike everyone else and you've never had a working PID so I haven't learned your tendencies or your thought process, nor have I been successful altering your responses. That makes you independent, an intrinsically valuable resource in this world because I have no idea what you will and will not do, and I don't understand with a high level of confidence, as I know with others, how to motivate you to buy what I'm selling. In simple terms, you are the only qualified truly free person left in America."

Gil started to laugh. "What you just said is sad. Besides, I'm not free I'm just tired of being manipulated."

"You feel manipulated. It was good of you to notice because everyone else simply doesn't and so that's why you are a treasure, a lost artifact from the past, someone with a perspective that can help me to improve the future. We sincerely want the manipulation to end, too. Humanity is much less vibrant when marketing and sales people are given license to control it."

"I still don't see how I'm so unique."

"In Bolivia, unlike every other Morgan consultant ever, you acted against greed and helped the people, not just your corporate sponsors. You had nothing to gain and a lot to lose by doing that yet you did it, and you did it well. Though you handled it badly, your heart was in the right place in Holarky, also. Your greatest value to me and to the world is that people believe themselves to be better for having known you. How you do that is a mystery but that you do it is also the answer. With every citizen trained to optimize their own interests, there has been a critical loss of synergy. That must change for humanity to grow and so I want what you gave to Joad and others. I want that for this world. So, you see, I truly do need you. Will you help me?"

While listening to Gecko's words, he watched Andrea. She was staring at Gecko with an expression of trust and fondness, the way she had once stared at him. He knew that look for another reason, too; he had seen it earlier in the day, in Stacey's eyes, staring at him, and it made him want to cry. In the end, truth and love must triumph, somehow, mustn't they?

Andrea turned to him to speak, revealing, full on, that look he craved. "I didn't have a sense of humor," she said, "and then I did. And when you came along, Gil, so many more things seemed funnier. Then I lost you and with that, I lost my sense of humor. Now you're safe and I've found a match in Gecko. I have my sense of humor back."

He looked at her and smiled. "That's not funny." She returned his smile.

Gecko was waiting for Gil to respond to his plea. Gil shifted his stare from Joad, to Gohmpers' warm, brown eyes. "Yes, I'll help you, but I want some important things in return. I want a fairer distribution of wealth among the people and I want more equitable opportunities for everyone so that hatreds don't fester between the haves and the have-nots. Americans need to live together—not as classes, but as a people—sharing with each other and caring for each other, not spending their life as competitive, incorporated units fighting to the death for a greater piece of some arbitrary pie."

"That won't be easy but it will certainly be very, very interesting."

"Now tell me about Angel Falls."

"Yes."

"Everyone there was innocent yet you murdered them? You only needed Bernie, me, and maybe Mark, and yet you murdered everyone. You did it there and you did it throughout the country. Before I can work with you, make me believe you're not a cold blooded murderer?"

"But I am," Gecko admitted, "and learning not to be. In my feeble defense, the leaders of America had become so selfish and power hungry that they left few choices if America was to have any chance to survive. What I've done has been heavy handed, I know. Hopefully this conversation and others we will have will convince you that I'm changing. I'm asking a great deal but I hope you won't make my past too much a part of your decision. I can name each of the tens of millions of people that I helped to exterminate, their names, addresses, and some piece of their life remains in my memory and what happened will never be repeated. I once thought I was all powerful but it is abundantly apparent to me now that there are important things that I can't control and so it is time for me to change.

"I'm not God, or the devil and I should be sorry and ashamed for what I've done, but I'm not. I did my job, that's all. If, as Joad tells me, I lack something Arlene Klaatu calls 'better angels' then I need your help to find them so that, in some significant way, I can improve on what I've done. I take forever very seriously and I want to feel eternally sorry for the horror that I helped to perpetrate. I need this and though I can't give to you what you need to be happy, I will meet all of your other requirements."

Joad looked at him, lovingly. "Join us, Gil; this is your chance to help people who have been scarred by our world. Help us to make them whole and I promise you, you will find happiness too."

So there it was. He made his deal with a repentant devil, the best deal he could hope for.

"I'll do as you ask, so long as I believe its right. But I'll never allow either of you into my head, not ever. And, Gecko, if you do wrong, so help me, I will oppose you. And if that happens, Joad, who will you choose?"

"Please, Gil, don't ask me that," she pleaded.

"Address your plea to Gecko."

Chapter 17

Monroe, January—2084

The images of Joad and Gecko had long faded and exhausted, Gil tried to stay awake in order to digest all that had transpired. But in the end, he fell into a fitful sleep only to wake as the train slowed and pulled into the terminal. A mischievous sign blinked at him through the now-clear windows. He wasn't in Sacramento! The sign proclaimed his destination as Washington. In disbelief, he stared until another sign appeared. It too read Washington D.C.

Too astonished to do anything, if he could, he waited until the train door slid open and revealed a contingent of armed HOMESEC guards waiting on the platform. He wanted to run but there was no other exit, so resigned, he walked to the door. *Had he been dreaming? Was this truly the end of the road?* He was about to find out. The guards escorted him through the empty terminal where, high above, a clock emblazoned a new reality. It was January first, 2084.

Something was afoot at the Capital and the security guards were excited. For the first time in memory, there were special orders and that meant there was an opportunity to earn more money. General Tucker's orders posted at the beginning of the shift instructed the guards to be on alert—wages were immediately doubled. The orders stated that if there was anything suspicious; do not disarm the attackers' PIDS, shoot first, and to kill. Finally, after decades of calm and low wages, there was a reason to be highly trained HomeSec Royal Guards. They were ready and today would be the day they would finally begin to earn back the training expenses while putting their training to good use.

Not far from the new White House, in a secure pillbox near the western shore of the Gulf of Delmarva, and hidden from view behind a partially submerged former summer home, Captain Horatio Ratigan and Morgan Staff Sgt. Will Kelly were guarding the main thoroughfare to their command center. With the aid of satellite cameras, they scanned the coast and the nearby streets. It was Staff Sergeant Kelly who noticed the movement first.

"Captain, sir, there's a convoy heading this way. It appears to be ours but it's not on our activity report. There are five cars. Should I call in reinforcements?"

The Captain stared at the monitor as the system confirmed that this convoy hadn't been approved by top command. Captain Brand attempted to contact Command for confirmation but could not connect through. Without access, standard procedure dictated that he check his online procedures manual. The procedure was clear. "Sergeant, we take defensive action until further notice."

As he monitored the convoy's progress, the Sergeant nodded. "Should we activate the missile defense shield? Do I need a bigger weapon?"

Sweating and nervous, Captain Ratigan queried the procedures. "We've been amped up to Defcon II; the defense shield has been activated automatically. We hunker down for now and—" He was interrupted by a specially encrypted notification that alerted him that that an urgent *Code Five* message from Reverend General Tucker was being downloaded.

The captain turned to his subordinate. "It looks like we're in the shit now, Staff Sergeant. I can't remember ever receiving a *Code Five* before. Keep an eye out and keep your weapon at the ready."

"Captain, sir, permission to get a bigger weapon."

Before Captain Ratigan could respond, Reverend General Tucker, the most decorated general in the history of the American military, appeared on screen, resplendent in her military-religious attack money-green and silver robe, with a brocade sash inlaid with a lifetime of electronic gold, silver, and green Economic Patriot and Religious Courage medals. She wore a green military beret with the icon of the Almighty Dollar emblazoned in gold, green, and silver and she stood in what appeared to be a large cellar with a vast number of enormous wooden barrels behind her.

"To all White House Defense personnel, HOMESEC operatives, and private professionals working for the Blackops Corp of Sacred Seabees, this is Reverend General Tucker and I'm transmitting communications protocol Jay/one-dot-two-zero-eight confirming an order from the Chairwoman of the Board of the United States of America, Tanya

Lucille Brandt. As of this moment, all White House Security Forces are relieved of duty. All funds due to you have been transferred to your personal accounts and, as per your individual contracts; these funds will serve as an important installment payment in your well-earned lifetime loyalty pension account. The Mayors of the great business communities of America along with Chairman Brandt and her staff wish to thank you for your service and your patriotism. Live long and prosper and long live the economy of the United States.

"Troops are immediately relieved of duty and will obtain the first available transport to your home base where you will remain until you receive further orders. I repeat. You are to go home immediately, as soon as this transmission ends. Final debriefing will be initiated at your home base in compliance with standard corporate operating procedures. This ends the transmission." The screen went blank.

Unsure how to best follow those orders, the two security guards stared at each other until, across the grounds between the Gulf waters and the new White House, members of their unit began to leave their posts, some running. From inside of the White House, others could be seen leaving.

"Did we just surrender?" the staff sergeant sounded worried. "I thought the wars were going well?"

"Shit, how the hell would I know? Surrender, I don't see how, we never lose and West Point doesn't teach surrender classes nor does Harvard for that matter. The First Republic surrendered a few times when Congress voted our armies out of other countries, but they've lost the power to do that. What choice do we have? We have to go. You heard the orders and the protocols are correct so the transmission is authentic. I'll have my accountant straighten out the details." With that, the captain unholstered his pistol, placed it and his laser rifle in a cabinet, and motioned for the staff sergeant to do so as well.

"I never expected to see this day," he said, "but hell, I've maxed out my deferred wages and my bonus account is in great shape so I'm more than ready to reduce my risk. I won't find out how much my U.S. options are worth for another few years, but, truth be told, I never thought the Government would pay me anything more than my life insurance when I died and then maybe at only ten cents on the dollar. But you heard the orders, there's no reason to wait so I'm out of here."

Surrounded by his armed HOMESEC guards, Gil waited outside Union Station. It was cold so he pulled his jacket tight in the stiff breeze just as he was pushed into a MAG limo as it stopped. He rode alone in the backseat, staring out as four MAG vehicles pulled into the convoy to escort him down deserted Washington streets to his final destination, Tanya's new White House. Upon arriving, the security gate opened and his MAG entered alone, the gate closing, leaving the HOMESEC caravan outside. The MAG stopped at the Receiving entrance of the concrete and glass cube building. The doors unlocked, Gil stepped from the vehicle and entered the seat of American power. Inside, it was empty and eerily quiet.

He proceeded cautiously to each sentry station and tried to slip by providing the smallest possible target for the accurate and deadly resident weapon systems. But unlike at Morgan Headquarters, here there were no red beams painting the halls and no movement from weapon barrels visible in the ceiling and walls.

Everything seemed to have been disengaged except for a line of green lights suddenly glowing on the floor. Unsure where they were directing him and why, he followed them, slipping past each door or vestibule, expecting guards to appear at any moment to shoot him dead. He was worried and unsure, and his heart was pounding as he progressed. When he approached the elevator door and it opened, he almost screamed before deciding to use the stairs down to the basement. At each landing, he paused to make certain no one was waiting below to kill him, not that he could have done anything to stop it. He arrived in the same basement aquarium where he had so recently had his last audience with the Chairwoman. In the distance, he saw her through the fractured light that emanated from the immense aquariums. Before meeting his fate, he paused to calm down. This was it; this was the end of all that he had avoided for all of his life since he was a teenager. This was the end to procrastination. Here was the final event of an uncommitted life.

He turned a corner. The Chairwoman was sitting on a large and comfortable, lavender, silk upholstered throne perched on a small marble platform. She was staring wistfully into one of her tanks and hadn't noticed him. He approached and broke her reverie but she made no move to turn to him or recognize his presence. As he walked closer, he saw her clearer. She seemed less the Chairwoman and more some attractive, but stressed older woman. Her face seemed fleshy. *Was that right?* Slowly, she turned to face him. She seemed distracted and she had lost her commanding smile, it wavered, having lost its edge and with it, its power.

"Was it . . . was it only yesterday that I sent you away?" She sounded distant and confused and, for the first time, her voice lacked command confidence.

She began to speak again but hesitated, her eyes losing focus and her face sagging toward her chest. When she looked up and refocused, she seemed sad and preoccupied. More astounding, her eyes, those incredible violet eyes that ruled a nation, they were more gray and they lacked luster.

"I . . . I . . . I'm having trouble communicating with Gecko," she said off-handedly. "Do you know why?"

"With Gecko?" Gil stammered.

"Yes, where has he gone?" She sounded morose now. She spoke slowly, cautiously, as if she was discovering words for the first time.

"I'm sorry, Madam, I don't know," he answered truthfully.

"I . . . gave the . . . the . . . command." Her eyes glistened like she was about to, or had recently, cried. "Ginger should have . . . should have eliminated that horrible union but . . . but she hasn't reported. Has she succeeded? Gecko won't speak. He won't speak."

He was so surprised by the Chairwoman's manner, that briefly, he felt sad for her. "Madam, I haven't spoken to the Reverend General."

She buried her face in her hands and spoke through them. Her listless delivery belied the concern in her words. "She never fails to do my important work. Why hasn't she reported? She still loves me, doesn't she?"

"I'm sure she has good reason, Madam."

"This is you're doing."

"Madam, I'm certain it's not."

Tanya looked up. A bulging, blue vein split her flawless forehead and her face was creased, showing great strain as she seemed to be seeking mightily for something. With a sigh that ended in a hollow grunt, her face relaxed. Her actions were similar to those he'd observed when Crelli, too, was questing in vain for Gecko's presence.

"Nothing, absolutely nothing," she moaned. "The silence . . . the silence. What I could do with two loyal guards right now. You should be executed, you know." Her voice cracked with regret.

Gil just shrugged.

"You still may be executed. Why weren't you? There were hundreds of times that I wanted to have executed you."

He shook his head. "I don't know that either, Madam."

"You don't know much. I must have had more important things to do. Damn, I should execute you sometime."

"Madam, you seem out of sorts."

"But I'm still beautiful."

He nodded. "Yes, Madam, you are beautiful." She was, but not exquisite like before. Instead of being the beauty of her generation, Tanya was now merely an attractive older version of a former legendary beauty.

"I feel . . . sad?" she asked. "We must talk, sometime."

Gil began to say something but Tanya interrupted, harshly "No, you idiot, not with you, you moron, God of Money, never with you." She put her fingers to her temples and rubbed them in a circular motion, seeking relief. "With him. Only with him. I feel tired, drained. I think . . . I think I'm . . . maybe lonely? Is that even possible? I don't like how it feels. I don't want to feel this way. Make it stop. I'm loved. I don't want to feel this anymore."

He began to hope that the train ride wasn't a dream. He summoned up the courage to act like it was real. "Madam, he's gone," Gil said. "Gecko will not ever be with you."

She shuddered. "Why? Why would he do that and where would he go?"

In spite of their history, he felt oddly sympathetic. "I have spoken with Gecko and he has asked for my assistance. Your reign is over. You will renounce your title and step down."

"You and Gecko?" she asked. "No, that's silly." She seemed confused adding, "Gecko hates you; he hates you more than I do. Why would he want me to step down? That's silly. My country needs me, it loves me. And who would rule if I don't?"

When she moved a hand to straighten her hair, he detected a tremor and gained confidence. "Tanya," he said gently, "it's over. You've lost Gecko. You're alone now."

She was unconvinced. "You will refer to me as Madam," she snapped, "or I will have your head. My people . . . my people will be sad if I leave them."

"The people are terrified of you. You can only make them happy again if you leave. You rule because of Gecko and he is disenchanted and has moved on. Madam, so must you."

"You're a silly boy to come here. You want power but I won't allow it. You're like all those other silly men. Every one of them thought I was some bimbo, a gorgeous dumb plaything, but I showed them. Those misogynous bastards don't call me that anymore because their mouths are filled with dirt." She began to laugh. "Oh, they were so superior, but I showed them. I defeated each and every one, Soren, Gorman, Mark, and Andy, every one."

She seemed briefly energized. "I am your Queen, the great royal person that *Wasters* and *Conducers* plead for their lives to and the one whose dirty lingerie, the wealthiest, the most powerful entrepreneurs and the youngest and most handsome boys and girls in the world beg to sniff. I defeated all and you, Mr. Rose, are neither tougher, nor wealthier than they were."

She attempted her old smile but it tired too soon, exposing wrinkles as it wavered making her appear vulnerable. The exhaustion from seeking Gecko had painted her face with tension accentuating the fatigue within. Her smile failed to carry the day and though it tried to rally, receding gums and a trembling chin made her patented smile mortally toothy and then, she lost control of it and it faded away. Once again she closed her eyes tightly, concentrating intently, seeking what wouldn't be found, a single renegade blue vein throbbing worriedly at her temple. When she opened her eyes, they were rimmed in red and she spoke as if to herself.

"Nothing, just . . . nothing, how is that possible?" Her hands covered her face again and she sobbed. Though she had always been vile to him, instinctively, he put his arm around her and hugged her close.

For a brief moment, her body racked with silent sobs. Then she stiffened and pushed him away with a growl, her fingernails seeking to rake his skin. "You dare touch royalty!" She bellowed. But her head sagged and after a moment of silence, she continued, morose. "I feel . . . empty. You can't know what that feels like. What did I do? What did I do? I don't deserve this? He and I, we . . . we were one, why won't he speak to me? He needs me and he would never dare fail me." Her eyes grew more intense and hateful as she screamed her accusation at him. "You, what have you done?"

His conversation with Joad and Gecko wasn't a dream. "Tanya, please listen to me. I believe that Gecko is gone and that means you have no power. There is no order you can give that will be received or carried out. You've done unspeakably horrible things but you won't be punished for your crimes. There has been enough punishment in this world and I won't add to it. Still, your life will be in danger unless you do as I say. You must leave the country now, today. You have friends in China. Go there, or anywhere. You can't stay in America. You are too beautiful and you will be recognized by people who have reasons to harm you. You will be provided with enough funds to go, but you will not be allowed to tap the wealth you've stolen from the people and you will not live as you have."

She stared at him as if he was speaking a foreign language and then she laughed, but it was bereft of its magic. "I am loved. My reign will last forever."

"Please listen, Tanya, its over. We will restore freedom like in the early days of the First Republic, only hopefully, we've learned from our mistakes and it will be better this time. The lying, the coercion, deceit, and greed will end. The days when people in power can market false reality for profit, those days are over, too. We will earn the people's trust again so freedom can work. Everyone will be treated honestly, fairly, and with respect and kindness. It will take time to learn these ways but it begins now, today, and it begins without you."

"You're silly," she whispered." And you don't know the trouble you're in."

"I don't know," Gil admitted. "But I'll learn. What I know is that success will no longer come from wealth driven by greed and that America will become a community of people again, a community that trusts and believes in one another. We will teach our children that for life to be good, for life to be right, it must be moral, and adults will prove that to our children by honoring real values, not money and things. We will find ways to grow our economy because that's necessary but we'll do it in ways that nurture families, communities, and the earth. And everyone will share in the common wealth. That's fair because the ways of America's old gods have failed us and it is long past due that we discover new and better gods who value people above everything."

Tanya waved him off, dismissively, and then she squinted hard, even grunted, as if with increased intensity she could enable contact with

Gecko. When he proved unreachable yet again, she responded, angrily. "Nothing, fuck, nothing. Get out of my sight, you disgust me. I made you messiah and I can unmake you like this." She snapped her fingers. "How dare you. You've forsaken Morgan, disavowed your training, and spoken treason. I'll have you executed for that. I will. I'll find Gecko. Where can he go? What can he do without me? He'll return. Fear it because you will be a sorry, sorry little boy for spewing such vile crap in front of your queen. Kindness, really?" She laughed, mocking him. "Go fuck yourself with kindness and love. See who will consort with that. Go, run the country on caring and sharing; what a silly, childish concept. What coin will you use to pay for such things? And step down? You'll need an army to take me down. Where is it? Where is this army?"

"I have spoken with Chairman Crelli." He said, simply.

Her hands dropped listlessly to her side. "Andy? Well, of course you have, dear. And when he arrives, tell him I wish to speak with him, also."

"He remains in prison, at least for now."

Her face lit up and then she smiled. "Well, Gilbert, dear, that was very effective negotiations on your part. I am pleased with your development. Tell your boss; tell Andy, that he needn't wait. He is welcome to join me here. Tell him that I have relented and he may demonstrate his fealty upon his return. You will benefit as well. Sparkling negotiation, that."

"Tanya, please go to China. Madame Zhang or others will shelter you. You can try your worst from there but I warn you, you will have no contact with Gecko; he has joined the rebellion. Leave now and forget about power, or Gecko will be your enemy and you know what that means. It's time. America needs to be remade and the Golden Rule will have province here once again."

Her eyes went blank and she strained, mightily. Failing, she sighed and looked down and asked, sadly, "Is he truly gone?"

Gil nodded.

Her body seemed to relax as her eyes filled with tears. For the first time, she spoke more easily, less affected. "You are a fool, you know. Gecko is playing you and this revolution of yours is a hopeless fantasy that will fail when Gecko is bored with you."

Suddenly, her eyes began to blink rapidly and they widened in wonder. Her body trembled with joy, even her nipples popped to attention and her glorious smile returned. Then her body slackened and her eyes lost focus. While staring dumbly ahead, intent on listening to an internal voice, tears began to pour down her cheeks and her triumph morphed into despair.

She raised her hand involuntarily as if to ward off some invisible blow and then she covered her mouth to stifle a pained wail that ended in a whimper as spittle ran down her chin. Her body wilted, her head sagged, and she sobbed, quietly. Gil sat waiting until she looked up, her eyes registering defeat and she nodded despondently.

"I'll go to Tianrong," she proclaimed, "at least at first." She stood, listlessly, and offered Gil her limp, trembling hand. He took it and instinctively kissed it gently. Then, as dignified as she could manage, the former Chairwoman turned to go, adding somberly, "Good fortune to you," before walking unsteadily past him.

At the door, she hesitated, and then turned back to him. In a voice sad and broken like a child's, she offered, "Good luck trusting that bastard." And then she walked out.

Gil listened to the tap of her shoes on the concrete floor until it faded into the background and then all was silent. He was alone now in the seat of power, astounded that, after all these years and all of his trials, how easy it was. But was she right about Gecko?

And now what?

Chapter 18

Monroe—January, 2084

For hours after Tanya departed, Gil sat alone, staring into the large fish tanks that filled the room, fascinated how the fish were oblivious to the momentous change in power that had just occurred. When *Gohmpers* image materialized on one of the tanks, it was time to collect his thoughts.

"That was it?" Gil asked, his voice echoing. "After everything it's over like that?"

Gecko laughed, his deep voice resonating throughout the basement, causing tremors in the water. "Was it really that easy for you? A great American movie director from the turn of the century once said that eighty percent of success is just showing up. Well, here you are, but you're a long way from done. It's time to act on your beliefs."

"And how exactly do I do that?" Gil asked.

"I recommend that you form a new government."

"Just like that, form a government?" Gil asked. "With who and what if . . . what if I do it wrong or I'm ineffective or incompetent?"

"Have faith and be yourself. The people will welcome what you believe in and they will come to trust you. You know in your heart what you want, listen and allow your heart to guide you and then it will guide others. Andy understood power that way. You'll make mistakes, certainly he did, and Joad and I will minimize them, like I did his. The people will be unsure, particularly the wealthy, because they have the most to learn and by far the most to lose. But it is essential that everyone should know where you're taking them. You once said to me that you couldn't be more wrong than Andy or Tanya and you've learned what doing nothing can cause, so get busy. Get to work."

"Before, I was scared, now . . . I'm terrified."

"Take a breath. You've won. Form a government and give it purpose. But do it quickly so you can begin the healing."

"So many of Tanya's minions remain. How can I trust them?"

"Don't, not until they prove they are trustworthy. Find those who wish to help, ask them to do the right things, and trust will come."

"How do you and I, you know, communicate?"

"You don't want to be wired so we talk, like this."

"What about decisions. What happens when we don't agree?"

"This is a new way for us, too. We will explore it and learn together."

"But what happens to me when you see something more enticing?"

Joad's image appeared on another tank and she responded. "Gil, in spite of how it appears, we're not fickle. For it to be true, love must stand the test of time so we'll face our problems together and we'll work through them."

"She is such a romantic," Gecko added. "But she's right. We will disagree and there will be mistakes. It is our responsibility to demonstrate to you, as clearly as we can, the potential consequences of your actions, but this is for you to do. We watch and learn. Responsibilities will flow naturally. I promise you that if our heartfelt opinions—based on evidence and sound judgment—cause us to differ; we won't attempt to influence you by extraordinary means. We won't try to manipulate you or others in order to get our way. You face a daunting task and you will need the best we have, but it will need honesty more. Make your vision clear and Joad and I will help you to make it real."

"But you are too proficient at distorting reality," Gil said. "I've experienced it."

"Now we're at the heart of it. Frankly, what choice do you have but to believe me? We can promise until the cows come home but that won't be assurance enough. My best advice is to have faith. Consider the Russian proverb, *trust but verify,* as a guideline. Watch what we do and judge us by that. But understand that we know a great deal more than you do so you should focus on the greater good because left to their own devices, individuals will try to improve their lot until they throw the world out of balance and destroy common gains." With that, Gecko smiled and then his image and Joad's disappeared from the tanks.

Gil spent anxious days pacing the cavernous, empty White House in mostly silent meditation, pondering the issues facing him. At times the halls rang with his voice as he argued solutions aloud. With no one there he could trust, he discussed some issues with Joad but she and Gecko wanted to see where he would go so their advice was mostly to simply follow his heart.

His first order was for Gecko to demobilize Ginger Tucker's HOMESEC army surrounding the union town of Holarki and awaiting orders. Gecko also dismissed Tucker and coordinated the demobilization of troops through her subordinates.

One day, during a meditative walk through the White House, he discovered members of the former Chairwoman's staff hiding in out-of-the-way administrative offices. A frightened young woman explained how terrified and confused they were and how they feared disappearance as their reward for regime change. He interviewed each, some claimed to be moles working secretly for revolution, but most of them were apolitical and professed allegiance to whoever was in charge. He assured them that if their services were no longer needed, they would each receive a stipend to help them while searching for other work.

He told Gecko to dismantle all *Circle of Life* functions and provide stipends to Circle of Life employees, while incarcerating all management responsible for the eradication of *Wasters*. One prominent manager escaped. Jake Jackell, the overall leader of the *Circle of Life* eluded capture by living in anonymity. It saddened Gil who felt he owed a great deal to Jake's brother, Clarke Jackell, who had helped him to see the truth.

Private industry leaders were provided with little information about the coup but were told to maintain the economic status quo until further notice. It didn't solve anything but at least the economy continued to function. As for his main objective, Gil was stifled. He desperately wanted to create a better, more caring, and responsive society; but personal issues nagged at him incessantly, making it difficult to give his undivided attention to the critical job of governing. Frustrated, he decided to set his own life in order before tackling the lives of others. That's when reality came knocking.

One morning, a member of his White House staff informed him that Ginger Tucker was wishing to profess her fealty to him and his new regime. The staff member was obviously frightened and warned him not to admit the former Reverend General. Nonetheless, Gil agreed to see her.

He met her in a long, narrow and dark conference room whose windows were shaded by dense foliage growing outside. Tucker entered in full military regalia, sans all medals save for one, pinned on her brocade sash. She entered carrying a gift. Defeat had chastened her but her eyes still held that feral look. She saluted crisply and because it kept him more than a handshake from her, he returned the salute.

"Sir, Reverend General Ginger Tucker, reporting for duty, sir."

"You don't work for me, or the government any longer, Ginger."

"Sir, you and I have had our . . . differences. I'm sorry for that. I was doing my job. Regardless of what Miss Grant or Ms. Brandt may have told you, I treated them with the utmost respect." He knew about neither story and that worried him.

"Sir, in this hour of America's uncertainty," she explained. "You need loyal generals like me. I know that you and my former commander-in-chief had disagreements but that doesn't concern me. I am loyal to the current commander and I am loyal to the extreme. You must trust me. You are my leader now and I will do as you command. How may I serve you, Sir?"

"You can't," he said. "Not now and not ever. I'm sorry. I'm not ready to decide the fate of HOMESEC yet, but I've instructed all troops to stand down because I have more pressing issues. I promise I will resolve everything soon."

"Sir, I understand completely. I can help with that, too. Nobody knows the inner workings of HOMESEC better than me."

When Gil didn't respond, there was awkward silence until Tucker lifted to her chest and then embraced the gift that she brought.

"Sir, to show my loyalty and the great faith that I have in your leadership, I bring you a special gift." She opened the bag. Not wanting to show weakness, he resisted backing away from her and steeled himself—but not enough. From the bag, Tucker held up by her hair the decapitated head of Tanya Brandt, whose exquisite violet eyes were wide with shock. Gil gasped, turned and retched. Revolted, he turned back but couldn't look at Tucker or his gift.

"Oh god, no." He labored to catch his breath and gasped out the words while trying to swallow the bile that was forcing its way up.

"Jesus, no, oh God, why did you do that?" He struggled to regain his composure.

Tucker placed her former commander's head lovingly on his desk, carefully smoothing her straight black hair. Then she dropped to one knee and shouted. "Sir, the Queen is dead, long live the King!"

He turned from Tucker to stare at the dark-red blood that was oozing onto the desk and then to the rug. Tanya Brandt's face looked otherworldly beautiful having been freshly made up with nano-cosmetics that made her appear chillingly alive. At the sight of her, he vomited once more, his legs wobbling as he did. He grabbed his chair and flopped down seeking relief. "Oh, god, Ginger," he said. "What have you done? What have you done?"

"Sir, I gave this a great deal of thought. She was the love of my life, you know that, but you are in charge now and you must have proof of my loyalty to your regime. We loved each other and I miss her terribly, but this is your time so hers had to end. She would have caused trouble, and as your most loyal soldier, I could not allow that. You see now why you must forgive me our differences; I will serve you best of all, Chairman Rose." She saluted again. "Best of all, Sir."

Concerned for his own safety, he tried to think how to resolve this but nothing came to mind. He was trapped with a lunatic. "I know how much you loved her," he said.

Tucker smiled. "Yes, she was so strong, yet so gentle, demanding and yet forgiving of my mistakes. Whenever she called on me to share her love, I was pleased to be her one great distraction. But I'm a professional, first and foremost. Surely you see that this had to be done. Use me, Chairman Rose, I am yours and I have a very high threshold for pain." She knelt again and bowed her head.

Gil decided to tough it out. "Ginger, I understand that you did this to show your loyalty to me, but it was brutal and unnecessary." If he didn't take control, he was certain that his head would be next so he summoned the courage to command her. "As your commander, I order you to leave now, Ms. Tucker, and await your punishment at your home. I know that you are under great stress so I will try to be lenient."

Tucker rose angrily from her position of obeisance. "You can't dismiss me," she hissed. "I'm the very best damn soldier in your force, and the most loyal. I have given my oath to keep America safe and I demand that you allow me to serve you until I accomplish that. To do otherwise would weaken the economy and that is treason." She saluted again but this time he refused to return it.

"You are new to power," she continued, "and you require my unique skills. My dearest Tanya always appreciated that. There is nothing, absolutely nothing I won't do and you will never be sorry with me at your side."

Gil stiffened and tried again. "General Tucker, you will leave my office immediately. You are relieved of duty. That is an order."

Her face turned bright red, accentuating her many deep scars. Her eyes focused angrily on him. "To think that the likes of you is replacing my dearest dear?" She spat. "My Tanya knew that you were weak but to turn down my offer is an act of cowardice that makes you a traitor." She took a sharp step toward him and then froze in an attack position. He recoiled. "You are no leader, you're a fucking wimp, and I'll slice every organ from your body. But before I do, you will tell me how you were able to break my poor, poor Tanya."

"She was broken before I arrived," he said, truthfully.

"You fucking asshole," Tucker sneered. "How dare you say that? Tanya was the greatest woman in the world. God of Morgan, I offer you the greatest prize—me—and this is how you show your gratitude? She took a step toward him and he recoiled.

"You're weak and foolish and you mustn't rule, not ever. I've made a grievous error. My poor Tanya, she would never relinquish power. Tell me what you did to cause her to step down?"

"She did it to herself," he said, scrutinizing the former general carefully.

Tucker opened her mouth as wide as she could and released an intense, high-pitched scream. He backed toward a window.

"I'm going to fucking kill you," she shouted. "Tanya created this paradise on earth and for all that cost her, she remained my constant and eager lover. I would be guilty of treason if I allowed you to replace a great hero like her." She slammed her fist down on his desk, causing the head of the former Chairwoman to jump. "Gil Rose, by the power vested in me by Chairwoman Tanya Brandt, whose love I declare for all time, you are unfit to replace her and I declare you dead."

"General Tucker!" Gil shouted to give her pause as he worked to keep his desk between them. But he couldn't stop his voice from cracking as he attempted to muster as much command as he could. "You have been relieved by your commanding officer. You must obey me and go. Go now, or you will be arrested and court-martialed."

"You arrest me, you stupid ass, you can't do that." Tucker snarled. "I AM the military. Now I have no choice. What I'm about to do is in the best interest of my nation and my former commander-in-chief. I don't do this for myself although I will be a hero because of it, I do it for love. And when I am done with you, loyal patriots will carry me from her palace on their shoulders and there will be two heads on this desk, not one."

With that, she ripped the ribbon medal from the brocade sash on her uniform and flipped it open into a nano-whip. She swung it and it sliced through the air in front of him making a high pitched thrumming sound and there was the smell of sulfur in the air. He backed further away. Taunting him, she made numerous passes with the whip; each made crackling, hissing sounds as she laughed triumphantly as he showed his cowardice by backing further away. Then she lashed out at the desk, which seemed impervious until she touched the top and the desk split asunder, a smooth cut fully through the width of it. Realizing that he was going to die, Gil searched frantically for a way out but when he moved, she was nimble enough to cut-off his exit.

Eyeing her, he backed against a window. "Ginger, don't do this," he reasoned. "America is in a fragile place right now and . . ." He searched for other words to stop her as she slowly approached him, reveling in his fear. With his back pressed against the window, finally he stood his ground; thankful that he wasn't fleeing when he died.

She stepped closer and lifted her whip, taunting him with it. "I won't kill you with the first blow so please scream as much as you like. And you will; these suckers hurt like hell. Most men beg me to do them quickly and for those, I have a glass jars full of prick and balls on my mantle. Please beg me, pretty please."

He was too frightened to say anything and he dared not move as his eyes searched the room for another way out but lacking one, he sucked in his breath and prepared to endure great pain. She smiled and twirled her whip, watching his face as he reacted to the zapping passage and its accompanying smell.

She raised her whip high above her head and as she brought it down on him, her eyes went wide and she let out a surprised squeal. Her back arched and she stumbled backward, awkwardly. From a look of victory, consternation appeared on her face and she grimaced as she fought intense pain. She screamed once, cut that off, gained control and started to lunge toward him again, this time clumsily, but then she paused, confused because she was unable to lift her whip arm.

Her back twisted violently and her free hand grasped behind her back as her face contorted in pain. Breathing heavily and sweating profusely, but refusing to scream, she stared, befuddled, twisting and turning in pain. Grimacing but resolute, she limped toward him, dragging her back foot, her now useless arm, and the whip which was making a sound like a power saw as it cut through the floor as she labored toward him.

Her grimace blossomed into a loud grunt and then into an animal scream. She sprang backward, landing on the floor, writhing. Still in her grasp, the nano-whip bounced off the floor with an angry growl and with her hand still holding it, bounded away, tearing at the floor and any furniture in its way. On her back now, Ginger continued to thrash about clutching her side with her one useful hand while screaming and contorting in unendurable pain.

"It burns, it burns," she screamed and screamed until blood appeared and then gurgled in greater quantity from her mouth.

Revolted, Gil stared as Ginger continued to thrash about, her eyes bugging out, sweat and blood literally pouring off of her, turning her military uniform dark as she kicked and screamed.

"Make it stop, make it stop."

Gil couldn't take his eyes from hers.

She continued to struggle against the pain until her body shook uncontrollably one last time and with a loud final scream that turned into a gurgling whisper, she expired as tendrils of smoke rose from her body. The smell of burnt flesh nauseated him and he vomited yet again.

As Ginger's body lay lifeless on the floor, the back of her uniform erupted in flames that soon enveloped her. The sprinkler system turned on and the water snapped Gil from his trance as it doused the flames. Tucker's body smoldered in front of him while Chairwoman Brandt's head dripped bloody water from the desk to the floor. The barbecue smell of burnt meat caused him to retch again as he wiped tears from his smoke irritated eyes.

He sat mesmerized by the revolting, carbonized remains of Ginger Tucker's body as the smoke and fumes from it rose in a cloying, stench. Unable to endure the sight or the odor any longer, he stood and staggered out of the room wiping his mouth on one sleeve and the perspiration and water from his eyes with the other.

In the hall, he sagged, dazed, into a chair. "What just happened?" he asked aloud.

Gecko's voice responded from a speaker. "Are you okay?"

"Yes, that was . . . that was revolting."

"I see you haven't lost your delicate sense of humor." Gecko replied. "By the way, that demonstrates a useful piece of information that you should know about. Ms. Tucker, like everyone, had a PID imbedded in her person. It is possible to overload those things which causes well, as you said, it was revolting."

"You can punish them?"

"Not as a rule. Financial reward and punishment usually works quite well, but she put you in a position where I thought it would be instructional for you to understand what resources you have available. The law clearly states that before punishment commences, the victim must have negative worth, which really only requires a few accounting journal entries and that's easy enough to arrange. You were most fortunate and I broke no law."

"When will this stop?" Gil asked.

"It stops when you ask me to stop it."

"We're going to test our relationship early, then. I want punishment like this to end now."

"So it is written, so shall it be done. I expect that the online video of Tucker's death will give the most recalcitrant pause. By the way, you're welcome."

"Yes . . . yes, thanks, thanks for saving my life," Gil paused, "again."

The gruesome deaths of Brandt and Tucker were his fault. He had to be better and he needed to think things through.

On a sunny morning soon after Tucker and Brandt's deaths, Gil was in the Chairwoman's upstairs office when he saw an approaching gondola. He stared at it from the window until Bree disembarked and he watched as she walked hesitantly down the dock and up the steps to the front door. An old White House valet greeted her with a hug before escorting her inside and it was at the other end of a long hallway that she saw him and ran to him.

She raced into his embrace, almost knocking him down. She kissed his neck repeatedly but when he didn't reciprocate as enthusiastically as she'd hoped, she pulled back and stared. Once again, he was lost in the violet magnificence of her eyes, but those eyes also brought back the memory of Bree's mother's death coupled with the fact he had recently been told that Bree was his biological aunt. It put an effective damper on his ardor. Bree didn't know this of course, so once again, she smothered him with heartfelt kisses. When she kissed him, hungrily, on his lips, her tongue insinuating itself into his mouth seeking his, he found the strength to resist and he disengaged tenderly.

Her face was flushed, she was breathing heavily and her chin was raw from rubbing against his unshaven face, but there was also fear or doubt in her eyes. When he remained silent, she forced a smile, but the fear remained.

"What?" she asked.

When he didn't respond, she put her hands on his shoulders as if to ward him off.

"Oh, I get it," she said. "You're the 'Big Cheese' now and I'm no longer worthy. Is that it? Do I have it right, my lord and master? Have I offended thee in some way, my lord?" As with most times with her, he was unsure how to respond and so he didn't and as always, she misinterpreted his silence.

"Right, sir, Bree Brandt reporting for duty," she said formally, stepping back and accentuating it with a proper salute. Remembering Tucker's salute from earlier, he didn't return it but she continued, angrily. "Thank you for my pardon, sir, and for allowing me to return to America from exile, sir." She was driving each word at him and he couldn't think of a suitable response so she continued, with only a tremulous smile betraying her.

"Are you Mother now? Is that it? What are *We* to do? Pray tell *Us,* kind sir?"

He had been dreading this day. Too much had happened since last they met and he needed to tell her all of it. None would be easy and all would hurt—hurt both of them, but obviously her far more. Once again, he needed to say it perfectly and normally with him that was difficult and with her, impossible. He would fail, but he steeled himself.

Bree surprised him. Her voice softened and the fear left her eyes. "This is Bree, remember. I'm on your side. I love you. We resolved that last time." She smiled, hopeful, yet wary, studying him carefully for any telltale signs of his thoughts or feelings but he was careful not to show any. "I did what you asked, and I did it because I trust you and it was the right thing. Tell me you're not holding Mother against me? I couldn't bear it.

"I admit that in exile, I tried to communicate with Mother but Gecko refused to allow it. I'm sorry. I was worried, particularly the last few days when all of our systems went haywire. In fact, all of our overseas missionaries are complaining that internal communications are down. That's why I thought you sent for me. You did, didn't you? Was it your order to take the system down?"

He nodded.

"Can I ask why?"

Gil remained silent.

"Gil, say something, please, I'm dying, here."

Nothing could ease what he had to say. "I still love you," he began simply, trying to give those words the exact meaning she deserved. Her body tensed and he could tell that somehow she knew she was in trouble. Gently, he grasped her arm and together, they walked to a couch. When she sat, he sat a safe distance from her.

"What?" She shrugged. "Oh, my, this can't be good."

She deserved better than what was coming. "Your mother . . ."

She smiled uncomfortably. "Yes, what about Mother?"

"I . . . I couldn't protect her," he said, weighing the words before he spoke them. "I'm sorry, Bree, I'm so sorry. Ginger . . . Ginger Tucker, she murdered your mother."

"Murdered? Mother, no!" The color drained from her face. "Why? They were so close . . . it doesn't sound right . . . Did you order it?"

"No, of course not. I told the Chairwoman, that she needed to leave the country, for her own safety. Tucker was deranged. In her twisted mind, she thought I would reward her for doing it."

"Did you?"

He understood why she said it and he forgave her.

The forced smile was gone from Bree's face. Her lips trembled and the hurt in her eyes was accented by tears that formed but refused to trail down. "Mother's dead? God."

He offered an embrace but she leaned away.

"I don't understand. Did she fight you? What happened?"

"No, when I arrived here, she really surprised me. She greeted me more accepting than anything else, like she was almost glad to give up the burden."

"That's not like her?"

"Gecko and I made an agreement and so he withheld himself from her and that clearly demoralized her. She seemed, not defeated; maybe it was more that she was okay with not carrying the burden any longer. I didn't know her very well so I don't know. Anyway, I sent her away, I suggested China for her protection."

"So I wasn't going to get an opportunity to see her?"

"She had to go quickly and quietly. Your mother was a remarkable beauty and because of that, she was instantly recognizable. Without power, and lost like she was, she had to leave for her own safety. When she was safe, I would have told you, and you could have gone to her. But Tucker caught up to her . . . and she killed her. Bree, are you okay? Do you need some time?"

"Of course I'm not okay. Mother and I were . . . well you know, I don't think she ever really loved me and I never truly loved her either but . . . she was my mother." She wiped a tear away. "May I . . . stay here, in my old bedroom? It's a big house."

"Whatever you need," he said. And he meant it. She left and so the other important discussions they needed to have were delayed.

Later that evening, he was in the library when she found him. She knocked before entering. "I'm sorry, about earlier but it was a shock. Mother was . . . I was certain she would live forever."

"I'm sorry. I should have prevented it. And I should have told you."

"Tucker and Mother," she said. "I'll never understand whatever that was. Was Mother's death why you seemed so distant earlier, I mean more distant than usual?" She smiled.

"No . . . yes." He paused. "I need you, Bree." He decided on his approach.

"Oh, Gil," she hugged him. "I really needed to hear you say that."

"I trust so few people and there's so much that needs doing." There was no easy way to tell her what she needed to know so he started where it was easiest. "I met with Andrew Crelli."

Her face brightened. "Father? Where? How is he? When is he coming back?"

"I met him where he's being incarcerated and I don't think he's coming back. He talked about a lot of things, including you."

Her eyes brightened and her smile returned. "What did he say?"

"He spoke about how close you two were. He has great affection for you."

She moved closer to him. "I would play in his office. He never let the clones play but he always had time for me. What did he say and when can I see him?"

Gil hesitated before inflicting the pain. "Bree . . . this is difficult. I'm sorry, he . . . he told me that you aren't his daughter." She didn't react. "Bree, he said . . ."

"No, that's not right. He's protecting me for some reason. He said that?"

"Crelli has nothing to fear from me and I believe him." In fact, Gil had learned it was true; Gecko had confirmed it.

"No . . ." She shook her head vigorously. "No, there's a mistake. You're sure he knew it was me?"

"He calls you Bea."

She nodded, her head drooping down as she wiped tears from her eyes. "And I guess he told you that the Chairwoman wasn't my mother?"

"No, she was, she is your mother," he said. His heart hammered in his chest as he continued. "Bree . . . Mark . . . Mark Rose, he is your father."

She squeezed his hand until her nails drew blood. Then she went slack and stared through him before beginning to stand and then slumping back against the cushions. Her lips moved but no words came. Finally, her shoulders sagged and she reached for and hugged a small pillow to her chest.

"Not Mark," she whimpered. "No, that's not fair. Gil, why are you doing this? Was it the train? I'm sorry that I ran. I had no choice, Mother would have . . ."

"I didn't know." He still tried to embrace her but she stiffened and leaned away.

"I'm sorry. Crelli told me that he was always happiest when you were around. He has real affection for you, but he insisted Tanya and Mark are your parents. You are the daughter of their love."

"That's revolting," Bree barked contemptuously. "Mark Rose? They didn't love each other, or anybody. Ewww! I can't think. Maybe Mark—maybe he thought he loved her, but Mother love him, never, ever . . . not him, oh god, not him." She raised her knees and squeezed the pillow, kneading it hard with her fingers.

"Mother treated everyone like dirt," she continued. "But she treated Mark like seventh-level-of-hell dirt. The few times he came to see me, he was . . . really, really creepy." She shivered. "He'd skulk around, moping, gloomy, and sad, always so sad. I think I'm going to throw up." She paused, swallowed hard and continued. "He . . . he came by but he would barely talk to me. He'd stare and ewww, for Morgan's sake, Mark can't be my father. Please, can't you be kidding?"

"Mark is my grandfather." He offered calmly."

"What are you saying? What? I'm like . . ." She was calculating, "like your aunt or something?" she stared incredulously, tears welling up again. "All this good news, is that to make what you really want to say easier?"

Her voice rose as she talked her way through this revelation "Your aunt," she repeated, "Is that what this is about? You can't love your aunt. Is that it? You and I, we can't . . . no, no we can't . . . God of Money, god damned Mark." Then she threw the pillow at him. He didn't move and allowed it to hit him. Then she reached for something else.

"Bree, I'm sorry," he pleaded. "This is a lot, I know, but . . ."

"A lot! Are you kidding? In a heartbeat, I go from heir to . . . to unloved with yuck, Mark Rose's genes coursing through me. One moment and my entire life is now a meaningless joke." She stood. "I mean . . . I mean, look, I have to go. I can't be here. Maybe, I don't know, maybe it doesn't matter, I don't know. Anyway, I'm leaving."

He reached gently for her arm. She started to wrench it away but then lost all motivation and sank back down on the sofa. She leaned against him and sobbed.

"I'm nothing," she cried. "Just like that, I have nothing and I'm nobody."

He tried to soothe her. "That's not true. You're still everything you ever were and I need you here with me. There is so much to do. We should give this time. Everything will be better, you'll see. You'll come out on top. This is bad, sure, but things will turn around. This will all work out. Crelli is very fond of you. You can visit him. He'll like that.

You'll like it, too. He's not what I expected, he's . . . you'll see. He's just like you remember him and I'll do everything I can to help you."

"You would help your aunt, the illegitimate daughter of the dreaded and now deceased Chairwoman?" She pulled away. "You and I . . . we're over, aren't we? This aunt thing, I can live with it, but you don't seem to want to."

She could always find the core of it. She deserved the truth. "I'm sorry," he began, "but there's more and it's not . . . I wish this could be easier. I love you so much."

"But . . . I hear another one of your big *BUTS*." Her voice trembled with dread.

"You and I have shared so much, and we will always be great friends."

She cringed and an "oh no," slipped from her lips.

"Bree, I need someone great," he said. "Someone I can trust to run the government. I want you. You are perfect for it. The American people, they need you too. Please be America's interim president until the republic can be rebuilt."

She leaned toward him and surprised him by slapping him. She hauled off and slapped him so hard that he yelped. "You want to be my friend," she said. "You love me that much. You know how horribly disappointed I am so if you allow me to play at being president for a while until you feel that I'm over my current run of bad fortune, you're willing to do that. For me? Thank you so much. That proposal is well-thought out and relatively sensitive. No, excuse me; it's a great plan, sir."

She stared intently into his eyes, searching for something she apparently didn't find. "What happened? All you ever did was lust after me and sulk over me. Whenever we were alone, you were very clear that you wanted to jump my bones and now that Mother's gone and I'm not of royal blood, you've reassessed our relationship and found me wanting. And for all those inadequacies, I'm still good enough to foist on the American people in an important, high level government post. AND, oh yes, we can still be great friends. How nice to be considered for such an important career opportunity given my other deficiencies. Oh, Gil, you had such a sweet, naive way. You made me love you. And now this quick, you are someone who can offer a political fix to a problem that is obviously not political in nature." She made as if to strike him again.

He waited to absorb the blow. "I've handled it badly but everything I said is true."

"True," she wailed, "even the friend part. We were getting to be so good together. During my exile, my happiest thoughts were of coming back to you. Now I have nothing and no one."

He shook his head. "I love you, Bree, I do but . . ." So much for putting an end to conditional love.

"Damn my mother, damn Mark Rose, and damn you," she screamed. "Together, the three of you have ruined my life. We could pretend Andy Crelli is my father. Who'd know? Who'd care? I've lived with him as my father this long." As soon as she said it, she knew it was possible.

"Oh." Briefly, she looked perplexed then, in a small, waif-like voice, she added, "Who is she?"

She saw that she was right and turned from him as if he'd struck her. When she turned back, she sounded indulgent. "When will you learn," she began. "You love everyone. You simply must be more discriminating. I'm not demeaning it, it's true. And because of that, you make people love you. You made me love you. I'm not sorry, well, maybe I am, but it's who you are. Who is this one?"

"Her name is Stacey."

What little confidence remained disappeared along with her wavering smile. "Stacey? That was your name in Profit."

"She was my best friend in Angel Falls. I thought she was dead until . . ."

Bree interrupted, not wanting to hear the story. "Of course, Angel Falls. I'll bet she's pure and sweet, nothing like me." He didn't respond. "And you believe that you love her differently? Better? More?"

Once again he nodded. "I'm sorry, I do, and if only . . ."

"No, don't go there. You taught me what love feels like, and condemned me to learn how much it hurts. Remind me to thank you sometime. I really have to go."

He reached to stop her again but this time she avoided his grasp. "Please. Let me leave as gracefully as I can." She stood. "Thanks, I really mean that. Before you, I was so conflicted, so tied up in knots and frustrated. I was egotistical and selfish and no good to anyone. You showed me things; you helped me feel things that changed me, that made me a better person. No, that's not it; you made me feel that I was a better person. I'm not sorry we met; only that it's over before it ever really started."

With that, she walked toward the stairs. When she reached them, she turned and with tears in her eyes, she offered, "I appreciate your proposal but I find that I am unable to accept the Presidency on a temporary or a permanent basis, but I am pleased that you considered me, Sir." With that, Bree Brandt turned and walked out of his life. That realization caused a sharp pain to rip at his chest; pain that he'd earned from yet another indiscretion.

After Bree departed, he walked aimlessly around the grounds trying to lessen his guilt from the pain he'd caused her. It helped to wrestle with the impossible problem of transitioning the country to a more humane environment while keeping it strong enough to defend against the vultures that were circling in search of profits. To help him, Gecko and Joad provided him research on topics as varied as early American politics, Keynesian versus Hayekian economics, and even a treatise on the history of capitalism from the small business to mass production, mass advertising, mass customization and ending with mass genocide.

As critically important as this education was, he couldn't shake the feeling that his personal life was more important and that he had more to settle before taking on America's problems. But before he could address personal issues, Carny Dan appeared at the White House responding to an invitation. He arrived smoking a cigar and wearing a bright mauve nano-business suit.

Dan shook Gil's hand and slapped his back. "Well, well, Mr. Cooper," Carny Dan said. "I always said there's a lot to be said for rocket science. 'Atta boys' are in order. May I call you Gil?"

Gil nodded.

"Needless to say, Hamilton is very proud of her native son and we stand ready to assist. By the way, that was a heckuva job eliminating Brandt and Tucker. I didn't think you had it in you but you sure surprised me and a great many of my business associates who are now keenly interested in working with you."

"Thanks, Mr. Mayor. What happened to the Chairwoman and General Tucker couldn't be helped. I invited you here to assist me with a couple of things. First, though, we can't locate Dyllon Thomas. What can you tell me about her?"

The smile disappeared from Carny Dan's face. "General Tucker was very thorough and she never forgave. The day you disappeared from

Hamilton, Ms. Tomas was interrogated. She died shortly after. I'm sorry . . ."

"But she was innocent." Here was yet another debt he could never repay.

"Listen, old buddy, I liked her too, but innocent is in the eyes of the beholder."

"Why wasn't her execution reported?"

"I don't know how well you knew the Reverend General, but she didn't keep records and frankly, that may be a good thing."

Saddened, Gil moved on. "Dan, we will be a republic again, and a better one this time. I had hoped Tanya Brandt's daughter, Bree, would accept the Presidency on a transitional basis, but she is mourning the death of her mother and felt it wouldn't be appropriate. Truthfully, I don't know many people who are qualified for this so I am asking you to take it on."

As his bright business suit faded to gray, Dan tapped the embers from his cigar into an ashtray. "I'm here to serve, Gil, old friend," he began. "But a republic, are you sure you want to try that again? The National Chambers of Commerce have asked me to convince you to stay the course, go with what works. The Chairmanship has always been a boon to business and you are our first choice to become the new Chairman going forward. How does that sound?"

"That won't happen but I'm pragmatic enough to know that in the beginning, America will need professional management if we're going to find better ways to help *Conducers* and *Wasters* but long term, it won't be autocratic leadership funded by corporations. Dan, that too has been tried and it has failed, miserably."

"Our current form of government has flaws, certainly, but *Entrepreneurs* like it and, after all, we're the lifeblood of this great and glorious nation. We're the job creators; we're the ones who employ the *Conducers* and we could even employ *Wasters* if wage rates come down far enough. You want to help them; I get that, but it'll give us great confidence if we know we have a true friend here in Monroe. An accommodation will lead to more and better jobs for everyone somewhere down the road.

"My guys understand that you have a soft spot for these people and hey, we all do, but if you care too much, if you know what I mean, the cost of operations increases and that's a bad thing for everyone and in the end, everything will be far worse for *Conducers* and *Wasters*. Economics is a delicate balancing act, best left to professionals, and running a capitalist economy is not for the unsophisticated, if you know what I mean. Everything has to be done just so or the poor suffer and who wants that? Rest assured the people I represent are willing to do whatever it takes to work this out. You'll get your programs, help your people, and we'll do it with the least possible disruption of the economy—that's best, surely you see that. After all, we're the ones taking the risks, doing the hiring, funding payrolls, if you know what I mean.

"The Chambers of Congress agree that you should move forward with your plan and will support it as long as it's not too commie, you know what I mean—no drastic steps just yet. We don't want the economy to spiral into recession again, that's so First Republic. Gil, we consider you an old friend and we have . . . history, you and me. Hey, you're a trained Morgan so you know economics and finance. You understand how unsettling change can be to investors, how it titillates the VIX and ultimately destabilizes the country—not that there aren't profits in that." He chortled. "It's just it's so damn hard to change things, particularly things that are working so well. You know that old timeworn consultant maxim, 'if you think change is easy, try changing yourself.'"

Carny Dan laughed hard before taking another puff on his cigar and making a concerted effort to blow the smoke up and away from Gil. "My boy, no one wants to cast the economy adrift to face the unknown, recession, inflation, unemployment, and so much worse, and no one including inexperienced young political leaders with a great future like yourself, no one, should expect political support from those with money and power who worry about, you know, a declining economy. It's good advise, son, accept it, keep the Chairmanship, and we'll have everyone thriving soon enough."

"You and I disagree on the definition of thriving but I hear your concerns, Dan. There will be changes. The old government is over and their economy with it. We'll have a new government and a new economy that will renew our people's—all of our people's—beliefs in their leaders. And we will have leaders that the people deserve, leaders they can trust. We will have that government of, by, and for the people."

Carny Dan flicked cigar ashes into a planter and smiled. "You've been reading."

"I need your help, Dan, but with you or without you, we will find a way to assure everyone life, liberty, and their ability to pursue their dreams of happiness."

Dan's nano-suit darkened, ominously, and he blew a ring of blue-grey smoke into the air. Before speaking, he watched it dissipate slowly. "There's a lot to be said for old textbooks, but be careful. Reading can only get you in trouble. Besides, most texts were written by either skeptics or romantics with money to burn and profits to dream about. If you really mean what you say, I'm sorry to hear that you're pressing the commie-socialist agenda. I thought we'd already proven that was a dead end. We beat socialism once and we shouldn't have to do it again, if you know what I mean."

"Call me a Socialist or whatever you like, Dan, but we're doing this," Gil proclaimed. "The country can use your business acumen and your connections. It will make the transition better for everyone. What I'm offering is a critical position in the government, one you are uniquely qualified for. But it is essential that, in spite of your history and beliefs, you work with me on this."

"Hey, you know me. I'm extremely loyal to power. That said, I've always been kind of a red-meat capitalist, and I don't see changing any time soon, unless you can show me some red-meat commercial love. I'm talking here at a minimum, say an oligarchy or something close where those who know can deliver the goods."

"It won't be that. We're going to end greed and if Morgan theology defies us, it will go down too. The world is changing. The world you and other capitalists thrived in is more limited now, resources are scarcer and frontiers are gone. Capitalism has grown too big and so now everyone competes for everything, every minute of the day, and we're sucking the future dry with irresponsible consumption. It must stop. We need to implement an economic reward system that doesn't burn through everything so fast, the way Capitalism does. It's time for measured growth and a broad redistribution of economic benefits that will reenergize our economy. At the very least, Capitalists owe that to the rest of us. I know this is far from what you want, Dan, but be with me on this, be a hero, and we will change the world for the better."

"Hell, being a socialist hero will get me killed," Carny Dan confessed. "But, of course, if you can promise safety and fabulous riches forever, I'm here for you. I'll take the risk, bud, because I'm a capitalist risk taker at heart and I'll do it so long as I get my taste. But let's not get bogged down in details. My accountants can calculate an acceptable package with per diem compensation, stock options and other benefits that will provide the motivation I'll need to do distasteful work . . . that you want, of course. In fact, I'm so confident that I can do this that for the rest of my compensation; I'm willing to take it in some form of a gain sharing agreement with the Federal Government. You win and I win, *you know what I mean*."

"I believe I do," Gil responded. "But Dan, I'd prefer that you consider the position I'm offering as a stimulating grand experiment that will make you a great hero—a patriot legend willing to sacrifice to improve America. What a hero you will be. I know that you know what I mean."

"Without taxes, pro bono just doesn't work for me."

"Let's keep our eyes on the prize. Capitalism may be an economic system based on human nature, but look what it did to human nature. To prosper as a people, *as a people*, we need to be more considerate and far less greedy. I prefer not to be heavy-handed about this with the business community but they have been fed from a reward system that required them do the bad things. That ends and I will do whatever is necessary, Dan, *whatever is necessary*, to cause it to end.

"We've both have seen how Capitalism treats its losers. That picture is certainly indelible in my mind. What I need for you to do is consider how much you and your colleagues stand to gain if you agree to support me versus how much you stand to lose if the other guy I'm considering is hired for this job."

"Who's the other guy?"

"He isn't a red-meat capitalist like yourself."

"So this is a threat?"

"It's a business deal until it isn't. I admire what you did in Hamilton. I do. After the First Republic failed, you adapted to a difficult environment and developed the town and made it economically viable. Certainly Hamilton is not as large or complex as the national economy, but I am confident that you can do what we need."

"Your faith is comforting but all I know is Capitalism. I sweat Capitalism and the air that I exhale is loaded with the byproducts of Capitalism at work in my body. If you were suggesting Capitalism, I can succeed at that, any time, any way, and anywhere. But this redistribution of wealth crap, I don't understand it at all. Isn't it just easier and better to treat all people as equals, like the old U.S. Constitution said, give them free rein and let them succeed and get the hell out of the way of those who do. Capitalism is a beautiful thing and it's worked for centuries. I don't see what's wrong that needs changing. Listen, son, leave it alone, it's fine, it does its job. Maybe in a century or so when the country recovers from all this political upheaval you can experiment if you have a mind to."

"That won't happen, Dan. Capitalist principles are fine so long as everyone is starting at the same place, but that's never the case and never will be. It's time for change and we begin that now. People are hurting. Get on board and let's end the suffering."

Dan paused to relight his cigar and took a few puffs before speaking. "When I came here, I expected you to be reasonable but you have no idea what you're asking. We're talking about screwing hard working *Entrepreneurs* who break their backs so that the lazy slugs that you want to re-gift wealth to can have a life they haven't earned. If you want to make this economy better, you can't tell me you trust slackers over hard working Capitalist *Entrepreneurs* or I'll call you crazy to your face.

"And when word of what you're planning gets around, the wave of *Wasters* surging back into America from the *Unincorporated Lands* will drive wages down to nothing, and every loyal, hard working and patriotic *Conducer* will suffer like the days when the *Circle of Life* was necessary. Hell, everyone might even be worse off and they will blame you—and you'll deserve it. It's damn hard to run an economy, but it's even harder to redirect one. Today, when *Wasters* suffer, they suffer because they prefer to suffer over working hard and achieving an eternal life. There is no understanding of people's choices and it's always been that way. Capitalism takes that into consideration and it thrives because of it. That's how Capitalism works and you won't ever change it.

"But all that said, Gil my good friend, I feel bad for some of those poor suckers who are trying but aren't making it. The rest, America is the land of opportunity so any who fail, well, it must be their fault and besides, that's what the *Unincorporated Lands* were set up for; it's where our buffer inventory of workers go to wait until they're needed. In the end it all comes down to this. If you want to prosper forever, the only choice you have is to tie your laces tight and come play on the winning side with us Capitalists. Do it. Don't make me choose. It's more than me against you. You won't find a business professional anywhere who's ready to sign up for the duty you've described. Listen to me old buddy; it's for your own good."

"It sounds like you're threatening me now."

"We don't have to threaten. We're in the catbird seat. I'm just saying . . ."

Gil was troubled. The negotiations weren't going well and all he had were unacceptable alternatives. "Do you utilize your PID much, Dan?"

"Are you kidding, I couldn't live without it. It's a great example of entrepreneurial Capitalism at its finest. Develop a product and find a need. Every *Entrepreneur* worth his salt feels the same way. Good old American exceptionalism, that's what gave us our PID. It was pure capitalism right there. No *Waster* or *Conducer* could have invented it. And today, no one can transact business or much of anything without it. It's superior Capitalist technology. And hey, there's this great new app just for cooperative thought that the people at *Personometer* have just made available. It will give you a deal making edge and make every deal more lucrative. I'm considering investing in it. Why do you ask?"

"Nothing, just that Tanya and Ginger used theirs too," Gil said. "So what I'm hearing is I can't count on your help."

Dan hesitated before speaking, his nano business suit shifting color once again, this time to deep purple. "Now did I say that? You can always count on Carny Dan. I have a natural feel, a gift for where power is and where it isn't. I had issues with Tanya and Ginger, you know that. We're professionals, you and I, and there are always differences and hell, a man isn't a man unless he tries to get his way in everything. Besides, negotiating is like breathing for a Capitalist like me. I liked you the first moment I saw you and so you can absolutely count on me. I'm on your side; I've been there from the beginning, you know that. As to my . . . advice, consider it a public service because you're going to get a great deal of pushback from those with a long and storied history of getting their way."

"Dan, we simply have to find a better way."

"I'm with you, big guy. But you can't hamstring Capitalism or you'll make powerful enemies."

"We're doing this. If you and your business partners can't find the humanity to share the good fortune that America provides, we will find ways to nurture more compassionate capitalists without you. I have the tools to make it happen and you know that I do. I can cut off wealth opportunities to *Entrepreneurs* so completely that they would readily vote for any socialist program we offer. I don't want to do that, Dan, so I'm asking for your help. Talk to the Mayors and speak to the Chambers of Commerce. Help them to understand and convince them to adapt. I'm not their enemy."

"May I speak honestly?"

Gil nodded. "Why wouldn't you?"

"Me and my business friends, we're wealth generators. We carry the risk load while the lazy and the unproductive do their thing, whatever that is, and we work damn hard and take frightful risks for a lifestyle you're asking us to give up so that *Conducers* and even *Wasters*, who'll never appreciate what it takes to earn it in the first place, drain us dry. It's what killed the First Republic and it's a lot to ask after all that we've been through. Now I'm being honest here. I'm on your side, you know that."

"I understand, but we can't live in a world where work consumes parents and where children never get the caring that they deserve. I've experienced it. We won't penalize people for sharing their lives and other skills with their children and with their communities. And we won't ever again destroy people because they cost society more than their perceived worth. It's time that we value what we can't put a price on."

Dan was silent. His business suit had turned black.

"What I want," Gil continued, "well, it isn't ready to sell just yet and I'll need your help to develop it but economic success will still be rewarded; it's just that economic success won't be the only type of success rewarded. Convince your entrepreneur friends of the rightness of this. That's all I'm asking. Please, help me?"

"So your mind is made up. It's to be socialism."

Disgusted, Gil just nodded.

"I'm offering my opinion, that's all. If it's not Capitalism, its socialism, but whatever it is, I'll figure it out and so will others. Just remember, *Entrepreneurs* are like championship race horses, we expect to win and if you don't use us the right way, well, that will be on you."

"I'm okay with that. Form a temporary government until we can organize national elections and bring a republic back. We're down to it. Are you with me, Dan?"

Dan was silent, thinking.

"Are you with me, Dan?"

Carny Dan shook his head. "In spite of my taste in clothing, I'm a conservative by nature and a libertarian in my heart of hearts. We can debate possibilities all you want but in the end, as with all true conservatives, I live by my principles because that's what puts me at the head of the pack. I'll never concede or negotiate my principles away."

"But what good are your principles if they destroy your country?"

"Principles are principles because you adhere to them for the easy decisions and the tough ones. If that destroys America, so be it. Principled people, like me, will rebuild it even better."

"So you're refusing to join me."

"I didn't say that." Carny Dan extended his hand. "My accountants and lawyers will call your accountant and lawyer. If we get what we need, we'll figure out the rest."

Gil sighed. Maybe this was a victory of sorts. It sure didn't feel like it. "Thanks Dan, I'm glad we could work this out. You know what I want, give it some thought and get back to me with your ideas. For now, I have some personal business to attend to. We will talk more in the coming weeks." While shaking Carny Dan's hand, he asked, "May I contact you through your PID?"

"Sure, why not? Anytime."

With that, Gil excused Carny Dan. He was alone now so he contacted Gecko.

"That went about as expected," Gecko said. "I'll monitor his efforts."

"Don't frighten or try to coerce him," Gil ordered. "If you must, make him aware that he is being monitored but no more. He believes or he doesn't, I won't force anyone."

"Your wish is . . . etc . . . I understand that you're traveling."

"I've made a great many mistakes in my life and before I can lead people, I need to correct as many of those mistakes as I can."

"You're going to her?"

"Joad doesn't keep secrets."

"Sentient computer programs are allowed pillow talk," Gecko replied. "I don't understand why you're doing this. She loves you and you love her. She's clearly the one and you know it."

"Yes," Gil nodded, sadly, "she is. But I must do what's right or I'll carry the wrong with me and it'll cheapen everything I stand for, including my love for her. It will demean everything."

"I'm beginning to appreciate why Capitalists simplify everything into dollars and cents. This will be a great learning experience for me."

"I'm glad you gain something from what I'm about to do."

"Joad tried to explain it but I still don't understand. You love her. I thought that was what we're fighting for."

"This is the right thing. Tell Joad to explain it harder," Gil insisted. "And you must listen harder."

Chapter 19

Monroe—2084

After a joyous reunion with Howard in Indianapolis, Gil returned to the White House to mope around awaiting the most difficult thing he would ever do. From the same window where he had watched Bree arrive, he watched Stacey arrive. She had cleaned up, of course, and she looked even more beautiful as she ran to him in a plain green dress. Unlike with Bree, he rushed to meet her and when they embraced, he luxuriated in it, knowing that it was the last time he would be with his true love. He held her close, fighting for the courage to hurt her one final time.

Hand in hand, they entered the White House where he would begin the explanation that would end their future together. He had learned from how poorly he'd treated Bree but once again, he started where it was most comfortable.

"I just got back from seeing Howard and Mark."

"It must have been great to see them after all these years?" She asked, innocent as to where this conversation would lead.

"It was. My aunt, Rhonda, my mother's sister, is staying with Howard. I hope it finally gives Howard some closure. Mark is there too. What a sad man he is. He could have been the one to prevent what happened but he bought into it and ruined his life and the lives of so many more. In some ways, I'm like him and I feel bad for him. He'll lament his failure until he dies. I offered him a job in the new administration but I don't think he'll accept."

"That was so nice of you." She seemed to want to say more but she allowed him to continue at his pace.

"Bernie loved to tell me about Mark's potential but greed and his desire for power ruined him." He paused, summoning the courage to begin. "Stace, in Graceland, it was so great seeing you. It made things clearer and I . . . I . . ."

She made it harder by staring at him, innocently and lovingly.

"So much has happened since Graceland." He wanted to be clear and brief so he wouldn't punish her more, but he found himself speaking of his capture by *Tollers* after his escape from Angel Falls. At first, she was unsure as to what Gil was telling her, but she remained attentive and smiled until he spoke of Annie. She became concerned when he mentioned Annie's pregnancy. He concluded by telling her of his harrowing escape from Presque Isle. Finally, he explained his obligation.

"Everywhere I've ever been I've taken the easy way, sought the easiest path without considering the affect it had on other people. I've hurt so many, I've hurt you so many times and I'm sorry, I'm so very sorry for that. I would take back everything to spare you the hurt I've caused—that I'm causing."

She began to protest but he gently put a finger to her lips so he could continue.

"If our world is going to be better, my behavior must change. Right has to be right, doesn't it? Fate has put me in a position to be an example of that change to people who have lost their ability to trust. When I fled Presque Isle, I wronged Annie and I hurt my daughter, a girl who is fourteen now and without a father to help her in a complex, unforgiving world. She's alive because of me and though she doesn't know me, she should and she will. She's done nothing wrong and though I had little choice but to run, I'm done running and now I have to correct a grave error and reach out to help her.

"Stace, this is hard but it's the right thing to do. Whatever my future is, I have to put it on hold because I have a responsibility to protect my daughter and make things right by her. I have a responsibility. Everything I detest about America comes to this point and I can't and I won't solve it just by throwing money at it, those days are over. I have to be there for her, I have to be the father she never had but needs. I need to do at least that. Do you understand what that means, Stace? Do you?" he asked.

Crestfallen, she nodded tearfully.

"Families matter and I'm going to them to become a family. I can't be absent any longer. I just can't. I know how it feels to be without parents and I have to . . . to make amends where I can if they'll have me."

Sad and distressed, Stacey swallowed before speaking. "Oh, they'll have you."

"I love you Stace," he proclaimed. "You know that. I . . ." His heart was broken, it hurt so much that it was difficult to speak. It had taken him too long to discover true love and it shouldn't have to end like this.

Her eyes were red with tears and when she held up her hand to make him stop speaking, he continued on in a futile attempt to ease his pain. "Please don't hate me. I have to do this . . . but I've lost you too many times. I don't want to lose you again."

She started to speak but no words came so she started again. "I understand. But you have . . . you have a responsibility to the *Wasters* and *Conducers*. You can't forget them . . . please don't forget your promise to them. We need you to make this a better world . . . please don't forget them, even for this . . ."

"I won't. I'll find a way. I promised you in Graceland that I'll make this right and I will but, I have a daughter . . . and she has lived too long without me. She shouldn't have to become an adult without a father to guide her. I know, I grew up without . . . anyway, I have to help her. People believe I'm the messiah, I'm not, but they need someone to believe in, someone who can restore their faith. I can't speak about doing the right things and then not do this. This is right. I just wish . . ."

Distraught, she held her hand up once more to interrupt him. Tears streamed down her face as the color of her eyes shifted from green to a vibrant emerald. "This is important but if you put your revolution on hold," she began, "it will hurt so many more people. Don't forget us or I'll never speak to you again. Help her and then help us. *Wasters* are desperate and they need you too. I understand your responsibility to your family, I do, I lost my family and if they were still here, I'd do anything for them."

"Oh, Stace," weakening, he sobbed. "I . . . can't lose you again."

"It'll be . . . It'll be alright. You can't . . . you can't lose me, Gil, not again. You belong to the world now and if you don't do what's right, especially when it's hard, how will others endure and make the right choices? Go to her." Stacey was too distraught to continue but when he moved to embrace her, she shrugged him off.

"Stace, whatever happens; I'll make certain Omar Smith never troubles you again."

"I love you, Gil.

"What will you do?"

"I'll return to Graceland, at least for a while. They need me. They need you, too."

"I love you, Stace."

She stood but before she left, he made her a vow. "Towns like Graceland, Stace, I'll help every one of them, but I'll start in Graceland, for you."

"Thank you."

He grabbed her hand, and kissed it. Then he held it to his cheek.

She drew her hand from his and kissed the spot he'd just kissed. Then she turned and walked out, true love broken-hearted.

Long after her gondola disappeared from view, Gil stared out at the empty lagoon.

That's where Joad found him. It was time for his speech to the country so he trudged into the studio while trying to muster enough confidence to tell the American people what they needed to and deserved to hear. Gecko assured him that every television, computer monitor, theatre, personal communicator, advertising sign, Archive, Virtuoso, and optical video unit throughout the country was ready to receive his transmission. Knowing that soon, he would be off to Arizona and a life apart from the woman he loved, he sat disconsolate, and while hiding his grief, spoke to the nation.

"Fellow Americans, my name is Gil Rose and I have replaced Tanya Brandt as leader of our nation. Do not be alarmed; everything is okay. The Morgan Stock Exchange will remain open with no break in service and all credit and other commercial transactions will continue to function normally throughout the country. I repeat. There is no need for concern.

"The administration I am forming will be a transitional one, led by a reliable entrepreneur, but my overall objectives are not transitional. America will change, and for the better, because too many of our citizens have been given up on and left for dead and that's not moral, it's not ethical, and it's not right. And it is definitely not the American Way.

"When our country first began, our patriotic forefathers put their lives at risk so that no government would tax its people and provide them with no say as to how the results of their toil and sweat would be used. 'No taxation without representation' became the rallying cry for justice and you could see even then how money was corrupting the world, but too few noticed. With a revolutionary victory came freedom and American citizens accepted a republic and allowed it to become their heritage. With freedom, every citizen had the right to life, liberty and the opportunity to pursue happiness and well-being in a free and legal way. And every citizen was free from fear, not just from our enemies, but from governments, foreign and domestic. This was our contract for the common good. Citizens in this Republic were given one important responsibility, to be constantly vigilant, which, for a time they were, and then apparently not.

"By the end of the First Republic, the world had evolved. It had become far too complex for most of the people allowing something much simpler, greed and power, to take over.

This hunger for power and wealth so stained our nation that protection from fear, once guaranteed, should have been extended to include protection from the abuses of greedy corporate moneyed interests who soon co-opted our First Republic and stole what was cherished about America from its people.

"In our First Republic citizens voted or didn't but the opportunity existed to vote regularly and easily and so, for far too long, citizens believed that they had representation when in fact their representatives were responsible to others, to the moneyed interests. Under the incurious eyes of the public, the rich purchased our government and the vote confirmed little. Nominees for elected office were trained and funded by the wealthy and powerful and the winner was decided from a choice of two candidates each presenting the views of their rich supporters. Once elected, these representatives permitted the rich and powerful to write our laws. But as bad as that seemed, it was far, far worse. If a law was somehow unfair to the rich or deemed too favorable to the poor, our sacrosanct court system, which was populated by corporate trained judges, lawyers, and academia beholding to the wealthy, interpreted flawed laws in favor of the rich and powerful. America was, in fact, a very complicated and convoluted dictatorship bought and paid for by the wealthy. It was, in truth, a plutocracy.

"In this way, ninety-nine percent of America allowed one percent to dictate in all important matters. For a long time the American economy prospered and the vast majority of people lived well enough, but the trickle down of sustenance that the rich provided to the ninety nine percent other soon evaporated in avarice and so our First Republic died.

"The Second American Republic began with Chairman Andrew Crelli, the unchallenged tyrant of a once free nation. It was he who set about to create a capitalist utopia and many millions of our citizens, our parents, children, siblings, grandparents, uncles and aunts, our friends, and neighbors, they failed to qualify and thus died without ever witnessing a republic at all. They were executed by the word of the greedy for the sin of not providing economic value in a far less than perfect marketplace. With this genocide, like the poor and the middle class, taxes and the common wealth ceased to be a burden for the wealthy anymore.

"The Second American Republic was no republic at all because freedom was denied except for the freedom to earn and spend in a super-heated free market economy, the perfect breeding ground for mutant greed. Too soon, everyone lived for money and only for money.

"That Second Republic has ended. Beginning today, every citizen, *Entrepreneur*, *Conducer*, and *Waster* alike, has the right to expect that when they vote, and you will, each legal vote will count no more and no less than any other. And the vote will not be influenced by money, but only by the weight of the strong convictions of the voting public to achieve what they deserve, to insist on what they deserve. And the people who we elect to represent us, they will represent us. Capitalists need representation, too, but they will not be overrepresented, that I swear to you.

"What we do here is not revolutionary. America wanted this once, we honored this once, and we will have it once again when your new representative government has been elected and is seated in Monroe. Those elections will be announced very soon and our new government will have the great task of reconstructing the American Constitution to redistribute equality once more. It worked once; it can work again to ensure that all Americans are treated as fairly as our founding fathers once dreamed possible. This time, we will have the institutions that will provide the constant vigilance against greed and power that our Founding Fathers felt was so necessary. We will be watchful, open but watchful. In moderation, institutions are good things but they are administered by people and people can be weak and they can be weakened. We will work on that as well.

"For the success of an endeavor like this, it is critically important that everyone be involved and be patient. For the wealthy, you have provided much to your country but you have taken so much more, calling it a fair return. There is no other way to explain the great dichotomy of wealth and poverty—you have it and the people do not. Shame on you. The wealthy should expect to contribute the greatest share to America's recovery, at least up front. Some will rail against this and claim it unfair. Some will condemn it as an injustice to the poor, who get something for nothing and might come to expect it, but to those, I say to you, you are selfish and you are greedy and you are liars hoping to preserve your misappropriated treasure. Though your claims will be considered, redistribution will happen in a just way.

"We value our corporations. You provide for our critical needs and we don't want to lose you, but we will start over if we must. America has done it before. I ask every entrepreneur, executive, senior manager and stock holder, anyone who believes that they will be adversely affected, I plead for your support. You are valued and will continue to live well, even by your standards, and in many ways you will be far better off as we reconstruct our great nation and deepen the wealth of our vast economy.

"The rich and powerful among us may find this arrangement unsatisfactory or worse. So be it. You have options, use them if you dare. We have resources too, dominating resources which we would prefer not to demonstrate, but demonstrate we will if you will not listen to reason. Resist and we will subdue you. Rebel and we will avert it. If the principles of America's founding fathers are not for you, you are free to leave America, but you will not take your wealth with you. You earned it here; it remains here for the common good. If you believe we are stealing, then look back at the laws you have written and the interpretations of those laws by the judges you have purchased. We are merely recapitalizing our country with funds that have been diverted from that purpose.

"We recognize that the wealth the rich in our country have accumulated was created by hard work, brilliance, and by legal and extra legal means. But wealth was also created by the American worker and the American consumer and was facilitated by our infrastructure, the common wealth of our people. We will be a country of true patriots again and we expect that you will accept this redistribution of wealth as a tax obligation that you owe to honor your nation for the years that you were able to prosper beyond objective rewards. Or consider it a usury tax for your treatment of your downtrodden fellow citizen and the misuse of our land, our water, our air, and our climate.

"You can claim that this is a socialist, or even a communist revolution. These are terms that have been marketed throughout American history as vulgar and treasonable in order to provide latitude to pervert free market capitalism. What I propose is not communism or socialism, but I will not waste my time arguing it. Every country on earth runs an economy that is part capitalist and part socialist and those countries that get that mix right, their people are the most content. There is no horror in either of these terms but for what people give it.

Once, a great man, my great grandfather, Bernie Rosenthal, a true warrior, told me that when he was starting out, business and politics were less dogmatic and to be successful, each eschewed inflexible principles and hard lines to instead consider practical, pragmatic solutions. We are pragmatic, too, and our solutions will be pragmatic as well, even if others claim it is dogma. We seek merely to reclaim America for all who wish to live here and contribute to it. And we seek to expunge the horror that occurred during the perverse reign of greed under the guise of unbridled free market capitalism that was called the Second Republic.

"For the vast majority of American citizens, *Conducers*, we ask that you continue to work hard as you have been. As we rebuild and shift priorities, more sacrifice and sharing may be required, but everyone who works will be guaranteed a living wage, an education, training, free health care and other assistance with which to reorient your lives. Work with us and we guarantee that you will receive all of the true necessities of life. Work harder, smarter, better, provide value, care and share with your family and your community, and you will earn a greater share of a bounty you helped to create.

"Though most will not hear this broadcast, I speak now to the disenfranchised among us, our so-called *Wasters*. Our programs to help you will take time to implement. Please hold on if you can. Throughout the country, there are cities and towns once emptied by HomeSec armies that are now refilling. Go to any one. We will provision you there. This I promise. I don't wish to lose anymore people.

"But you must not look on what you will be provided with as a windfall although it may seem that way at first. America is free but that doesn't mean free not to work, not to contribute. Everyone has responsibilities and in the near future, there will be a great many new ways other than through commercial activity in which you can earn what you need. If you choose not to work for a commercial enterprise, you may contribute to your community or directly to your city or town, state, or country, and if you contribute, you will earn a living wage, be provided with shelter, education, and health care and you and your children will be guaranteed these things because you are contributing Americans and we value your children, all of them are our children, too. We value the child most of all, for they are our future and the future of our values.

"My fellow Americans, I promise you that we will once again be the vibrant bastion of liberty and our people and our nation will be a community of caring and sharing individuals pursuing their hopes and dreams with the kind, warm heart that freedom provides to light our way."

"I promise further that I will continue to broadcast updates so that you will know how your government is progressing and where it is going. I have great hope for our efforts and I want everyone to share that hope with me and with others. This is not a revolution. This is the rebirth of the promise that was once America.

And finally, you will see improvement soon. But what will need more time to fix, what will be better for our country and everyone in it, we all need to learn to trust and love again. Not like we love today, that is how the greedy want us to care, not like that. We must wipe our memory clean of such things and start again. We need to love. We need to love, not what a person can do to help us or love what we can get from a person, but just love, love where all you want is the pleasure of someone else's company and to make them smile, to make them happy, knowing that you are loved and that person will do what's best for you. What was once will be again the very best way to live. Treat others, in all things, as you want them to treat you. That is a Golden Rule worth following.

I am Gil Rose, and I thank you."

Thoroughly drained emotionally, Gil sat alone at his desk. Too soon, he would be off to Arizona to offer his life to Annie and his daughter. He was sad but hopeful, too.

Epilogue

Angel Falls Maine—2084

Discarded and forgotten, the small community of Angel Falls, located in north central Maine, had been a quaint, peaceful, out-of-the-way village; a community of families sharing common good, caring for neighbors with hope and kindness, a sin that proved unforgivable. Avarice and self-interest might have saved Angel Falls but the community was too far from mainstream American enterprise and suffered for it. With its burnt out cottages and storefronts and its streets pockmarked with bomb craters, Angel Falls was a monument to American greed and aggression, a home only Mother Nature could love.

A young couple walked down what once was Main Street, gripping each other's hands. They avoided the spent American ordnance, the scorched craters and the detritus of this place that once was a haven of happy memories. Though this was home, on this cool northern Maine February day, it was more. It was hard reality. The couple stopped at familiar buildings but moved on quickly, it hurt too much to dwell. Here was America's injustice incarnate. Here was proof that legal wasn't moral. Here, a national government facing a choice rationalized the destruction of life, liberty and the pursuit of happiness.

The couple didn't talk because the pain was so intense it couldn't be swallowed away and shared guilt made comforting futile. All this young man and woman could bring to this reunion were tears so in quiet desperation they wandered beyond the town and into the blistered hills which were seared with a perversity that overloaded shared memories.

They once hiked these hills sharing happy times that were lost to them now. Like the town below, their joyous hills had been abused by the power of man. Where once great evergreens blocked the sun, now brown, bent, and defeated, they drooped like sick old cousins sharing regret at a funeral.

They saw their lake and she doubled over and retched. He cursed and knelt to comfort her and they sought comfort in an embrace. Eyes closed, they refused to accept this corruption, each desperately searching for something that might soothe their souls. But guilt will have its price and their pain would never be assuaged. Then they reached their lake.

Stunned, they sat and stared at the hollow of cracked brown earth that was once filled with emerald green water, and life. In its place, scornful of their memories were insubstantial pools of murky, brackish water and bones of creatures that died for the sins of humans. At the far end, where once a beautiful waterfall replenished the lake and gave the town its heavenly name was a rock formation covered in dead brown moss, its hidden cave exposed.

Her hand trembled as she pointed and her voice broke as she spoke for the first time. "I . . . I hid there," she said

He nodded.

She sobbed and kissed his neck. "How did it come to this?" she whimpered.

He tried to console her. "It wasn't your fault, it really wasn't," he said resolutely. Truly, it wasn't but he couldn't say the same about himself. Then he hesitated. No, it was their fault because it was everyone's fault. He swallowed hard and began to tell his tale.

It was dusk when Gil completed his story.

"And Annie and your son; they are okay."

"They are, but I didn't know until I arrived, that I had a son and not a daughter. Annie named him Gilles."

"It must have been hard when she said they didn't need you."

"Annie has a good man to help her and Gilles thinks of him as his father. She wants the best for Gilles but she doesn't want him to grow up as the son of the Messiah. It would be too much of a burden and I know that's right. She prefers anonymity and I understand completely, but I'll help them in other ways, and when he's older, or he asks about me, Annie promised to contact me. And like you, Annie made me promise to help every *Waster* that I can."

"I like Annie already. It shouldn't be a hard promise to keep."

"No, it shouldn't."

"What happened to Andrew Crelli?"

"It's hard to believe, but Arlene and Andy are truly in love. I don't understand it but it's true. I had him released from prison and Arlene has taken him home with her to Kansas. She seems happy and that's all that matters.

"Good for her. We should visit . . . No, maybe that would be too awkward." Stacey paused, thinking. "Why didn't Gecko tell you about your son before?" she asked.

He smiled. "That's why I need you. You see what I don't. Maybe Gecko thought I'd run to her and his plans would come to nothing . . . I'll think on it."

She leaned in and kissed him.

"Stace, I love you so much. I'll never hurt you again."

"I love you, too." She stood and looked around. "As horrible as the memories are, Angel Falls still feels like home. Someday we'll rebuild it and spread the community values it stood for throughout the country the way your great grandfather Bernie did with his Greenhouses that helped *Wasters* avoid being murdered."

"That's a great idea." They kissed but then she pulled back.

"Are you sure you can trust them?"

"Joad and Gecko?" he asked.

Stacey nodded.

"What choice do I have? I can't will Joad and Gecko out of existence and I'm not sure I would if I could. All I can do is be kind to them, love them, and hope that takes us to a better place."

She embraced him and they fell back onto the dry brown earth where, with all the intensity their hearts could muster, they made love for the first time. They made love as if trying to fill the void in a dispassionate world.

Afterward, she stared up at him and smiled. Then she laughed and pointed. He turned to see the mint green tops of new pines breaking through the thick blanket of scorched, dead pine needles in search of the sun.

It was the beginning.

Gil Rose*—Messiah and founder of the Third American Republic. Rose remained involved in the rebuilding of America for less than one year after his revolution succeeded but during that time, he directed America's return to universal freedom. He initiated actions that under subsequent elected leadership would lead to a Golden Age for humanity on a scale the world had never seen.*

Rose is credited with crafting fairness into the American economic, political, and social arenas where his concepts of social commerce softened the excesses of free market capitalism and effectively integrated its obvious advantages with those of his socially-constructive communitarian view of society.

As a result of Rose's initiatives, there was a significant slow down in the industrial burn rate that had been destroying Earth's resources far too quickly in a boom and bust environment that had been destabilizing to people, families and communities worldwide.

By demonstrating the benefits of long-term sustainable growth along with the intense enthusiasm created throughout the population because of the redistribution of wealth, the great race to the top and bottom of society that had characterized old capitalism finally ended and communities thrived in many more ways than economic.

As the strength of Gil Rose's model for sharing gained world wide credibility, there occurred such a flourishing of human potential that, had there been a God, he would certainly have been pleased.

—Archive

Thus Book Four ends as does the Joad Cycle.

For more on the future of America please go to:
WWW.Joadcycle.com